Upload

by Mark McClelland

For my wife Nancy
With all my love

Upload

independently published
by arrangement of the author

with special thanks to the BosMob, Dave Bowen,
and inspirational readers Drew & Valerie Burlingame

Printing History
Public edition v 1.0 published September, 2012
Distributed print edition v1.0 published October, 2012

ISBN 978-1-300-33561-0

Part I: R

CHAPTER 1

Tuesday, June 22, 2060

Raymond Quan awakened feeling alert and self-satisfied, well before his alarm was due to go off. He lay on his back, his bare arms resting atop the recycled-plastic quilt. He opened his eyes to the familiar darkness of his bedcell and immediately broke into a smile. The sweet taste of victory lingered from his brief but momentous fight the day before with another boy at the Home. With his right hand, he formed the leopard's paw fist, the tips of his fingers pressing into the meat across the top of his palm. He rolled to his left and threw a punch across his chest, certain it would end just shy of the bedcell's back wall. The brief ruffle of cheap papery sheets accentuated the crispness of his movement. He held the punch, reached a quarter-inch further, and felt his knuckles graze the hard plastic.

"That's your Adam's apple, Willm," he whispered in a drawn out, dramatically threatening tone. He kept his voice very low, knowing that Greg, his state-assigned younger brother, could easily hear him from the bedcell above.

Raymond had lived in room 212 of the Canal Street Home for Children of the State of Illinois for over two years now. When he was reassigned to Canal Street from the Joliet Home, he was fifteen. He hated the move. Home administrators told him he was being moved so he could be closer to his biological mother. She had supposedly complained that Joliet was too far away to visit—too far from the Hyde Park Recovery Center, where she had been busy recovering for nearly ten years now. By gridcab, it took about an hour to get from Hyde Park to his old Joliet Home. Now that he was at Canal Street, he was only ten minutes' ride away. In his six years in Joliet, she visited him once. She had yet to visit him at the new Home.

In truth, he didn't mind that his mother never visited. Her absence from his life provided a convenient source of suffering when he wanted to feel sorry for himself, but he really preferred to forget her. The one time she visited him in Joliet, it was plain that she didn't want to be there. It was probably some sign-of-progress hoop she had to jump through to stay at the recovery center, to continue whatever drug-laden therapy she was on. She had fidgeted constantly, throwing out random observations and rash judgements about the Home and its staff; the only direct words she could muster were empty apologies, by way of blaming his misfortune—and hers—on his father's having run off with another woman. "An *Asian* woman," she had said, practically spitting out the word in front of her half-Vietnamese son. "I always knew he would end up leaving me for an Asian woman. I'm just glad I've healed."

Not seeing her was fine. What he did mind was that—in order to fulfill her apparent ambitions of living out the remainder of her life in a state of self-deceived recovery—she had caused him to be moved. For this profoundly selfish act, he doubted he would ever forgive her.

In the first weeks, it had seemed that every aspect of the move was bound to be awful. Arriving at a new Home at the age of fifteen landed him among an age group of intense, often vicious competition. The state transferred him in late April of 2058, just a few weeks before the end of the school year—at a time when the children in the new home were bored and restless. And the Canal Street boys were tougher and more cruel by far than any he had known before. They spent most of their waking hours fighting for position or reinforcing dominance within their pecking order—which Raymond entered at the bottom. New kids always started out at the bottom, but Raymond had more or less remained there. His computer skills won him some respect among the outcast nerds and—more importantly—the adult caregivers. He gained rank among the bottom feeders and was left alone by the adults. But those same skills made him stand out. At Joliet, standing out because of his computer talent had been a source of pride. Here, it stirred hateful jealousy and made him a target. The birthmark on his cheek and being half-Vietnamese just made it worse. He arrived weak and afraid to fight, and the clique boys preyed on him.

Early on, he had tried to make friends with some of the kids in the lower cliques, only to make the sad discovery that these boys, who were kind to him one-on-one, turned mean in a group. He decided to operate alone, as best he could, and to keep a low profile. But his new Home offered little privacy. Conflict proved inevitable.

And last night, for the first time, he had stood his ground in the face of conflict.

One of the tough-boy cliques—known as the Face Clan for reasons unknown to Raymond—had talked him into gaming with them in the virtual chambers, during the pre-curfew free period. Raymond, typically excluded from the gaming sessions, reluctantly decided to give it a try. It was a medieval death-match game, in which everyone runs around a castle with swords and shields trying to kill everyone else. Except, in this case, they all started each round by pinning down Raymond, ripping his shield away from him, calling him Gooksy and Face Whore, then killing him. Raymond hoped at first that if he took his punishment like a man, they would relent and let him play for real. But after four rounds of this, he left his v-chamber and started to wander off toward the boys' dorm.

"Jesus, you suck, Gooksy." It was Willm, the cruelest of the clique, out of his v-chamber to further pursue his quarry. Raymond continued to walk away. "I'm not absolutely positive," persisted Willm, "correct me if I'm wrong—but I think you were the first one dead every single bleeding round."

It occurred to Raymond to point out that he had participated in only four rounds, but he had learned the painful irrelevance of reason. He kept walking, and was only ten feet or so from the stairs up to the boys' dorm when he heard Willm start running after him.

"Come on, Gooksy! You think I'm done with you?"

The familiar nauseating fear of what might come next arose within him. Should he run, or stand and take it? Would he be knocked down, kicked, elbowed, put in a headlock? Kneed in the kidneys? Or would he receive Willm's signature taunt, the slobbery wet finger shoved in his ear?

Then it occurred to him that Willm was alone. The rest of his clique were all still playing, their yowls and laughter audible even from this distance. This chance of catching Willm alone, combined with his recent karate training, sparked a fierce courage Raymond had never before felt. He turned, at what proved to be precisely the right moment; Willm's foot grazed Raymond's backside and angled off.

Raymond immediately recognized the opportunity. Willm was off-balance from his missed kick. He saw a clear shot at Willm's lean, jagged throat. His hand formed the leopard's-paw fist he had learned from his virtual karate instructor, and he stepped into his punch. The hard edge of his knuckles met the soft, vulnerable skin of Willm's neck, just below the Adam's apple, and drove the boy backward. Willm twisted to the side, stumbled, scrambled to his feet, and rammed shoulder-first against the wall, clutching his neck.

Panic shot through Raymond. He had just attacked a member of a six-boy clique. It was just a matter of time before they jumped him. They might even kill him.

Then he saw the way Willm looked at him. Willm's eyes were wide-open, shocked, even afraid, as he wheezed and gasped for air. The tall blond boy, with his tough-kid mohawk, leaned against the wall, looking at Raymond with a mix of anguish, surprise, and uncertainty. With a single punch, Raymond's cruel tormentor had been reduced to just another fearful boy.

Raymond felt sorry—he had really hurt Willm. But this regret vanished as a sense of power welled within him. He had really hurt Willm. He sensed Willm's uncertainty, and he knew it couldn't last long. He had to do or say something to seal the moment. He stood his ground and spoke as definitively as he could.

"My name is Raymond. Stop calling me Gooksy and I won't tell anyone I kicked your ass."

Without waiting for an answer, he walked down the hall and turned up the stairs.

o-----------------------------o

His exultant energy still burned within him. He turned in bed and looked to the clock in his headboard. It was 6:03. His work shuttle didn't come until 7:30. Plenty of time to train.

He reached up and tapped the face of his clock, and "Alarm off for today" scrolled across the display, followed by a low-tech 2-D animation of a boy drinking a bottle of Coca-Cola.

Raymond slid open the opaque blue curtain of his bedcell. The small dorm room's single east-facing window permitted the faint light of early morning, revealing the room's usual landscape of dirty clothes, empty MegaBlast bottles and Choco-Chompos bags, spongy yellow toy-gun ammunition, glide shoes, and musty towels. The endless mess was strewn about the floor, sitting precariously on the table's edge, draped over the rim of the aluminum sink, piled deep on the chair beneath the window. And every bit of it was Greg's. Raymond despised his ersatz brother. Greg was a loud, unthinking, graceless, overweight, pathetic, foul-smelling slob. At the Joliet home, Raymond had been lucky enough to have a room to himself. Here, privacy came only in the hours when Greg was away or asleep.

Raymond swung his legs out and sat up, kicking aside a pair of bright orange billow-pants to reveal a bit of floor on which to place his feet. He looked around the room, running his tongue across his morning-scuzzed teeth, and shook his head. He decided he wasn't going to put up with Greg's crap anymore. If he could take Willm, he could certainly put thirteen-year-old Greg in his place.

He flexed his right arm and patted his bicep.

Discipline, thought Raymond. *Self-control yields discipline, and the disciplined accumulation of power leads to freedom.*

He had composed this in his head the night before, as he lay awake, and repeated it over and over until committed to memory. This, he had resolved, would be his mantra. Self-control would give him the edge he needed to stand up against other boys in the Home, against fear and mediocrity. While others sought the low rewards of immediate pleasure, he would rise above.

He stood up, and the motion triggered the overhead lights to flicker on. He looked to the mirror over the sink, where he had long ago discovered a pinhole camera. He imagined someone sitting in a surveillance room—a guard or caregiver—seeing a monitor light up with activity in room 212.

"The lights don't come on so we can see," he muttered.

They come on so we can be seen.

He turned and quietly closed the curtain of his bedcell, conscious that he was under constant observation. He looked forward to his workday at Mr. Tate's house, where he controlled the cameras—where he could point all the cameras away from him and be alone.

This same desire to be alone had led to Raymond's karate training. There was an old, disused v-chamber in the second-floor study lounge that Raymond had decided to try out during his first Christmas break, when—in a State Home—it was especially hard to find time alone. It was this old v-chamber that really made him see a good side to his new Home. It was an old model, configured for educational use only, and was ignored by the other boys on the floor. Raymond had first tried it simply to escape, but he was intrigued when he discovered it had a karate training program, hidden within a catalogue of boring subjects like algebra and pottery. He was even more intrigued when he discovered he could hack it, bypassing the restrictions put in place for schools and children's homes.

He crossed the tile floor of his room with a skating motion, clearing a path through the mess to his closet, where his black exercise robe hung from its hook. It was a recent purchase, using money from the account Mr. Tate created for Raymond's robot-repair expenses. He slipped it on, relishing the silky feel of its absorptive lining, and checked its concealed interior breast pocket—he confirmed by feel that his Crown Series LX6 override, a magnetic device the size of a dime, was in its spot, hidden away.

Quietly, he exited his dorm room and walked down the hall, past the closed doors of other boys' rooms, to the study lounge at the end. Through the glass door he saw there was nobody in the room. He entered, weaved through the cramped tables and chairs—which were bolted to the floor—to the wood-paneled v-chamber in the corner. It was a fairly large unit, about six feet square, that felt oversized in this small room. To the best of his knowledge, he was the only person who actually used it anymore. Using the unlimited Net access at Mr. Tate's, Raymond had learned that it was an old British model, made by a now-bankrupt company called Crown Nanotronics—a company famous among hackers for weak security measures.

With a touch of the green "Unoccupied" button, the v-chamber door rattled sideways, jamming as usual. Raymond pushed it the rest of the way. He entered, pleased by the familiar lofty bounce of the floor, and closed the door behind him. A soft, low amber light turned on. There was no need for the light to be at all bright—there was nothing to see in a v-chamber while it was off. The interior was very plain. No buttons or screens or levers. Just black walls, floor, and ceiling, all cushioned for safety, in case of system failure while the user was being tossed about. Closer inspection revealed tiny holes on all of the interior surfaces—barely visible pinholes, in an extremely dense grid. Raymond had read that there were billions of even smaller holes, invisible to the human eye. He had also read about the mix of holography, electronet, and nanomist technologies used to create the virtual experience, but the details were beyond him. He knew that a powerful network of computers throughout the walls manipulated photons, electrons, and an unfathomable number of nanobots to create a virtual environment that looked, sounded, and felt very much like reality—so much so that the pedantic were always arguing whether it should be called virtual reality or temporary reality.

For Raymond, the term "virtual" still rang true. There was an obvious element of illusion in a contraption the size of a walk-in closet that allowed the user to see and navigate sprawling worlds. Most of the people and other creatures in virtual space were computer-generated, and conversations with them usually revealed their less-than-authentic personalities. Attempts at replicating smell were ill-advised, and Raymond was always noticing small details of physical reality that had been overlooked. He was profoundly aware that v-space was a hoax. It was a temporary escape to a world more pure, more fantastic, more desirable than plain old reality—temporary because one ultimately could not ignore the real world. One was inescapably bound to reality and all of its niggling maintenance problems—eating, bathing, defecating, looking after one's home—all of the work that a biological life-form must contend with.

The basic falseness of virtual reality was abundantly and painfully evident to Raymond. It had driven his family apart, as it had so many families. Addicts neglected their spouses, their children, and all of the implicit responsibilities that come with basic interpersonal commitment. Raymond had concluded at a young age that, for him, virtual reality would be a tool. A means of improving his life, not escaping it. Only if he could depart reality and move entirely into virtual reality would he ever release himself to it.

Raymond took the Crown Series LX6 override device from his pocket, crouched down, and allowed it to snap magnetically to the wall, to the right of the door. "Begin session," he said. "Admin mode."

The v-chamber made a faint humming sound as its ventilation system kicked in. The chamber filled with a haze of cool nanomist, and Raymond felt his body lift several inches. The space around him transformed into a long, old-fashioned carpentry workshop—the default space when in administrator mode.

"Monitoring override x-l-9-r-f-x," said Raymond. "Broadcast demo session."

"Acknowledged," responded the refined voice of an elderly British male.

With this command—an undocumented feature that the developers of this particular model never removed—Raymond effectively turned off the external monitoring of the v-chamber. The computer network at the Home monitored activity in the v-chambers, to prevent children of the State from breaking the no-sex/no-drugs rules. With the "broadcast demo session" command, Raymond was able to switch the outgoing monitor feed to a pre-recorded demo session, in which a pleasant little English boy goes for a pleasant bicycle ride through the Yorkshire Dales. Raymond could then do whatever the hell he wanted within the v-chamber, and only he would know.

"Give me the tropical dojo."

The space transformed instantly into an airy, wood-floored pavilion, covered with a high thatched roof and surrounded by palm trees. He stood at one end of the room, facing the center. Sunlight streamed in from his right. Finches chirped and warbled in the tropical forest outside.

"Give me Andrea." Those three words, and all of the anticipation that came with them, gave him a hard-on. Every time.

A young Caucasian woman appeared at the opposite end of the dojo, wearing a white gi. She was slender, about 5' 6", and had short dark-brown hair that hung in a clean angular line just above her full eyebrows. She looked to Raymond to be about twenty years old. He had chosen her first for her looks, while experimenting with the admin privileges. But he found that he also liked her fighting style. She moved swiftly, gracefully, focused on balance and use of space. She also hit with less force than the other instructors. Even with the v-chamber's impact dampeners, a sharp punch could smart.

She bowed to Raymond. He didn't respond. He knew it was a mindless bow, an animation detached from personality—her persona wouldn't kick in until he exited admin mode.

"Confirm monitoring broadcast," he requested. He wanted to be sure, before issuing his next command, that he was not being watched.

"Broadcasting demo session," responded the computer's admin response voice.

"Modify Andrea's outfit—no clothing."

Her gi vanished. Her skin was uniformly tanned, her body toned. Her breasts were small and firm, her thighs muscular. Raymond had touched her, and he loved the way she felt. But he had never had sex with her, or made her touch him. He had explored this v-chamber's capabilities with other women, curious whether it was possible—and it was. Even though the Home had ordered this v-chamber with educational programming only, the underlying anatomical models and personas were the same used in other Crown Nanotronics v-chambers. With admin privileges, one could make the simulated people do whatever one wanted. And Raymond had. But not anymore, and never Andrea. He preferred to tempt himself, to flirt with self-indulgence but stop just short. It was an exercise in discipline, part of the mastery of self that he felt would make him superior.

"Begin session."

o-----------------------------o

Raymond showered in the common bathroom, careful to choose the shower stall closest to the hook on which he always hung his exercise robe, so he could defend it from theft. He then returned to his room and dressed in his Workbound uniform—a blue-gray unitard provided to Illinois children who chose to participate in the state's work program. His wrist relay vibrated. He tapped it and a holographic text display popped up, a standard reminder from the Home network: "Don't forget to eat breakfast!" it flashed… "Only thirty minutes till your work shuttle arrives".

In all Illinois Homes, breakfast was mandatory, part of the Diet and Fitness Regimen. Pods, the child groupings intended to mimic families, were required to sit together with their primary caregiver. Each pod was supposed to consist of three same-sex sibling pairs, but the numbers rarely worked out. There were never enough caregivers to go around, so pods with fewer than six children were split up and mixed in with other pods. An adult, usually a woman, was assigned to a pod as its primary caregiver. The Primary was responsible for making sure all the children ate proper meals, had tolerably good hygiene, and basically got on okay in life. Pods with very young children were given a secondary caregiver, to help with feeding, bathing, and monitoring.

Raymond's pod was a six-child pod with no young children. There was Raymond, Greg, and four girls aged nine to twelve. The girls completely ignored Raymond and alternately loathed and were amused by Greg. Raymond had often wondered whether his life might be different if there were a boy his age in his pod, one he actually liked. But there wasn't, and at least the girls kept their distance.

When Raymond arrived at the pod table that morning, only Joe, the pod's Primary, was there. One of the many perks of the Workbound program was that it forced Raymond to wake up early, before any of the others in his pod. Of course, it also forced Joe to wake up early, as Primaries were required to be present throughout pod breakfast. Joe, a grumbly old black man who was never shy about sharing an opinion, had made it clear right away that he didn't like getting up early.

Raymond set his breakfast shake and banana down at his usual spot on the long cafeteria table and sat down, opposite Joe and one seat down. Joe sat with his eyes closed, slouched to one side with his cheek resting heavily against his hand. He was listening to something on his ear buds. Raymond was halfway through his banana before Joe noticed him. Seeing Raymond, he told his wrist relay to pause whatever he was listening to, and he looked thoughtfully at Raymond.

"So, how's the Karate Kid today?" asked Joe.

Raymond liked being called the Karate Kid. Ever since telling Joe about the karate lessons, Joe had been calling him that. It was apparently from some old 2-

D movie. Before "the Karate Kid", Joe had always called him Ray, or Baby Ray, or X-Ray—chummy meaningless names that rubbed Raymond the wrong way. Being called the Karate Kid was a little embarrassing, but it made him proud, too. Both the embarrassment and the pride arose from its being a nickname based on something that mattered to him, not just some random cute name.

"Not bad," responded Raymond. "What are you listening to?"

"One of them sports feeds. It's Nate Carr talking about Tobey Brown." Raymond's blank stare must have betrayed his ignorance. "Tobey Brown," explained Joe, "was one of the great three-goal-superball forwards of the '40s. Nobody could read the field and move like he could. Real shame when he switched over to football."

"I see." Raymond had no interest in sports, or any pop culture, for that matter.

"So, all's good?"

"Yep." Raymond picked the last of his banana out of the peel and popped it in his mouth.

"Well, I'll be right here."

Joe told his wrist relay to resume and closed his eyes again. Raymond drank his shake, watching two girls at another table and half-heartedly trying to overhear them as they listed off favorite v-worlds—favorites from among the comparatively narrow selection of government-run v-worlds used in schools and children's homes around the country. Raymond had heard of most of them, but had visited only a couple. He had his own v-world—Nurania. He had started building it in his abundant free time at Mr. Tate's. It was a private v-world, off the Net.

Maybe I should open it to the Net someday. Probably not—people would just ruin it.

As he drained the last of his shake, his wrist relay vibrated and displayed its annoyingly cheery animation of a smiling little bus screeching to a halt in front of a cute little house.

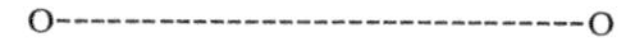

The work shuttle navigated its way north on Canal Street, its teenaged passengers uncharacteristically quiet, separated from their cliques and sobered by the early start of a new workday. The boy next to Raymond slept, and Raymond stared out the window. Chicago's downtown loomed large ahead, its skyscrapers icons of urban preeminence throughout pre-virtual civilization. Buildings over ninety stories tall, once the workplaces of thousands of office workers, remained as a testament to the value that centralized population once offered. They now served primarily as residential space. Raymond imagined a young Mr. Tate making his fortune in those buildings, back when they were cubicle mazes. Tate as management consultant, wearing a business suit, flying to other cities to meet with people, riding up and down buildings in elevators, hailing pre-grid cabs driven by people whose lives consisted primarily of driving other people around. Raymond looked to the front of the shuttle and imagined there being a special seat for driving, and a human driver controlling the shuttle. He wondered how they knew where to go, how they avoided hitting each other.

Raymond thought about just how old Nicholas Tate was. The old man had recently turned 85. That meant he was born in 1975, and that he had witnessed the infancy of the computer age. The computer industry had given Tate his wealth, incredible sums of money, made largely—as Tate had admitted, even bragged, to Raymond—through insider trading. Yet the money now sat ignored in low-yield investments while Tate lived his life in his v-chamber, in a nice but dated home far below his means. A vast suburban home with a one-acre yard. Which is where Raymond came in.

Tate hired Raymond to do routine maintenance work on the robots that tended his lawn and cleaned his house, and to do any housework that the robots couldn't do. It was a charity job, really—Tate could easily have hired cleaning and maintenance services. But he wanted to "give a young man a chance," as he liked to say. Raymond just happened to have been the lucky Workbound applicant to get the job.

It proved to be a dream of a job. He rarely saw Tate, who spent nearly every minute of every day in his big v-chamber in the basement. Tate granted him unlimited, unmonitored Net access, and encouraged him to convert the garage into a robotics workshop. Tate even gave him access to a special bank account, from which to fund the workshop. The few times that Raymond did see Tate, he had to endure the old man's magnanimity, out-of-touch advice, and putrid body odor, but it was a small price to pay.

The real kicker was that Raymond had been given a hacker's playground. Early on, his curiosity about the man had gotten the better of him. What did this old man do all day in v-space? Raymond listened at the door, as his mother had once listened at the door of his father's v-chamber. But Tate's was soundproof. He used his Net access to research the particular v-chamber model, to learn whether it might have security gaps. His research was fruitless at first, but he persisted, amazed by the amount of information available to him. His search led him to learn about other v-chamber models, including the old Crown Series beast in the second-floor study lounge. But Tate's proved to be a tough one to crack.

It was serendipity that ultimately showed him the way. Tate came storming into the garage one day in his tattered old bathrobe, complaining that his v-session had been interrupted by some silly warning about a medical alert system of some sort, and could Raymond take a look at it. Raymond looked into it and discovered that the v-chamber had a special subsystem that monitored vital signs of the user. If it identified a health emergency, it could contact a local hospital and request that an ambulance be sent.

To ensure that the subsystem was working properly, it routinely sent out a test message to the local emergency network. If the emergency network did not respond, the v-chamber would try again a few times and ultimately terminate the v-session. Which is what had happened to Tate. Raymond discovered that the real problem was simply that the emergency network was down. To appease Tate and allow him to return to whatever it was that so occupied him, Raymond rigged up one of his own computers to play the role of emergency network. It received the test signal, responded appropriately, and everything was back in order.

Then it dawned on Raymond that this little subsystem had to be aware of the user's activities in order to recognize a health problem. If he could just tap into it, he could monitor Tate's v-sessions and find out more about him. Within a few days, Raymond had it figured out. He told Tate that a possible replacement part had come in and that he needed to access the health monitoring subsystem again. He inserted a broadcasting repeater into the subsystem where it received its activities feed, then had Tate resume his session. Upstairs, in a second v-chamber, Raymond tried out his hack. Next thing he knew, he was experiencing Tate's v-world session, in full detail.

The voyeuristic thrill wore off pretty quickly, and Raymond moved on to a new goal. For years, he had been creating virtual personas—simulated people—with the objective of creating one so realistic that nobody would be able to tell it apart from an actual person. He had quickly discovered that the easiest way to do this was to record a real person and use sophisticated pattern recognition and replication software to "learn" the person's personality. But it took an immense body of data to come up with something decent, and he had never been satisfied with the results. Here was his opportunity. He could record Tate night and day, month after month. And so he did, and within a few months he had a remarkable likeness of Tate, complete with a rich body of self-knowledge. Including, Raymond soon realized, knowledge of bank account access codes.

A vague awareness of the shuttle's winding path westward pushed through Raymond's state of reverie. The shuttle had made many stops, at the restaurants, hospitals, and nursing homes where Raymond was pleased not to work. Before he knew it, he was watching the familiar homes of Tate's subdivision pass by out the window. It was a neighborhood of pretentious old brick homes, built in the 1990s for the burgeoning upper-middle class. The shuttle stopped at the end of Tate's driveway. The boy next to Raymond turned to the side to let him out.

Tate's home sat in the center of a perfect lawn. Though the wind was cool and carried a moist note of coming rain, the hot June sun shone on the grass, and on the green leaves of the mature, bushy maples that stood on either side of the driveway. A little round robot the size of a raccoon, built to look like an oversized ladybug, cruised across the lawn, poking holes in the soil with instruments attached to its head. Its back-and-forth progress was evident from the patterns in the grass. From the outside, one might imagine the house to give shelter to an idyllic, prosperous family living out the middle class dream of the 20th century.

Raymond underwent the retinal scan and voice recognition tests at the door, leftovers from a previous resident more security-conscious than Tate. Once in, he proceeded through the bright, soaring, tile-floored great room, and down a hallway past the disused kitchen and several closed-off rooms. He didn't even bother to call out hello—Tate never came out of his v-chamber before 10 AM.

Raymond proceeded through the door at the end of the hall, into the converted garage, where he spent the majority of his workday—his robotics lab. The lights turned on and ceiling panels slid open to reveal skylights. He crossed to the workbench, upon which were dozens of neatly arranged components, and performed his morning ritual. He took off his Home wrist relay and set it at the far edge of the work surface. It was a cheap black plastic thing, scuffed after only a year of use. From a shelf above the workbench, he took down his own personal wrist relay. It was a beautiful metallic relay. When turned in the light, its iridescent black surface showed hints of green and violet, like the feathers of a grackle. His Home relay could only connect to the Home's local network. With his personal relay, he was in full communication with the network in Tate's home, which in turn gave him unlimited access to the Net.

As soon as he put on his personal relay, a holographic display sprang to life. He was surprised—this meant that there was some high-priority message, perhaps a special request from Tate. He pressed a holographic button on the display to play the message.

"At 8:17 AM," said the relay's generic female persona in her invariably pleasant voice, "a health emergency signal was received. Shall I forward it to the local emergency network?"

Panic seized Raymond. If a medical team came to the house, they would see that he had tampered with the emergency subsystem on Tate's v-chamber. And they would know that he had hacked into it—that he was watching Tate's private life. He looked at the clock on the display. It was now 8:20 AM. The signal had been sent only three minutes ago. But those three minutes might have made all the difference—had he repaired the medical alert system, an ambulance would already be at the house. Now, if he did forward the signal and Tate were to die, the death would be attributed to Raymond's hack.

Oh my god. He's downstairs. He's in his v-chamber, downstairs, dying.

It occurred to him that the message could be a false alarm. He imagined Tate bursting into the garage, raving about the silly medical alert system, telling Raymond to just turn the fool thing off. Perhaps the original message would tell him more.

"Show me the message," he instructed.

An entire page of medical terminology appeared on his display. For a couple of seconds, he was completely baffled. The words "ischemic cardiomyopathy" jumped out at him as maybe having something to do with a heart attack. Then his doubts were erased. Toward the end of the message was the phrase "cardiac death imminent".

"Oh my god," he said aloud. "He *is* dying."

Basic human compassion finally kicked in. Somehow, he had never pictured being around when the old man died. He wasn't willing to call in outside help, but he at least had to go downstairs. Maybe there was something he could do. With long strides, he hurried back into the house, to the door at the top of the basement stairs. He pulled the door open and stepped down the first couple of stairs, then gripped the railing and paused. His bravado collapsed. He half expected some desperate zombie version of Tate to come up from the bottom of the stairs, clawing at him, pleading.

Raymond slowly descended the stairs, dazed by apprehension. In utter contrast to his imaginings, he found the basement to be quiet and completely still. The sparse furnishings were in their usual places, the space and its contents eerily unchanged.

The v-chamber's ventilation system hummed. The large black unit was ten feet square. Only the gap between its top and the basement ceiling made it seem like an object within a room, rather than a room of its own. The door was closed. Raymond walked around the end of the old double bed, a leftover from Tate's life before giving himself up so completely to v-space. On tip-toe, he approached the door, then paused again. He inched toward it, listening for sound, expecting the old man to burst out at any moment and reprimand him for the invasion of privacy.

Raymond's mind raced. What if Tate were dead? Nobody would know. Who could know? Was Tate with others in v-space when it happened? What would they have seen? The session should have terminated when the v-chamber recognized the health problem. Raymond was still recording Tate's sessions, forever refining his Tate persona—all he had to do was replay it, to see where the shutoff had occurred. Even if people had seen Tate die, how would they interpret it? It would most likely seem like the death of Tate's avatar, in whatever v-world he was in.

Paranoia seized Raymond. What if there were a surveillance system in the house that he didn't know about? Was there some way that the administrators at the Home could find out? Or could he just return to the Home at the end of the day and come back to work the next day, as if nothing had happened? He imagined himself having to take some crap job, like the other kids on the shuttle. Did anyone really have to know?

What am I doing?

Steeled for the possibility of finding Tate alive and in need, Raymond touched the door. It slid open. A violet light shone inside. A pair of boxer shorts sat in the center of the floor. Aside from these, Raymond saw nothing—the chamber looked empty. But the air was tainted with a sickly body odor, strong enough to defy the chamber's deluxe ventilation system.

Raymond stepped forward through the doorway.

To his right, on the floor, lay Tate, naked, legs folded under him, leaning against the wall. Motionless. The eerie stillness that Raymond had felt when he first reached the basement was magnified tenfold.

Raymond looked at the body. It looked as if the old man had been leaning his shoulder against the wall, then slid down. The violet light reflected off of Tate's bony shoulders and the bald crown of his head. It seemed such a pathetic end to this man's life of pride and ambition.

"You're dead, aren't you, Mr. Tate."

He paused, watching the body, as if Tate might suddenly gasp back to life. He started feeling light-headed. He backed out of the v-chamber. The door slid shut. He felt queasy, revolted. He made his way to the double bed, sat down on the bare mattress, and looked around at the mismatched furniture, oddly positioned here and there in the vast half-finished basement.

"This was no life," he said to himself. "He was done years ago. It's not like anyone's going to miss him."

His fleeting compassion for Tate faded.

He was just a dirty old man. So he's dead. It's not like I killed him.

His attention settled on the roll-away chrome-plated clothes rack, on which hung old pants and shirts Tate probably hadn't worn in years.

I can do this. Nobody ever visits the house. I just have to replace him with my Tate mimic. He's hardly ever in touch with anyone, except gamers and prostitutes—and they won't know the difference. I'll go home this afternoon and come back tomorrow, like nothing happened. And I'll quietly inherit his fortune.

"At this point, what else could I do?"

Raymond got up and reopened the v-chamber. He leaned against the chamber's door frame, crossed his arms, and took a deep breath. He started nodding to himself and chewing on the inside of his mouth, looking at the body as a problem.

CHAPTER 2

Friday, October 4, 2069

One afternoon, over nine years later, Raymond sat in his office at the University of Michigan's Life Computing Lab, doors closed, the lights dimmed. It was a spacious windowless office, sparsely furnished, an odd tinkerer's assortment of animal toys and disassembled robots in neat groupings on the beige industrial carpet. He wore his favorite computer terminal: an old matte-gray-metal noise-canceling helmet and a pair of black manuhaptic gloves. He had hacked into the private workspace of Tim Farley, one of the other software developers on the Human Mind Upload team, to take a look at Tim's progress on a project Raymond had wanted for himself—the creation of a new persona, known as "Hank the Handler".

"Figures he would use the Legrange lexicon," muttered Raymond disparagingly, skimming the persona's speech module. "Hank's gonna sound like a butler."

The team would soon be attempting, for the first time in human history, to upload the consciousness of a primate into a computer. If the upload of Bento, a terminally ill chimpanzee, were successful, the Hank persona would serve as Bento's handler in his new jungle v-world. Raymond had requested the Hank project, but he was the most junior developer on the team. Instead, he had been given the project of creating Bento's v-world, which he had knocked out in a single night. Tim had been working on the Hank persona for over a week, and Raymond was appalled by how crude it was so far. He wanted to scrap the whole thing and rebuild it himself. But he couldn't. Not yet, at least—not while it was in Tim's private workspace. Raymond already had a reputation for shredding and rebuilding the work of others as soon as it was released into the shared workspace. If he were caught making changes in a teammate's private workspace, he might lose his position on the team.

He moved his hands in his manuhaptic gloves, issuing commands in a sign language that he had created himself. It was a secret language that allowed him to communicate sensitive information while in plain view of others, one of his dozens of privacy innovations. The helmet was another of his creations. By using his own components, he could be sure there was no spyware monitoring his audio, video, and facial data.

His computer translated his gestures into commands, and soon he was skimming through Tim's design notes. He read the transcript of a conversation Tim had had earlier that morning with Ellen, the Chief Developer on the team. In the conversation, Tim explained a problem he had been having: when he tried to make Hank smile and talk while doing something with his hands, the persona would sometimes fail to react to visual events around him. In the conversation, Ellen guided Tim through a series of obvious things to look into, but together they had been unable to pinpoint the problem.

"Well, that's simple," said Raymond to himself. "The dumbass started with a customer service persona, and he probably left the peripheral awareness thread at its default priority."

Customer service personas were intended to have total focus on the customer, giving the impression of imperturbable dedication. Raymond took a look at the persona's root thread priorities and saw that he was right. He couldn't safely fix the problem, but he could help Tim to figure it out. He scripted Tim's design analyzer to point Tim in the right direction when he logged in Monday morning.

As Raymond continued to inspect Tim's work, he heard a voice whispering in his right ear. It was the voice of Scorpio, a persona he had created soon after he was released from the Canal Street Home and moved in full-time at Tate's. It was the voice most associated with Raymond's self-esteem, a voice more familiar than his mother's; Scorpio had been his fighting and adventuring companion in the v-worlds of Agakhan, Telemesis, and Seneca. Scorpio was Raymond's only confidant, and now served as the mouthpiece of Raymond's far-reaching surveillance network.

"Mosby," whispered Scorpio in his deep, dry voice. Mosby, his mother's maiden name, was Scorpio's nickname for Raymond. It was a name Raymond preferred to Quan, his father's family name. "Anya is headed to the break room."

Raymond closed his session with Tim's private network, tore off his helmet and gloves, and leapt from his chair. The break room was at the other end of the lab, and he didn't want to miss the opportunity to talk with Anya.

Anya Cordovil was one of the Human Mind Upload team's six scientists, not counting Bob Wells, Chief Scientist and head of the entire project. At age 28, Anya was the youngest of the scientists, only two years older than Raymond. Surprise had put Raymond off balance when he discovered that she was single—not married, not engaged, not even dating. Oddly, it was Darryl, Chief Tech on the upload project and all around super-geek, who first clued him in to her singleness. Darryl, a man bereft of subtlety, had been sitting with Raymond in the lab's break room, neither of them talking, when Anya came in to get a coffee. Facing away from them, wearing a black broomstick skirt and a bay cardigan, she bent from the waist to pick up a dropped stir-stick, then straightened up and shook loose her long black hair as she grabbed her coffee and left. As soon as the door closed behind her, Darryl let out a low whistle and turned to him. "Now just how is it that that girl's single? Someone needs to provision *that* resource."

Raymond had been attracted to Anya since he first met her, but he had always found her intimidating—she was so put-together and spoke so easily, with an air of authority made all the more impressive by the remnants of a Portuguese accent. Knowing she was single made her seem more approachable. For the first time in his life, he seriously entertained the idea of pursuing a girlfriend. After weeks of fantasizing about speaking to her, he finally got up the courage to do it, and he discovered that she was actually quite friendly. He had since managed to have several conversations with her, some of them unrelated to work—*personal* conversations. Raymond didn't have personal conversations with anyone. By his own request, he had a private office. He generally avoided partnering with others on development projects, and when he did end up pairing with someone, he talked only when necessary. He attended meetings, he responded to voice messages, he participated in work discussions. But he never broached personal topics—he frankly didn't care where most people lived, whether they had families, what their interests were, what they did over the weekend. And he responded to polite personal questions with polite superficial answers, keeping his carefully constructed façade of normalcy as simple and manageable as possible.

Anya was the exception. When she cordially asked how he was doing, he lit up. He had come up with a handful of safe topics, things he felt he could discuss without revealing his duplicitous life. He would tell her about his bike rides, or about whatever project he was working on at the lab. And she listened to him. She seemed genuinely interested in whatever he had to say, as if she had all the time in the world for him. He eventually hit on the topic of animals. They were both animal lovers, as it turned out, and she loved the work he did for the animals they uploaded, to make their lives more comfortable, more familiar. But the safe topics would come to an end, and he was left wishing he could come up with interesting questions to ask of her.

Not long after joining the upload team, Raymond had hacked into the security cameras throughout the lab, so that he could replace live footage of himself doing things he wasn't supposed to be doing with generated footage of himself innocently working. As a side benefit, he was able to spy on his co-workers. Only recently had this voyeur's tool really interested him. It allowed him to keep track of Anya, and sometimes he would watch her in the research labs and listen to her talk with others, hoping to get conversation ideas. But, face-to-face with her, the gap between reality and his fantasies of an intimate relationship seemed a vast, uncrossable chasm.

He had hurried to the break room the day before, just as he was now, only to find that Suma, the only developer on the team whom Raymond really respected, was already there. As he stood waiting for the drink machine to make him an almond vanilla shake, Suma and Anya got into a discussion about yoga. Anya mentioned that she had tried yoga a few times but had never been able to stick with it. Raymond, who had been doing yoga nearly every day for years, pictured himself becoming Anya's yoga trainer. He imagined impressing her with his discipline and spirituality. This fantasy had stayed with him the rest of the day, and had kept him up much of the night, until he finally convinced himself that he should ask her if she would be interested in doing yoga with him.

He walked now with long eager strides through the wide, brightly lit laboratory halls to the break room. Just before going in, he stopped to smooth his new shirt, a shiny black v-neck that he had had computer-tailored a little on the tight side, to show off his fit physique.

Anya stood by herself, her back to Raymond, looking at the project schedule on the wall. He could tell from the sound of the drink machine that her shake was nearly done. He walked around the table and chairs that occupied most of the room, crossed his arms on his chest, and looked over Anya's shoulder at the project schedule.

"Do you think we'll hit our target for the Bento upload?" asked Raymond.

"We have to," replied Anya with unexpected gravity. "He doesn't have much longer to live."

"Really?" Raymond's spirit fell. He'd caught her in a down mood. "Oh, wow. I didn't realize he was that sick."

"He's so weak." Anya looked at him with sad brown eyes. The privilege of her shared emotion felt like a gift to him. "I was with him last night. He's got a cold that his body just can't beat."

"Poor guy," said Raymond, sincerely touched.

"And all that's left between now and the upload is testing." She turned back to the schedule and shook her head. "Testing and re-testing. He's such a good little chimp. I can't stand the thought of losing him while we go through all this overkill."

She grabbed her mug from the drink machine and took a sip. Raymond asked for a mocha shake and the drink machine started working on it. They stood together for a moment, Raymond desperately wanting something else to say. He knew he was about to lose her. If the lull stretched even a few seconds longer, she would announce that she should go.

Anya let out a big sigh. "Well—"

"That was a big sigh," interrupted Raymond. "Sighing like that is a… can be a… sign of stress."

"Yeah, well—no surprise there, I guess."

Awkward pause.

"Do you ever do yoga?" asked Raymond.

"I've tried. You know, it's funny—Suma and I were just talking about yoga, yesterday. I love it, but I've never been able to stick with it."

"It does take discipline. You really have to make it a habit."

"So you do yoga?" asked Anya.

Raymond nodded and grabbed his drink. He was starting to have second thoughts, suddenly scared by the possibility that she might actually take him up on his offer.

"Do you go to a studio? Or do you just do it in a v-chamber?"

"Oh, a v-chamber." He wanted to go on to tell her about Nurania, but already he felt himself closing up. He wasn't used to sharing anything about himself. He could tell that Anya expected him to say something more, and he hated that he couldn't. He was so used to concealing the details of his life that anything even vaguely personal had to make it through miles of mental red tape before being approved for vocalization.

"I've tried doing yoga in a v-chamber," said Anya, taking up the slack in the conversation. "It just doesn't seem right to me. I mean, it's nice for lessons, but it always feels artificial. I like doing it in my living room. In my v-chamber, I'm always a little on edge, like I could be interrupted at any moment. I don't know, I guess I only feel in tune with my body when I'm in reality prime—nothing virtual."

"That's kind of ironic. Given you're an upload researcher, I mean."

Raymond's wrist relay vibrated. He glanced at it and saw that there was an urgent message for him from Scorpio. He tapped the display to acknowledge the notification and make it go away.

"I suppose," replied Anya. "Although, if I were uploaded, I guess the v-world would become my reality. I wouldn't be in a v-chamber, suspended in nanomist. But the v-chamber thing works for you?"

Raymond nodded. "It does." He made up his mind to tell her about Nurania, but just as he opened his mouth to speak, she started again to announce that she should go.

"I'm sorry," she said. "You were about to say something?"

"No, it was nothing. I was going to… never mind."

Anya looked at him quizzically. "You were going to say something about yoga?"

Suma entered the room. Raymond's instinct was to leave, to extricate himself from a group social situation where he might be the focus of attention.

"Hey guys," said Suma. She gave Anya a look that struck Raymond as teasing. "Did I overhear something about yoga?"

"It turns out Raymond is into yoga," said Anya.

"That's cool," said Suma to Raymond. He noticed her glance at his chest. "And you're probably the type who has no problem doing it every day."

"Not every day," he said. "There are some days where I'm just too busy."

"So, is it more of a workout thing for you?" asked Suma.

"No, I get that more from, um, karate and wing chun." Raymond mumbled the end of the sentence, embarrassed by the sense that he was bragging.

"Wow, that's really cool," said Suma. "I wish I exercised more. You know, isn't it unusual for a developer to be so physical? And yet you're this amazing developer, too. It's really impressive."

Suma crossed to the drink machine and asked for an iced tea. Anya and Raymond stood sipping their shakes. Raymond was torn between leaving and staying. His uncertainty about how to leave courteously made staying the default winner. Suma took her glass and relaxedly leaned against the counter.

"You were just saying you wanted to do yoga more often, weren't you?" asked Suma of Anya.

"Yeah," said Anya. "I just never make it a priority."

"You two should do yoga together."

Raymond stared at Suma, wondering whether she had actually just said those words. It was as if she had divined his fantasy, neatly boxed it up, and handed it to him—just as he was wondering whether it was something he really wanted.

"Suma!" scolded Anya. "I… I'm sorry, Raymond. I would never presume to impose on something so private."

"Oh, but—I mean, I…" Raymond was completely at a loss. He couldn't tell if Anya was trying to brush him off or merely being polite. But she could have left some time ago if she had wanted to.

Again Anya looked at him inquisitively. He felt she was trying to uncover the real meaning of the few words that escaped him. "You…" she coaxed tentatively.

"I wouldn't mind at all," said Raymond.

"Are you sure?" asked Anya. "I don't want you to feel obliged. You can certainly say 'no'."

"No, I'd love to." He locked eyes with Anya in an unmistakably meaningful moment, but bashfulness forced him to look away.

"Okay," said Anya. "I'll bring in yoga clothes on Monday, and we can try it some time next week. After work?"

"Sure," said Raymond. "Yeah, any day—just let me know."

"Then Monday," said Anya with a laugh and a shrug. "After work."

"Great—Monday," repeated Raymond. "I'll send you a v-world link, and you can… you can use one of the v-chambers here in the lab?" She nodded. "Alright. Great. I'll see you Monday."

He turned and left the break room, the remains of his shake in hand. He wanted to run and jump through the halls. The sound of excited whispering in the break room followed him. It occurred to him that he could play back sound from a security recording to hear what they were saying, but he decided it was probably best not to know. He would rather trust his sense that whatever it was, it was good.

As soon as his office door closed behind him, he jumped across the room and planted a solid kick in the practice bag that hung in the corner.

"I can't believe it. She likes me. And Suma knew it. They've talked—they must have. Oh my god. Anya likes me, enough that she actually told Suma. Oh my god!"

Raymond's wrist relay vibrated again. It was the same urgent message from Scorpio. He wondered what could possibly be so important. He ran a finger across the face of the relay and a holographic text message appeared just above Raymond's wrist. His grin collapsed.

CHAPTER 3

Monday, October 7, 2069

The simple purity of a Nuranian purple wren's crisp warbling echoed within Raymond's mind. He sat in lotus position, eyes closed, alone. He inhaled and exhaled fully, naturally, allowing the peace he had attained to seep through every muscle. The light gurgling of Orlea Brook, which surrounded him on three sides, felt as though it were within him. For the first time in three days, his mind was clear. Stress and exhaustion had given way to clarity. His worries had been set aside, and he felt ready now to lead Anya through a yoga session.

He opened his eyes. He was in Nurania, at his favorite yoga spot. He sat atop a small moss-covered rise at a bend of Orlea Brook, one of the red streams in the valley at the foot of Mount Golgora. The moss grew thick and soft, providing an ideal yoga mat. An old forest—home to hundreds of species he had created through the years—rose majestically all around him, wrapping his little spot in its vast sheltering embrace.

He unfolded his legs and tucked them underneath him, moving into Child's Pose. He bent forward at the waist, sinking further into the stretch with each exhalation. His forehead gradually sunk into the moss. The muscles in his neck felt relaxed for the first time in days, and the stretch felt hot in his lower back.

Self-control yields discipline, and the disciplined accumulation of power leads to freedom.

The mantra, conceived over nine years before, was still with him. It gave him a sense of gathered, focused, controlled energy, each time reminding him of his ultimate objective: to upload. He had carried the mantra with him through his time in Tate's home, following the old man's death; but only since learning of the upload project and enrolling at the University of Michigan had it taken on a sense of unwavering direction. It had fueled his intense drive to become a member of the project team. He had studied the publications and accomplishments of Bob Wells, the project's founder, with the sole intention of becoming someone Bob would find perfect for his team. He had enrolled in classes that would help him to understand all of the hardware and software used on the project, with no regard for the requirements of his declared major. And, two years ago, he had achieved his goal: he had been brought onto the team as a software developer.

Raymond stood gradually from Child's Pose into Mountain Pose. He would skip his usual relaxation cycle today.

"God mode," he instructed. "Teleport to the top of Mount Lidral."

The computer acknowledged his commands, and the environment of his v-chamber switched almost instantaneously. He braced himself against the sudden wind—he now stood atop a tropical mountain. The rocky slopes around him were steep and conical. Around his feet, wildflowers clung to bits of soil in cracks in the rock. From where he stood, he had a commanding view of the broad valley to the north, through which flowed a wide wine-red river.

Raymond spotted the flower garden he had created the night before, on a gentle slope along the near bank of the burgundy river.

"Teleport blink," he commanded.

He focused on the flower garden and slowly blinked his eyes. When he reopened them, he stood in the garden. The air was lightly perfumed with jasmine, a scent he had selected because most current v-chambers could faithfully reproduce it; he didn't want Anya's experience of the garden to be compromised by inferior hardware. Around him grew two acres of flowers, arranged in banks of increasing overall height. He had outlined the garden's perimeter with a wall of bushy trees from which hung long swaying strands of yellow-green leaves, a variety of willow he had created the night before. In the center of the garden was a small pond. Lily pads floated on the surface of the water, ample white flowers hovering over shiny green leaves. Little gold and amber frogs swam amid the roots, shimmering in the sunlight. Raymond scanned his creation, looking for anything out of place. He noticed a large rose bush in gushing bloom, and he felt that a lighter touch was needed.

"Replace the rose bushes with peonies," he instructed. The rose bushes disappeared, replaced by white peonies. "Make the peonies a bit shorter, and give the petals a pinker tint." The v-world engine carried out his commands. With the rose bushes gone, he was better able to see the flox that grew further back, and the softer color of the peonies gave the nearby dahlias a chance to shine.

He looked about nervously.

"I think she'll like it."

Raymond had created and destroyed many v-worlds since he first created Nurania, but this world had remained a work in progress ever since his teen years. Its underlying v-world engine had been upgraded many times, but the world itself had developed gradually, without the sweeping fickle changes typical of his other v-world projects. For a long time, he had dreamed of uploading and making Nurania his home, and he wanted it to feel natural and complete. Now that he might be uploading rather sooner than expected, he was grateful for his consistent, restrained approach to designing it.

Not only had Nurania been protected from whimsy over the years; it had also remained secret. It was his private sanctuary, never subjected to any criticism other than his own, an entire planet never seen by another human. Even now, just minutes before their scheduled yoga session, he was having second thoughts about sharing it with Anya. But it was his first date with a real woman, if it could really be considered a date, and he wanted to impress her.

He had dated women in public v-worlds, on the Net, but had never had a date with someone who was part of his real life. And his v-world dates weren't exactly dates. They were more like sexual rendezvous, in fantastically steamy settings, with women who may in fact have been bots. This was utterly different. Never had he experienced such a mix of hope and tremulous dread.

His thoughts returned inevitably to the intelligence relayed to him by Scorpio on Friday. Parts of the message replayed in his mind.

"The homicide division of the Illinois State Police has reopened the Tate case, at the request of family members. State Police Detective Trumbull has agreed to share records from the original missing person investigation with private investigator Arnold Murray."

One of Raymond's old listeners, spyware planted in Illinois police networks years ago, had recognized the significance of the reopening of the case and had fired a message to Raymond's surveillance headquarters, in his bunker in Minnesota. The message was flagged as urgent and sent to the private network in his motor home, which was registered to a false identity and sat concealed in a pole barn on his property northeast of Ann Arbor. There, the message was summarized and forwarded to his wrist relay. Tate's fortune was serving Raymond well.

Raymond hadn't slept more than a few hours since receiving the message. The entire weekend had been consumed hacking, listening, and data thieving, trying to figure out why the case had suddenly been reopened. He had to move carefully, making absolutely sure that none of his network activity could be traced back to him, but he was desperate for information.

He discovered that Murray had been hired by two of Tate's nephews just a few days before the reopening of the police investigation. A review of Murray's career showed him to be a smalltime Chicago P.I. Research into the nephews turned up nothing more interesting than a weak credit history, including a recent denial for a large loan. They were probably just fishing for inheritance money from their disappeared. But the fact that the police had agreed to reopen the case worried Raymond. Some new piece of evidence must have turned up. Why else would they bother to put staff on such an old investigation?

"Mosby, she's ready."

Raymond turned and saw that Scorpio stood behind him. The persona's avatar was that of an imposing man, tall, broad-shouldered, and grizzle-bearded.

He wore a long black leather coat and wicked-looking boots—black leather things with chromed buckles and trim.

"If I do come here with Anya, I can't have you showing up looking like that. From now on, in Nurania, you're a… blue jay."

The man disappeared, replaced by a brilliantly-colored little blue jay.

"Exit Nurania," instructed Raymond. "Take me to the yoga studio."

The flower garden dissolved, and Raymond stood in the center of an airy, British-colonial, wood-floored pavilion—the same virtual space in which he had taken karate lessons from Andrea, as a boy. This v-space, along with all of Crown Nanotronics' other v-spaces, had been released to the public domain soon after the company went bankrupt. Raymond continued to use this space for martial arts practice, and it struck him over the weekend that it would make a fine yoga studio.

Anya stood at the edge of the pavilion, looking out at the surrounding jungle. She wore loose black calf-length pants and a tank top, and her long black hair was up in a twist. Raymond, wearing shorts and a sleeveless shirt, realized he hadn't mentioned to Anya that the setting would be tropical. He walked across the yoga mats he had set out and crossed to where Anya stood.

"If you're warm in those pants, I can drop the temperature," said Raymond.

"This is a really beautiful setting," said Anya, still looking out at the tropical flowers and tall jungle trees. She turned to him. Her eyes and face already seemed softer than usual, more at peace. "Did you create it?"

"I copied it and made the jungle a little more lifelike. I learned karate in this space, when I was a teenager." He chose not to mention that he was a State Home child.

"The flowers are amazing. You're so good with jungles—I love the habitat you've created for Bento. You seem to give every detail equal attention."

"I have great tools." He considered making a joke about how his Vietnamese side gave him a natural affinity for jungles but cut himself off again. "So, I guess… do you want to get started?"

"Sure."

Raymond led the way to the middle of the room, and they sat facing each other on the mats, about six feet apart.

"Oh, I don't know if you heard me earlier," said Raymond. "Is it too hot?"

"No, I'm fine. These pants breathe really well. It's perfect."

A jitter went through Raymond's body. He couldn't tell how much of it was nerves and how much exhaustion.

"I've never done this before," he said. "Teach, I mean."

"Well, I'm an easy student. I've taken classes, I just have a hard time doing it on my own."

"Okay. I was thinking I would mostly just go through a routine I like, nothing too advanced. Stop me if you're unfamiliar with a pose, or whatever."

He led them through a routine that emphasized balance, stretching, breathing, and clearing the mind. He found that Anya was able to keep up quite well, and his mind started to drift. He had always pictured himself living alone in Nurania after he uploaded, free of human society and free from criminal investigation. Now, as he snuck looks at Anya's body, he imagined her visiting him in v-space. He imagined them in a secret relationship, making love on the moon-drenched beaches of Agakhan.

He finished the routine in Corpse Pose, with them both lying on their backs, eyes closed. He repeated the words of his virtual yoga instructors, talking Anya systematically through the relaxation of every muscle. "Soften the face. Soften the eyes, soften the tongue. Feel your eyes falling to the backs of your eye sockets. Feel your head sinking into the earth." Earlier that day, he had worried that she would find yoga hokey, but he found himself speaking with soul, in a rare moment of separation from self-consciousness. It made him feel close to her, at one with her, in a way he had never felt with anyone.

"Now feel your mind go blank. You are in the moment. You are not outside the moment, looking in. You are in the moment. Hear the birds. Let their song own your mind. Hear the breeze through the palm fronds. Not one muscle in your body is active. Your lips are soft, your cheeks are slack. There is only your breath and the peace of the world around you. Now lie like this, in silence. If your mind stirs, slowly bring it back and allow it to settle again. Focus on the birds, then release yourself to nothingness. Be at one with the moment."

He stopped talking and tried to let himself slip into the state of mind he had described. It was a state very familiar to him now, and one that he could usually attain quite readily. But his imagination was unstoppable. He imagined the weight of Anya's body on his, as if she were lying face-up on top of him. Her weight, motionless, on his chest and stomach, pelvis and thighs, pressing him closer to the earth. He imagined her with him in the flower garden he had made for her; he wondered what he could say to start the transition from here to there.

When he felt that a couple of minutes had passed, he slowly talked her out of the meditative state, into a position where she was curled up on her side, and finally into a seated position.

"Okay," he said, to indicate that the routine was over.

"Wow." She had a big sleepy smile on her face, a smile Raymond found infectious. "That was so nice. You're *really* good, Raymond."

He just smiled at her, not sure how to take the compliment.

"I wasn't expecting it to be so relaxing. I guess I was expecting you to be more into the strength-building poses. I had no idea you were so… spiritual."

The way the word "spiritual" came out, Raymond wasn't sure how to take it. It sounded like she might have meant it as a code word for "cheesy", but the look on her face made him think she was on the same wavelength.

"Wow. Thank you so much, Raymond." She slowly stood up, and Raymond followed her lead. "I guess we don't have to roll up our mats and put them away," she said with a chuckle. The dreaminess was already gone from her tone.

Raymond lifted his head slightly and spoke, an indication that he was giving a command to the computer. "Remove the yoga mats." The mats vanished.

"So, are you in the v-chamber in your office?" asked Anya.

"Yeah."

"I was thinking I might grab a bite to eat. Any interest in joining me?"

"Uh…" Raymond hesitated. "Sure." His idea of showing Anya the flower garden escaped his grasp that easily.

"Have you been to La Sevillana?" Her pronunciation of the Spanish was exquisite.

"No," replied Raymond rather dryly. He suddenly felt like he was being drawn into a dangerous undertow, and he didn't like it.

"It's wonderful. It's on Liberty, just west of Main. It's great for me—I live on the old west side. That's not inconvenient for you, is it? Where do you live?"

"I have an apartment on Kingsley, east of State." Strictly speaking, this was true—he did rent an apartment on Kingsley. He just didn't see it very often, as he preferred the secrecy of his motor home. "But, you know, I'm not sure I really feel like eating. I had a dinner shake around five."

"Oh, are you sure?"

Raymond rarely ate out, and this sounded like it might be a nice restaurant. The thought of flubbing his way through a fancy meal sounded awful.

"I just don't think I could eat."

"Maybe a glass of wine?"

"I don't know."

"We'll go for a glass of wine," she insisted, with a European flair for finality. "It's a lovely place—you'll love it. I'll just change and meet you in the lobby, and we can take a cab. Okay?"

The way she coaxed him make him feel childish.

"Sure," he replied reluctantly.

By the time Raymond got to the lobby, Anya was already there, and she had a little two-seater cab waiting outside. They climbed into the little bench seat together.

"La Sevillana," instructed Anya, and the automated car rolled noiselessly forward. "I love La Sevillana. It reminds me of my childhood home, in Portugal. We visited Seville quite often."

Raymond tried to break through the huffy mood he was in.

"Did you grow up in Portugal?" he asked. "Your accent isn't very strong."

"I lived there until I was seven, then off and on. My father's a science journalist, so his English is fluent. Why," she asked, putting on a thick Portuguese accent, "would you like for me to speak with a strong foreign accent?"

"Well… no," stammered Raymond, taken off guard by her playfulness. "You sound fine without one."

"Fine?" she mocked. "Just fine? Good—flattery is so boring."

Raymond looked at her and smiled with eyebrows furrowed, puzzled by her sudden change of stance. She looked back at him, and he turned away.

"You keep to yourself a lot, don't you, Raymond?"

"I suppose. Aside from work."

"It's not healthy to spend too much time alone. Humans are social animals."

"What if I don't like being with other people?" asked Raymond.

"Oh, I don't know," she mused. "It's okay to want to be by yourself sometimes, but too much just isn't good for you. Oh, look, we're here."

The little car pulled to a stop. Raymond wondered for a moment whether he was supposed to have paid for the cab, but the fare would have been automatically deducted from Anya's account. They climbed out, and Anya led the way into the restaurant.

Raymond was surprised to see that the place was full of people. It was a dark, cozy interior, a couple steps down from street level. It had the feel of an old Spanish restaurant. People were standing, talking loudly in tight groups around the bar. The atmosphere presented a sharp deviation from Raymond's concept of America as a country of people living out their lives in isolated v-chambers.

"Anya!"

A short, dark-complected, congenial-faced man in his forties greeted Anya with a kiss on the cheek. The man then turned to Raymond and offered an extended hand, much to Raymond's relief.

"Table or bar?" he asked.

"Table, please," answered Anya.

The man led them through a dimly-lit maze of little rooms and seated them at a small corner table. There was a stack of red clay dishes in the middle of the table, and a wire basket full of silverware and napkins. Anya picked up the wine list, and Raymond looked around him. Only in v-worlds had he ever been in a place with such energy.

"Red or white?" she asked. "Or maybe sangria?"

"Sangria?" asked Raymond.

"Sure," she responded. "Sangria always sounds good to me."

He meant, "What is sangria?", but he decided not to pursue it. Instead, he crossed his arms over his chest and looked around him, feeling very out of place.

"Is everything okay?" asked Anya.

"Yeah, sure." Raymond scooted his chair forward and set his left arm on the table, trying to make himself look more comfortable. It felt odd. He removed it and folded his hands in his lap.

Anya leaned across the table and spoke in a lowered voice.

"Raymond, are you nervous about something?"

He crossed his arms again and looked away.

"We can go if you'd like," she offered.

"No, no."

A waiter approached the table, and Anya ordered two glasses of red sangria. She started reading through the tapas menu. Raymond looked at her, wanting to say something, but he didn't know what to say. She looked up and met his eyes for a moment before he could turn away.

"I'm sorry," said Anya, again in a low tone. "Was I wrong to ask you out like this?"

"No, it's not that," said Raymond reassuringly. "I… I'm just nervous. I don't know. You must think I'm a freak now."

"Is it something about this restaurant?"

"Partially. I don't know. I… I think it's just…"

"Just… what?"

"I don't know," he shot back at her. He felt an awkwardness bordering on nausea; he hated the people around him, so beautifully comfortable; and all this ugly turmoil filled him with self-disgust. "I shouldn't be here. I don't know what I was thinking. You're a part of all this, and I'm just not."

He burned with an intensity he didn't understand, surprised that he had been able to speak. She seemed to study him, her eyes softly penetrating, and he held her gaze defiantly.

"I'm sorry," she said. "I had no idea." She stood up and held out her hands to him.

He looked up at her. "What?"

"Come with me." She shook her hands at him insistently. "Come on. I'm taking you out of here."

"But, the—"

"Don't worry about it. Just come with me."

He hesitantly gave her his hands and allowed her to pull him up. She led him out of the restaurant.

"Anya, what's the matter?" asked the man who had greeted her at the door.

"I'm sorry, we have to leave, Lucas. Tell Carlos I'll catch up with him for the sangrias."

"Is everything okay?" called out the man, but Anya had whisked Raymond past the man and up the stairs.

Outside, on the sidewalk, she didn't stop. She tightly held Raymond's hand, leading him at a run down the street. After a block or so, she slowed to a brisk walk. Raymond didn't know what was happening, but his mood had vanished; he was ready to throw himself at the feet of this woman's electrifying intensity. She led him on for several blocks, away from downtown and into a sleepy neighborhood. She turned onto a side street and continued to pull him along until they reached a small stone church. They walked along the low stone wall that ran along in front of the church until reaching a break in the wall. Anya led him through the opening, into a dark secluded statue garden.

"What are we doing here?" asked Raymond, voice lowered.

"I walk by this garden all the time," said Anya. "I thought it would be a nice place to get away."

"I'm sorry if I—"

She cut him off with a sharp "ssh". She led him deeper into the garden, around a small concrete fountain that had been drained for winter, to an arbor at the back. She released his hand and took a step away.

Raymond looked around nervously. It was only 7:30 or so, but it had been dark for hours. He felt as though they were intruding in the garden. His heart was racing with curious anticipation.

"Raymond," she said in a soft, caring voice, "what you said, about my being a part of all this but your not being a part of all this—it's not true. Things may feel foreign—"

"Anya, you don't—"

Again she cut him off, this time lifting a finger to his lips.

"Do you find me attractive?" she asked. She lowered her finger.

"Yes," he replied, without hesitation.

"You know how you were telling me to be in the moment earlier, when we were doing yoga?"

"Sure."

"I want you to be in the moment right now."

She moved toward him, to kiss him. He recoiled slightly, taking a half-step backward to keep his balance. He felt her cool fingers wrap around the back of his neck, he felt her soft lips on his. She kissed him, softly at first, then harder. He was rigid and unresponsive, taken off guard.

She leaned past him, her voice near his ear. "Have you ever been kissed like that?" She hugged him.

He stared blankly past her, dazed but enthralled. He shook his head. "I've never been kissed at all—not by a real woman."

She kissed him again, this time more gently, giving him a chance to respond. He felt the tension release from his shoulders. He tentatively reached up and ran his fingers over her hair. She held him more tightly, and he felt the passion of their kiss grow.

Anya gave him a last kiss and withdrew, smiling at him. He stood stunned. She took his hands in hers.

"I'd like to make you dinner some time, Raymond. And get to know you. Just let me know when you're ready." She kissed his cheek, released his hands, and walked quickly off.

Raymond watched her. He thought about going after her, but she had ended the moment perfectly. He sank onto a nearby bench and sat for a good long while, reliving her kisses and sorting through her words.

CHAPTER 4

Thursday, October 17, 2069

Raymond sat cross-legged in the grass, bathed in warm sunlight, taking an early lunch hour in the mini v-chamber in his office. He was flicking acorns off the base of the sugar maple about six feet in front of him. Buster, a gray squirrel uploaded at the lab earlier that year, clung head-downward to the trunk of the tree, looking distrustfully from acorn to Raymond to acorn, agitatedly jerking his bushy tail. Raymond noted the clicking sensation on his thumbnail as he flicked another acorn. It felt like it should, light and crisp. The level of detail achieved by his new v-chamber amazed him—he could see why the Nanograph physics engine was winning so many awards. As a test, he pushed his right thumbnail in with his left. The depressed area of his avatar's thumbnail turned white under the pressure, just as his own would.

"That is so cool," he said to himself.

He lay back in the soft, insect-free grass and closed his eyes, thinking that—if he lay still awhile—Buster might come down for more acorns. With his right hand, he made a gesture that indicated to the v-chamber's computer that he was about to give one of his private hand instructions. He then made the sign for the letter "A". His v-chamber recognized the command and responded by presenting an image via his retinal implants. He saw Anya in her office, from the security camera mounted above her door. She was reading from a tablet, her feet up on her footstool. He massaged his stomach muscles, sore from doing crunches, as he watched her.

In the week-and-a-half since their kiss, their time together had been disappointingly professional. They had eaten lunch together three times, each time by her invitation, but always with others. He sought her out in the break room once, but—alone with her—he found himself struck silent; his ignorance of what to say or how to behave filled him with aimless resentment. Her smiles and searching glances confirmed their nascent intimacy, but their conversations never strayed from the safety of work topics. Each time they parted, he was left wondering whether he could ever break through with her again, and how he could possibly express his desire to accept her offer of dinner.

He looked down at her now, at her long black hair hanging over the back of her chair, and imagined what it would feel like to sit next to her in her bed as she slept. He would feel so privileged to see this woman, so vital and engaged by day, in the vulnerable torpor of sleep.

A woman's voice startled Raymond: "Attention Uploaders." It was the voice of Janet, the lab's digital information assistant, speaking from the sky above the park. He opened his eyes, subconsciously seeking the source of the voice.

It was unusual for a Janet announcement to interrupt a personal v-chamber session. Raymond closed his eyes again, just long enough to see that Anya had looked up from her tablet, an expectant look on her face; she clearly had heard the announcement, too.

"I have an urgent announcement," came Janet's voice again, sounding large and distant, like a goddess speaking from the simulated heavens of Buster's park. "The Ethics of Science Worldcourt today issued its position statement on the uploading of a human consciousness into a computer, declaring that destructive upload of a human is fundamentally unethical and could constitute homicide."

Raymond sat up, sending Buster racing up the tree.

"Buster, this is not good," said Raymond, more to himself than to the squirrel.

Through the course of the past ten years, the ESW had gained a great deal of respect worldwide. The Naturalist movement, formed in the wake of the back-to-back technological disasters of 2059—the Manchester meltdown and the backfired attempt at rehabilitating the atmosphere over Antarctica—gained adherents with each new technological scare. The ESW was popularly viewed as a balanced and authoritative voice, as much in line with mainstream thinking as possible amidst such contentious issues. The position statement, indication of an increasingly Naturalist leaning in the court, was sure to have a deep impact on the largely corporate-funded budget of the Human Mind Upload Project.

Raymond jacked out, knowing his avatar's automation would kick in and keep feeding the squirrel for two more minutes then exit the park, lending a realistic sense of continuity to the squirrel's world. As he stepped into his office from his v-chamber, he continued to hear the news story, now from speakers around his office. He donned his favorite terminal, the gray lightweight helmet. His hands fell naturally into the manuhaptic gloves that hung like holsters at his side. He opened secret channels into the private informational world of Bob Wells, head of the Upload project, confident that his alterations to the lab's operating systems would allow him to monitor Bob's actions undetected.

Raymond checked Bob's private messaging inbox. Confidential communications from corporate backers followed close on the heels of the news from the ESW. Raymond skimmed them as they came in. All indicated that year-2070 grant money tagged for the Human Mind Upload Project—work for which

Bob Wells' name was known throughout the science and technology communities—would have to be pulled. The power of automated public-image management was at play. Across the board, corporate risk analysis software responded negatively to the ESW's decision. Bob would instruct his digital information assistants to appeal for reconsideration, of course, but there could be little doubt that the project's trajectory had just taken a sharp turn dirtward.

Raymond wondered how Bob would react to this turn of events. The man had over thirty years of research under his belt, much of which had pushed the boundaries of contemporary ethics. He was probably pretty used to this sort of thing. His work on the selective replacement of brain tissue with artificial lobes outfitted with radio transceivers raised all sorts of ethical concerns regarding privacy, human identity, and the possibility of brainwashing. His work on embedding encryption/decryption chips in the brain, enabling governments and corporations to "turn off" knowledge of sensitive information held by employees, had made his name anathema among privacy rights advocates. He had encountered such ethical roadblocks before, and it soon became apparent that he had anticipated this one; within an hour of the position statement's release, Bob had scrapped his "Plan A" budget and was bringing "Plan B" up to date, to account for the funding withdrawals. He could continue limited work on the project, probably hoping that the Naturalists on the ESW would be displaced in the years to come. He might even be able to obtain new anonymous funding, from individuals and corporations keenly interested in the outcome of his research.

Of course, their current work would not be called into question. So far, the team had successfully scanned and uploaded the minds of fruit flies, mice, rats, squirrels, dogs, and pigs. The ESW ruling said nothing about the destructive uploading of non-human primates. But the real money lay in human upload. The corporations funding their animal research were investing in the long-term payoff of human upload. At full funding, it might be years before Bob felt prepared for the first human upload. With budget cuts and the possibility of massive legal battles, testing was likely to grind to a halt, regardless how small the theoretical gap between chimp upload and human upload. Raymond felt a sudden pang of despair.

This whole thing could unravel.

It occurred to Raymond that Bob might even see a bright side to this turn of events. Competing projects worldwide would face similar budget cuts, bringing the field to a pause. This pause would give Bob some much-needed time to publish findings and to catch up with his other project, complementary research on the computer-controlled sustenance of a human brain—research deemed ethically acceptable—noble, even—by moderate Naturalists.

The one serious repercussion of the ruling for Bob, by Raymond's estimation, was that he would have to cut staff. Even though most team members were not particularly well paid, payroll and workstation leases were the most marginal areas of Bob's budget. He couldn't afford to sell off any of the team's expensive research equipment—he needed everything the team owned in order to continue working, and there was no way to safely cut corners on the maintenance of such mission-critical equipment. The first place to make cuts would have to be in staffing.

Bob had proclaimed many times how very proud he was of the team he had put together. Raymond watched now as Bob tweaked Plan B's personnel allocation. It came as no surprise to see that Anya's name was gone from the list. The past few days, she and Raymond had been discussing the project and its future, in light of Bento's worsening illness; Anya knew she frustrated Bob. He criticized her for being too eager, too emotional about her science. She was also inclined to think Bob viewed her as something of a threat, as if she might steal his thunder, using her father's science journalism connections to leak findings into publication before Bob was ready to publish his own papers.

Raymond wasn't surprised to see that Kim and Jake were amid the Plan B cuts, either; of the team's technicians, Darryl was the real expert, and Bob could bring in free student help if he had to. Of the programmers, Raymond was the obvious cut. He was the last brought onto the team, not even two years ago, and he didn't have a degree. Although his talent was obvious and his custom tools had measurably accelerated the team's progress, his lack of credentials would make keeping him unsupportable, especially since the other developers had all done cross-over work on Bob's brain sustenance project.

Even after dropping Anya, Kim, Jake, and Raymond, Bob's Plan B bottom line was still red. A text alert popped into Raymond's field of view, informing him that Bob was establishing a voice-visual connection with his digital assistant, to whom Bob had trustingly assigned one of Raymond's custom personas—that of a bustling, warm-hearted, middle-aged woman named Tina. Raymond tuned in, seeing and hearing roughly the same thing that Bob saw and heard through his pricey comm implants. Bob instructed Tina to gather his notes on the possible scientific benefits of the uploading of chimp minds and present them to various university administrators in hopes of garnering additional funding. "And Tina, we need to change the project name," he said. "Drop 'Human'. Present it as the Mind Upload Project."

"You got it, boss," replied Tina.

Raymond, listening from his office, was aware of Bob's every computer action. His software agents, enjoying the lax security of the university lab, monitored activity throughout the network. The moment Bob instructed his project management application to make the necessary adjustments for

Raymond's year-end termination, one of Raymond's planted agents recognized this as an alarm-worthy event. As Raymond thoughtfully watched Bob's edits, he heard Scorpio's voice whispering in his right ear.

"Mosby," whispered Scorpio. "You may want to take a look at Bob's project schedule. You want it?"

His hands still in the manuhaptic gloves, Raymond signed to Scorpio that he was already on it.

"You'll notice," said Scorpio, "that you're off the project as of December 19, just before break."

Raymond nodded. "Budget cuts," he muttered.

I need to figure out if I really can upload. I need to see Anya.

"Scorpio, have Puck compose a message to Anya. Something… clever. I want to take her up on her offer of dinner. Tonight, if possible."

"Mosby, you should tell her yourself. You do know that, right?"

Raymond was taken aback—Scorpio rarely offered advice. Even Scorpio recognized the cowardly avoidance in having a persona do his talking for him.

"I can't," said Raymond. "I've tried. I don't know how."

Raymond sat at his desk, massaging his temples, dwelling on the consequences of losing his spot on the team. Uploading was more than a dream for him now. It was his escape plan. He had originally joined the team to be among pioneers, taking part in research that really meant something to him. Intellectually, he saw uploading as a chance for the sick to escape their failing bodies, a chance for scientists to gain a deeper understanding of the mysteries of the human mind, a chance for humans to reduce their impact on the environment. It would facilitate space travel, allowing humans to beam their minds across the solar system in digital form. On a more personal level, it represented a means of entering a world wherein his imagination could define every aspect of his own reality. It would give him the opportunity to escape society, or create his own if he wanted one.

Now, uploading had a rather more urgent meaning. It was the beautiful way out of the fraud he had perpetuated since he was seventeen.

He stood up from his chair and started to pace. Adrenaline surged through his body. His hands formed fists. He eyed the kick-practice bag in the corner but consciously diverted his energy to scheming. He could not afford to lose his access to the scanning and uploading equipment. He suddenly had less than two months left on the project. Maybe he could wait, go into hiding, and come back when the upload research was further along—just break into the lab. But the longer he stayed away, the more the project would move beyond him, increasing the likelihood of a mistake. By the time he came back, he might not even know how to operate the scanner.

Bob might be willing to keep me on unpaid. I could monitor the Tate investigation. Who knows—maybe it'll blow over. Maybe they'll never come up with enough to arrest me. But what if I missed something, and the cops show up one day to take me away? Maybe this is just the motivation I needed to make my getaway now, while I have time.

The barriers to human upload had been discussed at length in team meetings. To Anya, the gap between chimp and human seemed trivial. The scanning hardware and raw computer hardware on hand were theoretically adequate. The greatest issues lay in the interrelation of scanned mind and simulated body. The approach to scanning they had taken thus far was first to monitor all major systems in the live source animal, then destructively scan the entire body cell by cell, with nanobots. Every cell in the nervous system was mapped into a highly specialized computer wherein the self-configuring hardware mimicked the behavior of the brain and all nervous pathways into and out of it. This computer then interfaced with a simulation running on another computer, a simulation of every other system of the body—muscular, skeletal, digestive, etc. This "body" simulation also provided the sensations of the virtual world in which the uploaded animal perceived itself as existing. All of the scientists on the team were pretty confident in the accuracy of the nervous system scan, but many unknown complexities lay in the neurohormonal effects of the body on the mind and vice versa. Bob Wells, himself a leading neurohormonologist, believed that their current simulation of neurohormones was a gross oversimplification. In their tests on small mammals, it had been difficult to judge whether the personality of the scanned animal matched that of its source.

Raymond had witnessed some very disturbing images in his two years on the project. He recalled the never-released images of Minnie, the uploaded beagle, when she first encountered the simulation of her loving real-world trainer and companion, Jesse, in her new v-world. Minnie sniffed at her, then cowered and ran. They tried the introduction over and over, thinking that the dog had experienced some kind of trauma, but there was no improvement. Jesse said it was as if Minnie didn't recognize her. Perhaps it was a problem with the memory scan, the researchers posited, causing Minnie to have no recollection of Jesse. Or was Minnie's computer brain not able to interpret the visual data it was receiving? Poor Minnie, whose real-world body had been destroyed molecule by molecule during the scanning process, suffered two real-world months of depression in her simulated world before Anya realized that their whole simulation of smells and olfactory receptors was vastly inferior to that of Minnie's natural life. None of the smells in her new world was anything like those she remembered, which, as it turned out, she remembered just fine; once the smell-related subsystems of Minnie's simulated physiology and environment had been appropriately enhanced, her reunion with the simulated Jesse was a squirmy, jumpy explosion of dopamine-crazed face-licking. The real Jesse, watching footage of this reunion, cried at the sight of it.

Although the team had ultimately figured out the nature of this problem and was able to solve it, there seemed to be thousands more such oversights awaiting discovery, especially for an animal so psychologically complex as a human. Similar problems had been encountered and overcome with every animal; improvements made to the olfactory system of Lentil the mouse had not been good enough for Minnie the beagle. It seemed quite likely that more problems would be encountered with Bento, the terminally ill chimp they planned to upload in the coming weeks. Problems capturing the complexity of a chimp's socialization seemed particularly likely. The researchers were optimistic about being able to quickly rectify any problems that arose, but they would not be available to fix the problems with uploaded Raymond; if he did upload, he sure as hell didn't plan to stick around the lab.

It had been assumed from the start that an uploaded human would not have exactly the same experiences. Consumption of alcohol, for instance, would not destroy the hardware that corresponded to brain cells. Alcohol would taste the same and might induce drunken behavior, but no one saw any point in simulating the physiological downside of neural damage. Where Bob argued that such shortcomings and unknowns would make the uploaded mind something other than human, Anya argued that the essential mental experience would be the same, and that the benefits of uploading already outweighed the risks for a person at high risk of an aneurysm, for instance. She argued that everything human would still be there, but there was the potential for life overall to be better. Where feasibility was concerned, she had pointed out repeatedly how similar humans are to chimps, arguing that—once the bugs had been ironed out in a few chimp uploads—the leap from chimp to human wasn't giant at all.

Raymond's conclusion, based on the meetings he had attended and his own understanding of how their proposed system would work, was that the system would soon be ready enough. Once uploaded, he reasoned, there should be nothing stopping the mind from altering the simulation of its body as necessary. So long as every aspect of mental perception could be controlled, the smoke and mirrors that made it all seem human were just a matter of cleverness. So, he planned to learn as much as he could from Anya, preferably without her knowing why he was so interested.

Of more immediate and fathomable concern, however, were the tactical and strategic issues of uploading himself—getting away with it, and escaping his crimes in the process. The computer that could hold his mind was a rare device indeed, and not something that could be emulated in real time—as far as he could figure—on some more common platform. It would take a massive collection of traditional computers to pull off what one of the neuristor-based computers (NBCs) could do, and the communications overhead among all those traditional computers would be immense, slowing or perhaps even ruining the magic of the human thought process. He knew of only four NBCs capable of hosting a human mind: the development, test, and production NBCs they planned to use for Bento the chimp, and the NBC being used by a lab in Berlin where researchers were attempting to create the mind of an infant from scratch and develop it at an accelerated pace into that of a young child. As much as he dreamt of being able to slip through networks, a refugee mind hacking its way nomadically into systems around the world, he would, in fact, have to rely on a single piece of hardware, custom-built to process information in the manner of a human brain. Which meant he would have to deal with the hardware maintenance side of things.

Keeping his host computer powered and safe would be his first concern. This was also the easiest problem to solve. He had been keeping computers going at his bunker in Minnesota for five years now, checking in on them only once every few months. The solar arrays and windmills there had thus far shown a zero failure rate. As for keeping the host computer safe, secrecy and deception—as usual—would be his greatest weapons. The tougher problem would be getting the machines there. He would have to perform the scan here at the lab and rely on robots to load the NBC into his motor home, which had gotten itself to Minnesota and back dozens of times. Unloading and installing the NBC on the other end could be dicey. An experienced listener and data thief, theft of physical property made him nervous. He couldn't stand the thought of his robots carting his future brain out of the university building, while his mind lay temporarily dead in storage media. He imagined one of the robots dropping some key component and accidentally crushing it. And the people… there would be so many people. Even if he waited until Christmas break, students and staff would still be in and out of the building at all hours. Physical exposure was a relatively foreign concern for him; the thought of it made him feel naked and scared.

Janet, the lab's information assistant, announced an all-hands meeting in the main conference room. Raymond wondered just how much Bob would tell. He headed out of his office as Ellen, the Chief Programmer of the team, was coming out of hers, just across the hall. Ellen Emami, a skinny nothing-but-business workaholic in her mid-40s, had been working with Bob Wells for many years. Raymond had looked into her background before joining the team, but had since forgotten most of what he had found. Nothing worth remembering, in his opinion. She was one of those programmers who seem to have been assimilated by the machines they work. Raymond only wished he could swap out her personality and replace it with one of his own creation. As they walked to the conference room, she asked him how his current tasks were coming along. He answered her directly, wondering whether she had even the slightest grasp of the significance of the ESW statement.

Eleven members of the thirteen-member team sat and stood in cramped assembly in the conference room. Bob Wells, a short pudgy man in his late fifties, stood at the head of the main table. His eyes closed and his lips moved slightly; he was communicating via his comm implants.

Raymond looked across the room to where Anya sat. She sipped a shake while reading from a tablet. A coffee-banana shake, for sure—that was her favorite. Raymond loved that she had a favorite, and took pleasure in recognizing that he knew what it was. He wondered whether an uploaded mind would experience that same pleasure, and it occurred to him to start his own journal of sensations, that he might test their presence if he succeeded in uploading himself. He immediately thought of the confusion of lust, tenderness, defensiveness, compassion, and joy he felt when he and Anya had kissed, not two weeks before, and wondered whether an uploaded mind could know such confused exhilaration. Gazing now at her beautiful face, he recalled the odd sense of relief he felt—while going through illegally obtained records on her personal background—upon discovering that she was genetically altered; it solved the mystery of her perfection. He smiled, wondering how it was that an anti-social natural child like himself could attract a beautiful gene-job like her.

She looked up and spotted him. As if reading his mind, she smiled back. She tapped a longish nail on her tablet, and Raymond felt a vibration in his wrist relay. He glanced down and saw he had a message from her. The subject line read "Eight o'clock". He looked back to her and nodded, smiling.

The conference room's wall monitors lit up as voice-visual connections were established with the other two members of the team, Jake and Tim. Jake's face came up on one. He was in a hallway somewhere, a University Broadcast monitor behind him. On the other monitor was the face of a cartoon polar bear, which Raymond recognized as one of Tim's goofy avatars. Bob took a moment to look around the room.

"Well, I expect you all know why I called this meeting. Jake and Tim," he said toward the wall displays, "I assume you're up on the news of the ruling?" Jake and the polar bear both nodded. Bob paused for a moment, preparing his thoughts, then launched into speech.

"The ESW has ruled that the destructive uploading of human minds is unethical." There was a heaviness to his tone that was unfamiliar to Raymond. All in the room were keenly attentive. "No one is willing to accept that the electronic copy of a human brain is sufficiently faithful. The implication, as I'm sure you're all aware, is that destructive uploading constitutes murder, although it'll be up to national courts to resolve this."

Bob paused, scanning the faces of those in the room. "You're probably all wondering what this will mean to our research. I would like to say that it means nothing—we could be years from human upload. We're just now entering the chimps phase, and this ruling has nothing to say about uploading non-human primates. But research doesn't happen without funding, and most of our funding is from corporations for whom chimp upload is worthless. From their point of view, this project is all about human upload, and this ruling makes that objective unethical. Which makes us a much less attractive investment."

Bob paused again, gathering his thoughts.

"I've taken the first step," he continued, "toward refacing the project, by changing the name to the Mind Upload Project—dropping the 'Human'. But don't worry… we still know what we're all about, and we'll just have to hope that some of the Naturalists on the ESW lose their seats in the next few years. Or, who knows, maybe we'll shift operations to Portugal, eh Anya?"

She raised an eyebrow at his playful jab, a "yeah-right" look on her face. Portugal was famous for sheltering non-mainstream researchers. Knowing as he did that Anya's position on the team was likely short-lived, it seemed like a mean comment to Raymond; he was relieved by her mild response.

Bob looked down at the table in front of him. "The unfortunate upshot of all this, I'm afraid, is that I can't retain a staff of thirteen for a chimp upload project. There's just not enough money for it." He looked up again, making brief eye contact with Raymond. "After year end, some of you will probably lose your positions. I know that's not far off… it's already October. I'm doing what I can to find new grant money, but we're suddenly a much weaker investment, and a risk to the public images of our investors. It will take at least a couple weeks before I can work out the details, but I wanted you to know the situation. I'm hoping I can convince some of the big players that it's still worth it to them. The decision could be overturned, or loopholes could creep in, in which case they would want to be backing the lead research team so they can be there when it pays off. But I'm not optimistic—not in the short term."

"Bob," asked Anya, "is there any room on your other team?"

"I'll see what I can do, but I can't make any promises. Naturally, I will do what I can to help anyone who ends up being cut. There's some related research going on here at Michigan, and I'm in touch with a lot of researchers elsewhere, as well. If I do have to let any of you go, and I hope I don't, I'll certainly do what I can to get you onto a relevant project. Other questions?"

"Bob," asked Ellen, "can you tell us a little about how you would decide whom to cut?"

"Sure. In fairness to you all, I should say that I have always been inclined to protect my scientists. Technical people generally have an easier time finding new positions. Their skills are more portable. That said, I'm also inclined to look out for the people who've been with me the longest." Raymond looked to Anya, and she looked back knowingly. The ones who had been with him the longest also happened to be the ones most willing to subjugate their own careers for the sake of his. "Dedication means a great deal to me. But please, I don't want anyone to get scared and bail on me before all the facts are in. I'm not gonna lift a finger to help someone who bails now, but I'll bust my ass to make life easier for anyone I have to let go. And I'd like to say that I am very proud of this team. Losing any one of you would be a great blow to our progress and to the comradery of the team."

"What makes you think the Naturalists will lose power in the court?" asked Alfonso, one of the scientists.

"Well, in all honesty, I don't see it happening any time soon. But ultimately, they will have to go. As you all know, I believe the jump from organic to digital is inevitable. We've already woven computers throughout the fabric of our society. We're at a point where we could pretty much let them take over, if we wanted to. I don't mean to come across as paranoiod, but if we're not careful that decision could become theirs. The only way to avoid being outmoded by computers is to merge with them. It's just a matter of time."

Bob thrust his hands in his pockets and leaned forward, looking down. It was body language that Raymond had come to recognize as a signal that Bob was about to wax philosophical.

"Life is all about the power of order," said Bob, calmly declarative. "The power to survive in the face of entropy. Evolution is the anti-entropy, and digital life is the next step. We don't want to give that next step away, to life-forms we merely created. We want it for ourselves, and a merger is the natural solution. There are plenty of people happy to hand the reins over to computers and live like pampered pets, but not me. We've built the vehicle that can take us to the next step, and it's just a matter of time before we get in and fire it up.

"Of course, the ESW may never approve of destructive uploading… they may never be convinced that it makes sense to destroy one life-form to create another. Human upload may be put off until we figure out how to scan a mind without harming it. But I don't think so. What we're creating is a powerful life-saving technology, not one that kills. There are just too many people who don't want to die. Uploading offers longer life, and a richer, cleaner existence. And, ultimately, there's no getting around it—the powerful people of this world can't bear the thought of giving up all the heroism of a new era to computers. Artificial life is already racing ahead.

"I tell you, once I get started…"

There were smiles and chuckles all around.

"To come back to the original question," said Bob, "the Naturalists are putting on the brakes, and that may be wise—destructive uploading today *would* be unethical. We're not there yet—there's too much risk. Frankly, I don't think Bento will be the same monkey on the other end of the upload. We're on the frontier of discovery. Mistakes happen. Ethics call for cautious progression here. But I feel like we're too close for caution to prevail for long… my guess is five years, max."

The meeting dissolved into small discussions. Raymond waited for Anya to stand and went to her.

"Well, this ruling came sooner than I expected," said Anya. Raymond nodded. "And things don't look so good for either one of us."

"No kidding," replied Raymond. "We'll have to talk. I got your reply."

"That was a sweet message you sent me."

Raymond looked tenderly at Anya, wondering what message his Puck persona had created on his behalf.

"Are you well-versed in Shakespeare, then?" she asked.

"I find a sort of vicarious pleasure there, I suppose." Raymond recalled the sexy Midsummer Night's Dream virtual mini-adventure where he had first come across the Puck persona. Shakespeare, he gathered, was some sort of flowery-but-clever soft-porn script writer. "I hope my timing's not too bad. The mood will probably be pretty serious tonight."

"No, no," she assured. "We won't let it get us too down. I'll cook a nice meal, open some wine… and hey—" She moved in, her hair drifting along his jaw line as she leaned into a whisper. "I'm really looking forward to getting to know you."

She smiled, gave his arm a friendly touch, and moved past him out of the conference room.

CHAPTER 5

The lab cleared out early that afternoon. Anya and Suma stopped by Raymond's office on their way out to see if he wanted to leave with them.

"Uh, no… I have some work I want to finish up."

"I don't know how you can concentrate," said Suma.

"I want to work through some of the problems that came up in the last test. If there's any slip in the Bento schedule, I don't want it to be because of me."

Raymond exchanged a somber look with Anya. The intensity of it electrified him.

"Well, you don't want to be late for dinner," said Suma with a teasing edge.

Raymond smiled and looked at the floor.

"I'll see you at eight," said Anya.

The pair left. Raymond returned to his "work". He had actually already finished fixing the problems from Bento's last test, and he was now busy putting together a map of the building's security system. He was not yet sure how things would unfold, but he expected to have to dupe the system sooner or later. Delight lay around every corner; the system's components were few and out-dated. He could trace a path from the lab's server room to the loading dock that passed only eight Eyes-and-Ears units, all ten-year-old models feeding their weakly-encrypted output directly to a single network node. Crack that node and nearly all of the building's sensory data was under his control. The node was on a secure, isolated network, but he had had agents in that network since his second week on the team. The only other security devices he could find were the DynaKey door-locks, alarms on all first-floor windows, and a log of the motion-detectors that controlled lighting and climate throughout the building's common areas. Once one was past the voice- and face-recognition devices at the entrances to the building, there was remarkably little security. Over the next few evenings, he would send out his favorite robot, Passe-Partout—a small monkey-like robot already a familiar sight around the lab—to create spatial maps of every area monitored by the Eyes-and-Ears units. Once he had the spatial maps, he would be able to insert whatever false images and sounds he wanted. "This is gonna be a joke," he said to himself.

But what exactly was "this"? He had only a vague plan in mind. He imagined uploading himself into an NBC, then having one of his robots carry the NBC down to the loading dock and load it into his waiting motor home. Then the robot would reactivate the NBC within the motor home. If the upload were good and the reactivation successful, he would hit the road in the motor home. It would drive him to his Minnesota bunker, where a robot would move his NBC in the basement. The bunker would be his home as long as necessary. The identity of Raymond Quan would be flagged as dead and therefore no longer of interest to the police. He would assume the legal identity of Ivar Svensson, who technically owned the motor home and the bunker. Ivar Svensson was a fictitious citizen of Minnesota—an identity Raymond purchased on the black market a few years back, as part of his money laundering scheme. Raymond Quan would be dead to the world and Ivar Svensson would come to life, a wealthy young hermit living unseen in a high-tech compound in the north woods. The highpoints of the plan were clear enough, but the details were a blur, a snowstorm of unknowns from which he wanted to take shelter.

His wrist relay vibrated, and his desk speakers made the call of a cuckoo-clock. It was 7:30, time to head to Anya's. He put on his biking jacket, a matte black windbreaker, and pulled up the hood, which was outfitted with audio input/output devices and a lightweight safety framework that served as a bike helmet. "Jack," he said—even his jacket had a persona. "Armenia." Armenian sacred choral music started to play softly within his hood. He double-checked the security on all of the personal devices in his office, then made his way through the hallways and front lobby to the bike storage room. He stepped up to his bike, the only one left in the rack, and placed his hands on the handlebar grips. The bike recognized his fingerprints and unlocked its locks, retracting them into its brushed alloy frame. He walked the bike out of the building, automatic doors sliding open at his approach.

Once outside, the choral music grew louder, his jacket automatically compensating for the noises of the wind and the ground and air traffic. He paused for a moment to look up Anya's address on his wrist relay. He expected the ride from the North Campus lab to Anya's apartment, west of Main Street, to take him about twenty minutes, without engaging the bike's motors. He got the bike rolling and smoothly swung his leg over, pedaled hard to build up speed, and headed toward the bike path to Central Campus.

Raymond sped along the bike path, through a rare stand of old trees that had survived the university's never-ending expansion. He emerged at the foot of Medical Campus Hill, the Huron River to his right. On this side of the river, towering above low residential buildings, stood the funky, organically-shaped Arbology—Ann Arbor's famous communistic arcology. It was a largely self-sustaining community of over fifteen hundred, built in the 40s, a diverse haven for urban farmers, co-op fanatics, environmentalists, Quakers, professors, art and architecture students, medical students, and enlightened capitalists. Raymond had originally figured Anya for an Arbology dweller. It seemed like just the right combination of radical and rational for her. As it turned out, she lived in a sleepy old neighborhood, ten minutes' walk west of Ann Arbor's quaint, lovingly preserved downtown—not far from the church garden where they had kissed.

There was a time when he would have balked at the thought of travelling twenty minutes to see someone whom he could reach almost instantly in virtual space. It was when he first came to the brick-and-mortar University of Michigan, five years before, that he learned to appreciate travelling through physical space, especially under his own power. He discovered something beautiful in the ability of his body to carry him across town, and he found this exercise to be more satisfying than running or biking in a v-chamber—even a good one. And now that he planned to upload, he felt he should savor the primitive richness of his organic life while it lasted.

By the time he reached Anya's neighborhood, he felt thoroughly invigorated. He imagined uploaded life being like this, only better. Uploaded, he would live in a world of his own creation. In Nurania, he could minimize the distractions and annoyances so abundant in reality prime and bring clean, personalized design to even the most mundane details of his life—and he would never have to leave it. He could live within it without the ever-present sense that it was false, that he would have to leave the v-chamber eventually, to eat or shower or use the bathroom. His mind raced with images of himself on an airboard, surfing the winds of Nurania's slammer season. He pondered the possibility of opening Nurania to the Net, allowing others into his home world. For so many years, he had lived with the nagging sense that he would never be able to finish creating the world. But, once uploaded, he would be able to work on it as much as he wanted, for as long as it took. His creations would truly become his life. Best of all, he fantasized about meeting Anya in cyberspace, the two of them in a secret relationship.

Raymond found Anya's address. She was in the ground floor of an old two-story home, carved up into apartments long ago. Raymond carried his bike up onto the wide front porch and checked the unit numbers. Anya's was the right-hand unit. He glanced at what he guessed to be her front window: warm incandescent light shown through sheer white curtains.

As he was locking up his bike, it hit him for the first time that as a digital life-form, essentially immortal, it would be awful to watch mortal Anya age and die. It could be twenty years or more before uploading became publicly accessible, if it ever did; and, even if it were available, she might choose not to do it. And what if she weren't satisfied with a lover whom she could only reach in v-space? He rang her doorbell, not wanting to think about it. A flesh-and-blood woman, wouldn't she want a flesh-and-blood lover? His upload would be exile. Thoughts of kidnapping her and forcing her to upload were flitting through his mind when she opened the door.

"Hey. Come on in."

It was a cozy one-bedroom apartment, awkwardly modified here and there to accommodate new technologies. Just inside the door, Raymond noticed a stack of empty delivery crates, ready for return. Like most people, she had all of her groceries delivered to her home by robotic carts, accepted into her entryway by a robotic security system.

Raymond stepped into the living room and was greeted with the smell of garlic and cooking meat. He found himself immediately put at ease. He felt as though he had entered a homey embrace—the space had such warmth. The richly stained wood floors and trim had a reddish-golden glow in the low warm lamplight. The decorations were mostly antiques—framed prints of works by Miró and Matisse, brightly colored art glass, a Calder mobile that hung from the ceiling, slowly spinning. Her v-chamber, a fairly new Panasonic, stood mostly out of view behind a three-paneled shoji screen.

"Go ahead and hang your coat up," said Anya, gesturing toward the line of coat hooks on the wall. She headed back to the kitchen. "I hope you're hungry," she called back to him. "I'm making a roast. And potato leek soup."

A roast—what a beautiful woman. She does things like cook roasts and make soup.

Again he was filled with the desire to savor the pleasures available to him as an organic life-form. Time with Anya made him aware of his deprived sensual experience, made him want to enjoy the details of the natural world for fear that they would not be the same in simulated form. And what could be more primitively pleasurable than eating the flesh of a cow—an actual cow? Anya was the key to a worldview Raymond had never really imagined. He found that the idea of eating roasted meat conjured a very basic sense of success within him. A very masculine notion of success. And it wasn't just the food, he realized. It was the thought of being served animal flesh prepared by a woman. A gene-job, sure, but a beautiful woman very much of this world. A real woman, with a heart that pumped blood through her body, a creature subject to the natural laws of the universe—with gravity to contend with, cells to nourish, and the chaotic damages of time to face.

Raymond thought he might be the first person ever to appreciate reality in just this way. He inhaled deeply, conceptualizing the flow of fluid air into his nostrils, beef molecules riding along and pairing with his olfactory receptors, receptors assembled during his gestation according to the instructions contained within his own DNA. He watched Anya walking back and forth in the kitchen and visualized her skeleton, held together by soft tissue, propelled by muscles controlled by her brain. Her bones would go on existing after the brain died. They might even end up buried in soil, to be broken back down into the basic building blocks of organic life. He imagined the skeletons of billions of women, buried all around the world. Bones, the remnants of matter that had been arranged into life—an arrangement that could only hold together for so long in the face of entropy. Then he imagined electrons and photons racing through a computer, duplicating the flow of information that crackled at a turtle's pace through the human brain, the electrons and photons merely representations of the complexity that is intelligence. He believed as Bob did that organic life was merely a vehicle of complexity, and digital life was the next step in the evolution of that complexity. And he was on the cutting edge, entering into a world that he believed was already populated by intelligent life—artificial life, complex automata, and the handful of animals that they had uploaded in the lab.

Raymond dropped into an armchair, pushing Anya's swing-arm reading display off to the side. He looked up at a high shelf across the room. The shelf, stained to match the trim, ran from one end of the room to the other, and was filled from end to end with books. Worn and darkened, they added character to the room.

"Do you ever read your books?" he called to her.

"Sometimes." She was busy in the kitchen, chopping and tasting, cleaning up, getting plates and glasses down from the cupboard. "Sometimes I tell my computer to shut everything down, and I light an oil lamp and some candles, and read a book. It feels good. It's like I've withdrawn from society for an evening, like I'm out of the system—alone."

Raymond wandered restlessly into the kitchen, and leaned against the door frame.

"It's good to feel alone sometimes," continued Anya. "Truly alone." She opened the oven, stabbed a thermometer in the sizzling roast, and checked the readout. "Ten more minutes," she announced. "Do you want to start with a glass of Cava?"

"Cava? What's that?"

"It's basically Spanish Champagne."

"Sure, that sounds great."

Anya took a small glass bottle of Cava out of the fridge. "I found this shop that sells Cava in antique-style glass bottles. It's so much more romantic than a temperature-controlled canister." She peeled off the foil wrapper and slowly, expertly popped the cork, shouting, "Voilá!" Raymond smiled and looked on with admiration. At the same time, he felt a vague discomfort, as though drawn into a dance, the steps of which he didn't know.

"Funny, I suppose," said Anya, as she poured out two glasses, "to be celebrating on the eve of such lousy news, but what the hell." She handed him a glass, then held her own up to toast, and he followed suit. "To the enjoyment of life, wherever it takes you." They tinked their glasses together. "And," she added with a smirk, "to my victory in getting Raymond Quan to come to dinner. Now drink up, because I have a special wine for dinner."

Raymond drank a mouthful of the Cava and found it to be very pleasant. Tingly and sweet at first, then a bit puckery, in a way that left him wanting more.

Anya set her glass down and tended to the pot of soup that sat steaming on her stovetop. "So… can you believe this ESW decision?"

"I know," said Raymond. "Although, I guess it shouldn't come as a surprise. People are so full of themselves."

Anya turned and nodded in agreement, but the look on her face told him she hadn't followed his line of thinking at all.

"People," said Raymond, struggling to identify the path to his conclusion, "have this concept that natural is good, and that humans shouldn't interfere with nature. As if we're outsiders. Religious people, especially—the whole idea that some willful, all-powerful being created the universe and inserted us into it, and there are rules about what we should or shouldn't do. I don't know—I'm not very good at explaining myself."

He wished he hadn't opened his mouth. It was immensely frustrating—he had such convictions on the topic, yet his ideas crumbled when he endeavored to express them.

"No, no," said Anya, "I see what you mean. People protect the sanctity of humanness as if it were inherently good. They're full of themselves—I see what you're saying. I think it's a self-defense mechanism. Whenever we approach a change that could redefine us, we put on the brakes. It's unfamiliar territory, and the unfamiliar scares us."

"Not me," blurted Raymond. He stopped himself. He wanted to say he would upload today if he could. Instead, he left it at that, standing awkwardly at the edge of the precipice he had just created.

"Oh really?" asked Anya. "What about… what about at La Sevillana? Wasn't that a little fear of the unfamiliar?"

"No, that was just…" Raymond trailed off, hesitant to speak his mind. He had the growing sense that his private thoughts didn't stand up well to exposure. But Anya gave him a provocative raised eyebrow, spurring him on. "That's just a part of society where I don't fit in."

"Don't fit in?" questioned Anya. "Or do you just need someone to invite you in?" Raymond didn't answer, and she was quick to move on. "But, generally speaking, people *are* afraid of the unfamiliar. I just wish they could deal with it some other way. People were reluctant to accept genetic engineering. Even by the time I was born, my parents were quiet about their decision to have me genetically altered."

Raymond feigned a look of surprise. "Wow. I guess that explains how you got to be so beautiful." The intention had been to flatter, but upon utterance the words sounded silly, possibly even insulting.

"Actually," responded Anya, "the genetic alterations were mostly health-related." She gave no indication of being either flattered or ruffled. She opened the oven and checked the roast.

"Just a few more minutes." She turned off the heat under the soup and took up her glass.

"Suma and I were talking about what will happen if the project loses funding. Have you given any thought to what you would do?"

Raymond wanted to spill everything he knew, to impress her. "I don't know." He thought about saying he would join an anti-Naturalist group, but it seemed too flip. He glanced at his wrist relay, to be sure he hadn't missed any new information regarding the progress of the Illinois State Police or Arnold Murray.

"You probably don't have to worry about it," said Anya. "Lord knows Bob would love to get rid of me. But you, with all the systems you've put together, all your cool tools—I would be surprised if Bob let you go. Even if you are the youngest. I would think Tim would go first—you could program circles around him, and he hasn't been on the team much longer than you."

"Tim's not that bad," said Raymond, taking the opportunity to come off as big-hearted. "He just has a hard time focusing on work. He has no discipline."

Anya leaned against the counter, drink in hand, and looked at Raymond, shaking her head. "Whatever the reason, he does a quarter as much work as you."

"I bet Bob would go strictly according to seniority," said Raymond. It was easy to come across as sage when he already knew Bob's plans. "Besides… sometimes I get the feeling Bob doesn't much care for me."

"Well, I can't see why not," said Anya, jumping to his defense. "You work like a dog for him—you're at the lab late all the time. You've come up with all sorts of innovations." She drained her glass, set it on the counter, and stepped over to where Raymond stood. She faced him straight on, and she squared his shirt across his shoulders. "You make toys for the uploaded animals, you create their worlds. You're sensitive, and shy, and sweet. I certainly can't see what's not to like." She trailed her right hand down his chest, then gave him a playful little shove. "Now, go sit down, and I'll bring out dinner."

Raymond smiled. His chest felt warm where she had touched it. Through his dreamy entranced state, he conjured the presence of mind to offer to help, but she refused.

He sat down at her two-person dining table and watched as she laid out the meal she had prepared, explaining it as she went: standing rib roast, from a range-fed cow, topped with peppercorns and served in its own juice; whole kernel corn drenched in real butter; a salad of pickled asparagus, artichoke hearts, hearts of palm, avocado, and roasted red pepper; two bowls of buttery, garlicky, potato-leek soup, garnished with fresh parsley; and hunks of torn baguette, for dipping in the soup. She even had a canister of Spanish Rioja, from which she filled two fine crystal glasses. When she brought salt and pepper shakers to the table, she found there was barely room for them.

Raymond gaped in awe. He laughed and exclaimed that he had never had a meal like this. And he hadn't had an all-natural meal in months. Not a single pill lay on the table.

Anya seated herself and raised her glass of wine to toast. "To the healing power of food."

"Ha—to the healing power of food," repeated Raymond.

The roast proved to be meltingly delicious, and was beautifully complemented by the soup. Raymond felt like a vagabond taken in from the cold. He savored every mouthful, closing his eyes and shaking his head, to the point that Anya just had to laugh.

"Have you really never had a good old-fashioned home-cooked meal?"

"Not like this. I mean, this is way better than the Thanksgiving meals at the homes." He was surprised by the word as it came out of his mouth; it slipped out so naturally. He sought to change the subject. "Do you eat like this often?"

"Not exactly. I enjoy cooking, but it's so much nicer to cook for someone else. I might make myself one or two nice dishes, but not a whole meal like this. And I haven't made a roast in ages. What about you? What do you eat?"

Raymond pictured his motor home kitchenette, the cupboards stocked with powders and pills, the freezer full of prepared foods. "Lots of shakes and juices and heat-and-eat dinners. Supplements. Chips. Fiber bars. And I eat out a lot, or bring home take-out."

"Does your apartment have a full kitchen?"

"No, I have a pretty small kitchen." *In my apartment. As for my motor home, the word "kitchen" hardly applies.*

"Do you enjoy cooking?" asked Anya.

"I never really learned to cook. My mother never cooked." He stopped abruptly, looked down at his plate.

Anya nodded at this and took a mouthful of the roast. They ate in silence for a while. Anya poked at her food and squirmed slightly, then looked at Raymond and spoke softly.

"I know you're not big on questions, but… you mentioned 'the homes'. It made me realize, I hardly know anything about you. I don't want to pry, but I can't help but wonder what you meant. You don't have to answer if you don't want to."

Raymond hesitated. Still unsure of how Anya would fit into his plans, he didn't want to say too much or the wrong thing. He didn't want the conversation to get too far. But he ached, and her voice was the comforting hand he craved.

"I didn't grow up in a nice family." He looked her in the eye as he answered her. The rare intensity with which he spoke made him feel as if he were bragging, towering over her, indulging a longstanding desire to speak pointedly on the topic of his separateness. As he tried to quell his emotions, he felt them transforming into a desperate, empty sadness. He swallowed and steeled himself, forcing nascent tears into submission.

"I'm sorry," said Anya. "You don't have to talk about it. I'm sorry I brought it up."

"No, it's okay." He looked her in the eye and surprised himself. "I want to be able to tell you. I've never told anyone."

Raymond set his fork down and leaned forward, his elbows on his thighs, his hands clasped on his lap—as if he were watching tiny motions in the meat juice on his plate. With his tongue, he worked out a bit of beef stuck between eye tooth and incisor, then cleared his throat.

"Well, I was born in Chicago. My mother was white and my father was Vietnamese, but born in Toronto. I grew up in a loft in Palmer Square, a poor little northwest neighborhood. My father was a v-world addict, and my mother was an alcoholic. My father could never hold a job, of course, and my mother got bored with jobs, so she never advanced. You know, just went from one to another. So there wasn't much money. I mean, I'm sure there was state money, but my father probably spent it online.

"They didn't fight much, but it seemed like my father was always in his v-chamber, and my mother would pace outside it and say things loud enough so he might overhear them inside. Always with a drink in her hand. Or a bottle. She couldn't deal with having him so close and yet completely out of reach. Me, I could just pretend he didn't exist."

"Oh, Raymond," cooed Anya, desire to help plain in her eyes. "V-world addiction is so tough on kids."

"It was tougher on her. She drank all the time." Raymond shook his head, remembering the sight of her. "She usually ended up sitting on the floor with her back to the v-chamber door. It was her form of protest. This feeble protest, like she hoped he'd try to come out, and would get pissed at her for blocking the door. But when she sat so close, she could hear him inside. She would bang her elbow against the door sometimes when she heard something. I didn't realize it then, but he was probably having sex with some woman in v-space, and my mother could hear it. It drove her crazy."

Anya was leaning her head on her hand by this point, clearly pained. She listened intently. The sadness in her eyes made Raymond remember his own past with a sense of compassion for himself that was utterly new to him.

"Finally, I woke up one night, when I was seven, because I heard a glass break. I got up and looked into the living room, and there was my mom, sitting against the v-chamber. She'd hurled a glass across the room, and she was sitting against the door, sobbing, wearing this really slinky red nightie. You know, like I could see a lot more of her than I wanted to."

Anya winced at this.

"All of a sudden," he continued, "she scrambled to her feet and tried to open the door. She got it part way open, then the door was suddenly jerked out of her grasp, and it slammed shut. She slipped and fell to her knees, her face against the chamber, an old black Panasonic. She whaled on the door with her fists, then opened it again, this time quickly enough that she got it all the way open. She started into the chamber, and I remember she said, 'Baby, please let me in!' And then she came sailing out, backwards, and she fell against this white plastic egg chair we had. And I saw my father's bare arm reach out from the chamber and pull the door closed. I watched as my mom lay sobbing, her head on her arms, lying on floor; I watched until she fell asleep, and then I went back to bed. And I remember, I lay awake and stared at the ceiling. I thought about the fact that my dad really did exist, and I tried to imagine what better place he must be in, that he always wanted to be there, and I wondered why my mother couldn't be there with him."

Raymond lifted his elbows onto the table. He leaned forward and touched his lips and chin to his hands, trying to stop them from shaking.

"And you've never talked with anyone about all this?"

He shook his head. "There was the State of Illinois guy, I guess, when he asked me questions. But that was different." His voice started to break.

Anya got up, came around the table, and hugged him from behind. She held him tight, saying "it's okay, it's okay." Through his watery eyes, Raymond saw that some of her long black hair was lying in the beef juice on his plate. He lifted it away and sniffed, then moved to stand up.

"I should go."

"No, no, no! That's the last thing you should do." She took hold of his shirt sleeve and led him into the living room, where she sat him down on the love seat. "Now stay put. Stay boy… stay." He sniffled and laughed. She sat down next to him, her feet tucked underneath her, and started to smooth his hair and rub his neck.

"I'm sorry," said Raymond. "We should finish dinner."

"Don't you worry about that. I can always reheat it." She petted him for a while. He was embarrassed that he had almost cried.

"So," she asked, "how did you end up in the state homes?"

He took a deep breath.

"My father left us to be with this Asian stripper named Mako, in Miami. I remember my mother telling me that over and over… that he ran off to be with an Asian stripper named after a shark." Anya kept petting him, making sounds of understanding but not saying a word. "So it was just me and my mom for a while. She drank like crazy. She would lock herself in her room and drink and cry. She didn't go to work for days, and she wouldn't answer when calls came in. I don't think she even called in sick. When she did go in, they fired her, and she came straight back, got piss drunk, and cried herself to sleep. When it came time to pay the rent, she filed for state aid. So a guy from the state came to look into her affairs, and he could see she was a wreck. He took us to a shelter and asked me questions about my home life. I thought he might send me to a better place if things sounded really bad, so I didn't hold anything back and maybe exaggerated here and there. The state took custody of me and became my legal guardian, and I was put in a home in Joliet. And that was that. The rest of my childhood, I was raised by the State of Illinois."

"Wow. I had no idea. That's a really tough childhood. It's amazing that you've gotten where you are."

She stood up from the love seat and went to the table. Raymond found himself instantly missing her, wanting her, watching her butt as she walked away.

"Do you want to eat more? You could eat there at the coffee table?"

"Sure. That sounds great. I'd hate to let it go to waste."

She brought their plates and glasses and bowls to the coffee table.

"I'm sorry," said Anya. "I know you didn't come over for a therapy session. We should probably talk about something else."

They didn't. Silence passed between them, and Raymond was fine with the silence, happy to have Anya near him. They finished their meal. She casually put her hand on his thigh, an expression of their sense of connection.

"Thanks for the meal, Anya. That was really, really good."

She smiled and thanked him for the compliment. "More wine?" she offered. He nodded. She refilled their glasses from the canister at the dining room table, brought the glasses back to the coffee table, then collected the dirty dishes and carried them off to the kitchen.

Raymond sipped his wine. He looked at the glass, the smooth surface of the wine—he wasn't shaking anymore. In fact, he felt a sense of peace, and he realized that it was because he had let Anya into his world. "A luxury I can't afford," he muttered.

Anya returned to the couch and settled in next to him.

"So," she asked with a gentle tone, "what were you working on this afternoon?"

Raymond pictured himself uploading, and he starting thinking about the possibility of the scanner breaking. "Persona stuff," he answered thoughtlessly. Perhaps worse than the risk of complete scanner failure was the possibility of a flawed scan, the errors undetected. He was vaguely aware of what Anya had asked. He sought some additional response, but his new train of thought had taken over.

"What sorts of problems do you think we might have with Bento?" he asked.

"All sorts of things. There are the usual scan problems. Unexpected patterns in his nervous system that cause the nanoscanners to halt or collide. The scan could miss some portion of the brain without our realizing it. Segments of memory could be lost, some percentage of the corpus callosum could be bypassed—millions of things could go wrong. Bento's brain is considerably more complex than any we've scanned so far. But, personally, I think the neural scan is so ingeniously simple that it's pretty much foolproof. Chimp, human—I think the neural scan is basically the same."

Raymond nodded, listening closely as Anya went on.

"I'm more worried about capturing the behavior of the hormones, neuropeptides, and neurotransmitters. This isn't a true physiological scan, after all. Sure, we're gobbling up everything as we go, but the nervous architecture is the only thing we're really mapping one-to-one. The rest of the data from the scan are employed statistically, to inform our simulation of the non-neural physiology. We don't have dopamine and serotonin flowing through these computer brains, and our simulation of their behavior could be way too simplistic for a primate brain. Uploaded Minnie seems like a well-adjusted dog, but the triggers for release and inhibition of neurotransmitters are a good deal more complex in a primate brain. We may get all the neurons in the right place, wired up just fine, yet completely fail to capture Bento's socially complex mind. And if we can't fine-tune the simulation quickly enough, Bento's mind could start to destroy itself, in a sense, as neural connections fade away and abnormalities arise."

"Isn't it possible to make a backup of the neural architecture at the time of the scan and revert to that neural backup once the physiological simulation has been ironed out?"

"Well, if we could cleanly back up and restore an NBC, that would be an option. But what are you going to back up to? There's no backup process for a neuristor-based computer. IBM is working on it, but they keep pushing back the availability date."

"At any given moment, every neuristor has a known value, right? Why can't it be backed up?"

"Sure, at a given point in time, every neuristor has a measurable value, but there's no way to tell each one to save state all at once. It's a massively decentralized, asynchronously self-adjusting computer, constantly attending to its computational efficiency."

"So, there's no way to freeze state?"

"Freeze state?"

Embarrassment engulfed Raymond's mind. He was only now realizing how basic a difference there was between an NBC and the computers he knew so well. His work had been solely in the traditional realm; only now was he glimpsing the depths of his ignorance. As if the mere utterance of his question weren't enough, here was her response, one of amazement at the uninformed nature of his question.

"An NBC," explained Anya, "has no central clock. Every neuristor acts asynchronously. It's like a network of two hundred billion nodes, each one a simple computer, capable of establishing thousands of trillions of network links. The pulse of an NBC is the pulse of the universe, the march of time. There's no clock to stop, and there's presently no way of broadcasting a 'stop' message to every neuristor. You could pull the plug, but that won't get you any closer to making a backup."

"Then how does IBM plan to make a backup?"

"Basically, they plan to add a meta-level to the whole machine—a synchronized reporting layer, interwoven throughout all two hundred billion neuristors, able to record a snapshot of the entire graph. But it would be more than just a reporting layer, because the process can go in the opposite direction, too—you prime the meta-level with state information, then tell it to load. In theory, the brain should suddenly undergo a complete change of mind and proceed from backup as if nothing had happened. But I'm skeptical."

Anya shifted, bringing a knee up onto the couch. It pressed into Raymond's leg; he scooted away to give her room.

"Well, then how do you load the NBC in the first place? I mean, I know how the data gets to the NBC, but how does it find its way into the right neuristors?"

"By applying the neural patterns as they're recorded by the nanoscanners. It's a mess, really." Anya shifted again, moving closer to Raymond. "There are a million or so entry points into the NBC 'brain', into which you start to pump the pattern data from the scan. The neuristors are set up to receive the patterns. What you end up with is an awful mess at first, until the patterns have all been completely applied. It's kind of like growing millions of tree structures, from the roots up, and expecting the leaves of the trees to mesh. If there's a flicker of consciousness at any point during that process, it's going to be one confused mind. Kind of like waking up in the midst of a dream. But everything seems to iron itself out okay. It may be registered by the mind as a bizarre trauma, but it shouldn't be—the patterns are such that nothing should make it into any form of memory until the final moments. And it can't really be considered a trauma if the experience isn't translated into memory—or directly damaging."

"So the patterns are recorded, right? I mean, during the scan, you record the patterns so that they can be pumped into the NBC?"

"Not exactly. The statistical summary of the non-neural physiological scan is recorded, but the neural architecture is never completely stored. It's stored in segments that roughly correspond to nuclei, modules, and lobes of the brain. Those segments are fed in upon completion. If the scan were to pause for even a second, already-scanned segments could become deformed, and essential links might never be made. But this hasn't happened since the fruit-fly scans."

"Okay, then the segments are recorded as they're formed, and then dumped. But if you could record all the segments, in the appropriate order, couldn't you then make a backup of the scan? You may not be able to make backups during the life of a mind, but at least you could have a backup of the source mind, from the scan."

Anya thought about this for a while. "I suppose," she admitted hesitantly. "I guess we've never seen the need."

"Well, you haven't had any disasters since the fruit flies. And it's never been you in that scanner, has it?" Raymond's voice cracked slightly.

"No. Obviously."

Raymond realized that his voice had grown louder, and he feared that he might be raising suspicions in Anya's mind. "But if it were… I mean, what about poor Bento? He's been a good chimp all his life, right? If we're going to scan his mind, don't you think that making a backup of the scan is a reasonable precaution?"

Anya reflected for a time and then finally reached out and put a hand on his shoulder. He realized that he couldn't move away from her; through the course of their conversation, she had shifted into his subspace so many times that he was backed against the arm of the loveseat. Her touch caused him to tighten up, then to relax somewhat, the tension of her proximity broken.

"That's brilliant. You know," she said, "I don't think I've ever seen you take such a passionate interest in a topic."

He looked away from her briefly, collecting himself. She awaited a response, an explanation. Her silence allowed him mental space in which to formulate some appropriately cool statement of position. He was aware of a lesson he had gleaned from years of deception: the closer to the truth you can come without touching on it, the more plausible your false position. His motives were large in his mind; he sought to chip off some key element of them, something that would serve his purpose. In parallel arose the possibility of saying something that would fit with Anya's role in his planned deceptions.

"I feel," he said in measured tones, "that we are closer to human upload than we realize. The ethics of chimp upload are not so far from the ethics of human upload. Therefore, we should deal with them seriously. And, to my mind, the only way to do that is to consider Bento's situation empathetically."

The energy of elation surged through him; his response was good. It fit. It was right. He felt as if he defied her grip on his shoulder, her attempt at controlling contact turned on its nose, yet he remained positively motionless. Some part of him was aware that her grip might not be intended as controlling—that his perception of the gesture might be distorted—but this awareness was remote. The wait for her answer was a sea of boundless and confident satisfaction.

Anya leaned into him and kissed his neck, her lips tugging gently at his skin. It was as if she were feeding on his mental rush, yet simultaneously contributing to it. His state of clarity and glee was amplified. His body felt powerful. He imagined himself slipping from the couch and delivering an astoundingly powerful roundhouse kick to some indeterminate foe.

"You're so right," said Anya at last. "Do you think you could implement that sort of backup? Do we have sufficient resources?"

An arrogant, self-satisfied ease arose in Raymond's mind.

"Oh, sure. No problem."

Anya stood up and went to the table, leaving Raymond where he sat, in his mental hot-mud bath. Again he found himself watching her butt, this time feeling as if she were entirely his.

"More wine?" she asked.

"Sure."

She brought the canister over and poured out two more glasses, draining the canister in the process. Raymond looked at his glass, considering the fact that he had drunk very little alcohol in his life. His concept of its effects were limited to the stumbling and slurring of virtual reality. He wondered now whether the Cava and the two glasses of wine he had already drunk might be affecting his mental state. While posing the question to himself, he picked up his refilled glass and drank from it, wanting to be sure he had experienced proper drunkenness before uploading. Anya sat down beside him again. She sat down such that her hip was placed firmly against his. She pulled his shirt out of his pants and slid her hand across his taut, muscular belly, her fingertips dipping just under his elastic waistline. He felt alarms go off in his mind; his penis filled with blood. He felt its taut skin shift within his pants, rubbing in small steps up the inside of his thigh.

"What about the dopamine?" he asked. "Isn't it possible to track the creation of dopamine and other neurotransmitters prior to the scan, to establish some sort of history?"

"Absolutely." She moved her hand up his stomach somewhat and slowly rubbed beneath his rib cage. The sexuality of the moment fizzled, converted to affection. "That's actually a big part of Bob's other project, on the computer-controlled sustenance of a human brain. But that project is only so far along.

Some of its findings have been useful to neurological surgeons, but the full-fledged support of a human brain by a computer is still a ways off."

"And the two projects should complement each other, right?"

"Well, the sustenance project should certainly complement the upload project. And, ideally, it should go both ways."

"So, if a human were going to be uploaded, they could undergo sustenance evaluation first. Establish a history for sustaining the brain via simulation, then upload the brain and apply the history."

"That's the ultimate idea," said Anya. Her hand came to rest comfortably just above his navel.

"And how far away do you think he is?"

"Oh, it's hard to say. The brain sustenance is only partial. It's integrated as much as possible with a real body. As much as is left of a real person. The difference in granularity between a sustained body and the simulated physiology necessary for an uploaded brain is hard to guess at. Statistically speaking, we're almost there. But statistics often leave out key details of reality; we could be overlooking some essential mental component, or we could have a simulated body that would leave an uploaded brain gasping for oxygen, bleating for proteins."

Raymond felt small and far from his destination again. Then, out of the blue, Anya asked him a question. "What do you believe to be your center?"

"My center?"

"Yeah, your center. The source of your person. The basis of your self-placement, your beliefs?"

The basis of my beliefs?

"I don't know," he said. "I'm not sure that's something I've ever really thought about."

His center had something to do with control, but he couldn't quite put his finger on it. Where others accepted their fate or the circumstances of their physical condition, merely reacting to the events of their lives, he made decisions in an attempt to control his life. But desire for control couldn't be the right answer.

"I guess…" He paused. "I don't know, I guess I would have to think about it. Right now, I think it's several inches below your hand."

Anya grinned.

"Okay," she said. "New question. This one's easier. Have you ever had a girlfriend?"

Raymond's head turned, and he met Anya's gaze. Her face looked open, innocent, inviting. He smiled. The primitive components of his mind started dumping hormones into his system, priming him.

"You know," he said, "I read once that the human face is capable of making over seven thousand facial expressions. But, for all the research that went into that number, I bet they missed the one that's on your face right now."

He wanted to kiss her, but he couldn't break through the inertia fast enough.

"Well, have you?" she asked again, her expression now mischievous, insistent, and elated.

Holding his ground and still looking into her eyes, Raymond shook his head 'no'. "I've been with women, mostly in v-space, but never what I would call a girlfriend."

Anya moved her hand up his chest, lifting his shirt as she went. She stopped just below his throat and gently pushed him back. He resisted for a moment, then yielded, sitting back into the cushion. His skin felt hot. She swung a knee over his legs, straddling him. Her breasts, beneath stretched soft fabric, loomed inches from his eyes. He looked up into her eyes, struggling against the feeling of powerlessness that washed over him.

Anya took his head in her hands, turned it to the side, and pulled it in against her. Raymond felt at once trapped and protected. She breathed deeply. He closed his eyes, inhaling the warm, unfamiliar scent of her cashmere top. She rested her cheek on the top of his head and spoke, her voice close to his right ear. "You're a very secretive man, aren't you. You've kept your hurt-filled past to yourself for… twenty-some years—is there no one with whom you're open? You're a good looking man, but you've never had a girlfriend?"

Alarms were going off in Raymond's mind, but somehow he felt safe—as if the intrusion couldn't touch him. A minute smirk pulled his lips to the side and lowered his brow. He inhaled slowly and deeply, savoring the faintly perfumed aroma of her neck, at the same time harboring a kernel of self-aware caution.

She leaned closer to his ear and whispered. "Raymond, I think you should be close to me tonight. I don't want to be alone, and I don't want you to be alone." She pulled back and looked him in the eye. "You don't have to say anything now, but I want you to think about it. When I go to bed tonight, you can join me or you can go—you don't have to say a thing."

She got up from the couch and took their glasses and remaining dishes into the kitchen. Raymond didn't move an inch. He was in shock. Such a flood of emotions. He recalled pictures of the flow of information up from the limbic system, the source of human emotions—pictures that showed how signals from the limbic system up to the conscious mind far outnumbered those sent down in the opposite direction. He imagined getting in bed with her and finding that she was naked. If he went to bed with her, he would definitely leave his boxers on. But what if she started to take them off—would he be able to resist her?

There was such abundance and promise in her offer, but he didn't want a relationship. Detachment seemed so much safer. If he stayed the night, he would end up in a position of implicit indebtedness. She would want him to spend more time with her, and she would want to know more about him. If she became a part of his life, it would muddy the waters, make everything more confusing. He couldn't afford to go soft. All his fantasies from before seemed tainted with danger now.

But was spending the night really going to cast him into the vortex of a relationship that he wouldn't be able to control? What if she wanted to have sex? If they had sex, there was no doubt about it—he would be in a relationship. Sex with a bot in a v-world was just a dirty thrill. Sex with Anya would expose him, make him a part of her. But he felt more alive when she was close, and there was no closer than making love. What if the upload failed, and he had missed this opportunity?

How could I pass this up? I just have to remain in control.

Anya was busy in the kitchen for some time, putting dishes in the dishwasher and cleaning up. Raymond eventually managed to get up from the love seat. He occupied himself with looking about the place, looking for eyes and sensors and computer components. He was intrigued by just how few security devices there were. The front door had a deadbolt and a brass peephole. There were no sensors on the windows and no interior eyes. Someone could break a window and enter her apartment with hardly a worry.

Raymond found himself starting to feel anxious without Anya in the room. He went to the kitchen and stood in the doorway, where he could watch her.

"You know," he said, "I really don't know that much about you, either."

"Then you should ask me questions. What do you want to know about me?"

"I don't know. The facts, I guess. You know—where you were born, the names of your parents. Do you have any sisters, or brothers?"

"I was born in Lisbon, Portugal. My father's name is Sean Flynn and my mother's is Maria Ornelas. My mother was a diplomat, so we traveled a lot. My parents moved from Portugal when I was seven, but we visited family friends there and in Seville many times, so I know—and love—Portugal and Andalucia. I had a younger sister, Amy, but she died five years ago. She was killed by her husband, just one year after they were married."

"Wow... her husband killed her?" Raymond squirmed a little, painfully aware of how wooden his reaction was. He hated situations where he knew he should express sympathy—he was never sure how to do it.

"He was in a bad car accident and experienced brain damage, but no one realized it at the time. She mentioned after the accident that he would sometimes act coldly towards her. As it turned out, he was afflicted with Capgras' delusion. I'd never heard of Capgras at the time. If I had, I might have recommended a brain scan when she mentioned his distant spells. It results from a combination of cognitive and emotional-recognition brain damage. Recognition paths involving the limbic system are damaged such that when you see a loved one, you recognize who they are but experience no emotional response. It feels odd to be with people you know, like it's not really them. The bonds of intimacy aren't triggered. You can recall the old bonds, you remember shared experiences, but the emotional memory isn't triggered. In classic cases, the Capgras victim—because of the combination of emotional-recognition damage with cognitive dysfunction—believes that their loved ones have been abducted and replaced with androids or holographic projections. Rob—her husband—killed her with a knife. In the middle of the night, in their bed, he slit her throat. He probably expected to find her neck filled with cables and motors. And when he didn't, he kept cutting and cutting."

"Oh my god, that's so awfully, tragically sad. What happened to him?"

"Fortunately, the crime was committed here, in the U.S. He was tried and convicted of second degree murder, but his sentence was left undetermined until a brain scan could be performed. The scans showed that he had, in fact, suffered brain damage typical of Capgras' delusion. He was given the option of life imprisonment or neurosurgery, and he chose neurosurgery. They were unable to repair the damage, but he was outfitted with chips that have allowed him to build new emotional memories. After a few months of additional therapy, he was let out on probation."

"Huh. It's great that that could be done, but it doesn't bring back your sister."

"No, but it doesn't bring back his wife, either. He's been on and off of antidepressants ever since."

Raymond shook his head in disbelief. "I'm so sorry." Anya stood drying her hands, the kitchen cleanup complete.

"So," asked Raymond, "was that what got you into brain research?"

"More or less. I was already headed that way. But I was headed several other ways, too, if you know what I mean, and Amy's death made all those other ways seem pretty silly."

"The same thing could happen to an uploaded mind, couldn't it."

"Sure. It's enough the same that I expect you could get an identical phenomenon. Assuming the uploaded mind is conscious and functional in the first place. But it's an extremely rare condition in humans, and we run around with our big soft brains encased in bone. Bone that doesn't even fit the way it ought to, because the evolution of our brains outpaced the development of our skulls. A photonic computer brain, safely mounted within an alloy case, is a lot less likely to suffer physical damage."

"And if Rob's brain had been a computer brain, your sister would still be alive. Is that how you ended up on the upload project?"

"Oh, no. I mean, that sort of thing has crossed my mind, but I'm more about the immediate research benefits. Research on an uploaded mind is much easier than on an organic brain. Every neuristor, before long, will be able to report its own activity. You can obtain a one hundred percent correct image of brain activity. Upload a schizophrenic mind, observe it, experiment with it, and you may finally be able to cure schizophrenia. Cure it, for real, without half a dozen side effects. Thousands of abnormal psychological conditions remain, only partially understood. An uploaded mind provides the perfect platform for understanding and, eventually, correction. Sure, I fantasize about a future in which uploaded humans evolve into something new, but my real motivation lies closer at hand."

"Have you ever thought about uploading yourself?"

Raymond immediately wished he could retract the question. He feared that he was treading too close to his plans for safety. But a thrill arose as he imagined cutting closer and closer to what lay within him, leaving a paper-thin shield that remained opaque to Anya's mind. The thinner the shield, the better.

"Sure, every time I'm on my period," replied Anya.

Raymond chuckled, relieved by her sense of humor.

"I mean," continued Anya, "I expect everybody on the team has fantasized about uploading, at one time or another. You watch a dog go into the scanner, and the next thing you know you're playing fetch and scruffing her neck in a v-chamber. Why couldn't that be you, you wonder. All your bullshit physical problems gone. Knee problems, colds, obesity, migraines, cancer, whatever, all gone. Immortality—what more could you ask for?" She leaned closer. "But what if something goes wrong? Then you've given up on your perfectly good life… because you were greedy for something better? Or what if it's only a partial failure? What if… your memories get wiped?" She shook her head and threw up her hands. "Can you imagine that? Have you ever kept a journal—like, media recordings?"

"Sort of. There was a time when I tried to create a computer persona that could serve as my duplicate in a v-world when the real me had to sleep."

"You mean a bot double that would continue your v-life for you?"

"Exactly. You know, so my double could carry on some mundane work for me. So I recorded myself telling all sorts of stories of my past in that v-world, so the computer persona would have a storehouse of information from which to draw, in case it had to interact with others."

"Did it take you a long time to make?"

"Oh, yeah. Months."

"Well, did you ever imagine it being destroyed? Total media failure—like if the building where it was kept burned down?"

"Sure, but I think that about every computer that means something to me. I'm always creating replication servers and remote backups and such."

"Okay, well imagine if you lost your whole recorded persona. Imagine your replication and your backups all failed, and everything was lost."

"Okay."

"Can you imagine how terrible that would be? It would be awful, right? Now imagine if your entire life memory were lost."

"Yeah, that would be awful."

"And that makes uploading a pretty big risk to take, right?"

"Sure."

"Well," said Anya, "that's a pretty good reason not to upload, as far as I'm concerned. I mean, you're risking your memory. Everything could be lost. Everything that makes you 'you'. I can see uploading if you have some terminal disease, or a mental condition that you think might be reparable after uploading. But if you're a healthy person, why take that kind of risk?"

"Uh, you did mention immortality?"

"Well, sort of. There's always the chance of hardware failure. But even if you were immortal, we're so conditioned for a mortal life span—don't you think we might not be able to deal with immortality?"

Raymond was still thinking of all the lovely reasons to upload, primarily that of avoiding the traceability of one's physical existence. Immortality and near-total control over one's environment seemed like nice side-benefits, at the moment. As for having a hard time with immortality, well, he'd cross that bridge when he came to it.

"I don't know," said Anya. "The idea of uploading certainly holds some appeal for me, but I'm not in this for myself. Of course, before long, I may not be in this at all, from the looks of things."

"Yes," said Raymond, suddenly checking his wrist relay. It was after 10:00. He was surprised to find that so much time had passed.

"It's getting on toward bedtime, isn't it," said Anya.

"It is. And, I don't know. I feel like I should probably go home." Raymond surprised himself—he was genuinely reluctant to stay, but he felt like he was using his reluctance as a weapon in a power game that he didn't understand.

"Home?" questioned Anya, sliding past him into the living room. "Home to your computers, no doubt?" She straightened a small framed photograph on the wall. "Surely your wrist relay can tell you whatever it is you need to know."

"Well, mostly. But, I don't know… I should go."

"Go?" She turned around and came back to him. She went up on her toes and leaned against him where he still stood, within the doorframe, her breasts pressing into his chest. "Go?" she repeated, a mildly devious challenge in the way she dragged out the word. "This isn't a fear of the unfamiliar, is it?"

He couldn't help but smile, keenly aware of the persuasion enacted upon him by her breasts.

"Okay," he said. "Here's a deal. You get ready for bed, and when you turn out the light, chances are I'll come in."

She dropped from her toes and shifted her weight away from him. "Oh, chances are," she said dryly. "Chances are? If you don't want to stay, you can just say so."

Raymond heaved a sigh and looked off to the side. He felt like an ass. "No… I'm sorry. I… I'm just not sure I'm—"

"That's okay." Anya took his hands in hers and gave them a squeeze. "I shouldn't rush you. But I really want you to stay. We'll just sleep. I really feel like we connected tonight, and I don't want the connection to end. Okay?"

Raymond nodded. She gave his hands another squeeze, then left, closing her bedroom door behind her. Raymond watched longingly after her, then wondered how it was that he had ended up so entranced by this woman. He redirected himself to the love seat and plopped into it, waiting for the lights to go out in her room. He felt at once duped and victorious. More than that, he was anxious. He had never slept with a woman, in the literal sense, even in v-space. There were places where you could do that, designed for real couples who wanted to remain virtually close through the night, but Raymond had never had cause to rent a v-room of his own. Now Anya, a real woman with a body of flesh from head to toe—and a beautiful, well-cared-for body, at that—was enticing him to sleep with her. What would it be like to wake up in another person's bed?

He looked at his wrist relay again. Still, there was nothing. He touched a small button on the face of the relay, to make sure he could still communicate with HQ; Scorpio responded with an image of a checkmark.

Raymond was surprised by how long it was taking Anya to get ready for bed. What was she doing? His mind drifted back over their conversation about uploading. He pondered the possibility of volunteering his body for Bob Wells' other project. His body could be scanned at a pretty high resolution without any harm. His physiology could be monitored and replicated in simulation, such that he might gain some useful details on the nature of his hormonal existence. The scan would even include most or all of his neurotransmitters, if he understood it correctly. The model provided would be of limited history and not of perfect resolution, but it might be of some use if he did manage to upload himself.

Anya's bedroom light went out. Raymond sat on the couch for a moment, staring at her door. He faced the decision of whether to stay or go—her influence could not be blamed now. He looked to her entry hall and thought of his bike, outside in the cold October night. He looked at his wrist relay yet again; comm indicators blinked, confirming his connection with the array of computers in his motor home.

"What a fool I would be," he said, shaking his head. And he stood up from the love seat, took the few steps to her bedroom door, and opened it softly. Noticing that no light came on in her room and that the light behind him did not go off, he sought a switch. He found one on the wall of the living room, beside her bedroom door, and turned it off.

In darkness, he undressed to his boxers, leaving his clothes in a heap near her door. He heard her breathing and moved toward the sound, reaching out in search of her bed. A damask comforter cover crumpled beneath his touch. Soon he had found his way under the covers. The sheets had a sweet, floral fragrance. He lay on his back, not touching her, eyes wide open. He felt her hand touch his, and she interlaced her fingers with his. He felt flannel against his forearm—she was wearing pajamas. He took a deep breath and smiled.

"Good night, Raymond."

"Good night, Anya."

He lay awake for a very long time. Eventually, Anya released her grip and turned away from him, curling up on her side. Her breathing grew heavy. He scooched up behind her, nesting his knees against the backs of her thighs. She moaned softly, and he took this to be an acceptance of his closeness.

CHAPTER 6

Tuesday, November 12, 2069

Raymond stood in his office, his eyes closed, smiling. He was watching a retinal feed of Bento eating some grapes on the floor of the jungle habitat Raymond had built, digital Bento's first meal in his new home. The scan had taken place at noon, and scientists had been performing basic tests on Bento throughout the afternoon, between his naps. The tests were duplicates of tests Bento had undergone in the months leading up to the scan, designed to verify the accuracy of the transfer. So far, aside from greater exhaustion than expected, the results were spectacular.

Raymond's wrist relay vibrated. He opened his eyes and glanced down at it. He had a message from Scorpio, flagged as important but not sensitive.

"What is it, Scorpio?" asked Raymond.

"A new version of your physio data was just dropped off in your inbox. Do you want me to do anything with it?"

Raymond had been gratefully accepted as a volunteer for Bob's brain sustenance project. They wanted to accumulate as many physiological histories as possible, and they were especially pleased because Raymond had agreed to submit himself to any scan, procedure, or probe they could come up with. In return, he was given copies of all the resultant data.

"Sure," responded Raymond, after giving it a moment's thought. "Plug it into both sims and let me know if there are any changes outside of tolerance."

He had already installed the team's physiology simulation software on machines in his motor home and his bunker. He had also installed copies of the software used by the brain sustenance team to substitute for a real human brain. The simulated copies of his body, connected to the simple brain-substitute programs, churned non-stop through 24-hour cycles of training and testing.

He closed his eyes again. Bento had advanced to the phase of his meal wherein he lazily, playfully plucked grapes from the bunch with puckered lips, one grape at a time.

Anya's voice came through the speakers in Raymond's office. "Are you watching this?"

"I am. This is fantastic."

"He nailed all the visual recognition tests, all the hearing tests, he's been up and around—I hadn't seen him up and around all week! And did you see when Doug first picked him up, to carry him into his new habitat? His eyes lit up! He recognized Doug's avatar immediately. Where are you? You have to come here!"

"I'm in my office."

"Come on!" urged Anya. "We're in Suma's office."

Raymond walked through the stark white halls of the lab to Suma's office, grinning the whole way. He had wanted to be with Anya, but he was so used to doing things on his own that he didn't know how to go about being included. Suma's office door was open, as usual, and Suma, Alfonso, and Anya all stood watching Suma's 3-D wall display. Raymond stepped in next to Anya and slid his hand across her lower back. The gesture felt awkward to him, but he had spent enough time with Anya in the past couple of weeks to know she would welcome it. And she did—she turned and kissed his cheek.

"We did it!" exclaimed Anya, utterly aglow. "Last night, I wasn't sure he would even be strong enough to withstand the anesthetics. Now look at him! We saved him! We saved his *life*!"

She cheered and hugged Raymond from the side. He wrapped his arms around her and hugged her back.

This gorgeous, popular woman just kissed me in front of Alfonso and Suma, and now she's hugging me.

"Oh, hey, Raymond," said Alfonso. "I have to say, I am so glad you had Bento's habitat ready ahead of schedule. Being able to take him into a v-chamber and introduce him to his new habitat, *before* the upload—it's just been huge. It basically eliminated the adjustment period."

"Sure," responded Raymond. "Yeah, it was really pretty easy."

Bento finished the last grape on the bunch and tossed the remains aside. They stood and watched as Margaret carried Bento over to his favorite toys, a collection of colorful boxes of various sizes, which Raymond had replicated for him. She set him down on the ground next to the boxes. He stood looking at them for a moment, then turned and held his arms out, wanting to be picked up again.

"Looks like he's still a little too tired to be playing," said Margaret, aware she was being recorded.

"I just can't believe this," said Suma. "This is so amazing. You guys, we should really celebrate."

"Yeah," said Alfonso, "it's already 6:30. We should cut out and go for dinner."

"There's this Indian place I've been wanting to try," recommended Suma. "It's a ways out, but it's supposed to be amazing. We could catch a glider."

"Sure!" said Anya enthusiastically. "You'll come, right, Raymond?"

Everyone turned to look at him, and he realized the significance of this moment.

"Sure," he said with a shrug. "Why not?"

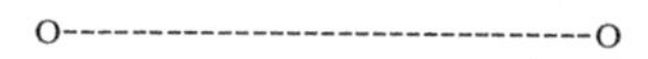

Raymond sat next to Anya in the forward-facing seat of a four-person glider, and Suma and Alfonso sat across from them, in the rear-facing seat. Raymond sat looking out the window while the other three compared notes on all the Indian restaurants they had ever been to. There was a joyous energy among them that was foreign to Raymond. It stirred mixed feelings in him; he was excited to be a part of it, yet he found himself looking out the window. The only Indian restaurant he had ever been to was India Express, his default choice for takeout, and it was dismissed with derision within the first thirty seconds of the conversation. They had moved on, naming over a dozen places he had never heard of, leaving him to relive the countless hours he had spent looking out the window of the Workbound shuttle.

I was so alone. I was even happy to be alone—I thought it was better. But I never learned how not to be alone.

He saw the lights of the Matthias Botanical Garden. He loved Matthias. He would bike there on weekends sometimes, to learn about the plants and get ideas for new species for Nurania, or just to get out of his motor home.

There's somewhere where I know how not to be alone.

Most of the docents at the garden were volunteers, and he had discovered early on that he knew a good deal more about botany than most of them. As he wandered the pathways, he would overhear curious comments made by visitors, and sometimes he would offer answers to their questions. He was reserved in his approach, careful not to annoy anyone, but once in a while he would find someone with a real thirst for knowledge. They would ask him question after question, eventually landing on one he couldn't answer, giving him a little research project to add to his list.

They flew right over the lot where he stored his motor home. He sat up in his seat to look down, to see if the roof of his pole barn was visible through the treetops. Most of the leaves were still on the trees, obscuring the dark rooftop.

"What are you looking at?" asked Anya.

"Oh, uh…" Raymond stalled. "There was a… weird light." It was the best thing he could think of. "Hey, I was just thinking we should go to the Botanical Garden some time."

"That's a great idea!" exclaimed Anya. "I love the Botanical Garden. How about this Saturday? Are you guys doing anything this Saturday?"

Raymond's relief at dodging any reference to his motor home was displaced by sheer terror. He had meant Anya, not the whole group.

"I think Saturday's wide open for me," replied Suma. Holographic displays popped up as she and Alfonso checked their wrist relays. "Yeah, I'm free," confirmed Suma. "I'll ask Tony if he wants to come."

"Oh, that's right," said Alfonso. "My cousin's baby shower is Saturday. But I should be free by three, if that's not too late."

"No, three's fine," said Anya.

"Hey, Tony," said Suma, talking to the floating head above her wrist relay. Raymond gathered from the way they talked that Tony must be her boyfriend.

Anya prodded Raymond playfully. "What a great idea, Raymond."

He smiled and waved her off, trying to hide the fact that he was actually mortified. Before he knew it, a five-person trip to the Botanical Garden had been planned, with dinner and bar-hopping to follow.

"Maybe we can go dancing!" proposed Anya.

"Oh, no," said Raymond, "I don't know how to dance."

"I'll teach you. We'll go to this salsa club I know in Detroit."

o-----------------------------o

The Botanical Garden idea thrust Raymond into a stream of activities he couldn't possibly have anticipated. Anya convinced him to join her clothes shopping after work the next day. "You'll need something… sexier, more going-out," she said, inadvertently causing him to call his entire wardrobe into question. They shopped together in v-chambers at the lab, bought a stack of clothing two-feet high, and Raymond had it all shipped to Anya's, to avoid giving any details about his living arrangement, with the excuse that she should see him try them on. Shopping together led to dinner together at La Sevillana, which led to drinks with some Columbian friends of Anya's at a wine bar, which led to a slightly unstable Raymond helping a rather drunk Anya get home, which led to the two of them making out on her couch until they both passed out. They had coffee together in the morning, Raymond showered in a girlfriend's shower for the first time, and they took a gridcab to work. They did yoga together that evening in Raymond's dojo-turned-yoga-studio, and again the following morning, this time with Suma. Thursday evening, Raymond joined Anya and Suma at a dark old bar called Del Rio, which was reportedly a revival of an even older bar, and spent most of the evening listening to them discuss family traditions, which led to Raymond's having to confess that he had no Thanksgiving plans, at which point Anya insisted that he join her for Thanksgiving dinner with the family of a professor friend who would be delighted to include him, she was sure. Friday morning, Anya joined him mid-way through his yoga session, at the end of which she invited him to join the science team for a lunch outing. By Friday evening, Raymond was exhausted, immensely relieved to learn that Anya had plans she couldn't cancel, leaving him on his own for an evening.

o------------------------------o

Raymond stepped out of Anya's bedroom and into her living room, looking down at himself in the outfit Anya had recommended for their Saturday outing.

"You look great!" exclaimed Anya. "Turn around." She made a sexy growling sound. "See, now that's how pants should fit. You've gotta get rid of all your baggy-butt pants."

"Okay," said Raymond without reluctance. "You see me wearing pants that don't fit right, let me know, and I'll toss them."

"Recycle," she corrected.

"Right, I'll recycle them." He glanced at his wrist relay. "It's almost three. We should get going."

They spent the afternoon at the Botanical Garden, Raymond impressing everyone with his knowledge of botany. He even managed to get a few laughs with his story of the docent who kept telling people to make sure they saw the giant "sequoia", which was actually a giant saguaro cactus. From the garden they piled into a gridcab and went to an ultramodern restaurant downtown, where they were joined by three more people, making eight. Raymond ended up across from Tony, who, as it turned out, had also done a lot of gaming in Agakhan, and they regaled each other with stories of their fights and adventures there. Dinner was finished with a round of Red Tridents, a wickedly strong, cinnamon-flavored, three-staged drink served in trident-shaped glasses, each tine stronger and more intense than the last. By the end of the third tine, Raymond felt like he could breathe fire if he tried.

"Detroit?" proposed Anya. "We can start at Pegasus—stick with the ultramodern theme."

This was immediately accepted by all. Everyone put their coats on and headed outside to catch cabs. Raymond and Anya ended up in a glider together with Alfonso and his girlfriend, a tall woman with a shaved head decorated with rhinestone spirals, who immediately proceeded to make out with Alfonso. Raymond watched out the window as they rose above Ann Arbor and entered the stream of airborne traffic headed east.

He felt a nibbling at his ear.

"You aren't going to stare out the window the whole ride, are you?" teased Anya.

Her breath smelled of cinnamon. She ran her fingers up the back of his head and started kissing his neck. He melted, his eyes closing. She breathed in his ear and whispered something in Portuguese. Through his tight new pants he felt her hand, feeling for his hard-on, and he opened his eyes, afraid that Alfonso or his girlfriend might see. They were too involved to possibly have noticed, but he shifted nervously all the same.

"Something about you," whispered Anya, "makes me want to be so sexy for you."

He smiled and looked away.

She affectionately rubbed his thigh. "I've been having so much fun with you," she said. "This week has been great." He put his hand on hers and met her dreamy gaze, and they cuddled the rest of the way.

The glider started to descend. Raymond glanced out the window and saw the lights of Detroit ahead.

"Isn't it beautiful," said Anya. "I love flying into the city."

"Have you ever done it on a hovercycle?" asked Raymond.

"No. Oh my god, have you?"

"Yeah, not long after I moved here. I used to rent a hovercycle on the weekends." He turned and looked at her. "We should do it some time."

The glider slowed to city traffic speeds, shifting right and left until it was in line with the top floor of the tallest of the old skyscrapers. It slipped smoothly alongside a docking station, then shifted left and locked in place.

"We're here, lovers," said Anya.

o------------------------------o

The group made their way through what felt like an ancient fog-enshrouded crypt, down crowded plaster-walled corridors, ethereal female voices whispering eerie bits of poetry. Raymond leaned forward, over Anya's shoulder.

"It's weird to feel underground but know you're so high up."

Anya stopped to pick up drinks from a cocktail waitress, turning to Raymond to ask what he wanted. He looked at the tray of crude clay goblets, full of what appeared to be different liquid metals.

"I have no idea."

She selected one of the goblets and handed it to him. "Mercury," she informed him.

He took a sip of it. It was thick like mercury but tasted like licorice.

They continued through corridors, eventually turning and climbing a long, narrow stone staircase. At the top, they emerged into a vast space, windows all around, tables and couches and bars in groupings around the floor. In the center was a hologram of a pegasus, flying in place. Raymond found himself underwhelmed, spoiled by v-world bars.

The group sat in couches around a low table, near a window overlooking the Ambassador Bridge. Raymond and Anya sat together in a love seat, close to Suma and Tony. They discussed their drinks and did a good deal of passing and sampling.

Raymond's wrist relay vibrated. He glanced at it and saw that Scorpio had some news about the project. Emboldened by liquor, he decided to take a quick look at the news. He closed his eyes and skimmed a summary relayed to his retinal implants. A paragraph of text appeared before him. The heading was all he needed to see: "Zootorium goes public with the uploaded-chimp deal." He had been watching the deal unfold since Tuesday, listening to Bob's private channels.

"So," muttered Raymond to himself. "It's public."

"What's public?" asked Anya. "What is it?"

"Zootorium," responded Raymond.

Suma turned and leaned in to hear what Raymond was saying. "Zootorium what?" she asked. The name alone was enough to raise concern.

"They just announced a deal. Bob caved. He signed a contract to exhibit two uploaded chimps."

Suma's jaw dropped. "No way! You know, he is so full of shit. How many times has he gone off about not blurring the line between a-life and uploaded life?"

"I can't believe he didn't tell us," complained Anya. "He's told us every time he *didn't* accept a deal with Zootorium. He's probably been working on this since the ESW decision."

"What's going on?" asked Tony. "What's Zootorium?"

"It's a zoo v-world," explained Suma. "All the animals are a-life animals, and Bob has agreed to give them exhibit time for an uploaded chimp."

Tony still looked lost.

"Artificial life," continued Suma, "is a type of digital life created from scratch, unlike uploaded life. It's really complex software, built up from—"

"No, no," interjected Tony. "I know what a-life is. I think I've actually been to Zootorium—I just didn't remember the name. But I don't get what's wrong with having an uploaded chimp in the zoo. Wouldn't they be paying for that?"

"They may be," said Suma, "but—"

"They are," confirmed Raymond.

"But a-life has no real *rights*," continued Suma.

"It's awful," said Anya. "People abuse a-life all the time. There's this whole fucked-up pseudo-science based on torturing a-life creatures. People use a-life to explore the limits of pain, hunger, dehydration—you name it, and they pass it all off as okay because they can always just kill the creature and restore it from backup. Or they say that humans created this new life-form, so we can do what we want with it."

"Most people make shitty gods," said Raymond.

"And Bob *knows* all this," complained Suma. "He's turned down Zootorium every time they've approached him, because he doesn't want to blur the line between a-life and uploaded life. We're losing the fight for a-life rights. He wants to make sure uploaded life gets a fresh start."

Raymond nodded in agreement. He had always been impressed that Bob had a strategy for advancing the rights of digital life.

"So," said Tony, "if the chimps are on display alongside a-life animals, the concern is that people will lump them all together?"

Suma and Anya both nodded in confirmation. Anya turned to Raymond. "Are there any details on how the exhibit will be handled?"

Raymond closed his eyes and skimmed the rest of the summary. "It says they'll be in a special part of the zoo where they show footage of real animals."

Anya and Suma looked to each other.

"That's not so bad," admitted Suma.

"Actually," said Raymond, "I guess that might be a good thing. You can accentuate contrast by putting two things next to each other."

"Organic animals and uploaded animals?" asked Anya, not seeing Raymond's point.

"No, a-life and uploaded," said Raymond. "Having them in the same zoo but in separate exhibits actually makes perfect sense—it contrasts the two."

"Still," said Suma, "I can't believe Bob did this without asking anyone. He's so full of himself."

"That is shitty," said Tony, "but if it brings in more money…"

"It will help us save more animals," admitted Anya. "At least we can drink to that."

She raised her glass, and they all toasted to saving more animals. Anya chugged the remainder of her drink.

"Well, what do you know—I'm empty. Drink up, Raymond, and we'll go get another round."

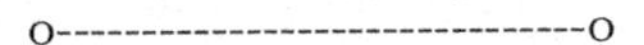

The party eventually progressed to another bar, a cheery little neighborhood place with an Irish pub theme. A trio played and sang traditional Irish songs. The louder setting caused the group to split up into smaller groups and huddle closer, to hear each other. Raymond found it difficult to listen hard enough to hear everything being said, and he ended up tuning out, nursing his beer, watching a couple of balding men buy drinks for a group of very attractive younger women.

"You need something stronger!" shouted Tony to Raymond. "You ever had an Irish Car Bomb?"

Raymond shook his head.

"You drop a shot of Bailey's in a pint of Guinness and chug the whole thing."

Raymond nodded, insufficiently experienced with alcohol to be able to imagine what this might taste like. But Tony treated him like a buddy, and Raymond liked Tony.

"Sounds great."

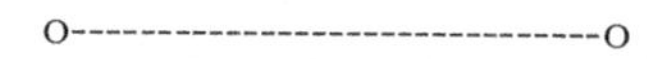

By the time Anya dragged Raymond onto the floor of the salsa club, he was far enough gone to try just about anything. Anya gave him some quick instructions, demonstrated the basic steps, and the next thing he knew, he was dancing, propelled by her strong lead. The sport of keeping his feet under him, combined with the enormous pride he felt at the mere fact that he was on the dance floor, proved to be riotous good fun.

"I'm dancing!" he shouted. "This is so fucking great!"

Unfortunately, the act of assembling words added a degree of complexity that was too much for his brain to manage. He lost his balance, fell into Anya, and would have taken them both down had it not been for the massive-bicepped latino man just behind Anya. The man turned around looking ready to flatten Raymond, but the stream of Spanish apologies that flowed from Anya's mouth saved him.

"Take a break," shouted the man to Raymond.

Raymond nodded largely in acceptance of this man's greater wisdom and happily followed Anya off the floor. They made their way to the bar and stood drinking water together.

"That was fun!" said Raymond. "I was dancing."

Anya beamed at his boyish excitement. They lingered at the bar awhile, watching people dance.

"Hey," said Raymond. "I saw v-chambers. Come here, I want to show you something."

Anya looked apprehensive.

"No, seriously," insisted Raymond. "Set your glass down. I want to show you something."

He led her through the club, to the wall where he had seen v-chambers. "Wow," he said. "These are two-person v-chambers, aren't they?"

"Yeah," responded Anya. "I don't know how clean they are."

Raymond ignored her hesitation and pulled her into a chamber with a green "vacant" sign. The door slid closed, there was a dull thunking sound, and a service persona announced that the chamber was locked. The space around them turned into a psychedelic little lounge. Raymond tapped his wrist relay and established a voice connection with Scorpio.

"Scorpio, open a public gateway to Nurania for me. Top of Mount Lidral."

"Are you drunk?" asked Scorpio.

"Shut up and do it," said Raymond. "It's just for a while." He chuckled and pointed at his relay. "I think I made him too smart."

Raymond fed the address of the new gateway to the v-chamber.

"Oh, my god," said Anya. "Are you going to show me your v-world?"

Raymond grabbed her hand as the space around them morphed into the top of Mount Lidral. Anya let out a little gasp. It was nighttime, and it took a while for their eyes to adjust to the light of the two crescent moons. Anya wrapped her arms around Raymond's waist.

"Where are we?" asked Anya.

"On top of Mount Lidral. Just a second. Close your eyes. God mode. Group teleport to Anya's flower garden."

They teleported to the center of the flower garden, next to the pond. Raymond was pleased that he could pull all this off, in his current state.

"Flower garden?" she asked.

"Open your eyes," said Raymond excitedly.

She drew a sharp breath. "How beautiful. Oh my god. You made this for me?"

"Remember when you first asked me to give you a yoga lesson? Well, after the lesson, I was going to bring you here. But you said you wanted to get something to eat, and it just kind of… didn't happen."

"You made this for me before we even did yoga the first time? Oh, Raymond!" Her voice cracked, and she threw herself into a hug. He grinned with delight. "So, show me around. It's so dark—it's a little hard to see."

"Oh, of course. God mode. I want red lanterns hanging from all the willow trees."

Red light erupted from globe lanterns in the trees around the perimeter of the garden. Anya applauded. Even Raymond was taken by surprise, the effect was so magical. He looked at Anya, in the center of it all, the first person to ever see his world, and he wanted as never before to kiss her. She turned to him, started to say something, and cut herself short. Her face softened, and her eyes seemed to come alive with the magic he felt. Her gaze fell on his lips, and he moved toward her, took hold of her, kissed her with confident, loving passion. Her kisses grew more and more intense. She ripped open the snaps of his shirt and stripped it off his chest. He felt her nails drag down his back. He pulled her closer, and they locked in a vigorous, lustful kiss.

She pushed away, stepped back. He moved after her, but she put a finger up to stop him. She lifted her dress up over her bare breasts, over her head, and tossed it aside. It flew about a foot and then dropped, and Raymond realized it must have hit the wall of the v-chamber. He looked at Anya, standing before him in nothing but lacy panties. An odd, intense mix of dizzy lust, awkwardness, and breathlessness at her beauty left him gaping, dumbstruck. He wondered whether the v-chamber was designed to enhance the beauty of its occupants, or whether she was really that beautiful.

She moved back in and kissed him. Her breasts pressed against his chest, and he felt an exciting visceral distinction between man and woman. He held her closer, ran his strong hands up and down her back, over the flare of her hips. She undid his pants, jerked them down. He shivered. His entire body quivered.

"Nobody's ever taken my pants off before," he said with a nervous chuckle.

She seemed to ignore his comment, stooping, kissing his stomach and hips as she descended. He felt like a little boy, standing there with his pants around his ankles. She ran her hands up the backs of his thighs, to the small of his back. He continued to quiver in spasms. She kissed his erect penis, and he felt it pulse full of blood. He closed his eyes, focused on his breathing, focused on the feeling of her hand as she slid it between his legs.

"I'm gonna come," he announced, and he felt the precursor shockwaves of orgasm. He wasn't sure where this was leading, and he didn't want to disappoint Anya by climaxing too soon. "I'm gonna come," he said again, this time more urgently, and he pulled away, trying to stop while there was still any chance of stopping.

"Raymond, it's okay. Try to relax. There's nothing to worry about—this is for you. I want to do this, for you."

o------------------------------o

Suma, Tony, Anya, and Raymond took a sleepy 3 AM glider flight back to Ann Arbor. Anya slept with her head on Raymond's lap, and he drifted in a state of delirium, petting her head from time to time. They stopped at Anya's apartment first, and Raymond and Anya went in together, no discussion necessary. They slept cuddled together in her bed.

Raymond awoke with sticky mouth and a blistering headache at 7:17 AM. He wavered into Anya's bathroom and leaned on the counter; turned on the cold water; cupped water in his hands and splashed it on his face; drank from his hands, rinsed his mouth out. He rubbed his temples, massaged the top of his head.

She gave me a blowjob. I can't believe she gave me a blowjob.

He made his way back to her bed and sat on the edge. Her face was slack, her mouth open. He brushed her hair away from her eyes, savoring the irony of her peaceful sleep; as she slumbered, forces she had unleashed tore through him, turning his life upside down.

He got dressed and lay on her couch, drifting in and out of sleep for about an hour. Still, she showed no sign of waking up. He grabbed his jacket, kissed her forehead, and left. He biked to a coffee shop and texted her as he ate a bowl of oatmeal: "Out to get some breakfast. Thank you for an amazing night."

His wrist relay went off. It was a message from Scorpio, urgent and very sensitive. Remnants of his fuck-all attitude from the night before drove him to retrieve the message and relay it to his retinal implants, regardless of the security risk of doing this in a public place.

"One of your lurker-agents in the Illinois State Police network was captured part way through transmission of a critical-priority message. The words 'bone chip' are all that got through."

Raymond's initial reaction was one of frustration. With one of his lurkers captured, he would have to shut down his police surveillance. He couldn't afford to risk leaving any of his other agents in the field; there was no way they would be able to trace one to him, but if more were caught, they might see a pattern. Then the significance of the message hit him.

"Bone chip."

The acrid odor of bone powder overtook him, a potent smell memory, which triggered recall of a day he wished had never happened. He heard again the gruesome, jarring sounds of bone against the gritty grinding stone. He remembered working all afternoon in Tate's basement, grinding the old man's bones, a crucial step in the painstaking disposal process. Every last bone, ground to powder and mixed with fertilizer, for robots to spread over the lush, suburban lawn.

How could there have been chips? It was all powder.

Then he remembered—there were chips in the grinder. But he had washed those out—he had worked so hard to clean the grinder, in the utility tub, before the Workbound shuttle came to pick him up.

The plumbing. What if some chips got stuck in the plumbing?

Raymond caught himself wandering down a path of conjecture. But what other explanation could there be? Something about bone chips had been entered into the evidence records of the missing person case—he could think of no other reason why his lurker would send a critical message. One of Tate's bone chips must have gotten stuck in the plumbing.

He pushed his oatmeal away, crossed his arms on the table, and lay his head down. He felt as though he should be thinking things through, planning his next step, but his mind was blank. There was a time when he would have taken this news in stride, merely chastising himself for his mistakes and adjusting his plans accordingly. Now, he found himself immobilized, brought to his knees by an unfamiliar weight: the despair of loss.

Anya, why can't I make my past go away?

CHAPTER 7

Friday, November 22, 2069

Raymond stood in his office, his arms crossed and his back against his mini-v, staring at the two-foot-tall holographic beaker on his desk. Its contents, the color and translucency of soy milk, gently bubbled at the surface, wisps of steam curling up and tapering to vanishment. The vaporization rate of this fluid was perfectly synchronized with the passage of time. For each of his remaining days on the project there was a white tick mark on the side of the beaker.

He created the beaker on the afternoon his release date was announced—October 21, the Friday following the ESW position statement. He hoped it would help him maintain the difficult balance between urgency and level-headedness. Already, the beaker was half empty. He gazed fixedly at the meniscus, smiling slightly at the accidental implication that present time is warped. It was now November 22. His official last day on the project was to be December 20, two days prior to Christmas break, but with Murray on his way to Ann Arbor and the Tate case at risk of being reclassified as a homicide case, Raymond would have to be gone much sooner than that.

He closed his eyes briefly, forcing himself to resume a mental scan of his life. He was trying to think of any possible missteps or loose ends that needed cleaning up, but he kept losing concentration.

"The motor home," he said, more with his lips than his voice. "I was thinking about the motor home."

The obvious place to start was its v-chamber, just off the tiny bedroom at the rear of the rig. This was where he did most of his personal work. But he had been through it a hundred times. He couldn't bear to dwell on it further. He pictured the bedroom next, as if exiting the v-chamber: the built-in bed, clothing, gadgets, cleaner bots, meaningless personal effects. There were the memory chips he sometimes used to transfer data between work and home, but he had wiped those clean and double- and triple-checked them.

His mental exploration jumped to the dinette. On the table were his plans for the weeks to come, written out on antique paper, which he intended to burn in a week or two. But it occurred to him that it was cocky to leave the plans out, to assume that his motor home was safe from investigation. As careful as he had been not to reveal the motor home to others, there was always the chance that Murray or the police knew more than he suspected. He would have to take care of those notes.

He wasn't sure why he had written them out on paper in the first place. He was vaguely aware of some romantic association with scrawling out one's grand schemes on paper, but it was more a matter of wanting to be completely safe from hacking. Whatever the reason, it no longer made sense. He had to accept that he was now just as susceptible to physical investigation as he was to the prying software of police hackers.

His thought process was again derailed, his focus falling back to the beaker.

Bento had been undergoing psychological tests for almost two weeks now, and they were going extremely well. Tests of his reaction to the sight of a snake confirmed that his emotional memory remained intact; he leapt and climbed to a high spot in his habitat, where he jumped and screamed and threw loose objects at the snake. His diet and sleep habits conformed to those he had exhibited in biological form. His gestures and moods appeared similar. He had even returned to playing with the colored boxes, his most favored toys.

Raymond pushed off from the mini-v and started to pace slowly, his arms still on his chest. In less than an hour, at 1:30 PM, the team would attempt to upload a second chimp, a female named Molly. Molly was to be the first of the Zootorium chimps. Via his access to Bob's personal computer network, Raymond knew that Bob had just put in a request for more chimps, though he had promised Zootorium only two. Which was why Raymond didn't feel bad about the catastrophic upload failure that was soon to be entered into the scanner logs.

His pacing grew more intense. He ran a hand through his hair, struggling to keep his mind from jumping uselessly from thought to thought. It was a source of great anxiety to him that Murray had purchased an airbus ticket to Ann Arbor. The timing was especially irksome—Scorpio had notified Raymond of Murray's travel plans earlier that morning. Murray was due into Ann Arbor by airbus the next morning. As if his mind weren't already spinning fast enough with the details of his plans for the night. Now this.

What exactly was it that had triggered Murray's visit to Ann Arbor? The day Raymond's lurker was tagged, he had dismantled his State Police listening network. As a result, he couldn't be sure how much they knew. But it was obvious he was their hottest lead.

He ran through the saga of his fraud. Each month and year that passed made the events seem hazier and hazier, more safely distant. Self-disgust arose within him each time he recalled his one grave error—not giving the nephews full power-of-attorney on Tate's emergency account. It was the money therein, locked away from them, that motivated them to investigate the fate of their wealthy uncle.

The mistake had really been threefold, which made it all the worse. First, there was the issue of not granting the nephews full power of attorney. This was a matter of a clerical oversight on his part—he had merely failed to fill out the forms correctly. Second, he forgot to check the anonymous mailbox that he had set up to allow the bank to contact Tate, who was ostensibly off in some remote tropical location with the girl of his dreams. Had Raymond checked that damned mailbox in time, he would have found a message from the bank informing him that the nephews had attempted to access the account and failed, and he would have been able to grant them access. Third, he had been ignorant of the bank's regulations. He wasn't anymore. Once a missing person report on an account holder had been active for over a year, that account holder was locked out of the account, unable to make modifications to or withdrawals from the account without visiting a bank outlet in person and passing a series of identification tests. A missing person report was filed for Tate a month after Tate supposedly ran off with his dream girl, and the account was sealed a year later.

Now the nephews wanted access to it. In order to gain access, they either had to wait another two years—at which time Tate would automatically be declared dead—or they had to provide proof that Tate was already dead. And the nephews weren't willing to wait.

Had I avoided any of these mistakes, the nephews would have had gotten access to the account and gone on their merry way.

Raymond struggled to stop dwelling on the past. He needed to face his current circumstances with a clear head. Hope flashed through his mind—what if Murray's trip to Ann Arbor were a coincidence?

"Great," he murmured. "Delude yourself to safety."

A text message came in on Raymond's wrist relay—a message from Anya addressed to him and Suma. It was time to prepare for the scan. One set of anxious thoughts replaced another, and the subconscious agitation grew more intense. As he closed up his office, looking for the millionth time for anything that might give him away, he imagined himself as a digital life-form, safely residing in a hi-jacked communications satellite, orbiting the Earth. Not wanting to be late, he sighed deeply, resigned himself to the risk of having missed something, and made his way toward the Scan Lab.

"Hey, Raymond."

Raymond turned around to see Suma walking quickly to catch up with him. Raymond stopped to wait for her. She smiled at him. As frazzled as he was, it was still nice to see her—her air of control and good cheer was contagious, and he found himself smiling back at her, releasing his worries into her warm gaze.

"So," she said, "it's time for me to learn your system."

"Oh, yeah, that's right." Raymond had forgotten that he and Suma were going to go through his procedures together during this upload. She would be taking over his responsibilities associated with the actual upload process, and Tim would pick up any maintenance work on the other software tools that Raymond had created.

She caught up with him and they walked down the hall together.

"I can see you've really been thinking about it," she joked.

"Yeah, well—you've already seen most of it. It's really not that big a deal. You even helped build some of it."

"True, but I'll feel better once we've gone through a live run together. I was looking through your 3-D display for scan and upload progress. It's really good."

"Oh, thanks. It was just a modification to a 3-D model I made for a v-world a few years ago."

"Well, it's really good." She laughed mildly on the word "really". "And it's a touch that nobody else would have added. I was talking with Anya and Jean-Michel about your feedback display work. They're so impressed. I mean, you do in a day or two what it would take anyone else on this team weeks to do—we just don't have your visuals background. It's really a shame you're leaving."

"Oh, you'll still have Tim. He's good with visuals."

Suma looked at Raymond with a raised eyebrow. "He's good at goofing off."

"There is that…" As Raymond trailed off, he placed his hand on the fingerprint scanner at the entrance to the Scan Lab. The doors slid open and he and Suma stepped through.

The Scan Lab was a fairly large lab. From his 3-D mapping work, Raymond knew it to be forty-two feet by thirty-eight feet, give or take a few inches. It was a brightly lit windowless room at the heart of the building. There were two doorways—the one through which Raymond and Suma had just entered, and the one that led to the animal holding chamber. In the center of the room, under a track of spotlights, was the scanner. It was a sleek piece of equipment, a long charcoal gray pedestal with a transparent yellow dome cover that was open at one end. Around the perimeter of the room were mobile computer stations, where team members could monitor the upload. Dominating one wall was a floor-to-ceiling display, currently showing a live feed of Bento's living environment. Bento could be seen on a low tree limb, looking idly down at the ground as Rona, a female a-life chimp, preened him.

Roughly half the team was already present in the lab. The scientists on the team all wore white lab coats. Raymond spotted Anya, standing at her usual station on the other side of the room, next to the main wall display. Ellen was with her, the two of them discussing holographic charts. Raymond crossed through the center of the room, where Darryl and Kim stood at one end of the scanner, running through results. Kim looked up at him.

"Our final run, eh Kim?" asked Raymond as he passed her.

"Yeah," she responded, "and just when we've got the whole thing running smoothly…"

Raymond reached Anya's station, and Suma came up next to him. Anya and Ellen continued their discussion. They were going over test results for the simulated physiology that would become Molly's body, once her mind was uploaded. They ran through details, confirming one result after another. Raymond loved seeing Anya in her lab coat—he loved the air of authority it gave her.

"Hey, Anya, what's up?" asked Raymond.

She looked up at him, meeting his eyes with a look of distraction, her brow slightly furrowed. "Oh, I just wanted you two to know everything's on schedule. You should go ahead and run through the controller tests." She looked back down at her screen.

Raymond lingered for a moment, then crossed back past the scanner to the controller station. This was the only fixed station in the room, the others being mobile for reuse throughout the building. The controller station consisted of a single adjustable touch-screen, atop a charcoal gray pedestal that matched the base of the scanner.

"Okay," said Raymond. He touched the screen to activate it, and it lit up with a complex array of controls and feedback panels. He grabbed the top of the screen, pulled it up a couple inches, and tilted it forward. "This, obviously, is the control station. Everything you have to do can be done from here."

Raymond ran through a series of tests to make sure the scanner controls functioned properly, explaining to Suma the purpose of each test, what results to expect, and how to deal with failures. As he described the various possible trouble spots, he imagined performing the upload on himself. From the beginning, he had accounted for the possibility that the upload would have to be performed without human interaction.

"If you look through my code," he explained, "you'll see that everything has a fully-automatic mode. I've even created automated procedures to handle nearly any failure case that can occur. But, by default, it's set to await manual confirmation or override. The auto version is there for the sake of testing—so I can force a hardware failure and see how the system will respond without having to be in two places at once."

Suma nodded, accepting this explanation without question. All tests came out positive.

"Okay," continued Raymond. "Next comes code analysis, to make sure the code base for the scan and upload is the right one. Obviously, we don't want any untested code to be included in the build for a run like this. In fact, in this case, everything should match the code base used for Bento's scan. This is probably the most important step in the entire process."

Raymond ran code analyses on all the control modules, smiling to himself as version control falsely confirmed that the feedback and logging modules had not been modified since Bento's scan. *Why, that's odd*, he joked to himself with familiar self-satisfaction—*I modified them just last night.*

"So, everything checks out fine, and that's about it. Now, you just hit this icon or say 'Home', and it takes you back to the main control panel."

Ten minutes prior to the scan, the doors to the animal holding chamber opened, and Doug and Margaret wheeled Molly in on a gurney. Her prone, motionless body was spotted with derms, feeding a mix of anesthetics and nanoscanners into her bloodstream and throughout her body. By the time the scan started, she would be so thoroughly anesthetized that no straps would be needed to hold her still during the scan. For his own upload, Raymond had imagined himself being inside the scanner before applying the derms and self-anesthetizing. But now, looking at how many derms were on her, he realized he would be too cramped inside the scanner to reach his legs and feet. He would probably have to do it all sitting on the gurney, then have one of his robots push him into the scanner and initiate the scan.

Bob Wells entered just a few steps behind Molly. As Doug lined her up for transfer onto the scanning table, Bob stepped over and placed a hand on her forehead. "Be a good girl for me, Molly."

At five minutes, the wall display that had shown the feed from Bento's v-world switched to a five minute countdown. Molly was transferred to the scanner, the top section of the gurney sliding directly onto the table. Raymond watched the motion closely, in anticipation of his having to train one of his robots to do the same.

"Bring up the monitors, Raymond," said Bob.

Raymond pointed out to Suma a button on the main control panel, then pressed it. Large holographic displays on either side of the scanner lit up with spinning chimp-shaped grids showing the positional status of the nanoscanners. The team had found that the scanners behaved somewhat differently from body to body, making it essential that the actual scan be triggered at the correct moment. With help from Anya, Raymond had trained the controlling computer to recognize the correct moment, but Bob liked to maintain override power, in case of abnormal conditions. From the holographic monitors, it could be seen that the nanoscanners had made their way through most of Molly's body. Those that had come in contact with the nervous system sent off signals indicating that they recognized their position in the body. These signals were sensed by the scanner and portrayed as magenta points in Raymond's holographic displays. Molly's nervous system took shape before them, a complex network of threads throughout the body, all leading to the brain.

"Ready on the ignition, there, Raymond?" asked Bob.

Raymond nodded in response. His left middle finger was poised over the scan-initiation button, while his right index finger was poised over the abort button. Just as the holographic displays showed complete pre-scan positioning of the nanoscanners, the voice of the controlling computer called out a three second abort period prior to automatic scan initiation. Raymond looked to Bob, who gave a positive nod, and he lifted his hands from the control panel. He was pleased to see his automated system work properly yet again.

"Commencing scan," announced the computer.

The whole nervous system scan would take about thirty seconds, and the scan on the rest of the body—which would be used to verify and possibly to enhance the existing physiological simulation—would take a total of about two minutes. Molly's brain death, a somewhat subjective occurrence, was announced by the controlling computer just moments into the scan. Raymond waited apprehensively for his false failure report. He wondered again whether the scan failure would be a significant setback to the team. They would probably chase their tails for quite some time, trying to figure out what the hell went wrong. And they would probably end up replacing some of the hardware components in the scanner. But would it be considered a transgression of animal rights? His simulated raid on the lab would make it *look* like a big animal rights issue, but would it actually become one? Until a few moments before, Molly had been terminally ill, as Bento had been prior to his scan. Bob had argued that the upload could be considered a medical procedure, an attempt to extend the life of the animal. Given the apparent success of the scans performed thus far, his argument had been upheld. But with this seeming failure, would his argument be dragged under the public spotlight and reconsidered? Might the team be charged with malpractice by the Lansing Zoo? Not likely, thought Raymond, as the procedure was accepted as being experimental, and had been fully authorized by Molly's legal guardian—the city of Lansing, Michigan.

The clock ticked away. Reports on the progress of the scan were promising. An occasional two-beat vibration in his wrist relay indicated to Raymond that his agents were successfully recording the scan data, rapidly encrypting it and socking it away in computers all over the Net, using a dozen "verysafe" hacked accounts, for later reassembly and upload—upload into one of the NBCs that Raymond planned to steal that night, under the falsified auspices of an Animal Liberation

Army (ALA) break-in. Everything was in place. At 11:00 PM, he would box two NBCs and ensure that they were safely loaded into the cargo bay of his delivery robot, while his agents fed the building's security system with footage of an empty lab and empty hallways, making his activities invisible. His delivery robot would cart one box to University Property Disposition and add it to the outgoing mail there—along with corresponding database records indicating the shipment of a small centrifuge—and the box would be shipped to the Minnesota post office box of one Ivar Svensson. The other would be delivered to his motor home, this second NBC being the one that he planned to upload into. He was okay with the idea of uploading Molly into a remote machine, sending her mental data across the Net via hundreds of network paths, trusting that it would all make it to its destination. But the prospect of sending his own mental snapshot over the Net disturbed him. There was always some remote chance of it being intercepted, and he didn't see any point in running that risk.

With the NBCs packaged and on their way, he would then head to Anya's to make an unannounced romantic visit. Through the night, his robots would re-map the building, updating his existing maps to reflect displaced chairs, carts, and other miscellaneous equipment. Then, at about 3:30—while Raymond was fast asleep with Anya—his agents would feed the building's security system with his homemade footage of ALA members entering the building, breaking into the lab with high-tech lock-breaker devices, dropping the two NBCs into bags, and smashing the contents of the bags to bits. As the ALA members appeared to depart the building, alarms would be triggered. If all went as planned, police officers and university security personnel would arrive at the building, review the night's footage, and arrest known ALA members for questioning. Meanwhile, his two NBCs would be on their way to Minnesota.

"Catastrophic failure detected."

Raymond's racing mind was interrupted by the voice of the controlling computer.

"Unknown hardware failure. Terminating transfer of neural architecture." Raymond heard Suma gasp next to him.

"Terminating transfer!" shouted Bob. "Terminating transfer! What the hell is that?"

The holographic displays showed that the nanoscanners had just finished the nervous scan and were proceeding through the rest of Molly's body, turning it into a deconstructed pudding as they went. But a wall display showing activity in the NBC revealed that flushing patterns had already been released from a million entry points, clearing the NBC of the ostensibly bad data.

"It's flushing!" shouted Bob. "Shit! Raymond, what the hell is going on? The transfer should have carried through! We yanked the flushing procedure ages ago!"

Raymond stood staring at all the displays of the controlling computer, shaking his head. "I don't know!" he shouted back. "Version control checked out okay. Everything should be just like the Bento scan."

"And there's nothing we can do, is there?"

"No," said Anya. "Once flushing patterns have been released into the NBC, there's no stopping them."

"Well I'll be damned."

They stood and watched helplessly as Molly's hairy body started to shimmer with motion. Her skin tone faded to gray in splotches, the splotches expanding and joining until what was left on the scanning table looked like a sagging pudding, roughly chimp-shaped, covered with loose hair.

The holographic displays vanished. Bob rolled the gurney up to the scanning table, aligning it such that it snapped into place, and slid the table surface out of the scanner, back onto the gurney. The sludge-like remains of Molly's body jiggled with the motion and melted out of shape.

"Poor girl," said Bob. "That's not how it was supposed to work."

He started to head out of the scanning room, then stopped, whirling about angrily. "Get what's left of her out of here. Whatever failed, I want it fixed or replaced within 48 hours. And Raymond, goddamn it, I want to know just how it is that the flushing procedure is still in place. I made it very clear, a long time ago, that we were to salvage as much of a failed upload as possible. This is unacceptable. Near as I could tell, the scan was finished when that failure occurred. One of you damned programmers may be responsible for the death of that chimp." He pointed at Molly's remains. "That poor goddamned chimp." His voice started to break. He stormed off, but turned again at the door. "And not one word of this gets out of this lab—understood?"

Everyone present looked to each other as the door closed behind Bob. Raymond noticed that his wrist relay had stopped pulsing. A green light on its display indicated that storage of Molly's mind capture had completed successfully. He let out a big sigh. The thing had been carried off. He glanced at Anya and their eyes met. Before he knew it, the hint of a smile had leaked over his lips. What sort of villainy would she imagine if she were to see him smile at such a moment, not knowing what he knew? He looked down at the controls in front of him, then abruptly turned and walked out of the room, without so much as a look at Suma, hoping that Anya had overlooked his brief expression of victory.

Raymond found himself nearly racing to get to his office, to privacy. He wanted to explode—he had carried if off! But control was of the utmost importance now. More than ever. What would he say if Anya questioned that smirk? Perhaps he should bring it up to her, to explain, rather than wait for her to question him.

Back in his office, he paged her, requesting a voice connection. She did not respond immediately. She was probably still in the scanning lab, cleaning up, maybe talking to others about the catastrophic failure. Perhaps he was being blamed. Of course he would be blamed—nobody else would associate their own activities with possible failure, as nobody else had been near the flushing code in over a month. Blame aside, it was natural that his teammates would suspect him of being responsible. He was the one closest to the problem. Whatever others thought of him, Raymond was certain his case was bulletproof. Nobody would be able to detect his handiwork with the version control software. The error would ultimately be attributed to some rare flaw in the complexity of the software. He couldn't linger on this. He needed to move on to his plans for the evening; he needed to monitor the departures of his teammates, making sure that the coast was clear for his late-night activities.

"Raymond?"

It was Anya. She was initiating a voice-video connection. Raymond responded.

"Oh my god, you were so right," he said.

"Right? Are you okay? I felt like you were on a completely different wavelength in the lab. Right about what?"

"Right about the risks of uploading. Remember we were talking about uploading?" Judging from the screwed up face Anya was making, she still wasn't quite following. "It's just that you were saying the risks are still too great—that you don't really even think about it, because you have so much to lose. I don't know. I guess that conversation was just fresh on my mind. I thought you were probably thinking the same thing."

"Not exactly. Raymond, what the hell happened there? I just can't believe the flushing patterns kicked in."

"I don't know. I'm looking into it. I've seen version control go haywire before. Somehow, old code crept into the latest build. It must have been in the Bento code, too—but it wasn't triggered, because the scan went smoothly. I'm going to run a version control audit, to see what happened."

"Oh my god, I can't believe this. Molly. I can't believe—poor, poor Molly." Anya's voice was cracking. "You know, there's a chance she could have been cured? She shouldn't have even been in that lab."

"What?"

"She could have been cured. With gene therapy, with something. I don't remember. I just remember reading through her files, being surprised that the Lansing Zoo gave up on her."

"You've said that about other test animals, too."

"I guess."

"Zoos can only afford so much. Even if there were other options, uploading may have been the most reasonable."

"Maybe. I'm not so sure. Listen, a bunch of us are going to go to Central Campus, probably to the Customs House. There's no way we can just go back to work. You can come if you want."

"No, I need to look into this. Bob's going to be all over me. I need to figure out what happened. I think I'm going to check into my v-chamber for the night, work on this in total solitude."

"Okay, but don't stay up all night. You can always stop by my place if you want."

"Thanks, Anya. I was hoping you'd say that."

"Yeah, but I'll probably come in tomorrow and find you asleep in your v-chamber. I'm gonna run. Good luck."

"Thanks. Hey, can you tell Suma that I need to work alone on this? At least for a while."

"Sure."

o----------------------------o

Raymond launched himself into the kick-practice bag in the corner of his office. He was dying to load Molly's mental data into an NBC, to see if his capture of the scan was clean. He wanted the evening to be over. He whaled on the bag.

"Discipline," he said to himself. "Think."

He sat down at a terminal and banged out instructions to Scorpio to monitor activity throughout the lab and to let him know when it emptied out. He also instructed Scorpio to check in with him at 9:00 if anyone was left at that time, in which case Raymond would have to alter his plans. He then started to run an inventory of all the procedures necessary for the evening to go smoothly.

His wrist relay vibrated, indicating that Scorpio was trying to get in touch with him. Raymond put on his light helmet terminal and his hands slipped into his manuhaptic gloves.

"Mosby, Murray has left you a voice message. Play or summarize?"

"Play it."

The voice of a middle-aged man came on. Raymond immediately noticed a slight Chicago accent.

"Mr. Quan, this is Arnold Murray, private investigator. I'm calling in regards to events that took place several years ago. Involving a Mr. Tate. I'd like to meet with you, to ask you a few questions—it seems you were the last person to make direct contact with him, and some of his relations are concerned about the nature of his departure. If you could get together tomorrow, that would be great. I understand you work… at the university. I'd be happy to meet you at your convenience. Over lunch, if that works for you. Give me a call."

Raymond took a deep breath, then let out a long sigh. He took his helmet off. "Shit." A face-to-face meeting? He dreaded the prospect. He would have to prepare…

Or would he? Years had passed. Raymond could claim to have forgotten a lot of what happened. Murray couldn't expect him to have details of all that had happened. In fact, too much preparation might make him seem nervous. Murray couldn't probe too deeply, under the circumstances. He would have questions for Raymond, and might ask him to provide details in follow-up meetings. What would Murray ask? What could he hope to gain face-to-face? More than information about the past, he would probably be looking for an impression of Raymond's personality. The thing Raymond had to think through was his own story, as he had presented it in the past. He didn't want to think about his past. He needed to focus on his work for Bob and on his plans for the night. But he knew that soon he would have to push through and work out the details of his story. The longer he could stall the investigation, the better; he couldn't afford to make a stupid mistake.

CHAPTER 8

That evening, Raymond worked in his office mini-v. He sat in a Scandinavian recliner, working away, his hands in his lap, his legs extended in front of him. His hands moved as if he wore manuhaptic gloves, giving instructions to the computer, but in this v-space gloves weren't necessary—his movements could be sensed without gloves, and the air around his fingers felt viscous, providing subtle feedback to his gestures. His eyes were closed, his retinal implants providing him with a view of his data world. Occasionally, he spoke, giving the computer verbal commands where it was faster than signing. Generally, he avoided speech commands, because of the risk of being overheard. But within his v-chamber, with nearly everyone gone from the lab, he occasionally allowed himself this luxury. He dictated headings for the report he was finishing up.

All around him, lost on him while he had his eyes closed, was a beautiful wilderness view. This was Raymond's favorite workplace, a mountain-top viewing station at the crest of Mount Golgora, in the Faralon Range, a hundred miles or so south of Nurania's equator. He was in the center of a small, circular room, surrounded on all sides by glass. The red cedar beams of the roof rose to a point above him. It was an architecture feasible only in a v-world, the roof resting directly on the windows. Outside, clouds passed by at eye level. A landscape of lush valleys sprawled in all directions from the base of the mountain, lustrous red rivers threading their way through rich green foliage.

His hands lay dormant for a while. Eyelids closed, he stared at his work, exhausted. He had put together an initial report on the state of the lab's version control software, based on an audit of the last six months, covering all software modules related to the flushing code. Having completed some additional file system handiwork, he could now support that the flushing sequence had been absent on the Monday evening prior to Bento's scan, and that it was suddenly present at 12:03 AM Tuesday, the next day, with no record of anyone having committed a change. He would point to overnight maintenance as a possible source of the oddness. And, thanks to support-forum complaints from the past few months, which he had posted himself under false names, he could now point to reports of similar behavior experienced by other users of the same software. Only a highly-qualified security expert would have any chance of tracing his modifications to version control, and even then Raymond felt that he stood a good chance of escaping the tracker's eye. All that could ultimately be proven, he believed, was that the operating systems of the lab's computers had been tampered with—a measure that Raymond had taken long ago, to circumvent some of the defensive measures of the self-aware operating systems in use at the lab. Even then, it would be impossible to determine who had carried out these low-level security breaches, as he had logged on using a shared administrative account to perform them.

Through the blur of mental exhaustion, he suddenly realized that he had been hearing a tapping sound for some time. Opening his eyes to see what was making the glassy tap-tap-tap sound, he saw a blue jay. It struck him as a familiar bird, but he couldn't think why. He stared at it for a moment, watching with puzzlement as it looked at him and tapped again, this time with slower, larger, more deliberate head motions. Then it dawned on him—it was Scorpio. Raymond had long ago restricted Scorpio's access to the mountain-top office, to reduce interruptions. As a bird, about his only means of interrupting Raymond was by pecking at the window.

"Oh shit. Scorpio! The next time I come here, remind me to make your interrupt a little more conspicuous. What's up?"

"Bob has not yet left the building," came Scorpio's voice from overhead.

"What time is it?"

"9:03 PM. You asked me to let you know if Bob had not left by 9:00 PM. I executed my interrupt for 187 seconds before gaining your attention."

"Is anyone else in the lab?"

"Aside from yourself, Bob is the only person in the lab."

"What is he doing?"

"He is working on a text document. It appears to be a press statement about the failed upload experiment on Molly."

"Right. I guess I'm not the only one working late."

Raymond made a quick hand gesture, as if turning off a faucet somewhere in front of him, and the simulation ended. Amber lights came on in the v-chamber, he stood up, his chair vanished beneath him, and the haze of nanomist dissipated into the v-chamber walls. He exited the small chamber, crossed to his office chair, donned his light helmet, and slipped his hands into his manuhaptic gloves again.

Raymond looked through the press statement that Bob was working on. It appeared to be complete. He checked the last-modified timestamp on the document; it had not been touched for over fifteen minutes. Bob was probably staring at it, digesting the catastrophe that had befallen his project. Raymond checked for other recently accessed documents. He found a voice message that Bob had sent to a man named Stewart Richardson at 7:45. Skimming through it, Raymond found it to be a dinner cancellation.

"Who is this Stewart Richardson?" he asked Scorpio.

"Undergraduate professor of computer science, here at Michigan. Computer vision specialist."

In the voice message, Bob had made no mention of the afternoon's disaster. Raymond guessed that this Richardson couldn't be a very close friend—Bob was a man inclined toward sharing the details of his life, and wouldn't have been able to contain himself with anyone more than a professional acquaintance.

"Nothing interesting," said Raymond, mostly to himself. "He's just staying late, shifting balance after a heavy blow."

"Instructions?" asked Scorpio.

"Postpone all events in the schedule by ten minutes for now. Signal me twenty minutes before event number one."

Event number one was the duping of the lab's internal and external surveillance systems to make it look like Raymond had taken his bike from the bike storage room and left the building, leaving the lab empty. He didn't want it to seem like he stayed especially late, and he didn't want his real facial expression to be captured on his way out of the building—he was afraid of how nervous he might look.

"What's the weather like?" asked Raymond.

"Clear, forty-two degrees Fahrenheit."

"Good." Raymond had prepared clear-weather footage of him leaving the building and was glad he would not have to take the risk of adding weather effects.

Raymond kicked back and started thinking about what he should do. He wanted Bob out of the building, out of the picture. He figured he could wait Bob out, drive him out, or entice him out. Waiting him out was the most desirable option, of course, but Raymond had to come up with one or more backup plans in case Bob didn't leave. The least risky would be to postpone the entire operation until another evening, but Raymond was anxious to get Molly's mental capture data uploaded into an NBC—his own upload hinged on the success of this crucial step, and he was all too aware of how little time lay between now and his last day on the team. The possibility of postponing the entire upload plan crossed his mind—postponing it until after he was gone from the team—but he had already concluded that being distant from the research team would cripple his efforts; he needed to know where everything stood so he could deal with known risks, and he needed the security advantages of being an insider. So, between driving Bob out and enticing him to leave, which was the better option? Raymond started listing out his options, using finger motions in his manuhaptic gloves to create two columns of choices.

"Let me know if he goes," he instructed Scorpio.

Raymond filled Column A with driving-out choices: simulate climate control problem to make it uncomfortable to remain in his office; simulate system or application failure, to prevent him from completing his work on his own workstation; kill the lights in his office; simulate a network security breach and have Janet issue a warning that any sensitive documents should be closed; have Janet start reading off random news reports at high volume, to irritate him and cause him to doubt the stability of the systems. He filled Column B with enticing-out choices: simulate a call from Bob's girlfriend, asking him to come over (not good, because he would almost certainly find out that she had not actually called); simulate a text message from Bob's home security system, informing him of a prowler (similarly bad); display subliminal messages via Bob's workstation to make him hungry, in the hope that he would go home for dinner; have Janet recommend to him that he go home and continue his work after a good night's sleep.

All sorts of other goofy ideas floated through his head, but only these made the list. Of these, he thought the options involving Janet were most reasonable. He could have her go haywire, then suddenly issue an alert of a network security breach; this would add to the overall sense of chaos in the computer systems, and—after tonight's simulated attack by the ALA—it would seem to Bob to fall in place perfectly. He would conclude that the network security breach had resulted in outsiders gaining access to his press statement, which had then led to immediate action on their part.

"I wish I'd planned it this way all along."

Raymond set about hacking into Janet's control system. It was a trivial hack, taking advantage of several backdoors he had opened over the past year. The key, as usual, was to cover his tracks, and he had long ago figured out how to move unseen through the lab's systems. Within a matter of minutes he had hijacked one of her subprocesses and had her loudly broadcasting excerpts from an environmentalist news feed, her voice booming throughout the building.

"In a summary of the results of her three-year study on the island of Borneo, Dr. Talmus of the University of California at Berkeley reports that species repopulation efforts on the east side of the island, carried out over the past decade, have met with limited success."

As Janet prattled on, Raymond inserted a code hook in the hijacked subprocess that would allow him to remotely terminate the news feed and start the network-security-breach announcement via a signal from his wrist relay. He then walked quickly through the halls of the lab to Bob's office. He noticed his heart pounding and slowed down, trying to calm himself. He knocked on Bob's door, afraid his adrenaline rush would give him away, but it was too late to worry about that.

"Just a second," came Bob's voice through his office intercom. "Okay." The door opened, sliding noiselessly into its pocket.

Janet continued her high-volume reading of the news feed.

"Any idea what's up with Janet?" asked Raymond.

"What?" hollered Bob.

Raymond tried again, raising his voice to be heard. "Janet! Any idea what's up with Janet?"

"No, no. Very strange. What has you here this late?"

"Working on the version control audit, trying to figure out what the hell happened this afternoon."

"Great."

Janet paused, between stories.

"Listen," said Bob, "I hope I didn't scare you too bad when I blew up earlier."

There was an awkward lull, in which Raymond had the sense he was supposed to say something.

"You found anything?" asked Bob.

"Well, I—"

"Recent attempts," resumed Janet, "to reduce the Antarctic melt rate appear to be showing positive results, although debate continues regarding the possibility that this year's colder winter at the South Pole was due to natural climatic patterns."

Raymond walked into the office so Bob could hear him.

"They're preliminary findings, but there is no record of anyone committing a change. Yet I can pinpoint when the flushing code was brought back in. It happened at about the same time as some systems maintenance work. I can only guess that there was some systems fluke."

Bob nodded largely.

"The Argentine research team," continued Janet, "reported that by damming some of the Antarctic melt-off, they had increased evaporation and thickened local cloud cover. It is posited—"

"And what the hell is this?" shouted Bob, pointing at the ceiling. "I get the feeling our systems are all coming unhinged. I asked her to stop – no response."

"I'll look into it. I've never known a DIA to flip out like this. Could just be a screwed up filter."

His hands clasped behind his back, Raymond triggered his wrist relay. Janet's reading of the news story stopped mid-sentence. There was a pause. Bob and Raymond looked at each other with shared quizzical expectancy.

Janet's voice returned, this time at normal volume. "Please close any sensitive materials. A network security breach has occurred. I repeat, please close any sensitive materials. A network security breach has occurred."

"What the fuck!" yelled Bob. He switched on his terminal, which was partially visible from where Raymond stood, and hastily closed the various documents he had been working on.

"I'm on it," said Raymond. "I'll make sure our network is locked down."

Raymond raced back to his office, closed the audit report documents he had been working on, verified that his hijacked process had died, then busied himself with network analysis tools, pretending to hunt for a breach. The office door opened, and Raymond turned to see Bob. Visceral fear seized Raymond; it was very rare for Bob to enter his office. Bob walked in and stood looking over Raymond's shoulder.

"What do you see?"

"Um… nothing. I'm closing down all channels. I don't see any sign of entry."

"Isn't there a system log or something that can tell us what triggered Janet's message?"

"There should be, but I don't see anything. There has to be something."

"Janet?"

"Yes Bob," came Janet's voice.

"How did you find out about the security breach?"

"Please clarify."

"You announced a security breach a couple minutes ago. What made you make the announcement?"

"I have no record of making any announcements in the past hour."

"What?"

"I have no record—"

"I heard you, Janet. I meant… I heard you make an announcement, just a couple of minutes ago. Or rather… I heard an announcement made using your voice. Do you have any record of relinquishing control of your vocal program?"

There was a pause. Raymond sat frozen, staring at the speaker closest to him, stunned by Bob's move to take control of the situation.

"I have record," responded Janet, "of losing contact with a subprocess. The first failed attempt to contact the subprocess occurred 127 seconds ago. Loss of a subprocess sometimes occurs when the process is hostilely captured and terminated."

Raymond winced. Bob continued his line of questioning.

"Is this a common occurrence?"

"The statistics available to me indicate that this has occurred 44 times since I was last reinitialized, 238 days ago."

"So, that could just be some innocuous bug."

"According to quality assurance records, unexpected termination of subprocesses happened zero times during 710 hours of testing."

"But that's just QA," said Raymond to Bob. "Live usage is generally more problematic."

"True. So, either this is a bug that wasn't uncovered in testing or someone has been hacking our DIA on a regular basis. Shouldn't a central operating system be able to tell us whether one of Janet's subprocesses was taken over by another process, and who owned that process?"

"I don't think so," lied Raymond. "That much process monitoring would be a major drag on the system. And you would end up with a huge, unmanageable body of data. In a high security system you might be able to do that, but in a university lab, there's generally no point in dedicating those kinds of resources to process-level history."

"Janet, can you trace the process that killed the subprocess in question?"

"No. Historical tracking of inter-process interrupts is an unavailable function."

Unavailable because I yanked it.

"Well," asked Bob, looking to Raymond, "is there any other sign of someone hacking our network?"

"I'll keep looking, but I haven't seen anything. Even with all the security measures in software today, it can be nearly impossible to track down a good hacker. For every security measure there's at least one countermeasure."

"Listen, call me at home if you find anything, but don't stay here too late. Just make sure Net access is locked down. I plan to get someone in here to look into this breach and tighten things up. There's gotta be some comp-sci grad student out there who would be overjoyed to dig into this stuff. Oh—when do you think you can have that version control audit done?"

"Tomorrow."

"Good. Thanks, Raymond. I don't know what I'd do without you."

Raymond smiled and nodded.

So is that why you're kicking me off your project?

Bob left, and the door closed behind him. Raymond sighed with relief. The remainder of his night's work seemed easy, downright fun, after dealing with Bob personally. He slipped his hands into his manuhaptic gloves and blindly instructed Scorpio to signal him via wrist relay when Bob had actually left the building. Scorpio responded by moving Raymond's right thumb and index finger into an "okay" sign.

Raymond pushed away from his desk and leaned back in his chair, his legs stretched out in front of him, his hands folded over his stomach. He took a deep breath and let out another long sigh.

"Well, my ass is on the line now," he muttered.

What if Bob's new security person were good? A good security person would find his operating system alterations and rebuild the system with all standard logging and security features in place. It felt like his plan had backfired. But Bob probably would have brought in a security expert anyway, after the simulated ALA break-in, to figure out how the ALA had caught wind of Molly's failed upload. In fact, this might actually be better; Bob now had every reason to believe that there was a network security breach. He might now assume that the information had been obtained by an outsider directly, where he might otherwise have suspected that someone on the team had leaked the story. Were Bob to suspect a leak from someone on his staff, he might initiate the staff reduction immediately.

Raymond was confident that he had covered his tracks well enough to prevent anyone from tracing security breaches to him. However, he needed to reel in all of his agents tonight, to be safe. Which meant he would no longer be able to monitor Bob's personal communications and workstation activities. It would also make it much tougher to dupe the lab's security systems, as he would be doing this evening. But did that matter? After tonight, he would have an NBC for Molly and one for himself—after tonight, his stealing would be done. He still needed more data to set up his own physiological simulation, but he had legitimate access to that. The next two weeks would consist primarily of preparing his motor home and bunker for life after upload. The only access to the lab that he needed now was up-to-date knowledge of the scanning equipment and access to the scanning lab on the day of his upload, both of which came with his position, while it lasted.

His wrist relay went off, indicating that Bob had left the building. He set about retrieving his agents, double-checking that his tracks were covered, and verifying that his robots were busy re-mapping the lab, to reconcile his false footage of the lab with the current positioning of chairs, doors, tables, and lab equipment. It was critical that—when the night was over—no sign of his activities remain. It occurred to him that he would also have to take his light helmet and manuhaptic gloves home. A security expert would see custom hardware as a red flag.

At 10:30, his relay pulsed three times—the false footage had kicked in. As the lab's security system recorded false video of Raymond leaving the building, the real Raymond made his way through dark hallways, pulling on a pair of silk gloves to avoid leaving any fingerprints. Motion sensors reported his movement to a deaf building-maintenance network node. Lights that would have normally brightened at his approach remained low. He was invisible to the system.

Exhilarated by his success, he broke into a jog. He entered the loading dock and opened the garage door, and his waiting delivery truck backed itself in and opened its rear hatch. Footage would show an empty loading dock and an empty driveway. Raymond grabbed two empty shipping boxes from the cargo bay of the truck, dropped them onto a nearby dolly, and took off through the halls with the dolly.

By 11:00 PM, right on schedule, the boxes were loaded and on their way across North Campus, one to Property Disposition and the other to his motor home. The deed was done. Raymond closed the loading dock, returned to his office, and filled his backpack with potentially incriminating personal items: helmet, gloves, surveillance gear, and a handful of memory cards. Fifteen minutes later, after making an unrecorded exit from the building, he hopped on his bike and headed off into the night, to Anya's.

Raymond chose to engage his bike's motors. He streaked down nearly-empty streets, reaching 50 miles-per-hour on the straight-aways. The thrill of speed and the rush of cool autumnal night air were delicious. He found himself craving Anya. A now-familiar fantasy flooded his mind—one that had moved from Agakhan to his own v-world, from moon-drenched beach to tropical tree-house. He imagined himself lying with her in a crude structure of rope and wood, amid the wet, sprawling foliage of an orangey Nuranian evening, pulling her close to him as a slammer-season storm faded into the distance.

Abruptly, the fantasy ceased, interrupted by conscious concerns—what was the likelihood of her joining him after he uploaded? He imagined her risking everything to be with him. Or spending nearly all of her time in her v-chamber, afraid to upload but unable to live without him. Delusions, he told himself—all delusions. One minute he would imagine her joining him, and the next he concluded that—once he uploaded—he would have to cut all ties, completely concealing his Net identity to prevent the authorities from tracing his communications and discovering his location. Even if she knew how to reach him and could join him, would she? Maybe once the technology had been proven, years from now. But not any time soon, and maybe never. He had to accept that. Should he even be seeing her any more? He pushed the bike faster, flying through the intersections of her residential neighborhood, such that the demands of keeping the bike under control conveniently displaced his capacity for reason.

He saw that the lights were on at her apartment and indulged himself in a sense of relief, a sense of home. He rang the bell. It was the first time he had shown up at her apartment unannounced. Fear of finding her with another man shot through him, but he subdued his imaginative jealousy, assuring himself that she had too little room in her life for another love interest. He wondered for a moment whether he should be looking into a video camera somewhere, then caught himself, remembering that she had an old-fashioned brass peep hole.

She opened the door. She was wearing the same cream-colored wool cardigan that she had worn to work that day. It made her look mature, he thought. He found the look to be very attractive, but it made him feel comparatively boyish, and it put him off.

"Raymond! Are you okay?" Her face was screwed up in a look of shock and concern.

He stared at her, nodding, puzzled by her reaction. There was something wrong with her eyes—they looked swollen. She stepped outside, drawing him into a long, tender embrace, the door standing open. He realized that she must still be thinking of Molly and the failed upload, and he remembered that he was supposed to be tired from a night of hard investigation into the source of the problem.

"Come on in," she said at last. "I'm so glad you decided to come over. I'm sorry I'm such a wreck—I've been crying all night." As she closed the door, he stepped past her into the living room.

"Oh… I'm so sorry to hear that," he said, working out how to carry himself and how to react.

"It's okay. I was just doing some reading. Some old articles that my father wrote, about famous setbacks experienced by scientists and technologists through the years."

"Your father? Oh, that's right—he's a science journalist, isn't he?"

"Uh-huh. He keeps claiming to be retired, but he can't stop writing. The one I was just reading is about some of Isaac Weisberg's early work."

"He was the designer babies guy?" As soon as the words were out of his mouth, he worried that Anya, a gene-job herself, might take offense. She didn't appear to.

"Yeah. He was one of the first doctors to practice genetic manipulation purely for the sake of aesthetics."

"Oo—this sounds bad."

"It is. There's actually a disease that was named after him. I don't want to go into it… it'll just make me cry again. But a bunch of his first babies, mostly done for movie stars back around 2015, turned out to have a severe form of schizophrenia. It was heavy on the hallucinations, and it showed up in children as young—" She started to break up. "As young as six. Can you imagine that? Six-year-olds, hallucinating?"

"Wow." Raymond had no idea what to say. He felt a twinge of guilt—he realized just how hard she was taking Molly's apparent death. He wanted to tell her what had really happened, but he couldn't. "He must have felt really bad."

"To say the least." Anya wiped her eyes and took a deep breath. "I'm sorry. I don't mean to get you more down than you must already be. How did your search go?"

"Not bad. I mean, I think something got screwed up during nightly systems maintenance, a while back. I can't trace it, exactly, but the flushing code wasn't there, and then all of a sudden it was. Audits showed no sign of anyone committing changes that would have brought the flushing code back into the build, so it looks like there was no human error."

"Then we still don't know what actually went wrong, and whatever happened could happen again."

"Uh, sure, but now that we've seen that it can happen, it shouldn't be too tough to put in safeguards to prevent it from happening again. We can set up our own validity checks on the source code."

"Yeah, I guess. I just can't believe it happened. It's so sad."

"I know. And it looks like somebody outside the lab may have found out about it."

"What!"

"This evening, while Bob and I were still in the lab, there was a network security breach. It looks like someone has been listening on our network."

"Who? Data thieves?"

"Maybe. That would make sense, I guess. Since the ESW ruling, we've been spotlighted in a bunch of articles. Could be someone hoping to sell insider information. Could be subversives—Naturalists. Could just be some random hacker. Who knows?"

"And Bob was there? He must have had a fit!"

Raymond gravely shook his head, playing up the sense of drama. "He was not a happy man. I guess he was working late. Probably trying to figure out what to do after today's failed upload."

Raymond felt the urge, as he often did, to tell Anya about his ability to watch Bob's work, to brag about his skills as a listener. He wanted to tell her exactly what Bob had been working on, even beam a snapshot of his work to a terminal in her house. It was an urge that he was used to suppressing, but it seemed closer to the surface, harder to move past. He wanted to show off, to impress her, but he couldn't; this was not some harmless, mischievous hobby.

"I'm sorry," said Anya. "I haven't even given you a chance to take off your jacket. Hey, do you want to go for a walk or something? It might be nice to get some air."

"Oh, I would, but I'm really tired. I was actually kind of hoping I could maybe crash here… would that be okay?"

"Okay? You're so funny. I've had to beg you to stay in the past. Of course you can sleep here tonight. Take your jacket off. Sit down. Have you eaten?"

"No, but I'm not really hungry." Raymond took his jacket off, and Anya took it from him and hung it on a hook. He wandered toward the sofa, but remained standing. Knowing that Bob would probably call him upon hearing about the break-in, he wanted to go straight to bed to get what sleep he could.

"Are you sure you're not hungry?" She crossed to where he was standing. It seemed she wanted to be near him, to touch him. "I made a big pot of minestrone the other day. You could have a bowl of soup, and I could slice you some sourdough. Doesn't that sound nice?"

Raymond's wrist relay vibrated, indicating that the NBC headed to his motor home had been successfully delivered.

"Um, sure. That does sound nice. I guess I should eat something."

Anya headed off to the kitchen. Raymond stood about, feeling an odd mix of overload and emptiness. How very strange to be in the home of this innocent, dear woman while in the midst of such a critical step in his plans. It gave him a perfect alibi, but it felt wrong. He was vaguely aware that reserving information from her in this manner was subtly eroding his respect for her. It made it seem as though she were far away, a person who just happened to be in the same Ann Arbor home, unwittingly a tool in his plan. He wanted to console her, but anything short of telling her the truth would just make him feel more empty. Such detachment while being with this woman about whom he had such intimate fantasies made him feel guilty, listless, dangerous. He shouldn't be with her. He walked to the kitchen doorway, intending to excuse himself. If he remained with her, he would break down. Something would slip.

"I—"

"Do you want your bread lightly toasted?"

As she asked this question, she too was headed for the doorway. He started to shake his head.

"I should—"

He cut himself off. She looked at him with searching concern, and he was afraid of making her unhappy. She reached her hands out for his, but he made no movement in response. He had to go—he couldn't let her stop him from going.

She dropped her hands to her side. "Are you okay, Raymond? What's wrong?"

He looked away from her, to the side, then shifted his gaze to the floor. A short breath of exasperation escaped him.

"Honey, what's the matter?" She moved in to hold him, and he backed away.

"Listen, I'm sorry. I really should go."

"No! I mean, no, please don't go." She took his hand from his side and started to lead him to the sofa. He resisted, but she didn't let go. She leaned her weight away from him, pulling him toward the sofa. She looked at him and stuck out her tongue, still pulling him. He laughed, reluctantly allowing himself to be pulled along.

"Anya," he pleaded, "you can't do this. If I say I should go, you have to let me go."

"Not like this. You're going to sit down and tell me what's on your mind. Then, if you still think you need to go, you can go. But you can't just show up, brighten my night by asking to stay, and then up and leave without explanation. Now sit down and tell me what's going on."

Raymond plopped down on the sofa and stared blankly across the room. He exhaled pointedly. Resentment stirred within him.

"Okay," said Anya. "You can start by giving me a clue. One or two words. Whatever comes to mind."

Raymond resisted. He took a deep breath. He certainly couldn't tell her the first thing that came to mind.

"Okay, if that doesn't work," persisted Anya, "how about this? I'll ask you questions, and you can just tell me yes or no. Is it something I did?"

Raymond made a motion to get up, but Anya pounced on his thigh, pushing him back down into the sofa.

"Anya!"

"It's something I did, isn't it?"

"No," whined Raymond, shaking his head. He still didn't look at her. How was it that he had imagined this being a simple, cozy escape? What sort of alibi would she offer if she could see right through him?

She folded her feet beneath her and leaned her head against his upper arm, reaching a hand tenderly across his chest.

"Raymond," she said softly, "it feels good to have you here. Please stay. You don't have to talk." She rubbed his chest. "I don't want to lose you."

He took another deep breath. His mind was a spinning, writhing mess.

"I don't want…" His voice cracked slightly, and his eyes suddenly watered. "…to lose you either."

But I have to lose you.

He felt her hand press his chest harder. She cooed and leaned into his arm. Through force of will, he managed to prevent himself from crying, driving all thoughts from his mind and opening his eyes wide, looking away from her.

"Oh shit! The soup!" Anya jumped off the couch and raced toward the kitchen. Half way there, she stopped and turned around. "Stay right there! I'll be right back!"

Raymond could hear her as she turned off her old-fashioned stove.

"You probably don't feel like eating?" she called.

"Not really. I'm sorry."

"No, no, it's no problem."

Raymond glanced at his wrist relay. It was 11:50, and he had not yet received confirmation that the other NBC had been successfully entered into Property Disposition's outgoing delivery chamber. It was supposed to make the midnight pickup. He stood up from the couch, restless, just as Anya came back into the room.

"You're leaving, aren't you."

"No, I'm just really tired. Is it okay if I crawl into your bed?"

"Okay…" She sounded rather tentative.

"I'm sorry, Anya, I just don't feel like talking."

"That's alright. Give me a kiss, and then you can go to bed."

He gave her an obligatory peck, to which she responded with another searching gaze.

"Whatever is on your mind," she said, "it must be serious. I really wish you could share it with me."

"Well, I can't." That came off much more sharply than he had intended. She looked at him with disbelief. Somehow it felt good to hurt her, as if he had received validation of his original intention to leave. But it was an odd note to end on as he made his way into her bedroom. "I'm sorry, Anya," he said, affecting sincerity. "I just want to be near you tonight. I'm really not even sure what's wrong."

She hugged him.

"I want things to work between us, Raymond," she said, holding him. He was taken aback by the weight of her words. "You can't keep closing me out. I know you have a hard time being open with me, but you need to know that I'm here for you."

He stiffly hugged her back, his perfunctory manner an inadvertent defense mechanism—somewhere deep within, he equated emotional detachment with power.

"Okay," he said, aware that the closure was purely superficial.

He headed into her bedroom. Resentment stirred within him. He considered getting into bed with all his clothes on, as a signal to her of just how much he could close her out if he wanted to.

That'll just drag it out.

He violently undressed, threw back the covers, and crawled in. Moments after pulling the sheet up over his shoulder, he felt his wrist relay vibrate. He pulled his arm up out of the covers and saw what he was hoping to see: a green smiley face winked at him—the second NBC would be on its way to the bunker tonight. It was 11:57 PM. He confirmed receipt of the message and tucked himself in again. Knowing that one more hurdle had been cleared was reassuring. It took the edge off of his irritation.

His fuming mood relented, and he started to wonder why he was angry. He couldn't figure it out. He felt like a child, his emotions out of control. Her words and touches replayed in his head as acts of oppression.

Anya entered the room, undressed, and joined him in bed. He didn't stir. She said his name softly, but he pretended to be asleep. She snuggled up behind him and gently kissed his shoulder. Within a few minutes he felt her breath grow heavy and fall into the rhythm of sleep.

Raymond didn't know how long he had been asleep when his wrist relay went off, but it didn't take much for it to awaken him—the first vibration brought him to full alertness. He looked and saw that it was 4:08am. He had received an alert from Bob, as expected.

He slipped carefully out of bed. Anya's sleeping body showed no sign of disturbance. He walked into her bathroom and closed the door, took a moment to wake up and get in character, then initiated a voice connection with Bob.

"Raymond, I need you to come to the lab. There's been a break-in."

"A break-in? You mean another network breach?"

"No, someone broke into the lab, and they destroyed two NBCs. It looks like it was the ALA. I need to know everything you found out about the security breach. I need you to get here as soon as you can."

As Raymond walked back into Anya's bedroom, he heard her groggy voice ask him who he was talking to. Not wanting to deal with her, he told her only that it was Bob, and that he wanted to know more about the security breach. He kissed her forehead.

"You have to go? Can't you just talk to him about it?"

"No, I need to go to the lab. Go back to sleep. I'll fill you in tomorrow."

CHAPTER 9

As Raymond coasted toward the lab, eager to escape the damp night chill, he noticed a tall silhouette in the lab's entryway, behind the exterior glass doors. As he drew nearer, he saw that it was a police woman.

"That didn't take long," he said to himself.

He stood up on his pedals and smoothly dismounted as the bike rolled to a stop. The woman watched but made no motion to open the door for him. He made eye contact with the two red lights of the security sensor above the door and spoke his name, "Raymond Quan". The doors slid open, and he rolled his bike into the entryway, hoping he wouldn't have to exchange words with this statuesque representative of civic authority.

The outer doors closed and the inner doors opened, but the woman stepped in Raymond's path and held up her wrist, on which she wore a standard-issue black police wrist relay. Raymond dutifully looked at it, aware that it was scanning his face and comparing it with the photo on record under his federal registration.

"ID please," she said flatly. Her voice was low and devoid of emotion.

Raymond brought his own wrist relay up, placed his right thumb carefully on its face, issued a few commands, and heard the police relay chirp to acknowledge receipt of data. His nerves fluttered a bit as she monitored her relay, apparently waiting for confirmation. He glanced at the badge on her shirt, which identified her as an officer of the Michigan State Police Department.

"Okay, you can go in. Straight to the main conference room. All offices have been closed. You'll see—just stay clear of the taped-off areas."

He proceeded into the empty lobby, and the inner doors of the entryway finally closed behind him.

Yellow tape was everywhere. The only passage not taped off was the hall toward the center of the building. Even the bike storage room was off limits, so he wheeled his bike down the long hallway. As he walked past the scanning room, the door opened and out glided a hovering metallic orb, at eye level, bristling with gadgets—a police sniffer bot. It picked up speed and zipped down the hall in front of him. The scanning-room door remained open for a time, and through it, in the center of the otherwise dark space, he saw another orb, fanning an array of lights over the scanner. The door closed.

Raymond let out a low whistle, taken aback by the speed and thoroughness of the police response.

Bob stood in the conference room with a tankard of coffee, wearing running pants and a faded University of Michigan rain jacket. He faced the main screen, which was blank. Seated nearby was another police woman, in her mid-thirties, pale, with a neatly cut bob. She slowly shook her head as she read a document on the tablet in front of her, occasionally tapping the screen. Neither noticed him.

"This would be a lot easier," she said, seemingly to herself, "if the university would allow campus-wide surveillance." Her words were evenly spaced and delivered with a mildly aggrieved tone. Raymond felt an innate positive response to this woman.

"Thank god," responded Bob with an edge of contempt, "for the rare bastion of privacy."

Raymond walked his bike into the room and leaned it against a wall. It made a soft thunking sound as he locked the tires, drawing attention to his arrival.

"Oh, Raymond," said Bob. "Thanks for coming in. Ms. Brody, this is Raymond Quan—"

The main screen lit up, interrupting Bob's introduction. Ms. Brody smiled courteously at Raymond, then turned to face the screen. A clean-cut young man in a traditional white dress shirt, the sleeves of which were rolled to the elbow, looked out at them from the screen.

"Sorry I had to duck out," he said. "Is this Raymond?"

"Yes," responded Bob. "Just arrived. Raymond, as I was saying, this is Ms. Brody. She's with the state police. And this is… I'm sorry…"

"Michaels," answered the man on-screen. "Agent Michaels. Okay, where were we, Detective Brody?"

Raymond swallowed hard.

Agent? FBI? It's 4:30 AM, an hour after my little staged break-in, and the FBI is already involved?

"Right, well," said Ms. Brody. "I've gone through every step of the initial procedure you sent. You should have all of the security video by now?"

"Yes, we have the security video, the network logs, and the lab's personnel records, and I'm working to assign an analysis team."

Raymond stood blinking. It baffled him that the FBI showed such keen interest. There was evidently some political significance far greater than he realized. Perhaps some Naturalist in government had been dying for a reason to shut down the project. Or maybe the FBI was merely a vehicle for stealing the team's research, to trade, or use for their own purposes. Whatever the explanation, Raymond had attracted an infestation of the very federal agents he had spent so much of his life carefully dodging.

Agent Michaels was looking away from the camera on his end—off to the side, most likely at a display.

"So," said Bob to Ms. Brody, "I'm guessing that the FBI will be taking the investigation from here?"

"No," answered Brody, speaking directly to Bob. "In a case like this, involving the property of a state-funded institution—"

"Actually," interrupted Michaels, "the answer in this case would be yes." He looked up from his display. "An FBI team will be arriving on-site at 8:00 AM, and you will be relieved, Detective Brody."

From where Raymond stood, he couldn't see Brody's face. But he saw her head tilt slightly downward, and he was quite certain that Michaels had just received a look.

"I'm sorry, Detective," said Michaels in a politely conciliatory tone. "I do appreciate the work you've put in this morning. The Bureau relies on the work of men and women like yourself, able to respond quickly and carry out the crucial first steps of investigation. But I'm afraid—"

"Agent Michaels," interrupted Brody, "I do appreciate the sense of self-importance that comes with a Bureau position such as your own." Raymond couldn't help but smile at her cuttingly deadpan sarcasm. "But you will find," she continued, "that I am a woman not easily intimidated." Michaels opened his mouth to speak; Brody merely spoke louder. "You will also find that I know policy. Very, very well." She turned to Bob and resumed her initial answer. "So, in answer to your question, the FBI and I will be conducting independent investigations. I will of course share all of my findings with the FBI, and I can only hope that Agent Michaels will do the same for me."

"Ms. Brody—" started the FBI man on screen.

"That's Detective," she corrected. "Detective Brody."

"Detective Brody, your—"

"Thank you," she interrupted again.

"Detective Brody, your spirit is certainly… admirable. And, according to policy, your answer is accurate. But you may find that your notion of policy is a bit naïve."

Raymond looked to Bob, expecting him to weigh in, but Bob stood silently by.

"Now, Bob," said Michaels. "It will be necessary to interview all members of your staff."

"Of course. As I said before, you have my full cooperation, and I'm sure that goes for everyone on my team, as well."

Michaels turned in Raymond's direction.

"Raymond, you were closest to the network security breach last night. I would like to ask you a few questions, if that's alright?"

Raymond hesitated for just a split second. "Sure, of course."

"It's okay, Raymond," said Bob. "I've told them about all the work you put in last night. They just want to ask you some questions."

"Okay," said Raymond.

"And Bob," said Michaels. "I will have to ask you to leave."

"Oh, sure, sure." Bob made a point to walk past Raymond on his way out. He put a hand on Raymond's shoulder and spoke to him in a low tone. "Raymond, I want you to know how grateful I am. I apologize for putting you in this position. As soon as this is over, I'll do everything I can to keep the pressure off."

Bob headed out, closing the door behind him.

"Okay," said Michaels. "I—" He looked to his display. "I'm sorry, I'll be back in a second." The screen went blank.

Brody turned sideways in her chair, to face Raymond. She gestured to the chairs next to her. "Please, have a seat."

Raymond sat down. He shifted his seat a bit, not sure which way he should face.

"How old are you?" she asked.

"Twenty-six."

"Twenty-six," she repeated. She looked him over with a scowl of focused scrutiny. He felt like he was being read. Her gaze lingered at the right side of his face. "Is that a birthmark?"

"Yes."

"I like birthmarks. Very distinctive. Your parents never tried to have it repaired?"

"No," replied Raymond, nervously shifting away from her. "No, my parents couldn't afford cosmetic surgery. And when I was in state homes, uh… it's not in their budget."

"I see."

The screen lit up again. Agent Michaels was back. "Okay. Now Raymond, we have the lab's network logs here, under analysis, but I'd like to ask you a few questions about what happened when and how you reacted. Just to provide some context."

"Okay."

Michaels went on to ask Raymond questions about Janet's unusual behavior, the security breach announcement, what steps were taken to lock down the network, and how Raymond went about reviewing the logs for information. Raymond answered the questions as coolly and thoroughly as he could, careful to keep his story consistent with what he had told Bob earlier that night. Part way through, Ms. Brody received a page on her wrist relay and left the room. She returned a few minutes later, resuming her position next to Raymond.

When Michaels had finished, he asked whether Raymond would mind proceeding with a standard FBI interrogation. "To get it out of the way," said Michaels. Raymond agreed to undergo further questioning, and Michaels went on to ask some routine personal questions, regarding his school and work history, his address history, travel abroad, and criminal record. Raymond answered the questions as accurately as he could, except where his current address was concerned: he gave the address of his apartment, even though it was hardly home for him.

"Now," continued Michaels, "I'm going to ask you a few more probing questions. You have the right to refrain from answering these questions, as you did all previous questions. But I should warn you, Raymond, that if you choose not to answer these questions, you may be subject to more rigorous personal investigation."

"Okay," said Raymond.

The questions covered illegal drug use, affiliation with political organizations, affiliation with terrorist groups, contact with foreign governments, espionage activities, and affiliation with cult religions. Raymond answered all of these questions truthfully. He was starting to feel like a pretty clean-living young man. Then came the questions about organized crime.

"Have you ever come in contact with an individual or individuals whom you knew to be participating in some form of organized crime, such as gambling, drug trafficking, money laundering, or the unlicensed sale of firearms?"

"No," replied Raymond.

A lie—I just lied to an agent of the Federal Bureau of Investigation.

"Have you ever participated in some form of organized crime, such as those I just listed?"

"No."

Lie.

"Were you ever to knowingly come in contact with an individual or individuals whom you knew to be participating in some form of organized crime, such as those I listed, would you report this activity to the authorities, as previously defined?"

"Yes," replied Raymond. "Absolutely."

"Thank you, Raymond. As a member of the lab's staff, you are automatically a suspect in a federal criminal case. Within 48 hours, you will be asked to come back, and you will be given an FBI monitoring device. This device will allow us to track your movements, freeing you to travel anywhere within the United States. Until you have been given this device, you are required to notify the FBI of any plans to travel more than twenty miles from the city of Ann Arbor. You understand?"

"Yes."

"Okay then, you're free to go. Thank you for your time and your assistance in this case. We will contact you when you need to come in."

The screen blanked out. Raymond took a deep breath, then started to stand up.

"Wait," said Detective Brody. "I'd like to ask you a few of my own questions. I know you must be tired, but would you mind, Raymond?"

"Well, sure. I guess."

"Thank you so much."

Raymond sat back down. He wore an exaggerated look of exhaustion, trying to make it clear that he wanted this to be done as soon as possible.

"I find your work fascinating. What's it like to work with uploaded minds?"

Raymond's wrist relay vibrated twice in quick succession, indication that the robot butler at his bunker had taken delivery of the NBC. The stolen goods had arrived at their destinations without a hitch, even sooner than he had expected. He had attained his goal, but now he was face-to-face with a police detective, about to undergo another interview, and the other NBC was sitting in his motor home, red-hot evidence of his guilt.

"Well," responded Raymond, "I'm really more of a tools guy. The scientists do a lot more with the mind, directly."

His own mind was still on the NBC in his motor home. He wished he had sent both NBCs to the bunker. He had chosen to keep one local—the one that he planned to upload into—because he didn't want to risk sending his own scanned mental data over the Net, as he had Molly's. He was afraid it might be traced, or even lost. But, with the FBI and the State Police on the case, the risk of their finding the NBC in his motor home seemed far higher.

Raymond suddenly realized he wasn't paying attention to Brody.

"But isn't it just amazing," she was saying, "to think of transferring the mind of a living animal into a computer?"

"Oh, yeah, definitely," he responded automatically. Then, in his mind, he replayed what she had just said, and realized that he actually had something intelligent to say. "Although, it's, um, it's not exactly a transference. It's more of a copy."

"Yes," said Brody. She drew the word out, nodding sagely as she said it. The curl of a smile turned the ends of her thin lips. "Yes, I suppose it is more of a copy. I understand you've uploaded a chimp?"

"Yes, we have."

"Amazing." Her eyes were locked on Raymond's in a way that he found very engaging. He felt like she was studying him, like she was immensely interested in everything he had to say. "When a creature's mind is uploaded, a chimp's for example, does the chimp then live in a virtual world?"

"Yeah. I actually do a lot of the v-world design."

"Really? Wow. Have you spent time with animals that have been uploaded, then?"

"Sure, of course." Raymond felt himself getting excited. He wanted to tell this woman he had just met all about what it was like. But he held back, wary of her motive for questioning.

"The body of the creature is destroyed, right?"

Raymond nodded.

"And when you're with the creature after it's been uploaded, do you feel like you're with the original creature?"

Raymond deliberated, thinking first of the animals that had not seemed at all themselves after upload. "Usually," he responded. "The process has gotten better."

"Sure," she said, seeming to understand. "It's experimental. There are bound to be problems. But when it works, they seem like themselves? I mean, there are a lot of nuances to an animal's personality. They're all still there?"

"They seem to be."

"And yet, it's a machine, simulating an animal. The line between life and machine must be a complete blur for you."

"Oh, there is no line," he blurted.

Her expression didn't change, but she was silent. Raymond could tell she was digesting his response. Part of him wished he could take it back.

"I suppose you would have to feel that way, wouldn't you, in order to be a participant in this sort of research."

Raymond didn't respond.

"Animal rights groups that are against destructive uploading must really frustrate you," sympathized Brody.

Suddenly Raymond saw where she was going. Intuition told him to hide as little as possible.

"They do, but… only a little, really," he said reflectively. "It's more that I don't understand where they're coming from. I mean, why can't they see that uploading makes life better for these animals, not worse. Of course, there have been accidents, but this is a pioneering research group, and the animals that died are like, little pioneering heroes."

Raymond winced at this phrase, "little pioneering heroes". He was clearly too tired, and shouldn't be talking, especially to a police detective.

"I see," said Brody. "So, you see uploaded life as being better?"

"Well, yeah. Your mind is freed from your body, which is what breaks down. It's just like anything else digital. It doesn't break down." She sat listening to him, still looking at him with those studying, fascinated eyes. "And the world is better. You can make a v-world anything you want. Exactly the way you want."

"That seems like a *lot* of work."

"Sure, I guess. But when you're done, you get to live in the world of your dreams. And if your dreams change, you just change your world. If you want to be a space explorer, you can. Or a pirate, or an artist, or—whatever you want."

"But you're still a part of this world."

"Not really. Not if you don't want to be."

She slowly shook her head. "Oh, but you *are*. Do you really not see that? You're in a computer, and the computer is in the real world."

"Obviously, but—"

"It's like living on a boat in bottle," she continued, interrupting him. "You can pretend the boat's on the ocean, but what if someone knocks the bottle off the shelf?"

Raymond wanted to explain about his bunker, and all the precautions he had taken, but he needed to keep his guard up. "We take good care of our servers. Nobody's going to knock the bottle off the shelf."

She looked at him with penetrating scrutiny. "Are you forgetting what happened tonight?"

"Well okay, there are risks, but most of the animals we've uploaded have been sick and likely to die in a matter of months."

"I see." She started to pack up the few materials she had with her. Raymond was unsure whether this meant that he could leave. Just as he started to stand, she spoke.

"Oh," she said, in an off-hand manner. "There's a man outside who's waiting for you. Said he was a private investigator."

"Really?"

"Yes, I thought that was interesting. I told him he could wait for you, if he wanted. Said his name was Murray, I think. Do you know him?"

"No. I mean, I don't know him, but I know who he is, I think."

"Well, I'll walk out with you, to be safe."

"Oh, no, don't worry about it."

"It's on my way. Really." She stood up. "If you're not sure who he is…"

"No, I think I know. This private investigator guy from Chicago has been trying to get in touch with me." Raymond stood up and walked to his bike.

"Wow. A private investigator. Do you know what it's about?"

Raymond stalled for a moment while unlocking his bike. What could he say? If he withheld information, there was the risk that Murray would reveal the deceit in the course of conversation. He had to stick to the half-truths.

"It's about this guy I worked for, years ago." Raymond walked his bike out of the conference room, Brody just behind him.

"A private investigator from Chicago," she asked, "following up on a connection that is years old? At…" She looked at her wrist relay. "5:30 AM?"

Raymond shrugged, as if this were as bizarre to him as it was to her.

As they walked back toward the lobby, Raymond glanced longingly down a taped-off side hall that led to his office, wishing he could whisk the contents of his office away before they made it into the hands of FBI data analysts.

The unadorned walls and bright lights of the laboratory hallway felt foreign and threatening as Raymond approached the lobby, Brody beside him. A spasm shook him abruptly, leaving him hollow, a haze of disorientation dominating his consciousness. He dropped some of his weight onto his bike.

Then he saw Murray, standing next to the police woman who had been standing in the entryway when Raymond arrived. He was a mostly-bald man, a bit shorter than Raymond, hands thrust into the pockets of a floor-length silver raincoat, wearing heavy-framed industrial-orange glasses long out of fashion. Raymond's mind clicked back in place.

Murray did not step forward to meet Raymond. He just stared at Raymond, dramatically expressionless.

"Trouble from every direction, eh?" said Murray, hands still in pockets. Raymond detected a stronger south-side Chicago accent than he'd noticed in Murray's voice message. It seemed exaggerated, as if it were a deliberate reference to Raymond's childhood.

"What do you want, Mr. Murray?" asked Raymond.

Raymond noticed a sniffer bot hovering high in a far corner of the lobby. His conversation with Murray was being recorded.

"I thought I might find you here. You're not very obliging where interviews are concerned, Mr. Quan."

"I'm sorry. I'm very busy, and frankly I don't see the point. I long ago told everything I know about Mr. Tate. It was all recorded by the police. If you need my consent to access the recordings, I'll happily give it to you."

Brody stood at Raymond's side. Her presence made him anxious, but her clear-headed logical nature lent him a degree of confidence—as if it had spread to him by contagion.

"Face-to-face," said Murray. "I need to see you face-to-face. Do you have some time now?"

"Mr. Murray," interjected Officer Brody, "it's 5:30. You're on a case that's how many years old?"

"It's an unsolved missing person case, ma'am, and I've been hired to crack it. Mr. Tate was last seen by this young man five years ago. Until the case is closed, every moment counts."

"That sounds very noble. Could you beam me your investigator's license?"

The private investigator reached into his jacket, and Brody brought her wrist up to inspect his license. She tapped on the face of her wrist relay a couple of times, nodded, and lowered her wrist.

"So," she asked, "why the sudden interest in this case? This missing person, was he wealthy?"

"Quite," responded Murray, and Raymond nodded in confirmation.

"And somebody's after his money?" asked Brody.

"Family's looking for peace of mind," responded Murray.

"I see," said Brody. Raymond was pleased to see her gaze boring into someone else. "Five years… and his funds are still off limits? His money must be in off-shore banking. How did he go missing?"

"His family received a message from him saying he was running off with some girl, off to some remote corner of the world."

"And were his banks asked to contact him?"

"Yes ma'am, and that's where things get fishy. For a long time, the banks couldn't contact him. Then all of a sudden they report that he's been in touch."

Raymond was starting to get edgy. "Listen," he said. "This is all very interesting, but I'd like to get home and get some sleep."

"And where is home?" asked Murray.

"You can look it up."

"I did. Seems you're not home very much."

So, Murray had been doing his homework.

"Yeah, well, I have a girlfriend," said Raymond. It slipped out so easily. The last thing he wanted was to drag Anya into his criminal investigation, but she made for such a convenient excuse, and somehow he felt like his having a girlfriend meant he couldn't possibly be a criminal.

"How about if I give you a ride home," offered Murray. "We can talk on the way."

"I don't think you get it. I'm tired, and I don't want to talk to you. Unless you have a subpoena, you'll just have to wait."

"You don't have to worry about him running off," said Brody. "The FBI will be keeping tabs on him for this case. Let him get some sleep. I'd love to talk to you more about this case."

Raymond felt another wall drop in the elaborate trap that was closing him in. If Brody dug far enough, she might start to see connections between the Tate case and Raymond's current work with v-worlds and artificial life. He might soon become her lead suspect—if he wasn't already. But he decided to take his out and headed for the door.

"I'll be by later," called Murray. "Once you've had your beauty sleep."

Raymond didn't respond. He rolled his bike out the front door, eager to get away.

CHAPTER 10

As Raymond exited the lab, rolling his bike along beside him, he was affronted by the chill pre-dawn air. He paused, uncertain of exactly how to proceed. The fallout of his actions astounded him. The FBI had seized control of the lab, and now, no doubt, news of the break-in was being broadcast worldwide. His workplace would soon be a media focal point. So many alarms had gone off in his mind by this point that he looked around at the familiar campus scene and felt lost. His carefully fostered anonymity was in a shambles.

He saw only one option. He focused on the leading arc of his front tire as he rolled it forward, stepped his left foot on the pedal, and swung his right leg over the seat, headed for the motor home.

His bike ride went a long way toward clearing his mind. Fear and self-doubt faded, replaced by a matter-of-fact acceptance of his situation. He made a point to take a circuitous path, in hopes of shaking any person or thing that might be tracking his movements. He turned left onto Nixon where he would normally have continued on Plymouth. He did not engage the bike's motors. The rhythm of physical exertion gave him welcome relief from his cluttered thoughts. He took back road after back road, regularly checking over his shoulder to make sure he was alone. The sky started to lighten, the stars overhead disappearing. He turned down a secluded, private dirt lane and rode the last quarter-mile to his home: the windowless pole barn that housed his motor home.

It was a simple metal structure, painted pine green, concealed in the middle of a ten-acre wooded lot northeast of Ann Arbor, in Superior Township. He had purchased the lot by way of Ivar Svensson soon after deciding to come to Michigan. There was an old home on the lot at the time he bought it. Raymond had it bulldozed, had the lot re-landscaped for privacy, and had the pole barn built. He also filed for a permit to build a little stone cottage, to satisfy the suspicions of anyone who might wonder at the disuse of such valuable property.

The supple, newly fallen red and yellow maple leaves softened the sound of his bike tires as he rolled down his gravel driveway. It was unseasonably warm for November, even in light of global climate change. He unlocked the side door by which he usually entered, rolled his bike in and leaned it against the wall, and locked the door behind him.

With the door closed, it was very dark. Fine lines of faint morning light came through a ventilation grate high at one end, and through the very narrow gap around the big garage-style door. The motor home, a shiny metallic self-driving vehicle about thirty feet long, occupied most of the interior space. There was one strip of concrete floor where Raymond had entered, on which he had an old weight bench, a space for his bike, and an assortment of tools. At the far end of the strip, just inside the little package delivery hatch, he could just make out the edge of a box.

So, so stupid.

He slowly maneuvered around the weight bench, his eyes still adjusting to the dim light. He knelt down on one knee and set his hand on the box. It was the box he had loaded into his cargo bot the night before—a sturdy cardboard box, about two-feet-square.

"What a price I paid for you," he said. He shook his head and blew a little snort of disgust.

He wrapped his arms around the box and stood up with it. It was light for its size, maybe fifteen pounds. He carried it to the door of the motor home, lifting it up over his head to get it past the weight bench, then set it down. He unlocked the metallic door with a fingerprint check and a 9-digit code, and it slid open. He grabbed the box and stepped up into his kitchenette, where he set the box down again and heaved another anxious sigh.

The interior of his motor home was more robotics lab than home. The space was cluttered with robot limbs and sensors, hundreds of pieces of hardware. Every surface was pristine, cleaned daily by small hovering cleaner bots—it was a very clean mess. Raymond looked around. Typically, he didn't mind it. But in his present state, it added palpably to the stress.

Panic betrays guilt. I can't afford to panic.

He knew he had to remain balanced and circumspect. The FBI was all over the lab, and his work computers, including his mini-v, would be subject to search and seizure. His meticulous management of sensitive data was about to be put to the test—all he could do was worry, and he didn't have time for that. He had only a few hours in which to get his affairs in order and leave the motor home. Murray would be stopping by his apartment soon.

"If I can just get my shit together and upload, they'll see my suicide and close the case."

He checked the time on his wrist relay. It was 6:10 AM. The first thing to take care of was to finish Molly's upload, to make sure his whole plan could work. But first, a shower to clear his head.

His gaze fell on the hand-written plans that sat on his dinette table. "Well, I won't be needing those." He glanced over them. There were so many steps he would have to skip. In a little subsection of the plan, he had listed three items he wanted to scan into Nurania: the shirt Anya tore off him in the flower garden; a monkey-headed plastic stir-stick from a bar they'd gone to; a hummingbird robot he built when he was eighteen.

"Oh well."

Off to one side was a note, "surveillance install," a reminder to install surveillance eyes at Anya's and at the lab, in case he needed to monitor activities back in reality prime. Toward the end of the plan was his motor home ride to the bunker. He shook his head. With the FBI on-site, there was no way he could take this NBC to the lab, upload into it, cart it to Minnesota in the motor home, and expect to get away with it.

He looked at the piece of paper, aware that his exhaustion was cluttering his thoughts, obscuring the right course of action. If the FBI were to find his notes, they would have no problem piecing together his whole plan. Of course, if the FBI found the piece of paper, that would mean they had also found the motor home. Which would mean they knew he lived in a secure motor home registered under a false ID, on property officially owned by that same false ID. This alone was crime enough to put him away for years. Never mind possession of the NBC itself.

He found himself suddenly awash with fear again. His anonymity was gone, leaving him utterly exposed. At present, he was fairly certain nobody knew of the motor home, and nobody knew how to contact him except through his university network account. It was critical that nobody know of the motor home. Once he uploaded, the false identity of Ivar Svensson was his ticket back to anonymity. The link from Raymond to Ivar had to remain unknown. He needed to finish the few remaining steps that demanded the secrecy of his motor home, then avoid it as much as possible. He couldn't afford to be tailed to this location.

Raymond looked at his plans again. They were useless now. He took them into the pole barn and burned them, grinding the blackened flakes of ash into the concrete.

He climbed back into the motor home and locked up. He headed to the back, starting to take off his clothes as he went. In his bedroom, he stripped naked, tossing his clothes on the bed. With a vocal command, he started the shower in the bathroom. A winged cleaner robot dropped from the ceiling of the bedroom, hovered for a moment, then descended to the bed to collect his clothes and carry them to the laundry.

In the shower, Raymond found himself scheming again, trying to figure out how to perform the scan and sneak his mental data out under the noses of the FBI. It was then that he realized another tool at the disposal of the FBI: satellite surveillance.

"Oh my god—how bleeding stupid can I be? I'm so screwed."

The university itself banned the use of public surveillance cameras, which is why Raymond hadn't been worried about there being exterior footage of his illicit delivery of the first NBC to Property Disposition. But the FBI probably had satellite coverage of the entire planet. How much of it could they store? All of it, probably, but for how long? Would they have records of recent satellite footage? If they did, they might be able to trace back to 11:00 PM of the night before, when his delivery robot carted the stolen goods across North Campus to Property Disposition, then to the motor home. Regardless of their ability to retain footage of the entire planet, they would certainly be able to watch him now, and they would see him ride his bike from the lab to the pole barn, thereby linking him with Ivar Svensson.

"They've already had hours to review data. It could already be too late. Shit, they could have watched me ride here… unless, maybe it was too dark out." Could satellites "see" at night well enough to track him?

He skipped the rest of his shower, hastily dried himself off, then pulled on a pair of boxers and entered the v-chamber in his bedroom. He said the word "workstation", and the interior of the chamber transformed itself into a dense array of displays and inputs. Raymond sat in the chair that appeared behind him and it slid forward into position. His hands fell into manuhaptic gloves modeled after his real ones. With a combination of speech and gesture commands, he created a list of agent IDs. These were software agents of his that resided on weakly-secured network nodes throughout the US and Canada. He would disperse his encrypted communications among these agents, making the origin very difficult to trace. He had memorized the credentials and network addresses of all his most secure agents; were his own systems ever compromised, no record of his most secure data could ever be found.

Having set up his channels of communication, Raymond contacted an acquaintance he had successfully avoided for nearly three years, a man he knew as Manolo. Manolo doubtless had many other aliases, but this was the one he used among respected fellow hackers. Manolo in turn knew Raymond as Celia. Raymond had learned early that Manolo had a soft spot for shrewd, in-the-know women, and he had adopted the persona of a short-haired, all-business, all-in-black Hispanic woman. Raymond had only ever sought one real favor from Manolo, but had spent months establishing a rapport and offering small favors before making his request. In this time, Raymond learned just how dangerous Manolo could be. Once Raymond had what he wanted, he had made himself scarce. Happily, he had not heard from Manolo since.

Raymond had also learned that Manolo had a soft spot for enemies of the FBI, and it was for this reason that Raymond turned to him now. To request a meeting with Manolo, Raymond posted an unremarkable image of a sunset on a Net site that purported to be a place to share vacation stories. Embedded within that image, spread out in a pattern known only to a few trusted friends of Manolo, was a message that named a v-world location and a time for the meeting. Raymond then fired off a watcher process to await a response, which would come in the form of a slight cropping of his sunset image. If more content were trimmed off the top of the image, it would indicate that Manolo had agreed to the meeting. If more were trimmed off the left or right edge, it would show how much earlier or later the meeting had to be, respectively—five minutes per pixel. And if more content were trimmed off the bottom, it was no go, and it would be up to Raymond to attempt an alternative meeting.

Having delivered his calling card, Raymond started doing some research into the capabilities of FBI surveillance. What he found gave him a glimmer of hope. There were privacy laws in place that prevented them from accessing detailed footage without prior cause. Furthermore, tracking movement at night was said to be problematic. However, they would definitely be able to track his movements during the day. And there was no telling what sorts of loopholes existed in those privacy laws. Agent Michaels' comment to Detective Brody about a naïve understanding of policy came to mind.

"So, how to get out of here," he said aloud. "I need to ditch this rig and sell this property. I'll ship the second NBC to Minnesota the same way I did the first, and I'll just have to upload into that one remotely. Which means I definitely need to know whether remote upload works. It's time to fire up that brain of yours, Molly."

There was no way he would be able to sleep. His mind was spinning way too fast. He stayed in his v-chamber and reviewed the steps necessary to complete Molly's remote upload. First, he needed to inventory all of her mental data, stashed away in various accounts, and transfer it to the datastore at his bunker. Second, he needed to initiate the diagnostics suite on Molly's NBC, to make sure it was ready to receive her mental data. Third, he needed to instantiate her simulated physiology, which would run on a server connected to the NBC. He would give her new body a trial run, then put it on hold, awaiting its corresponding brain. Fourth and finally, he needed to start the flow of mental data into the NBC—the remote upload.

All of Molly's mental data proved to be in order, and Raymond was successful in transferring it to the staging datastore in the bunker, from which it would be loaded into the NBC. He felt a weight lift away as he cleaned out all the hacked accounts he had used to store the data; it was one more traceable step covered over. He continued with his work. Just as he fired off the NBC diagnostics suite—the second step—he heard Scorpio's voice.

"Mosby, the sunset image has been cropped. The left-side crop was greatest, by twelve pixels."

"Twelve pixels—that's an hour early! Crap, that means he wants to meet me now."

The v-chamber lifted Raymond out of his chair as it transitioned to a dark location in east Delta Nuevo, a city of about half-a-million on the Sea of Anxiety, in the public v-world of Telemesis. Several years before, when Raymond was more active in the underground, Delta Nuevo had been a favorite location for surreptitious dealings, and—to the best of Raymond's knowledge—it had never attracted the attention of government listeners.

The scene transition put Raymond in a small, dark, unadorned room, lit only by a flickering violet light that emanated from the floor. Most often referred to as lobbies or static gateways, the room was an entry chamber, a known location through which one may enter a v-world. As lobbies went, this one was especially minimalist. There was a single door out of the room, with a retinal scanner beside it. Loose wires protruding from the top of the scanner sizzled and sparked—evidence of a novice attempt at bypassing identification. Raymond wondered whether the scene in Delta Nuevo might have turned newbie.

Raymond naturally reached for his hip, finding Celia's trusty disruptor pistol holstered on a female hip that curved out rather wider than his own. He wasn't expecting trouble, but it was a necessary precaution. Violence on Telemesis had an element of realism unusual for v-worlds. Death was permanent—if the v-world deemed you mortally wounded, your avatar would be banned from reentering. It was possible to return to the world under a new guise, but Telemesis was tough on newcomers. Even for those with powerful allies, starting over was difficult. Weapons licenses, work permits, and currency were strictly controlled by the fascist government of Telemesis, and its all-bot police force was immune to bribery. But, because it was run by an off-shore consortium that closely guarded the privacy of its members, the payoff outweighed the risks for those seeking secrecy.

Raymond looked down at himself and saw he was wearing a tight, high-gloss, black, zip-up one-piece—a latex cat suit. "Not exactly low-profile," he said to himself. He heard his own voice as that of a gruff Latina. He was quite used to alternate voices, but he hadn't had a female avatar in quite some time; it would take a bit of getting used to. "Clothing change: I want my gray mechanic's one-piece, from Fischer's." The clothing change was instantaneous. He was now wearing a beat-up mechanic's suit with a Fischer's badge high on the left arm. Fischer's was the maintenance shop where Celia had gotten her start on Telemesis, fixing used gliders, hovercycles, robots, generators, and whatever else came into the shop. The technology of Telemesis was mostly the same as that of reality, with the addition of more frequent space travel and more exotic weapons. The atmosphere, however, was grittier, more bleak. Especially in Delta Nuevo.

"Scorpio, you there?" asked Raymond, tilting his head downward to speak into a voice receiver in his mechanic's suit.

"Affirmative," came the response. It was a response that only Raymond would hear, for Celia owned a much-coveted aural implant. It could receive signals from real-world sources, to which he could respond via transmitters sewn into her clothing. In other v-worlds, a continuous private connection with the real world was standard. In order to enter Telemesis, it was necessary to give up certain basic v-chamber features; in order to connect with the real world, one had to advance far enough within Telemesis to obtain rare and expensive hardware. Celia had won hers in an illegal robot-combat gambling arena. At present, this was especially handy—Raymond wanted to record his conversation with Manolo, so that he wouldn't miss any of the details.

He stepped up to the retinal scanner, which was really just a prop that triggered his v-chamber to provide login credentials; it would not scan Raymond's retina. Whoever pulled the wires clearly didn't realize this. He leaned forward, looked into the eyepiece, and saw a sweep of red light. The lobby door slid most of the way open, then stuck, then closed part way, stuck again, and started going back and forth. Raymond side-stepped through while the door was mostly open and stepped out into a dark alley. The door slid shut behind him.

He heard a glider above the alley, and a light swept over him. He looked up and saw a police cruiser, probably checking for lobby-killers—people who attack isolated avatars as they enter a v-world via a static gateway. This was a common tactic among gamers seeking money, weapons, or status, and the Telemesis law against it was occasionally enforced. Raymond's hand rested on his disruptor as he watched the light sweep down the alley. Seeing no one, he headed for the street.

The alley let out on Escutcheon Street. It was essentially as Raymond remembered it, a narrow street dominated by small industry, with bars and cheap restaurants here and there, catering to the after-work crowd. There were no weekends in Telemesis—work schedules were tailored to the needs of the individual—so the laborers' bars were rarely crowded but never empty. The rendezvous point was a barbecue joint called Cookout, just a block south from the alley. Raymond checked his wrist relay and saw that he was nearly five minutes late. He started down the sidewalk with long strides. A few people walked in and out of bars, but the sidewalk was mostly empty. Street traffic was sparse, mostly crapped-out old hovercycles. Raymond was relieved; the street seemed essentially the same as when he was last in Delta Nuevo.

He spotted the Cookout sign—a retro image of a man standing over a kettle grill—and started to get nervous. He wasn't entirely sure what it was that he wanted from Manolo. He wanted to know more than he already did about FBI surveillance capabilities, and he wanted the access necessary to alter recordings of his movements. More than anything, however, he wanted an ally. He was afraid, and he wanted to have someone he could turn to if things got bad—someone who could help him stall the FBI investigation long enough to pull off an emergency upload, if need be. He came to the glass front of Cookout, a deep, narrow restaurant, dimly lit, with tall booths along the right-hand side. Not surprisingly, Manolo was not visible from outside.

He'll be in a booth at the back, facing the door.

The door slid open, and Raymond headed toward the back. He reached the last booth having seen no one he recognized. He checked his watch again. He was seven minutes late. Had Manolo come and gone in that time? It was unlikely. Raymond sat down in the booth at the very back, facing the door, where he had expected to find his contact. A waitress came back to serve him. He accepted a menu but told her he'd get her attention when he was ready to order.

"Mosby." It was Scorpio's voice in his head. "The sunset's gone."

Something had gone wrong. Manolo had withdrawn the sunset image, a courtesy that he didn't grant everyone. But Raymond wondered what was up. He wondered whether Manolo had found something about Raymond that worried him—whether he might already be tainted, a man to avoid.

"I'm sure it's nothing," said Raymond to himself. "At least he pulled the sunset."

Raymond considered leaving Telemesis immediately—jacking out right there in Cookout—but remembered that instant-outs were strongly discouraged in this v-world. If he were to leave without going through a proper exit, his avatar would become a bot for the next 24 hours, leaving Celia highly vulnerable. If she were killed in those 24 hours, he would find out the next time he tried to come in. He got up from where he sat and walked out of Cookout, headed for the gateway through which he had entered.

When he turned the corner, back into the alley, he ran right into a tall, white, muscular thug wearing ripped denim pants and a dirty white tank top. After hardly a split second's hesitation, the man spun him around and put him into a choke hold. The brute's movements were strong, fast, and precise. Raymond tried to speak, but the choke hold was too firm. Not knowing his foe's intentions, Raymond could only assume the worst. With a twist of his foot, laser punch-blade knives slipped noiselessly out of Celia's sleeves, the handles falling naturally into his grasp. He brought both his arms over his head, reaching back for the man's ears; the laser blades shot out on impact, cutting through the man's skull with a crackling, popping sound. Raymond thrust the blades upward, cutting all the way through the top of the man's head. The arms around his throat went limp, and Raymond was pulled off balance as the man slumped to the street. He fell onto one elbow, then rolled away, retracting the blue blades that now shown in the night. He scrambled to his feet, his back against one wall of the alley, dropped the laser knives into tool pockets along Celia's thighs, and pulled out his disruptor. Overhead, he heard the sound of an approaching glider. Search lights hit the other end of the alley and started sweeping toward him.

"Mosby, the sunset is back." It was Scorpio's voice again. "The time is now."

His disruptor still in hand, Raymond stepped out onto Escutcheon Street again. The sidewalk was empty. He looked back down the alley. The search light had stopped in front of the gateway. He looked up and saw that it was a police glider. Someone was about to come out through the gateway, he realized, and the police were simply providing cover. Estimating that it would be at least ten seconds before the newcomer entered the scene, Raymond dashed back to the body of his attacker and searched the man's pockets. He found nothing. Then he noticed the man was wearing a leather necklace. He ripped it from around the man's thick neck and pocketed it. He then stepped back, dialed up the power setting on his disruptor, and fired; the man's body was vaporized.

The search light swept down the alley toward where Raymond stood; the police must have seen the burst of his weapon. At the same time, he heard the gateway door open. He made an all-out sprint across Escutcheon Street and ducked into a bar that had heavily tinted windows. It was a dark bar with no more than a dozen customers. It smelled of Telmerian spice cigarettes; the smell seemed artificial, reminding Raymond that he was in a v-chamber. Without concern about raising suspicions, Raymond turned and watched through the window. The police glider appeared over the top of the warehouse across the street, then settled down to street level. Raymond took the necklace out of his pocket and looked at it. From the black leather strap hung a rough-hewn medallion, made from a soft metal, perhaps tin. A crude T-shape had been punched into the metal at a 45 degree angle.

Raymond pocketed the necklace and looked out the window again. There was a man talking to the police now. Escutcheon Street had been deserted when Raymond looked down at the necklace; the man had to have come from the gateway. From this distance, he couldn't quite make out the man's face. He wondered whether it was Manolo, disappointed that his trap had failed. But if it was a trap, it couldn't have been Manolo's—it was too poorly executed.

"Something going down?" came a male voice from behind Raymond. Raymond turned to see a young man in mirrored sunglasses, his wavy hair greased back, his black shirt half-unbuttoned. On his chest was a metal medallion just like the one in Raymond's pocket.

"There was a disruptor blast in that alley," responded Raymond, "then—"

"Shit, that's…" The man's voice trailed off.

"You—" Raymond turned to the man, but he was headed out the door. As Raymond watched, the man who had been standing next to him crossed the street and joined in the conversation. The man pointed to the bar, and the other three men looked to where Raymond stood.

"Not good," said Raymond to himself.

The man who had entered through the gateway lowered his head and spoke. Someone behind Raymond, inside the bar, said "What's up, boss?" Raymond recognized that this was no coincidence. He dropped to the floor as a disruptor blast blew out the window of the bar. The shot had come from behind him.

Raymond leapt through the now-missing window, rolled out of the way of another scorching blast, then took off at a dead sprint down the street, away from Cookout. He weaved and dodged, two blue beams of police laser fire narrowly missing him. He dove behind a delivery truck. He heard the footsteps of a man pursuing him, also running. Somewhere shy of the truck, the footsteps stopped. Raymond drew his pistol, dropped to the ground, and saw what he had hoped to see: a pair of feet. He fired. A cry of pain pierced the silence, and a body dropped to the ground where the feet had been. It was the man in sunglasses. Raymond fired again. The body was vaporized.

Raymond heard the police glider revving up. He scrambled forward and peered around the corner of the truck. The glider was headed toward him, and the man who had entered via the gateway was going into the bar. He would be coming out with backup, no doubt—the bar was probably a guild hangout. It was just Raymond's luck that he would get mixed up with some thug gamers' guild when he had real work to do. The big goon he had killed in the alley was probably the avatar of some 14-year-old kid v-worlding on a Saturday morning, working his way up by running protection for a guild leader who didn't want to get jumped at the gateway.

"Scorpio, any word from Manolo? Am I too late?"

"No word."

As the police glider moved overhead, Raymond rolled underneath the truck, out of view from above. He heard the glider continue down the street and turn down an alley—the obvious place for him to have run, he figured.

"Scorpio, create a new user with my Fenton account, give the user this same avatar, and push her through the gateway."

"Acknowledged."

Within a few seconds, Raymond saw a woman identical in appearance to Celia walk out of the gateway alley. At the same time, four men came out of the bar, weapons drawn.

"Run her south," instructed Raymond.

The Celia clone took off running to the south. An array of weapons opened fire from in front of the bar; she didn't get far. The group of men hooted and high-fived each other, then returned to the bar.

Now, to sneak past while their backs are turned.

Raymond crept out from beneath the truck and jogged as quietly as he could to the edge of the bar window. From inside, he heard men calling out drink orders. He casually walked past the bar, looking across the street so that anyone looking out would see the back of his head. He broke into a run again as soon as he was past the blown-out window, and he ran all the way to Cookout and entered the restaurant without pausing.

Once inside, he saw a short Hispanic man rising from the last booth. Their eyes met. The man made an exaggerated motion to look at his watch, then looked at Raymond disapprovingly.

"My apologies," said Raymond, once the two of them were seated. "I ran into a guild." He took the metal guild emblem from his pocket and showed it to Manolo. Manolo, a middle-aged man with receding hair and sloped shoulders, unfolded his plump hands to reach for the emblem, then waved it off with a gesture of disinterest.

"Yes, yes," said Manolo with a note of mild annoyance. "Hammers are everywhere."

Raymond looked quizzically at him.

"You don't know the Hammer?" asked Manolo. His eyes narrowed slightly, but his voice sounded off-hand. "Big cross-world guild. Fee-based, but nothing too steep. They get a lot of kids, kids who like to think they're dangerous. You been out of it?"

"I suppose so. I've been doing my own thing."

"That's good to hear." He nodded approvingly. "Something big?"

"Pretty big. Nothing public, but it's big for me."

"And you've run into trouble."

"Yep. I guess you get that a lot?"

Manolo nodded. The waitress came to take their order.

"We'd like some peace and quiet," said Manolo, "and a side of onion rings." He handed her a small fold of cash and smiled after her, then turned to Raymond again. "So, Celia, what's your situation?"

"I've got the Bureau on my back, and I want to conceal my physical movements. Outdoor movements. I don't want them to know where I sleep at night."

"What's your surveillance status?"

"I'd like to know."

"I'll need your IID."

Raymond hesitated. It had occurred to him that Manolo might ask for his international ID, but he was hoping that there was some way around this.

"I'd like access to do the digging myself."

"Access?" Manolo broke up laughing. The laugh trailed off into a smile of fond pity. "Access, oh that's funny. You've never gone this high up, have you,

Celia? It's not like I can just hook you up with a node address and some credentials and you're on your way."

Raymond met and held Manolo's gaze. He debated lying, he debated skirting the question. He shook his head 'no'.

"Bureau authentication is basically crack-proof," explained Manolo. "People granted the sort of data control you're talking about have auth implants that perform DNA verification against the surrounding cells before coughing up the necessary certificates. These Bureau systems are under a mile of barbed wire."

"Damn," said Raymond, genuinely impressed.

"And these implants self-destruct if they lose contact with the approved DNA, so you can imagine how hard it is to get your hands on one."

"Yeah." Raymond considered making a joke about entering a high-security FBI facility carrying a severed head, but he was neither stupid enough nor respected enough to make light of his situation. "So," he said matter-of-factly, "you have an insider, and he needs to know who I am before he can help."

Manolo nodded. "Precisely."

"Okay," said Raymond. "I'm not sure I'm going to be able to get what I want, then."

The waitress came back with a basket of onion rings and tossed it on the table between them. Manolo proceeded to dig in. Raymond grabbed a ring, but he was too nervous to eat.

Manolo ripped a sheet from the roll of brown paper towels that sat on the table. "Okay," he said, wiping his fingers off. "We'll start with your surveillance status. Then what?"

"I want records of my outdoor movements within a specific area wiped out."

"During what period of time?"

"The last two years."

"Two years! What the hell are you trying to hide?"

"I told you—where I've been sleeping."

"You think they don't already know that?" Manolo chuckled.

"Nope."

"Then I've been mistaken about you. You're an amateur. There's no way they don't already have an address for you." Manolo returned to the onion rings.

"Oh, I'm sure they do. I just want to make sure it's the wrong one."

Manolo looked at him in disbelief, a bemused grin on his face. Raymond met the look straight on.

"I know we've never talked money before," said Raymond, "but I could certainly sweeten the deal."

Manolo disparaged the offer with a lift of one eyebrow.

"If you're right," said Manolo in a considered tone, "then I could really use someone like you. Give me your IID. If the Bureau doesn't know about your hiding place, I'll wipe out records of your movements myself."

"Okay, here's the deal. Nearly every day, I ride my bicycle to a motor home in the woods. I want to make it look like I stop underneath a rail overpass and never go any further. You follow?"

"Sure. You want to make it look like you've been living under an overpass. And you don't think they'll see through that?"

"Doesn't matter—I'm just buying time. If I give you my IID and the coordinates of the overpass, can you take it from there?"

"Sure. That is, if you're right about them not already knowing where you live."

"You'll find the coordinates and my IID in the canals of Amsterdam, in one hour."

Manolo slid the remaining onion rings off to the side, indicating that they were done. They stood and shook hands.

"Now," said Raymond, "if you want to avoid any chance of getting mixed up in a messy scene, you should probably leave first."

"Right."

Manolo left the restaurant, and Raymond went to the women's room. He spent a few minutes in a stall, then made his way out to Escutcheon Street. His hand rested on his disruptor as he exited Cookout. Outside, there was no sign of unusual activity. No police gliders hovered overhead, no sirens could be heard, nobody was standing watch on either side of the street. He walked to the corner and took a look down the alley. It was empty. The Hammers must have bought the death of his avatar double. He jogged to the gateway, stepped through the half-open door, and exited Telemesis.

CHAPTER 11

The v-chamber returned to a workstation, and Raymond dropped into the office chair that appeared below him. He heaved a sigh. His eyes burned, his heart raced, and he was covered with sweat. He opened the v-chamber door, walked to the kitchenette, and had his shake machine make him a banana-espresso shake. As he drank it, his thoughts drifted to Anya.

"Oh, crap." He suddenly remembered telling her he would be in touch. At the moment, the thought of talking to her seemed like hell. But she would probably worry if he didn't at least let her know he was okay. He walked back to his v-chamber workstation with his shake, sat side-saddle on his office chair, and spoke a text message for her, letting her know he was exhausted and would be spending the day sleeping. He sent it, then downloaded some random image of an Amsterdam canal, embedded his IID and the rail bridge coordinates amid the pixels, and posted it on the same site where he had posted his sunset meeting request.

Raymond sighed deeply as he made the mental adjustment to pursue his next bit of work. He spent a minute with his eyes closed, breathing deeply, combating fatigue as best he could. If he did succeed in uploading, the need for sleep was a requirement of life he intended to eliminate.

He connected to his bunker network again and went over the results of the NBC diagnostics. All tests had come back positive. He proceeded to the third step: initiating and testing Molly's simulated physiology, to make sure it was ready to be paired with her brain. He first started a crude brain-sim process that would serve as a placeholder for her uploaded mind. Next, he started the physiology process. As all subsystems of the physiology came to life, signal traffic between the brain substitute and the physiology increased. Soon, the physiology appeared to have reached a balanced state that corresponded to that moment when one's consciousness releases a dream and recognizes reality. Raymond then started a test suite that simulated external forces acting upon the body—changes in temperature, oxygen level, and other environmental conditions that should trigger measurable responses. All results were positive. He proceeded to test reflexive responses to direct physical stimuli—a hammer to the knee, a bright light in the eye. The tests and their expected results were well documented and easy to run.

He skipped through, performing only those tests he felt were most important, and within fifteen minutes he was satisfied that all was in order.

"Scorpio, has the Amsterdam image been taken down yet?"

"Yes."

Manolo had received his IID. It could already be in the hands of the FBI insider. A jolting shiver ran through him. He felt so exposed, and was no longer in control of his success factors. But he saw no other way to avoid an obvious connection between him and his precious Ivar Svensson identity.

"Okay," he said to himself. "Focus on the tasks at hand." He glanced at the clock on his upper workstation display. It was already 10:00 AM.

All was ready. It was time to upload Molly's mental data into the NBC. He put the physiology simulation into a ready state and terminated the brain substitute. It was time to plug in a real brain.

Whenever he worked with remote hardware, Raymond liked to have a video feed of the hardware itself. It was a sanity check, to make sure the hardware wasn't smoking or sitting in an inch of water. He had one of his robots look over the NBC that was to house Molly's mind, and he watched its video feed as it performed a brief inspection. Everything checked out okay. The bunker server room looked to be in order, as usual.

Within his v-chamber workstation, Raymond set up a window into the v-world that would be Molly's new home, so he could watch her awaken. When Molly awoke, she would find herself alone in a v-world identical to the one he had created for Bento, right down to Bento's favorite toys—Raymond had not had enough time to create a replica of Molly's teddy bear. That she would have no companions worried him. Bento had received constant attention from the scientists, and was eventually introduced into a community of a-life chimps. The introduction had not gone well at first, the a-life chimps treating Bento as an outsider. They hooted threateningly, driving him out of their community, even throwing stones at him. But, eventually, Bento had been adopted into the community at the bottom of the male hierarchy. Raymond wanted to give Molly a community, too, but he had not thought to grab a copy of the a-life chimp code before stealing the NBCs, and now the FBI had it all locked down. He might be able to find public domain code that would work, but he couldn't know how long it might be before he would have time to pursue this.

"Hank—I'll give her Hank the Handler."

Raymond drained the last of his shake and triggered the upload. A 3-D display of a brain appeared before him, showing the signals sent out by the neuristors as they came to life. Molly's mental data, so carefully recorded and mapped during the scan, was moved into position in its new brain. Patterns of light spread quickly up through the primitive core of the brain, then through both hemispheres of the display. One lobe after another came to life, activity spreading outward from center. Finally, the cerebral cortices lit up, indicating that Molly might be gaining consciousness. Raymond nervously drummed with his feet, repeatedly looking to the array of warning indicators. They remained dark. The physiology simulation came out of its ready state—the connection between mind and physiology had been opened. The brain started to receive sensory signals and send directives to the body. Raymond noticed movement in his window on Molly's v-world, and he turned to see her stirring to life in her new home.

He tried to imagine what Molly was experiencing. The last thing she had known, she was an ill chimp undergoing some new treatment, sleep spreading through her body as the humans shaved her and applied patches to her skin. Now she was waking up in an environment that was probably a lot like the zoo primate house she had known most of her life, except there were eighty-foot bamboo walls instead of a metal fence, and a forest canopy far overhead. Molly was waking up alone, but with a body that felt healthy. He wondered whether she was able to detect how foreign the environment truly was, whether something might seem fundamentally wrong to her.

Raymond found himself wanting to be with her, to interact with her. He had often wanted to touch her during her time at the lab, but was not permitted to. Now there was nothing to stop him: he stood in his v-chamber, closed the door, and was transported into Molly's v-world.

To enhance the experiential coherency of the v-world, he had given it a static gateway. Like most lobbies, this one was a small, unadorned room with a single doorway. A faint yellow light emanated from overhead, and the door glowed a rich shade of green. He touched the door, and it slid open. He stepped through. The humid, tropical air felt like silk against his skin. The ground was soft beneath his feet. The forest around him was dense with narrow sleek-barked tree trunks. Birds squawked and sang somewhere above him, obscured from view by the thick foliage. Raymond knew the floor of the v-world to be precisely one acre in size. It was mostly tropical forest, with a stream that flowed through one corner, coming out beneath one eighty-foot-high bamboo wall and disappearing beneath another. Were Molly ever to plunge into the water in hopes of swimming beneath the wall and away, she would find a mesh of reeds barring escape, a seemingly natural barrier in a profoundly unnatural environment.

Raymond walked along a path to the center of the space, where he found Molly sitting on the ground. The shaved spots were gone, her hair coat fully intact. He approached her slowly, holding out open hands to her. She gazed complacently at him, her head slightly lowered. She made no motion to flee. He wondered what her life must have been like that she would not be struck with fear at the sight of an unknown human. Or perhaps this was some side-effect of her upload?

He moved in closer, and she held her hands out to him, much as he held his out to her. He took this as a sign that she wanted to be picked up. He squatted down, let her wrap her hairy arms around his neck, and stood up. He found her to be far lighter than expected—his avatar apparently had super-human strength, a convenience for the researchers. She wrapped her arms and legs around him and leaned her head against his cheek.

Her peaceful, complacent nature disturbed him. She seemed downright depressed. He wondered whether it was possible that some basic spark of vitality had been lost during the upload. Or perhaps she had simply been in a funk because of her illness, and she had not yet had time or opportunity to discover that her body was a healthy one now. He would have to read more of her background notes. Maybe she needed a playmate or a favorite toy, or maybe it was just a matter of time.

"Computer, is there any mention of a favorite food in Molly's records?"

"Oil palm nuts," whispered a female voice in his ear.

"I want a pile of oil palm nuts on the ground in front of me."

A pile of small nuts appeared in front of him. He gently lifted Molly away from him. She clung to his neck, her grip very strong.

"Okay," said Raymond.

He crossed his feet and carefully lowered himself into a cross-legged seated position. He then scooched around and showed Molly the nuts.

"See? Look at those yummy nuts."

Her head turned slightly, but she showed no real interest in the nuts. He shifted so that his right hand was free, resting her weight in his lap but keeping his left hand on her back, to comfort her. He reached out and picked up a nut, then lifted it up and placed it next to her nose. She pulled away slightly. He lowered his hand, not wanting to annoy her.

"What's wrong, girl?"

Something was odd, and he realized he had expected her to be a little smelly. She wasn't—in fact, he detected no scent at all. Raymond wondered whether this was a failing of the v-world or a shortcoming of his v-chamber. He had been careful to use the most advanced v-world engine they had. Perhaps it was just a matter of the default settings being off.

"Computer, I'm not registering any smells. Run the basic smell diagnostics and calibration suite."

"Running. Complete."

Raymond got a sudden whiff of chimp odor. It reminded him of the animal holding area in the lab, only not as pungent. He held the nut up in front of Molly's nose again. This time, she released her grip enough to free one arm, and she took the nut in hand. She then started to look around at the ground. She looked to one side, then shifted so she could look to the other side. Whatever it was that she was looking for, she apparently didn't find it, as she dropped the nut and went back to leaning her head against his.

Raymond wondered whether he had missed some other calibration process. He was surprised that they were not run automatically, only now realizing how much tweaking Anya and the other scientists must do after first instantiating a new v-world.

"Computer, Molly was looking for something on the ground when I gave her the nut. Do you know what she would have been looking for?"

"There is mention of hammer and anvil stones near occurrences of the phrase 'palm oil nut'."

"Of course—nutcrackers. Tools. You're a smart girl, aren't you Molly?"

Raymond picked up another nut, then stood up from his cross-legged position and walked Molly to the stream. The stream bed was lined with stones, and there were more scattered along the bank. He held the nut up for Molly, and she took it in her left hand. She then looked down at the stream bank, and swung down from Raymond's neck, apparently having found a stone she thought would work. She selected a broad, flat stone, picked it up in her right hand, and set it a short distance from the stream. Still holding the nut in her left hand, she made her way up and down the stream bank, examining stones. Eventually, she found one that was large and oval-shaped, and she carried it over to the first one. She placed the nut on the flat anvil stone and gave it a whack with the hammer stone. Her technique was good; the shell of the nut split away, and the meat inside was exposed, only slightly mashed. She dropped her hammer stone, picked up the nut, dug out the meat, and placed it in her mouth. She then showed Raymond a big toothy grin and started to make her way back to the pile of nuts.

Raymond took the opportunity to wander around a bit. The space seemed a little small. It had been designed to make it easy for the researchers to observe and interact with Bento when he was uploaded. Raymond decided he would enlarge it if he had time. For now, to give Molly something more to look at, he would create a window onto Nurania.

"Computer, open a gateway-window to Nurania. Within this habitat, place the window in the center of the east wall. Unbreakable, completely transparent, ten feet wide and six feet tall."

He walked to the center of the east wall and saw a window. The other side was pitch black—he needed to define the other end of the gateway.

"Computer, jack out, avatar exits via gateway immediately."

The jungle scene disappeared, and Raymond found himself in his v-chamber, in the pale amber glow of its default lighting.

"Nurania, god mode. The tree home in Nalixia Rainforest."

The scene changed immediately to a tree house. The floors and walls were of masterfully lashed wooden poles. Overhead, a roof of huge overlapping leaves lay over a teepee-like arrangement of gracefully curved beams. There were shuttered windows on all four sides, and a trap door in the floor.

"Flight control," said Raymond. A small controller appeared in his right hand. He pushed forward and flew through the wall of the tree house. He hung in mid-air amid dense foliage. He lowered the controller and flew down through the foliage without disturbing it, dropping slowly below the forest canopy. He nudged the thumb-joystick further forward, and for a moment the forest was a blur.

Raymond looked down past his feet to the forest floor, some 80 feet below. He knew that a community of gibbon-like creatures lay to the east. He had created the a-life species when he was about sixteen, but had planted them in Nurania just a few years ago. Directly below him was an area of forest that lay at the edge of their territory. He decided it would be a good place to drop Molly's one-acre habitat. There was plenty of room to grow into someday, the climate and flora were similar to that of the habitat, and Molly might enjoy watching the creatures of this region.

"Clear a one-acre square centered below me, ceiling level with my feet, floor level with the current forest floor." The trees around him vanished. The forest floor was replaced with a matte white surface with a grid of thick orange lines. "Gateway-fill this space with Molly's habitat." At his feet appeared a one-acre slab of black; the upper exterior surface of Molly's habitat had never been defined. He pressed a button on the flight controller and his weight came to rest on the black surface. "Place a drainage grid on this surface." He was elevated six inches, and the surface beneath him turned into a grid of mesh-covered gutters that ran to the edges of the acre. "Atop the drainage grid place ten inches of substrate, contained by bamboo support walls at the edges of the acre." He was elevated again. Now he stood atop dark soil. "Seed the soil with tropical mix three." The surface of the soil was covered with a randomly distributed assortment of seeds. He considered placing a protective covering over the seeds, to prevent birds from eating them, but decided to let the simulation take its course. He had never created an artificial mesa like this, and he wasn't sure what would come of it.

With a push of the controller button, gravity vanished again. Raymond flew to the center of the east edge of the new bamboo-walled mesa, then dropped straight down its sheer face. Below him he could see ant-eaters feasting on the insects that had been pushed out of the acre that was previously there; Raymond had his v-world set to a preservationist mode that prevented his construction from killing any of the animal life. When he reached the forest floor, he hovered a few inches above the insects and looked in through the window. The ant-eaters ignored Raymond while he was in god mode, voraciously inhaling the bugs as they attempted to crawl or burrow to safety. Through the window, Raymond saw Molly on the other side, curiously smacking the simulated glass. From outside, there was no sound. Raymond saw that she could see him; she grew agitated at the sight of him. She opened her mouth and leaned against the glass, then started hitting the glass forcefully. It broke his heart to see her there, encaged, wanting to get at him.

"You're going to have to hang on, Molly. I can't let you into Nurania yet. I don't know what might happen."

He wondered whether the window was a good idea. It seemed cruel to inform her that there was a world outside her habitat.

"Fill the window with opaque bamboo wall, the same material used for the rest of the wall."

The window vanished, replaced with bamboo wall that blended flawlessly into the whole of the mesa wall.

"Insert Hank the Handler into Molly's habitat. Jack out."

Raymond found himself in the amber glow of the v-chamber again. He took a deep breath, trying to shake off the image of Molly banging on the window.

"Sleep. I need sleep."

He stripped and crawled into bed, turning off the lights with a voice command. He felt hot and cold at the same time. He balled himself up in the fetal position, trying to fight off the shivers of exhaustion.

CHAPTER 12

After about half an hour of tossing and turning, his mind racing with thoughts of how to get rid of the motor home, Raymond heard Scorpio announce an urgent message from an FBI agent named Berman.

"Play it."

A man with a droning nasal voice informed him that his presence was required at the lab, no later than 3:00 PM. Raymond looked and saw that it was 12:15 PM now.

There would be no time for sleep.

"You also have a message from Anya."

"Play it."

Anya's voice came over the speakers, asking where he was and whether he was okay. She had tried to contact him at the lab, but he wasn't there.

"Tell her I'm sleeping. I'll see her at 3:00, at the lab."

He spent the next couple of hours making arrangements to dispose of the motor home. He found a black-market buyer who specialized in such business. "Buyer" was an ironic term, as Raymond would have to give up the motor home and pay a handsome fee on top of that. But the deal was quick and relatively painless. In a few days, the motor home would deliver itself to its new owner. It was to be delivered to a repair shop in nearby Ypsilanti, called Jim's Garage. Officially, an insurance company would pay for the vehicle, as if totaled in an accident. It would be stripped of all personal belongings, painstakingly cleaned, and either scrapped or put into service doing who knows what. Raymond decided he would worry about selling the land itself after he uploaded, if at all.

Then there was the matter of getting the second NBC to the bunker. Raymond called his delivery robot to the motor home, loaded the cardboard box into its cargo bay, and scheduled a second nighttime delivery to Property Disposition. If all went well, the NBC would arrive at the bunker early the following morning.

"Mosby." It was Scorpio's voice, coming from Raymond's wrist relay. "You're expected at the lab in fifteen minutes."

Raymond stood in his bedroom, staring at his v-chamber. He was struck by how odd it was to hear his wrist relay while in his motor home. Typically, he would have been contacted via the motor home's comm system, but cleanup routines were rapidly depersonalizing the entire motor home. His v-chamber would soon know nothing of Nurania, nothing of his underworld dealings. The shake machine would have no record of his preferences. The climate control system would be restored to factory defaults. From the kitchen came sounds of robot components twitching, humming, clicking through the self-tests that followed deprogramming.

It occurred to Raymond that Scorpio had contacted him by his secret name, without first confirming that it was safe to communicate openly.

"Scorpio, this location is no longer safe. The lab isn't safe." Raymond paused. The digital heart of his home was being dismantled. "Nowhere is safe."

"Acknowledged. Records updated accordingly."

Raymond suddenly craved a favorite song, an old song sung by a woman, in a language he believed to be Bulgarian. He didn't have many artistic associations, but this song had a strong connection for him. It represented the sad isolation he now felt—the hollow, ringing, cutting comprehension of how far apart he was from the rest of the world. He wanted to hear it, to have it reflect and amplify his state of being, but even his music collection was gone from here now, wiped out by the cleanup routines.

"Ten minutes," said Scorpio.

"Okay," said Raymond. "No time for self-indulgence."

He looked around at his depersonalized home and felt like a ghost, already departed. For a moment he didn't like the feeling, but he quickly turned it inside out. He was going to a better place. Separation from this place gave him a sense of power.

"It's like flying," he said to himself. "This is me getting off the ground."

He grabbed his coat and left.

As Raymond approached the lab, he saw that there was a crowd outside the front doors. Students mostly, but there was a media truck in the parking lot, and several police cars. He thought about trying the service entrance, but it would surely be closed. He rode onto the sidewalk and started to dismount while coasting in, standing on his left pedal. He wondered again how much information the FBI had on him. And the police. And Murray. Were they all cooperating? Might they arrest him on the basis of his sketchy past? They couldn't, legally, but was that enough to stop them?

What did it matter? He was in too deep to run.

Murray—shit, I never went back to my apartment.

As he walked his bike through the heart of the crowd, escorted by FBI agents, all eyes were on him. Media bots swarmed mid-air in front of him, bumping and edging contentiously for the most effective angle. An angry-looking man in his 30s glowered at Raymond and called him an ape killer. Others repeated the epithet. The slur meant nothing in particular to him, but he was unprepared for the emotional impact of a mob. One particularly tough-looking undergrad girl, dressed in black and green, her eyes filled with youthful rage, spat out a single word as he passed: "cannibal". He recognized her intent, and unthinkingly shot her a dirty look. It was a reference to an underground animation about a villainous man with a destructive-upload device, shaped like a 20th-century canister vacuum with a piranha-head attachment. The man goes about sucking people up with his scanner, uploading them into little edible storage devices, then eating the wafers, believing he will somehow gain "massive karma" by doing so. Raymond wished he could stop and debunk all the deliberately twisted imagery used to portray uploading in underground art.

People from the media shouted questions at him, which he ignored completely. He wondered whether such questions ever provoked response. He stared straight ahead and proceeded down the lane opened for him by FBI agents. As he reached the edge of the crowd closest to the lab, a face caught his eye. It was Murray.

"You weren't home," he said, raising his voice only slightly, to be heard over the noise of the crowd. And Raymond couldn't help but hear. "You weren't home," repeated Murray, "and you weren't at your girlfriend's. Do you know who *was* at your girlfriend's?"

Raymond looked at the door of the lab, determined to show no further response. He had always wondered why such mobs even tried to get a reaction, when it seemed so easy to ignore them. He understood now how difficult it is not to take the bait when the mob really knows their quarry.

o-----------------------------o

Inside the lobby, one of the agents took Raymond's bike, assuring him it would be well looked-after, and directed him to the conference room. Raymond struggled out of his jacket as he walked through the halls. The conference room was as full as Raymond had ever seen it. Everyone on the team was present, as were several more FBI agents. It was standing-room only. Bob stood at the far end of the room, next to a young man in a white shirt, Agent Michaels. Several others stood around, leaning against the walls. There were scattered conversations, but voices were lower than usual.

Raymond spotted Anya, standing at the end opposite Bob, and headed toward her. She turned, and her face melted into a look at once worried and accusing, her eyes appealing but her head-tilt one of worried aggravation.

"Sorry," he whispered to her. "I was up so late, I needed the sleep."

"Who is this Arnold Murray character, and who the hell is Nicholas Tate? You look awful. Have you slept at all?"

Agent Michaels directed another agent to close the doors, and the room fell silent, saving Raymond from having to respond immediately.

"I'm Connor Michaels. I am an agent of the Federal Bureau of Investigation, and I will be heading this investigation." He paused, his slowly fidgeting fingers the only sign of his nerves. "Now, I don't know what you may have heard thus far, but chances are there is already a great deal of misinformation, so I'm going to run through the events that have occurred."

He went on to lay out the events of the night before, as reported by Bob and Raymond and as recorded by the building's security systems. He presented the details in a circumspect manner befitting a detective. Raymond soon tuned out, looking about the room. The agents mostly had their eyes closed, probably taking the opportunity to review case data via retinal implants. But everyone else watched Michaels with rapt attention. Raymond noticed a closed metal case on the table in front of Michaels and wondered what it might be.

No Brody.

Raymond looked around the room again.

No police at all—just FBI. And no mention of cooperation with the State Police.

"We have collected and analyzed all data in the building's security systems," said Michaels. "Here's a brief clip of the perpetrators breaking into the building."

On the same big screen where Raymond had first seen Michaels that morning, his own carefully crafted break-in footage now played. Michaels narrated the clips. Several people gasped when the footage of the activists destroying the NBCs was played. Raymond looked around the room and felt the collective shock of the team.

God I hope I know what I'm doing.

"Based on these recordings," said Michaels, "we believe this was a crime of very focused destruction. The criminals appear to know where they are going, and they do not destroy anything other than these two thus far unused NBCs. It would seem these units were selected because they were not hosting uploaded minds. The perpetrators worked with a degree of expertise uncommon among criminal activists. Thus far, no organization has come forward to claim this as a victory of their own, although many have expressed ideological support.

"Now, it is Bureau policy—and, frankly, basic investigative policy—to expect inside help in a job like this. I'm not making any accusations here, but I want you all to bear this possibility in mind as you reflect on what has happened here. This is a crime of grave proportions, and any assistance in identifying those responsible will be greatly appreciated."

Michaels stepped up to the table and opened the metal case. He turned it around so everyone could see its contents. Inside were rows upon rows of plain metal rings.

"Surveillance rings," muttered Raymond.

"Did I hear someone say 'surveillance rings'?" asked Michaels. Raymond was taken aback. There was no way Michaels could have heard him from across the room. Raymond looked around for a moment, then realized that Michaels had indeed heard him, somehow. Without waiting for a response, Michaels continued.

"That's right. These are surveillance rings. As suspects, you will all be required to wear one. Until this investigation is over, you may not take off your ring for any reason. These rings will record and broadcast your location and your heart rate. If you are caught travelling more than fifty miles from the crime scene without FBI authorization, you will be arrested and placed in FBI custody for up to thirty days. Does anyone have any questions?"

"Yeah," said Anya. "I have a question. What ever happened to civil liberties?"

"I will say again that you are all now suspects in a Federal investigation. These rings serve to prevent you from escaping due investigation. I will provide you all with documentation explaining your rights, but I want to clear up some popular misinformation regarding surveillance rings. They have no audio or video capture capabilities. They won't record your conversations, they won't record your activities—I assure you, they are in no way an invasion of privacy."

Anya nodded in false acceptance, and a murmur went around the room. Bob took the opportunity to examine his shoes.

"Now," continued Michaels, "I will say it again. You are not to remove your ring at any time. If the ring loses contact with your skin, agents will be deployed to locate and retrieve you immediately. Don't take it off in the shower, don't take it off to go swimming. If you do, you're in for a surprise. Removal of your ring with intent to escape FBI surveillance is grounds for arrest and is in and of itself a crime subject to penalty of up to one year in prison."

Again a murmur went around the room. But as Agent Michaels called people up, one at a time, he met with no resistance. When it was Raymond's turn, his body seemed to move without his willing it to do so. To falter now would be a tacit admission of guilt. He placed his right hand in the silver finger-measurement mitten, as everyone before him had done.

"Which finger?" asked the agent helping Michaels.

"Middle." It was as close as he was ever likely to come to giving the FBI the finger, in person.

A ring was customized on the spot. It was a plain metallic band, still warm as it was slid over his finger.

"Raymond." It was Bob. Raymond looked up and saw genuine apology in his eyes. "I'm sorry you're so wrapped up in this, and I want to thank you for everything you've done. Since you were here this morning, you don't have to stay for the one-on-one interviews."

"Okay. Thanks." Raymond started to turn away, then stopped. "Hey, I noticed Officer Brody isn't here."

"Yeah, she's… she won't be on the case anymore."

Raymond nodded, as if this made sense.

"Thanks again," said Bob. "I'll be in touch if we need you here again."

"You mean…"

"If you haven't heard from me, you don't need to come in on Monday. The project is on hold."

"Oh," said Raymond. "Okay."

He walked the length of the room, back to his spot, spinning the ring, looking at the ground. Inside, he felt as though four new walls of the ever-tightening trap had just fallen around him. Yet, somehow, he was still confident he could escape.

Anya looked at him expectantly.

"I've already been through the questioning," said Raymond, "so, Bob said I could go."

"No way are you getting out of here without some explanation. Raymond, a private investigator came to my apartment looking for you."

"It's nothing," he assured her. Raymond wanted to grill her for details—what did Murray ask her, and what did she tell him? But he knew she'd sense his concern, his guilt. And what did it matter, anyway? "It's an old missing person case," he whispered, "about this old man I used to work for. That's the Nicholas Tate he mentioned. I just happened to be one of the last people who saw him."

"Why does that not make me feel any better?"

Raymond was keenly aware of the presence of people around them, and of Michael's heightened ability to hear.

"Listen," he said in a lowered voice, "I can tell you about it later, when—"

"And somehow this has never come up before?" Anya lowered her voice, too, sensitive to Raymond's desire for privacy, but her frustration came through no less clearly.

"I didn't want…" Raymond drifted off, not sure what to say. He was tired of having his history exposed. "Listen, this isn't the place. Can we talk about it later?"

"Oh, we're gonna talk. And you're not going to like it."

She turned and walked away, excusing herself as she slid between people to get to the other side of the room. Raymond watched her go. He wanted to respond with righteous anger, but found himself struck sullen. He noticed Suma looking at him, surprised and questioning. He shook his head and shrugged—as if Anya were being needlessly dramatic. But inside, he felt her justification all too fully, and the shame of it staggered him. Tears rushed to his eyes, and with long strides he fled the room.

In the hallway, he broke into a run. His office was still off limits, and he wasn't sure where to go. He turned the corner, headed toward the lobby, and saw that there was still a crowd outside. *His* crowd—for his actions had brought them here. He hated his crowd. He veered to his right, and leaned heavily into the wall, wishing he could disappear.

He closed his eyes and wiped the scant tears on his shirt sleeve. He pictured himself with Anya, in her apartment, being pushed out by her attacking words as she berated and insulted him. And he, deserving it all, thrust out of the life of this beautiful, beneficent woman. Murray's words, "Do you know who was at your girlfriend's," echoed in his head. He had perceived them as an empty jab, but what if there had been someone else there? What if she had already started seeing someone else, trying to stanch her disappointment by finding someone better? He ran through the list of men in her life and pictured her kissing them, taking off her clothes for them, putting her hand on them as she had him, to see if she made them hard. Hatred and jealousy stirred nausea in his stomach and turned his mouth dry. He felt on the verge of throwing up.

"Sir, your bicycle."

Raymond opened his eyes to see a young FBI agent, about his age, offering him his bicycle. Raymond thanked him, and the man discretely returned to his post in the lobby.

Raymond took a deep breath and started rolling his bike down the hall. He was through with Anya, he told himself—he was headed for a new life. A new life, free of his past.

As he rolled his bike out the front door, the young agent came to his side, mouthing words into an unseen microphone, and escorted him out of the building. Raymond lifted his head and looked through the crowd, past them, to the trees in the distance, at the entrance to North Campus. He noticed a man moving across the front of the crowd toward him—Murray again—and continued to look into the distance ahead.

"I saw your mother," said Murray, raising his voice to be heard over chants of "ape-killer". Murray walked in parallel with Raymond, to his right, on the other side of the FBI ribbon. "I went to the Hyde Park Recovery Center. That's where your mother lives—did you know that?"

Raymond walked faster. Murray couldn't keep up with him, having to push his way through the crowd. As Raymond reached the far edge of the crowd, he swung onto his bike and engaged the motors.

o------------------------------o

Raymond sat in his black silk bathrobe, alone, on his rented black fake-leather sofa, his feet folded underneath him, staring at the undecorated white wall of his Kingsley apartment. The shades were drawn and the lights were off; the darkness was a semi-successful attempt at muting the stark emptiness of his essentially uninhabited space. He looked down at the surveillance ring on his finger, which he had idly been spinning.

There was a rapping at the door, for about the thirtieth time. When Raymond had arrived at his apartment, he had stripped and gone straight to bed. But he had never quite managed to fall asleep. The loud knocking, accompanied by Murray's south-Chicago accent, had begun just as he began to drift. His wrist relay started going off soon thereafter, with the text message, "I know you're in there."

"He's not going away," said Raymond to himself. He unfolded his legs, arose from the couch, and padded silently across the thickly carpeted floor to the front door. He left the chain in place and opened it a couple of inches.

"Murray," he said through the door, squinting at the light, "if you don't go away, I'll call the FBI."

Raymond felt a cold draft along his thigh and wrapped his robe more tightly around him.

"I had the good fortune of meeting your mother," said Murray.

"Yes, you mentioned that. Now go away."

"Your mother. Don't you want to hear how she is?"

Raymond looked off to the side, exasperated. Perhaps if the man had a chance to blabber on for a while, he would go away.

"She didn't have much to say," continued Murray, "but she seemed like a good woman. A good woman who's experienced a lot of pain." He paused, looking Raymond in the eye. Raymond accidentally met his gaze for a moment, then looked away again. "You don't know your mother very well, do you Raymond?"

Raymond felt a mix of anger and embarrassment rise within him. He focused on keeping a straight face. He noticed that his lips had tightened; with some effort, he was able to relax the muscles.

"This isn't about my mother."

"No, no, granted. But you know something, Raymond? You can tell a lot about a person by getting to know his parents. And getting a sense of how he feels about his parents. I had the opportunity to look through the visitation records for your mother, and I didn't see your name. Not once."

Raymond stood still, trying to show no reaction. "Mr. Murray, I don't appreciate you probing into my personal life. If you want to ask me about Mr. Tate and the work that I did for him, that's fine."

"She didn't talk about you. I thought that was pretty interesting. You know what she talked about?"

Raymond looked down at his bare feet, which were getting rather chilly, expecting Murray to answer his own question. The silence was irritating. He finally looked up. Murray raised his eyebrows slightly. Raymond fell for it. His mouth opened and words came out.

"Okay, what did she talk about?"

"Death," said Murray, nodding. "She talked about death."

Again, a long pause. Raymond responded, his restraint failing him.

"Sure. My mother's probably terrified of death. She's so weak, so selfish."

"Quite the opposite. I've found that troubled, broken-down people *crave* death. What terrifies them isn't death—it's *dying*. The pain you have to go through on the way to death. It's killers who fear death itself."

Oh, so this is where he's going.

"Killers," repeated Murray, drawing the word out for emphasis. "As a matter of honor. Or ego. They don't want to end up in the same place as the people they killed. I guess it's sort of a failure complex." Murray shifted his weight, leaning slightly nearer. "Now I'm not talking about thugs or heat-of-the-moment killers. I'm talking about the thinking kind. The kind who rationalize their crime."

"I'm sure this is all very interesting for you. Sounds like you have a pretty morbid job."

"It can be morbid. Sure." Murray's attitude changed abruptly, and he took a step back. "I've done a fair amount of homicide work. Lots of bodies." He turned to the side. "Have you ever thought about what you would do with the body, if you killed someone?" The sun glinted through Murray's breath.

Raymond tightened up. Now more than ever, he knew Murray was looking for a reaction.

"Um, no? When I was a kid, maybe. You know, kids like to talk about gruesome technical stuff. I remember this kid asking me whether you could vaporize someone with a laser."

Raymond felt like his answer had come off well. But how sharp was this guy? Could he see facial motions that Raymond couldn't even feel himself making? Did some eye movement or head nod give away the fact that this was, in fact, a matter to which he had given a great deal of thought? Maybe Murray had surveillance equipment that recorded and analyzed facial expressions and verbal intonations.

"Listen, I'm tired, I'm getting cold, and…" Raymond's wrist relay vibrated. "You're wasting my time."

Raymond looked down and saw a text message: "Meeting request from Manolo." He looked at it for a moment. This was the text message of a direct contact. Manolo had never contacted him directly.

"We're not quite done yet," said Murray.

"I'm sorry, I need to answer this message."

"I'll just be a few more—"

"No," interrupted Raymond. "This is ridiculous. There's no reason I have to put up with the third degree from some morbid, pseudo-psychological PI. If you need my help with your case, email me your questions and I'll be happy to answer them."

"I'll tell you something," said Murray. "I think you know more about what happened to Nicholas Tate, and you should get it off your chest. You're a young man, Mr. Quan. Guilt does strange things to a person. You're a young man," he repeated. "You don't want your whole life to be tainted by guilt. Happy people are innocent people."

Raymond closed the door.

"Get rid of the guilt," shouted Murray, "or it will *define* you."

As Raymond walked to his bedroom, his wrist relay went off again. It was Anya.

"Hello?" said Raymond, loading the word rather more than he had intended.

"Raymond, we need to talk. Can I see you?"

"No. I mean, not right now. I don't need to listen to…" He trailed off, not liking where he was headed. He was automatically trying to make her look like the bad guy, and he wanted to be bigger than that.

"What, listen to me bitch about how you hide everything from me, how you run—"

"No, Anya, Anya. No! That's not what I meant. I'm sorry. I feel like I've… reached a turning point."

"Good for you, Raymond. I hope you have. But I can't take it anymore. I was afraid there was something big behind all the mystery. And there is, isn't there? I should have known better. I guess I thought you just needed to be brought out, to be loved. But I can't take being lied to, being left in the dark. I'm sorry Raymond. I don't think I can spend time with you right now. And I can't see how we're going to do the Thanksgiving thing. I don't know. I think I need to be away from you for a while."

"Okay."

Silence.

"Okay?" asked Anya.

"Yes. Okay. I can see why you're fed up. You're good and caring and patient. You've reached out to me. And I can't open up. You want a sharing, healthy relationship, and I can't give you that."

"Yes, that's… pretty much right," she said skeptically.

"You don't get enough back from me," continued Raymond. He hadn't thought through much of this, but he suddenly felt as though he were holding a model of their relationship at arm's length, describing its obvious flaws. "You want a healthy relationship, and you've found someone better." An accusatory edge slipped into his voice; the model turned to dust.

"What? What do you mean I've found someone better?"

"You have, haven't you?"

"Are you suggesting that I've been seeing someone else?"

"Well, have you?"

"What, did you see me having coffee with someone and conclude that the man must be a lover? Are you fucking watching me?"

Raymond felt very silly. The only basis he had for his accusation was a vague suggestive comment from a private investigator who was trying to get under his skin.

"That's it, Raymond. That is it! You're a fucking freak, and I can't deal with it anymore. I need to move on. Goodbye."

"I wasn't saying you were actually—"

The connection dropped.

"Fine!" yelled Raymond. "Fine. I *am* a fucking freak. I'm a freak—I don't belong. It's time for *me* to move on, too. Goodbye, fucking world."

Twenty minutes later, Raymond was in a v-chamber arcade. The manager, a college kid for whom Raymond had done some favors over the years, was happy to let Raymond patch an encryption module onto one of the v-chambers and reroute its network connection, no questions asked. Raymond fired up the old chamber and—as Celia—was soon in Celia's repair shop in Delta Nuevo. Rats scattered when he turned the lights on. He hadn't been to the shop in ages. He was a little surprised that his lease was still good. The auto-renew feature must have actually worked. He paced now, nervous, wondering why Manolo would want to meet.

The buzzer seethed and popped, followed by the sound of skittering rodents. Raymond walked downstairs, checked the security screen, and saw Manolo standing just outside.

"Come in."

Raymond gestured for Manolo to lead up the stairs, then followed.

"Your tools are dusty. You *have* been away a long time, haven't you."

"No, I hire a service to spread a fine layer of dust everywhere."

Manolo paid no heed to his sarcasm. He wandered, looking about, picking up tools and inspecting them with a degree of interest that struck Raymond as an affectation.

"So," said Manolo, turning a small radial cutter in his hand, "I did a little research into your background. Looks like you've covered your tracks pretty well through the years. You came up pretty clean. According to Bureau records, you live at 727 East Kingsley Drive."

"I've been careful."

"But not careful enough… or you wouldn't have come to me." Manolo turned and faced him straight on. "So what is it? It's something to do with this upload project you're working on."

As careful as Raymond had been, so much of his life was out in the open. All it took was an IID, and Manolo could discover his real name, his address history, his place of employment, his school records—and much more. And of course Manolo would know about the upload project—it was all over the news. Raymond chose not to respond. He took a deep breath and narrowed his gaze, wondering what Manolo's motive might be.

"So, let's see," continued Manolo, starting to wander around the shop again. "You want Bureau data scoured—you must be hiding from the Bureau. The Bureau is all over your little upload project, because of a network security breach and some missing hardware."

Raymond winced at the word "missing". Had Manolo surmised that the equipment was missing, or was it described that way in FBI reports? Raymond's false footage had shown the NBCs being bagged, smashed, and carried away. Had they not bought the footage after all?

"Very valuable hardware," continued Manolo. "The sort of thing one might want to steal. To sell, perhaps… but you don't seem the type. So I asked myself, 'Why else might he want top-dollar research hardware that he already had access to?' You want to take the research in your own direction, don't you? The journals all say you're years from being able to upload a human. Do you think that's true?"

"Absolutely."

"Really? *Years*? That's a shame. A lot of great people are going to die in the next few years—people who wouldn't have to die, if they could upload. Does that weigh on you?"

Raymond shrugged. "You get used to it, I guess. I mean, we're moving as fast as we can. But we don't know that it will ever work for humans. And with the ESW decision—"

"You realize what it would be worth, don't you? I'm not just talking money. What wouldn't a dying man give to drink from the digital fountain of youth? With the power to upload even one person, you would command the attention of the world's most powerful people. I mean truly powerful people—the likes of which you probably don't even know about. You don't realize what you have on your hands, do you? Of course not—how could you?"

"It's not like that," scoffed Raymond.

"No?" Manolo's keenly perceptive gaze slid past Raymond's every defense, inspecting his inner thoughts as easily as he did Celia's tools. "Are you sure?"

Raymond felt himself wither. He looked away, and he hated himself for being weak—for putting himself in a position where he was no longer in control.

"And then we have this motor home where you've been living," continued Manolo, stepping away again. "Parked on property owned by one Ivar Svensson. There's a motor home titled to Ivar Svensson, but there's no record of him—"

"Listen," interrupted Raymond, trying to assert himself. "I'm tired and my girlfriend just dumped me. Let's cut the bullshit. You've got a nice handful of puzzle pieces. You think you've got something on me, and what—you're looking for something more from me? Thus far, I've counted you as a friend, Manolo. I would hate to see you forfeit my good opinion of you."

Manolo smiled wickedly.

"What the hell do you want?" asked Raymond. "Cash? You've never struck me as a man hard-up for cash."

Manolo moved towards him, still holding the cutter. "You don't think I'd blackmail you, do you?"

Without breaking eye contact, Raymond made sure he knew where Manolo's hands were.

"To be perfectly candid, Manolo, you don't seem above blackmail."

Manolo laughed at this. "It's simple, Raymond. What I want is very simple. I want you to know…" He leaned forward and spoke into Raymond's ear. "… that I have you by the cojones."

Raymond leaned away and took a step back, still tracking Manolo's movements.

"I don't want you as an enemy," continued Manolo, relaxing his delivery. "Who needs more enemies? And I bet you could fuck a dude up pretty good. But when I need you as an ally… you catch my drift?"

"Sure." Raymond felt his muscles relax. "That's only reasonable. You've scratched my back. I know how it goes."

"Alright then. We have an understanding."

"Tell me one thing," said Raymond. "How much of all this does your man on the inside know?"

"Not a thing."

"And you still agree to all the cleanup we discussed?"

"Of course. It's taken care of. I just wanted to… make sure you understand my position."

Raymond nodded. "You make yourself very clear. Now, I'm sorry, but I really must be going."

"Not to worry. I can show myself out." Manolo walked to the top of the stairs, then turned. "I too am a busy man. Though perhaps not so desperate."

As soon as Raymond heard the door close behind Manolo, he looked to the ceiling, closed his eyes, and—shaking his head—quietly swore over and over.

He jacked straight out from Celia's shop, leaving her to clean the place up. He didn't much care what happened to her at this point. It was time to upload. He had every reason to leave this world, and only one reason to wait.

Raymond arrived at Anya's apartment on bike. As expected, he saw no light through the windows. She had left him a message, apologizing and saying she would be out for the evening with Suma, and maybe they could talk things through afterward. It was only 9:30 now, and she had said she would probably be back by 11:00, but Raymond knew she was rarely home before midnight from her outings with Suma. He rapped his cold knuckles on the door, to make sure she wasn't there. No answer.

Time to say goodbye.

He rolled his bike around back, crunching through dry leaves, and leaned it against the rear of the house, just beneath her kitchen window. Making sure the bike was stably situated, he stepped gingerly up onto the frame, bringing him level with the window. He lifted the screen up out of its slot, lowered it part way to the ground, and dropped it in such a way that it fell away from the house, to minimize noise. From within his jacket he produced a thin-bladed knife, a favorite tool he rarely had the opportunity to use. He slid it between the outer and inner frames of the old window and popped it up with the palm of his hand. Flakes of paint fell onto his wrist, felt ticklish against his skin. In less than a minute, he had the lock open and the window up. He returned the blade to its inner pocket and pulled himself through.

Once inside, he dusted himself off, closed the window behind him, and stood in the kitchen, listening. He heard slowly throbbing ambient music from the upstairs apartment. The quiet whining and whirring of Anya's old refrigerator. The ticking of the antique wall clock. Nothing to indicate that he was not alone.

He walked into her living room, tossed his jacket on the sofa, and entered her v-chamber. A soft yellow light filled the small interior space. The door closed behind him and the unit turned on, gently lifting him off the ground. The air warmed, his feet landed on what felt like a hard tile floor, and a room took form around him.

Bright morning light filtered through sheer white curtains that lifted and fell with a breeze. The air smelled of sea salt. Gulls could be heard outside, and the crash of ocean surf. The walls were papered with a quaint floral print of purple and yellow flowers.

The space had the architecture of an old home, but the décor of a commercial space. There was a wood-framed reception window in front of him, on the ledge of which sat an old-fashioned metal hotel bell. He looked around him. There were several doors, open windows at either end of the room, a narrow wooden staircase up to the second floor. Next to the hotel bell was a little iron business card holder. Raymond looked at the front card, noting that the elegant calligraphy was in a foreign language—Portuguese, he guessed.

"I'd like to leave a message for Anya," he said. He expected to be transferred to a standard v-chamber service interface, but there was no change.

"Admin mode," he said, hoping to bypass this program, which was apparently Anya's default interface. Instead, a short, smartly dressed, middle-aged woman stepped up behind the reception desk. Her black hair, streaked with gray, was pulled back tightly away from her face. Her movements were slow, but graceful and deliberate.

"I'm sorry, sir" she said in a warm, lush Portuguese accent. "I didn't hear you come in. Do you have a reservation?"

"I'd like to leave a message for Anya."

"Of course. Just a moment." The woman moved to one side and picked up a pen and paper.

"Oh please," moaned Raymond. That was not the sort of message he had in mind. "Exit world. Jack out. Close program."

The woman tilted her head and leaned toward Raymond, her eyes narrowed in a look of utter consternation.

"Exit bleeding world," said Raymond. "I want to leave a voice-visual message for Anya."

"Young man," scolded the woman, "there is no need for such language. There's a comm booth just down the beach. Out that door, to your right. It's just past the ice cream stand."

The door to which the woman pointed swung open, and in walked a Mediterranean-looking man, a little older than Raymond, with wavy black hair, wearing tailored light gray slacks and a loose-fitting white linen shirt, finely detailed with vertical stripes. The man entered smiling, but his appearance hardened as he comprehended the situation. He crossed to the reception booth and tentatively greeted the woman in what sounded to Raymond to be Portuguese.

"And I suppose," muttered Raymond, "that you're Anya's virtual Latin lover."

The man turned on Raymond and shot him a severe, disapproving look.

"Who are you," he asked in a thick accent, "and how do you know Anya?"

"Listen, can you tell me how to get out of this program?"

The man's look turned to one of exasperation. "There is a newbie entrance for a reason. Do you not know how to operate your v-chamber?"

"Very funny. As if you didn't know that this is Anya's v-chamber."

"How should I know whose…"

The man trailed off. It suddenly occurred to Raymond that Anya's default interface might be a public v-world, and that the man to whom he was speaking might be the avatar of a real person.

"But, you must be Raymond," said the man.

"I am so sorry. I, um, I mean, what I would like to know is how to exit this v-world."

"Hail a cab. Or go to the bathroom. Every cab and bathroom is a gateway."

"Right," replied Raymond, drawing the word out. He turned to the receptionist. "So, is there a bathroom I could use?"

Soon Raymond was out of the v-world, at a standard v-chamber interface, feeling vexed and embarrassed. And angry. He struggled to subdue his jealousy. For all he knew, the man was just some guy she had met online.

And at this point, what does it fucking matter?

"Voice-visual message for Anya," he instructed.

The space changed to look like a public comm booth. One wall was taken up by a feedback screen, on which he saw an image of himself. On the opposite wall was a plastic seat, bolted to the metal floor.

"You may begin," announced a generic female service voice.

"Could I get something a little less austere?" asked Raymond.

"Would you like to select from the menu of available comm booth environments?"

Raymond rolled his eyes.

"Will I be able to edit this when I'm done?"

"Yes," replied the woman. "Shall I start over?"

"No. No. Okay." Raymond shifted restlessly, looked at the floor, then at the feedback screen. "Well, Anya, I'm in your apartment, and you could walk in any minute, so I'd better get started. I wanted to give you a proper goodbye."

He had composed bits and pieces of his goodbye to Anya in his head, but he found himself drawing a blank now. He ran his hand through his hair.

I'm saying goodbye to Anya forever, and I have no idea what to say?

"Okay, start over," he instructed.

"Starting over. You may begin."

Raymond looked himself in the eyes and took a deep breath.

"Anya. If you're seeing this, then my attempt to upload failed. Which means I'm dead, I guess. And I'm sorry. I don't know how hard you're taking it. For all I know, you might feel relieved. Like you can move on, with a clean slate. No, I… Well, never mind that. I'm sorry I risked my life, and I want you to understand why I did it."

Raymond sat in the plastic chair and leaned forward heavily, his elbows on his knees.

"First of all, you should know how much I love you. I know I have a way of screwing things up. Things never seem to go quite right. I'm just not what you need in a man. I can't be. I hide too much, I know." He smiled, lowered his gaze momentarily. He was starting to feel like he was really speaking to Anya. "And I give too little, I guess." He nodded at this small self-realization. "You give a lot, and I give too little."

He leaned back and crossed his arms, his gaze drifting.

"I know it's gotta be frustrating for you—dealing with me, I mean. I've never been able to be open with you, partially with good reason. Now, I might die soon." He felt something catch in his throat. Saying it out loud, to another person, it suddenly seemed real.

He looked into the eyes of his mirror image. "I might die. I don't know if I've ever really understood what that means. And if you're seeing this… what I'm saying—it must be so frustrating, dealing with me. But you tried. You're the only person I ever came close to opening up to. I wish I could have. But… well, you're about to see why I couldn't."

He ran his hand through his hair again.

"Remember I told you how I grew up in state homes? When I was fifteen, living in the Canal Street Home, I got this job, as the groundskeeper/repairman for a rich old retiree—Nicholas Tate, the missing person that the PI was asking you about."

He told her a little about Tate's background, how he spent all his time in a v-chamber, and what it was like to work there.

"Once in a while, he would come upstairs and want to talk to me. He would ask me about my life, how bad things were at the Home. He was always fishing for gratitude. I think he wanted to feel good about himself, like he was doing something for the real world, like he felt guilty for all the time he spent in v-worlds.

"Tate set up a special account for ongoing expenses and gave me money to convert the garage into a workshop. I used some of the money on things for myself, but mostly I was just excited to have this awesome workshop."

Raymond recalled having wanted to switch some of the details around. He knew this recording would end up being used as evidence against him, and he wanted it to seem like Tate had died a couple years later than he really had; if the police knew when Tate had really died, none of the money-laundering Raymond had done early on would make sense. He shifted in his seat and continued, pretty sure he had the story straight in his head.

"When I turned 18, I was released from Canal Street, and Tate let me stay for a while in his house, until I could find an apartment. He made my job a full-time position, and he said I could work on my projects when I wasn't doing work on his house. Looking back, I guess he was pretty generous with me. I mean, by that time, I had the place running by itself, and I spent my time screwing around. I had all sorts of projects going. I was working on personality sims, natural language, robotics, a-life—that kind of stuff. I guess I was always interested in the line between man and machine.

"I started working on a persona replica of myself—I think I told you about it once. It became my obsession. I would spend entire days in Tate's old spare v-chamber, teaching my replica to be more like me. I eventually got it to a point where people in public v-worlds couldn't tell whether they were talking to me or it.

"It was when I discovered I could hack Tate's v-chamber that things took a bad turn."

He told the story of how he discovered he could hack Tate's v-chamber by tapping into the emergency recognition system.

"Once I had access to his v-chamber, I realized I could record his sessions and have an endless source of material for training a replica. I had no idea what I would *do* with a Tate replica. It was just this challenge, to make a copy of him without his knowing."

He chuckled and smiled.

"It turned out to be way harder than the replica of myself; Tate had like eighty years of life behind him. And he talked more. I tried new approaches, and I went deeper into the psychology than ever before. In the process, I discovered my Tate replica had learned Tate's bank access codes. I was tempted to drain off some funds for myself, but it seemed like a stupid risk. I mean, look at what I already had.

"A long time went by, and things were pretty good. Then, one morning, I got a medical alert on my wrist relay. I had never hooked Tate's v-chamber back up to the emergency medical network. I was afraid to—if there ever was an emergency, they might come to the house, and they would see I had hacked his v-chamber. I guess I figured someday I would finish the Tate replica, and *then* I'd remove my hack and make things right again."

Raymond crossed his arms over his chest and sat back. It felt weird to lay out his whole story to Anya, but he wanted to give the police everything they needed to close the case and be done with it.

"So I got this medical alert, and I didn't know what to do. What if he were to die? What would happen to me? Where would I go? Or could I not mention it, and just go on taking care of his house as if nothing had happened? It's not like anyone ever came to visit him in person, and his v-world relationships were mostly with people he paid for pleasure, or with gamers, and they wouldn't much care if he disappeared. In the few v-worlds where Tate did have real friends, my replica could just pick up where he left off, and nobody would know the difference. I could go on living on Tate's money… what was the harm?

"Of course, I wasn't sure he was really dying. What if it was just a minor heart attack? I went downstairs, scared as hell, and I opened his v-chamber. I didn't know what I'd do if he did need help, but… well, that turned out not to be an issue."

Raymond looked down, losing his train of thought as he remembered the old man, dead on the floor of the big v-chamber. He leaned forward and folded his hands.

"And that was it, Anya. All of a sudden, I was in the midst of serious crime. It wasn't murder, exactly, but the old man was dead. Negligent homicide, I guess. And then I made it look like he was still alive. I fed my Tate replica a story to cover for his brief absence, I taught it to make jokes about going senile whenever it was asked a question it didn't know the answer to, I gave it access to the v-worlds where Tate had friends, and I let it loose.

"That was August of '63," lied Raymond, careful to adhere to his false timeline. "I watched Tate's replica in action. Over time, I started to worry that it wasn't believable enough. The senile jokes came too often, and people seemed a little suspicious. I tweaked the replica to be more surly, to piss people off and make it seem like Tate was losing it. To drive people away. I gradually backed out of all remaining relationships. By the summer of '64, the replica was only online a couple times a week. I started to cash out his accounts, and I finally had the replica inform Tate's few living relatives that he had decided to run off with a woman and might never return.

"From that point on, my entire life was based on fraud."

Raymond stopped for a moment, looking himself in the eye.

"My entire life—fraud on top of fraud."

He shifted, collected himself.

"So, I had command of this fortune, but it was money I couldn't spend, or I might give myself away. I decided to lie low for a few years. I enrolled here at Michigan, with the goal of joining a research team where I could satisfy my love of personas and v-worlds. Then I heard about the upload project, and my dream of escape took form. Not escape from my crimes. I mean escape from a world that seemed like it had no place for me. Until I met you.

"Just when life started looking up, I learned Tate's nephews had hired a private investigator to look into the old man's disappearance. In fact, it was on the Friday we first made plans to do yoga together that I found out the missing person case had been reopened. I kept tabs on the investigation. For a while, it seemed like they had nothing new on me. Then the missing person case started to look like a homicide case, and I knew I had to move fast. If I'm caught, my prison sentence could be ten years. Probably way longer, with all the hacking and fraud. And who knows what they might do to my brain, in the name of behavioral reform."

Raymond paused and took a deep breath. He was through with the spin and the lies. He was just talking to Anya now.

"I probably shouldn't have let our relationship go as far as it did. As soon as I found out the case had been reopened, I should have ended it. But I couldn't help myself, Anya—I'm in love. I know you could probably never love me, after all this. I can't blame you. I mean, look at who I really am. You're probably kicking yourself for ever even liking me. But I… I want you to know that I love you, as much as someone like me can, I guess. Being with you, I've seen what it feels like to be close to someone. I feel like you made me a real person, for the first time in my life. If my past were different, maybe… maybe things would have worked out between you and me. I don't know. Maybe, years from now, we would have uploaded together. I wanted it to work. It just… couldn't. And now you know why."

Raymond moved to stand up, then realized he had forgotten the original impetus for making this recording. There was one more lie to be told.

"Oh—hey. What's left of Tate's money is in an offshore account. If you get this message, then I won't be needing it. Please forward this message to the Ann Arbor police, and make sure it makes it to Arnold Murray. He has a reward coming."

In actuality, most of Tate's money lay in the accounts of Ivar Svensson. What he had doled out for Tate's nephews was a fraction of the original fortune. Raymond rattled off all the information for the account, so that Tate's relatives would be able to access it. He only hoped it was enough to satisfy their greed, to bring Murray's investigation to a close.

"Well, that's it. I'm glad I got a chance to tell you all this. If I'm lucky, you'll never even see this. But, you know, it felt good just to spill it all. It's been locked up inside me, all this time, and now it's free. If I'd never met you, it would have remained locked up forever. I hope everything that sucks about me makes sense now. It doesn't make me any less fucked up, but at least now you know."

A surge of sentimental intensity welled up within him. His eyes started to water. He opened them wide, swallowed hard, and looked off to the side, trying to shake it off.

"I guess that's it. Goodbye Anya."

He stood up.

"Stop recording."

o----------------------------o

He configured the message to be delivered in three days, then stood awhile, taking in the gravity of the moment. His outpouring left him feeling wrung out.

It would be nice to rest a bit in Anya's apartment. He checked his wrist relay and saw he still had plenty of time before she was due back. He stepped out of the v-chamber. Cautiously, he shuffled through the dark living room to the sofa, touched the cushion to make sure there was nothing on it, and sat down. He took his shoes off, folded his legs beneath him. Drawing in long breaths, he concentrated on calming his mind, absorbing the slow easy groove of the ambient music that still played in the apartment above. The darkness of the room felt warm and fluid. He drank it in. The world felt close around him, and he welcomed its contact. He imagined Anya curled up next to him, her head in his lap, awake but silent.

Tonight—tonight I upload. I'll never be in this apartment again. I'll never see Anya again.

He looked around the room. Everything seemed so placid. He turned the surveillance ring on his finger, around and around. He focused on the feeling of the smooth metal gliding over his sweaty skin as he slid the ring down over his knuckle and back.

I wonder if I'll sweat when I'm uploaded.

A peaceful acceptance of his imminent departure swept through him. He was ready to leave. He imagined the calm within him as sand settling out of water, turbulent water allowed to swirl itself to stillness. He sat back and closed his eyes, just for a moment.

Raymond was jarred out of sleep by the sound of keys in the front door. He sat up with a jerk, seized for a second by panic. It was too late—if he ran out now, Anya might be weirded out and call the police. He slipped his shoes on, then attempted to settle back down, but tension lingered in his shoulders and neck. He would just tell her he came over to talk.

He heard an unexpected voice, a woman's voice. The door opened.

"I don't know, Anya." Raymond recognized it as Suma's voice. "I'd rather see you with someone more—"

The light turned on, and Suma was cut short by the sight of Raymond. Anya started, letting out a small gasp.

"Raymond!" scolded Anya. "You surprised me!"

Raymond stirred, sat up. "I'm sorry."

"Wait a minute. How the hell did you get in here?"

Raymond shrugged his shoulders playfully. "It's not tough."

"Maybe I should go?" offered Suma.

"You broke into my apartment?" shouted Anya, ignoring Suma.

Raymond shrugged again, this time as if about to explain something away. But he didn't know what to say. He was stuck at the disconnect between the clean getaway he had planned and the excruciating situation he had gotten himself into.

"Raymond, you can't just break into my apartment! Jesus Christ! If I wanted you to come and go as you pleased, I'd give you some bleeding keys!"

"I said I'm sorry," said Raymond miserably. He stood up. "I'll go, okay?"

"No, that's not okay!" yelled Anya. "Every time there's the slightest hint of conflict, you decide it's time to leave! I'm tired of it! How about you grow a pair of balls and actually talk to me for once!"

I just did.

Raymond melted into utter despair, staring at the wall.

"Listen," said Suma, trying to make her exit.

"Raymond," said Anya, her voice softening somewhat, "what were you thinking?"

"I…" He trailed off. He wanted to tell her it would all make sense in a few days, but he knew that such mystery would just make things worse.

Suma started to leave, but Anya stopped her. "Wait, Suma. Let me give you the book." Anya crossed the living room and selected a book from one of her bookshelves. Raymond looked to Suma, embarrassed. He sought some sort of consolation, but she simply looked away.

Raymond wanted to get away. This was the last time he would ever see Anya, and all he wanted to do was leave. He felt like he was drowning in his own dysfunction. He sizzled with angry disappointment, and was completely at a loss for how to express it. As Anya walked back and handed Suma the book, he realized that Suma would leave in a few seconds, and he would be alone with Anya. He saw no good outcome in staying. And Suma's words echoed in his head: "I'd rather see you with someone more…"

He grabbed his jacket from the sofa and headed for the door.

"No you don't!" admonished Anya.

Raymond continued to the door, then turned.

"I wish things could have been different, Anya." He stepped outside and slammed the door behind him. He walked down the porch stairs, pulling his jacket on as he walked, then started around to the back of the house to get his bike. He heard the front door open. "Raymond!" called Anya, her tone loaded with a frustrated plea.

Raymond turned around. It wasn't Anya's voice that stopped him. He had seen something. A car, parked just down the street, with two dark figures inside. As he watched, the doors of the car opened.

"Raymond, what's wrong?" asked Anya from the porch. "What are you looking at?"

That's it. They're onto me.

Raymond hesitated no longer. It was the FBI, or Murray—he didn't care which. As he took off around back, a light shone on him from behind. He broke into a sprint. Around the corner of the house. His bike still rested against the building. He grabbed the handlebars, swung onto the bike, and pedaled hard. He started to go around the house the other way, but heard footsteps—they had split up, coming around either side of the house.

Raymond heard Anya yelling his name. She sounded scared.

"He's on this side," said one of the men. "Sounds like he's on a bike."

The man's voice was close. Raymond made a split-second judgement—he was trapped. If the man had a gun, he would have plenty of time to make a clean shot.

Raymond tweaked a burst of the bike's motors and raced forward, straight for the corner of the house. The man came into view, weapon raised.

"Freeze!"

In one perfectly timed motion, Raymond lifted his weight onto the handlebars and nailed the bike's front brakes. He shot head-first through the air and smashed into the man, landing his elbow in the man's face and his knee in the man's stomach. An instant after the impact, a shot was fired. Raymond heard Anya scream in terror.

When Raymond hit the ground, his knee ended up in the man's chest, and he felt ribs crack. Raymond's momentum carried him sliding forward, past the man, and his bike landed in the grass next to him. The man rolled onto his side, groaning in pain, and reached around to fire on Raymond again. But Raymond was too fast. He spun around on all fours, out of the line of fire, and pulled the blade from his jacket. He leapt on the man like a cat and brought the point of the blade down on the man's gun arm. The fine alloy blade slid through muscle and into the soil. Raymond grabbed the gun from the man's hand, stuffed it under the waistline of his pants, and scrambled for his bike.

From the corner of his eye, Raymond saw the second man come tearing back around the front of the house, gun in hand. Raymond ducked his head down and ran his bike back along the side of the house. Anya screamed "Raymond" over and over. A shot was fired, and Raymond felt a streak of burning pain across his right shoulder.

Behind Anya's house was a low concrete wall, on the far side of which was a parking lot for a small apartment complex. Raymond sped toward this low wall and dexterously swung his bike over it. He pedaled between two parked cars, turned, and engaged the motors. The bike surged forward. He braked hard, turned down the alley that led to Liberty Street, and revved the motors again.

Liberty was a robot-only street, clearly marked by a strip of blue lights down the center of each lane. A light traffic of unmanned delivery vehicles, big and small, flowed ceaselessly in both directions, wirelessly communicating their locations and intentions to one another. Typically, any non-robotic vehicle would cause traffic to stop, as a safety precaution—a problem Raymond had solved long ago.

"Robot mode," he said into his jacket. His jacket communicated with his bike, which silently joined into the radio chatter of the robots. He slipped into traffic, fell in behind a large truck, and issued another command into his jacket collar: "Robot shadow". The bike locked in on the closest vehicle—the truck—and used its navigational communications to shadow it, allowing Raymond to safely tail the truck as long as he wanted. He reached back and felt his shoulder, assessing the wound. It stung like hell, and his hand came back bloody, but he still had full strength and range of motion.

The men who were after him were almost certainly FBI. And if the FBI were onto him, they would probably disable his access to the lab. They might even have agents at the lab before he could get there. But his only chance of escape was uploading. He had narrowed his own options to one, and it was now or never.

He suddenly remembered the surveillance ring. He glanced at his hand, on the handlebars: the ring was gone.

The ring. Shit—they weren't onto me. My ring must have come off. I must have been playing with it while I was sleeping, and it came off, and they were sent to find me.

He screamed "fuck" at the top of his lungs and revved the bike. He pulled into the middle of the street and pushed the bike as fast as it would go, zipping between robot vehicles inches away on either side.

Maybe there's still a chance. Maybe they won't expect me to head to the lab.

Suma's words came back to him. "I'd rather see you with someone more…" More what? More open? More giving? More mature? More healthy? More balanced? More socially acceptable? Suma could see he wasn't right for Anya. He'd always been a misfit. Soon, he'd either be dead or living in a world where he didn't have to fit in—where he could make the world fit him.

One problem, two possible solutions—each as elegant as the other.

He streaked across town, reaching speeds that exceeded his capacity to control the bike. He was aware of occasional glider traffic overhead, but not once did he see a search light. He heard sirens in the distance, but they didn't seem to be following him. And he was moving too fast to allow him to check behind him. Traffic on the road to North Campus was light, allowing him to cut across lanes as he pursued the optimal line through the sweeping curves. He was relentless in his pursuit of speed, exhilarated by his utter fearlessness.

The lab came into view. There were no sirens, no hovering police gliders, no agents at the door. He jumped the curb and skidded along the sidewalk to the entrance. The door opened at his approach. He glanced behind him and saw nothing.

He ran down the hall, ducked under investigation tape, and proceeded straight to the scanning room. The doors recognized him and opened. He cast his bike aside and walked directly to his post at the scanner controls. His heart raced, his body ached, his face tingled with windburn.

"What the hell," he said aloud. "They really weren't onto me after all." He pulled out the stolen gun and set it down, logged into the controller, and started the scanner warm-up process.

"Commencing warm-up," announced the female computer voice.

He started to strip his clothes off. He would have to apply some of the derms now and just hope he could work through the haze of anesthetics. He stepped into the animal prep room and started going through cabinets. "Derms, derms, derms," he said, digging through labeled boxes. He found the stack he was looking for, grabbed an armload of boxes, and took them back into the scanning room.

As he started to apply derms to his calves, he checked to make sure the nightly source-code backup was still scheduled for 3 AM, as this was his ticket past the FBI lock-down. He noted that most scheduled processes had been disabled, probably to make the investigators' lives easier. But they hadn't touched the source backup, because it included the result logs of ongoing tests. He configured the scanner to send a copy of his scan data to the test results datastore, without logging the copy action. He then rewrote from memory a simple cleanup script, to cover his tracks.

"What the hell?" called out a man from behind him.

Raymond grabbed the gun and whirled around. Bob stood in the doorway. Raymond aimed the gun at him.

"Lock down the building, Bob."

"You're nuts if you think this is going to work."

"Lock down the fucking building!"

"Take it easy. It's just you and me, Raymond."

"Bullshit. Lock it down or I blow your fucking head off. I know the FBI tightened this place down. Let's have it."

Bob issued a series of commands to seal all entrances to the building.

"Raymond, I'm not here to stop you. I've told the FBI to stay away. I was notified that you'd taken your ring off, and Michaels told me you were headed for the lab. Raymond, I want this to work. I'm here to help you."

"I don't have time for this. You're stalling for time. Get out of the scanner room."

"Raymond, I mean it—I want to help you. You're out of your head, but if there's any chance this could work—"

"Out, Bob!" shouted Raymond. "I don't need your help. Get out and lock down this room."

Raymond fired a shot at the floor in front of Bob, sending him scrambling for cover.

"Get out!"

Bob ran for the door. As soon it closed behind him, Raymond resumed his work.

A quick tour of the system's security services showed that the FBI had beefed up security at the operating system level. They would know that his scan data had been written to version control. But, as Raymond had expected, they hadn't upgraded security on the version control system itself—he could make it look like the data had never actually made it.

But it needs to look like I thought this would work. I need an NBC, here in the lab.

He configured the scanner to send its primary copy of his data to Bento's NBC. It would look like he meant to replace Bento's mental data with his own, but failed. No harm would come to Bento.

"Warm-up complete," announced the computer.

"Commence scan on my verbal command."

"Acknowledged."

Raymond added derms to his chest and arms.

"Janet," said Raymond. "Is anyone in the building?"

"Only you and Bob."

Raymond felt the derms starting to take effect. He was losing muscle control fast; he was likely going to need a shove to get him all the way into the scanner. He suddenly remembered his monkey-like robot, Passe-Partout.

"Janet, send Passe-Partout in here. And can you let me know if anyone enters the building?"

"Sure, Raymond."

As soon as Passe-Partout was in, Raymond started to barricade the scanner room doors, but his knees buckled. He staggered back to the controller station, grabbed the boxes of derms, and carried them to the scanner. He sat at the mouth of the scanner, placed derms on his hands and face, then more on his legs and stomach and chest.

"Commence scan when I lose consciousness."

"Acknowledged."

"Passe-Partout, push me the rest of the way in."

He tossed the gun on the floor and lay back. His clever robot dragged a chair over to the scanner, hopped on, and gave Raymond the last shove he needed. He lay under the yellow dome, the details of his plan running through his mind. His mental data would be backed up to a remote university server along with the rest of source code as part of the nightly backup. His agents would then relay it across the Net, as he had done with Molly's mental data, and wipe the data from the university server. The only remaining trace of his scan would be the falsified failure logs.

He thought of the last sound he had heard from Anya, the sound of her scared voice calling his name over and over. The end wasn't supposed to happen like this.

The burning pain of his gunshot wound was gone. A cold numbness spread up from his feet, and he started to feel alternately heavy and weightless. Thoughts broke into fragments. He was starting to fade.

He heard Janet's voice. He heard her voice saying words. He heard the word, "entered". This seemed significant for some reason, but he didn't know why. More words followed. He struggled to grasp them, like fish in dark waters.

"Grateful… we… pioneer… watching… we…"

Janet was saying "we". Janet shouldn't be saying "we".

Part II: R_2

CHAPTER 13

Raymond's mind stirred, but he found himself in a state completely devoid of sensation.

Where am I?

Nowhere.

No feeling, no light, no sound.

The struggle to inhale. No air. No lungs to fill with air, no muscles to expand lungs, no chest to rise and fall.

No body in need of oxygen.

Where am I?

Words. Words, but neither lips nor tongue to form them. Yet, there was an "I" to think the words, to pose the question. And the words came readily.

Where am I, where am I, where am I, where am I.

It felt good to generate words. They came crisply, instantly. He pictured them in print, on a page. Page after page, filled instantly, with an awareness of every occurrence of the phrase.

No sensation. No place. No body.

Raymond suddenly recalled his attempt to upload, his desperate attempt to escape. The sound of Anya yelling his name, the pain and fear and concern in her voice. The blade he drove through the man's arm. The gunshots. His encounter with Bob in the lab. Lying in the scanner, waiting to lose consciousness so the scan could start—it couldn't happen fast enough, and seemed to take forever. But it was in the past now. It must have worked.

The mental scan must have worked, but I have no body. Did I forget to start the body simulation? No, it was set to start before my mental data was uploaded… but it must have failed. Or it could be running just fine but the brain-to-body connection failed, leaving me in a void.

Oh my god—it must have worked. The upload worked. My name is Raymond Quan. I am human. I am computer.

He wanted to laugh, but he had no body to do it. He pictured a little cartoon dog laughing in yippy little barks, slapping his knee. He imagined angrily putting the little dog in a box, jealous of its ability to laugh. But even in the box, the dog just kept laughing.

Okay, I need a body.

He thought through possible problems with the body simulation. The most likely problem, and the easiest to solve, was that the initialization process which was supposed to connect the body to the brain had simply run at the wrong time, and needed to be run again. How could he re-run it?

He had installed a listener program, between the NBC and the body simulation, that would pick up all muscle-moving brain signals. These signals would in turn be translated into input device events, as if he were wearing his manuhaptic gloves and his terminal helmet. This way, the same brain signals that moved his simulated fingers could create computer commands, allowing him to connect with the outside world.

But if I don't have a body... what if that listener program isn't working?

By force of habit, he made a hand gesture that meant he wanted Scorpio's attention. Nothing happened.

Of course nothing happened. How would I know if anything happened? No feedback.

He thought through the commands that he would have to issue in order to re-run the program to connect his body and his brain. He then willed nonexistent hands to move appropriately, carefully running through the sequence of steps. When he came to the last step, he paused. Was there anything he had missed? He thought through everything again. With a building sense of anticipation, he danced his imaginary fingers through the quick, subtle motions of the last command.

Seconds passed—seconds brimming with possibility. Possibility gave way to doubt, which gave way to disappointment. Nothing was happening. Had he forgotten some crucial command? He ran through the steps again in his mind. What could he have missed?

It didn't work. It's not working. How could it not be working?

He pictured the bunker's server room, his mind running in an NBC in the middle of the floor, connected to nothing. Machines running all around him, hosting his v-worlds, hosting his body, monitoring the bunker's internal and external systems, all stupidly waiting for his brain to join the party.

What if I'm stuck like this forever, in a digital coma?

What had gone wrong? He had set up everything so carefully. His mental data had clearly made it to the NBC—he was up and running. Which meant the NBC had to have been on the network at some point.

Unless I'm dead, and this is my cruel afterlife. Or—oh my god, what if I was captured? What if the FBI captured my mental data before it ever left the lab, and now they're trying to figure out how to wind up the monkey and make it work?

He pictured Anya working with Agent Michaels in some secret FBI laboratory, explaining to him what the various mental signals meant, pointing to holographic neural graphs, saying, "From this activity, we know that Raymond is experiencing fear." He pictured Michaels leaning in and kissing her neck, just behind her jaw, the way Raymond had sometimes, as she slept.

No, no, no. He tried to shake the image. *It wouldn't be her helping the FBI. She believes too much in the rights of digital life. No, it would be Bob, scoring points with the feds so he can continue his research.*

I'm panicking. I can't panic.

What if he simply hadn't done the commands correctly? Maybe he hadn't willed his hands to move in the right way. It hadn't felt wrong to him, but without feeling the feedback of his manuhaptic gloves, it was hard to tell. He ran through the commands in his head again, then imagined motioning through them. He faltered part way through, starting to doubt that he was right at all. He considered starting over, but he wasn't sure what state things would be in if he stopped now. He continued, making each motion more slowly and deliberately, until the last command was complete.

Raymond had always imagined himself waking up horizontal, in bed, in the dimly lit little v-world he called Home Base. That was, after all, how he had programmed it to happen.

Suddenly finding himself vertical, standing in the heat and humidity of a tropical jungle at midday, he immediately started falling backward. He staggered, attempting to get his feet beneath him, and ended up in a backwards run, which terminated abruptly when the back of his head hit something hard. His bare left shoulder jammed up against a rough unyielding surface, but his right side kept going. He put his hands out to catch himself as he spun backwards to the ground, and he landed heavily on his right hand. Acute pain shot through his wrist, and he let himself fall onto his front, naked on the forest floor.

He heard the flapping of wings high above him, and the eerie trill of frightened ikki-ikki birds—a species he created. He rolled onto his elbow and lifted his head to see the telltale blur of white wingtips as the flock dispersed into the jungle canopy high above him.

"Nurania."

He rolled onto his back, the grit of decaying leaves pressing into the exposed skin of his back, his butt, his thighs and heels. A broad smile broke across his face, in spite of the throbbing pain in the back of his head—at least now he had a body. Beside him, the trunk of a Nuranian blood tree soared a hundred feet or more above him—the tree that had so abruptly stopped his backward run. Its huge pale silver leaves, lined with fat red veins, spread across the sky.

"Nurania," he said again. His pleasure was mitigated by an ominous sense of displacement. This was not where he was supposed to be. He was supposed to wake up in Home Base.

He went to stand up, but put too much weight on his right wrist. Pain shot up his arm, and he collapsed onto his elbow.

Pain. What a pleasure to feel pain. This fundamental connection between body and mind assured him that his simulated body was properly integrated with both the world around him and his new brain. He gingerly assessed the damage. There was no bruise, no swelling. It was probably a pulled muscle. He shifted his weight to his left side and used his left arm to support himself as he stood up.

"I did it—I uploaded."

He wiped the dirt from his palms, then held both hands up to look at them. They looked like his hands. He looked down and saw his own body. His almond skin, hairless chest, flat pectorals, dark nipples. The simulation of his flesh looked and felt flawless. He thrust his pelvis forward and felt his privates swing. He held his right arm against his ribs and threw a punch with his left, his fingers sliding tangibly through the humid jungle air. All felt as it should. "I'm digital. Pure goddamned digital." He inhaled deeply, his nostrils alive with the rich organic scents of the Nuranian jungle.

"Wait, my shoulder." He reached back and felt his right shoulder, where he had been shot. There was no sign of the wound. "Of course… my body simulation was created healthy."

He brushed the leaves and dirt from his whole body. Arriving naked fit nicely with the birth metaphor, but he would need some protective clothing.

"God mode. Clothing store, jungle theme."

Raymond stood there, expecting to be transferred temporarily into a jungle-themed clothing store, where he could select an outfit for himself. Typically, the transfer was instantaneous.

"Repeat my last command," he instructed.

Nothing happened.

"Am I in god mode?"

No response.

"God mode, with confirmation," he instructed. Still nothing happened. His shoulders fell and he tipped his head back. "Shit." Never had he experienced a basic failure in Nurania's command system.

What if… what if it doesn't recognize me as me?

"Who am I?" he asked aloud.

From behind him, he heard the trill of an ikki-ikki bird. He turned around and scanned the treetops, but saw nothing. He suddenly felt alone, vulnerably alone, and the feeling frightened him. "I wasn't supposed to start here," he muttered. "I was supposed to start in Home Base."

He looked around him again, wondering where in Nurania he was. There were many jungles on the planet. This could be any of several. Nurania was a planet of nine continents, warmer and wetter than Earth, and more prone to storms. He looked to the sky and realized he had already recognized, subconsciously, that it was blue. Blue meant calm. During slammer season, the sky was generally an orangey yellow, and would become a mix of orange, maroon, and violet during storms. Strong slammers could bring prolonged winds of over eighty miles per hour, with tornado-strength gusts. Naked, without shelter, he would stand little chance of surviving a slammer.

He thought about making the hand motions to disconnect from Nurania. Doing this should return him to the very simple Home Base v-world that was supposed to be his base v-world. He couldn't imagine a malfunction that would have made Nurania his base v-world. If he disconnected from Nurania, that might land him in Home Base… or he might end up nowhere, a bodiless brain in a void, as he had started out.

He needed access to the operating system of the computer on which Nurania and Home Base ran, so he could diagnose the problem. From Home Base, this was easy—Home Base included a copy of the workstation he usually used to control his network. But Nurania was his escape, and to keep it free from interruption he had never incorporated his workstation into it. Except from his mountain-top workspace, but the connection from there was temporary, created specifically for his work sessions.

He was reluctant to exit Nurania, afraid he might lose the connection to his body. But what was the alternative? If he didn't get out and gain access to the operating system, he would be stuck in Nurania without god mode, a powerless citizen of a made-up world, for the rest of his life. Which, without the ability to interact with reality prime, could be hundreds of years, until one of his computers crashed, or the bunker lost power, or some other catastrophic failure occurred. He had always pictured his life in Nurania as one of creating and enjoying his own personal paradise. His current situation was clearly the unacceptable result of some oversight.

"I have to fix this sooner or later. I might as well deal with it now."

He made the hand gesture that would indicate to the v-world host software that he wanted to exit Nurania. And waited.

"Exit world."

He looked around him. Nurania, world of his own creation, felt strange and threatening, as if it had taken on a life of its own and turned on him. He repeated the exit gesture and command over and over, to no avail. He tried god mode again, he tried old override commands he had long ago disabled, all to no avail.

"What the shit? Is this some sort of hell?"

It was entirely possible, he suddenly realized, that he had in fact died when the nanobots destructively scanned his body, and this was his afterlife.

The perfect hell. A ghost, powerless in a world of my own creation.

But that didn't feel right. This was such a plausible continuation of his life, how could it be the afterlife? Something must have gone wrong with his upload—this was the simplest explanation.

He wondered whether he could die in this world. V-chambers included safeguards to prevent any real injury. But what would happen if a slammer wind were to lift him from the ground and throw him against a tree? Was his body simulation capable of withstanding fatal damage? Previously, he had thought of this as a purely academic matter. He had expected to have access to the operating system, and the ability to modify his own physiology simulation. And, within Nurania, he had expected to have god-mode powers, which alone were enough to prevent physical damage. Now, if he withstood fatal levels of physical damage, what would happen? Would his brain return to the nowhere where he started? Would his physiology reboot, giving him a second chance? Nothing was as he had expected.

He looked at the ground. He wanted to sit down. His complete lack of direction was making him tense. But he didn't want to sit naked on the ground's decaying leaf matter. He resentfully recalled the imaginings he had long nurtured of his first moments in Nurania: surfing the winds of slammer season on an airboard, cutting into blistering winds, dropping into storm clouds to feel the thrilling blast of moisture on his skin, the refractive violet air thick with impurity-free water vapor. He had imagined sensations of undiminished intensity attainable only as a digital life-form.

Raymond looked about at the straight tree trunks, branchless for the first eighty feet or so, wishing he had made them climbable. He was mentally exhausted from the insane series of events leading to his upload, and he wanted to arrange himself carefully on thick tree branches and fall asleep, as Robinson Crusoe did his first night on the island. His thoughts drifted to his days in the Joliet Home, where his primary caregiver sometimes read to him when he was young. Those days felt precious to him in a way they never had before. In hindsight, they seemed so safe and simple. If he hadn't been relocated to the Canal Street Home, where would he be now? Would he have eventually adjusted to life in Joliet, made friends, turned out normal?

"I drove a blade through a man's arm. An FBI agent, but he was just a guy doing his job. And Bob… if he hadn't wised up and run for the door, I would have killed him."

He suddenly remembered hearing Janet's voice as consciousness faded, and the feeling that her words didn't make sense. What was it she had said? He remembered her saying "we". And something about being grateful. And "pioneer"? Was it really her voice that had said these things? It didn't make sense that she would say "we". Who could the "we" have been? Bob had said something about agent Michaels, and telling the FBI to stay away. Maybe it was Janet's voice, but it wasn't really Janet—the same trick Raymond used to drive Bob out of the lab. Could Bob have hijacked the Janet persona? That didn't seem likely. What about Michaels—he could have done it. But why? And why would the FBI listen if Bob told them to stay away? What authority did Bob have over the FBI? "Pioneer?" That seemed like a Bob word. Why would Bob tell the FBI to stay away in the first place? Had he suspected Raymond would try to upload, and he wanted to see if it might work?

They were one step ahead of me, and I bet they captured my mental data before it made it out of the lab. But I'm in Nurania… how would they have gotten hold of Nurania? They would have to know about the bunker. The satellite footage must not have been cleaned up in time. The feds traced me to the motor home, unraveled the Svensson link, and seized my hardware at the bunker.

He looked around him, expecting to catch a glimpse of someone hiding behind a tree. "What is this?" he asked in a loud voice. "Did you bring me to life to get a confession out of me?"

There was no answer.

Or maybe Bob cut a deal with the feds. If the upload worked, maybe they would give him the green light to continue his research. In some government lab. That would explain why they kicked Brody off the case—they didn't want her to blow the whistle on their shady deal.

"What do you want from me?" called out Raymond, and promptly felt silly for doing so. He was jumping to conclusions. It was just as likely—probably more so—that he had goofed something up and was stuck with the consequences. But Janet's words did seem weird… could he have been dreaming as the derms pushed him over the edge? In the past few days, paranoia seemed to have gotten the better of him. His judgement, it seemed, was not to be trusted.

I was bleeding ready to kill Bob!

"I need sleep. When was the last time I got a decent night's sleep?"

He sat down, arms folded across his knees, and tried to ignore the discomfort of his seating arrangement. He took a deep breath and sighed. Had he really thrown away whatever chances he might have had with Anya for *this*? Maybe he could have convinced her to give him the time he needed to open up, to get used to having someone in his life. It had felt so good to spill everything to her in his goodbye message. What if he could have done that without having to run away?

I didn't throw away my chance with her. I never had a chance. I screwed things up before we even met, and it was stupid to even try to have a relationship. I should be in jail now, for all the shit I did. In jail, locked away. Instead I'm here… and at least here I have a decent chance of finding a way out.

He lay on his back, with the thought of sleeping. But his mind was restless, and he started thinking of the giant spiders and centipedes he had created for his jungle ecosystems. He found himself in a world of his own dark, mischievous inspirations, turned inside out. Desire for novelty had informed many of his decisions as he had gone about inventing Nurania. Novelty, without straying too far from the familiar. Even though he had never actually intended Nurania for public consumption, he had often imagined some hapless Net wanderer straying in. He recalled his own satisfaction at creating lush, beautiful environments that would lull the unwitting visitor into a state of trustful appreciation, only to be shocked by an unexpected encounter with a frog-tongued giant ladybug, scorpion-tailed squirrel, or acid-spitting sloth. Now all that clever child's play would be the stuff of nightmares—there was no way he could sleep here.

For lack of anything better to do, he stood up and started to walk. Gravity, or rather the simulation of gravity, carried him absent-mindedly down the slight grade of the jungle floor.

This is my world.

But the notion provided no solace. This was a foreign world. For the first time ever, he recognized his arrogance in thinking of this as a world of his creation. From his mind had sprung the basic ideas of Nurania, but the vast majority of the world's details were computer-generated, many of them details he had never even noticed. This world had fit his abstract imaginings, but a trillion other worlds would have fit just as well, their subtle differences escaping his gross human capacity for understanding.

He stopped and felt the bark of a golber tree. He was pleased at least to know the name of the tree. But he did not know this particular tree. Its bark, nearly black, was covered with an intricate pattern of overlapping hexagonal bark scales. He ran the palm of his hand over the rough surface. There were a few golber trees that he did know, in areas special to him, but there were millions he did not know, and never could know.

A true god, with transcendent knowledge, would know them all.

His feet carried him further down the gentle slope, the pricking pain in his soles a welcome, present intensity in a state of existence that he didn't understand.

A deep rumbling sounded from somewhere in front of him. The trees around him wavered as from an earthquake, and a groundswell put him off balance. Afraid he might fall, he got down low. Ripples of reverberation shook the entire jungle around him, and branches fell as the trees abraded each other up in the canopy layer.

An earthquake?

It was a feeling he had never associated with Nurania.

From somewhere in the distance, ahead of him, there came the resounding sound of a colossal explosion. He looked up. Off to his right, a patch of sky suggested the presence of a clearing in the jungle canopy, a chance to see out. He broke into a run, wanting to see the source of the explosion. The patch proved to be further away than his initial perception would have suggested. Winded, he slowed to a fast walk, then quickened his pace again, to a jog. He had a strong sense that the break was too high up for him to actually be able to see anything, but a vague hope led him onward, haphazardly navigating uneven ground and leaping over fallen trees. Lesser explosions could be heard in the distance, and the ground continued to rumble beneath his feet.

As he neared the opening in the jungle canopy, something off to his right attracted his attention. There was something on the ground, next to a tree. A sense of déjà vu came over him—he had been here before, or had imagined being here. The hole in the canopy seemed familiar, and he suddenly recognized the long elliptical shape of the item on the ground. It was an airboard. He slowed to a walk, looking around him. There was something about this place. He felt as if he had walked into an old dream. He moved toward the airboard, drawn to it. The dream started to come into clarity. He had imagined a place like this, a jungle—himself, slipping through the broad leaves of blood trees to land his airboard. He had imagined it, but had he ever actually done it?

The airboard lay amid low soft green ferns, nosed into the thick jungle topsoil. He seized it and pulled it out of the ground, ready to be angry at its failure to operate. But as soon as he righted it, parallel with the gentle slope of the hillside, it pulled downward into a stable hover, several inches off the ground. He reluctantly stepped his right foot onto it, expecting the worst, but it didn't budge. He shifted his weight slowly onto his right leg, rising onto the board, and arrived at a standing position without problem.

"This is better," he declared.

He squatted down, grabbed the sides of the board with either hand, and leaned forward. The board reacted to his shifting weight as expected, moving forward over the ground. He pulled up and leaned to the left, the board rising and turning with him. Glancing down over the edge, he saw the ground twenty feet or so beneath him. He curved gently around a tree and continued to climb, headed for the break in the canopy. He tried hard not to think about how high he was flying—a concern he had never had when visiting Nurania in a v-chamber.

Upon clearing the treetops, he carefully pulled the board to a hovering stop. A light breeze blew, and the air felt less humid at this height. In the distance, he saw the source of the explosions, and in the same moment he recognized where he was: he was near the southern edge of the Faralon mountain range, and to the north, beyond Mount Lidral, Mount Hawthorn had blown its top and was spewing fiery orange lava into the sky. A great cloud of ash and dust was already spreading to the east. The shaft of red-hot geologic gore surged higher and stronger. An unfathomably large chunk of rock broke away, hurtled through the air, and dropped to the ground near the base of the mountain. A plume of earth rose up from where the rock cratered. Red-hot rocks and lava rained down in the distance, and Raymond could see smoke rising where forest fires must be burning. Never had he seen such destruction on Nurania.

"This is hell."

CHAPTER 14

Nurania was not the only world Raymond had ever built. As a child, he created many v-worlds, deleting them and starting over, again and again, refining his vision and his skills through trial and error. With a single command, an entire world could be erased. Typically, this was done without remorse: Raymond the creator was not pleased with what he had created, so he would smudge it out of existence and start over. But as time went by and he became more invested in his creations, he started to take out his disappointment and frustration on his hapless digital worlds. Like an artist slashing his canvas, he would rise above a continent, unleash a meteor shower on it, and watch it go up in flames. Or he would stop time, introduce a surreal mile-thick layer of liquid nitrogen into the upper atmosphere, then unstop time and watch the vast icy devastation. As the technology available to him improved, his worlds grew richer and more lifelike, and their ultimate destruction more terrible. With one v-world in particular, Biloxia—an island city of gentle, semi-intelligent cat people—he grew bored, ran out of ideas for ways to improve it, and introduced an airborne flesh-eating virus. He then walked in god-mode among the Biloxians, watching as they turned to one another for help, frightened by the first gruesome signs of the illness. The virus progressed rapidly, and the mayhem and suffering that ensued provided none of the twisted amusement that Raymond sought. He was struck by the expressions of surprise and aimless accusation on the faces of his creatures. These memories never faded, and his relationship to his digital creations was forever changed.

Nurania never experienced such petulant wrath. It was sacrosanct. From the start, he had moved cautiously, with an eye for the permanence of his actions. Now, as he squatted on his airboard watching rivers of lava run into the jungle northeast of Mount Lidral, he imagined unsuspecting animals caught in the maze of fire that spread through the trees, and his eyes filled with tears.

"This can't be happening. How can this be happening? What twisted nightmare is this?"

He sat down on his board, his legs dangling over either side, and looked to the sky.

"Who's the god of this world?"

Perhaps there was no god; perhaps he had inadvertently thrown himself to chance, trapped in a godless world on a server isolated from reality prime, completely unknown.

He slumped way forward, his elbows on the board, and let his head hang. What had happened to his world, and how was it no longer his? Something had gone terribly wrong, and he had no access to the mechanisms at play.

He looked over the edge of the board. The uppermost branches of the tree beneath him were about ten feet away, and the ground was probably a hundred feet below that. If he were to roll off and let himself fall, he would surely suffer physical damage sufficient to kill him. But would he actually die? What would happen to his mind? Would he simply be kicked from Nurania, returned to the void from which he had entered? Without trying it, there was no way to know. There was no one he could ask. There could be no stories of what had happened to others, for none had come before him. Likewise, if he did try it, there was no one else who could benefit from the knowledge gained by this life-endangering experiment.

Perhaps the world itself contains some clue as to what's gone wrong.

Now that he knew where he was, he also knew he wasn't all that far from where he had planned to enter Nurania after his time in Home Base. Maybe an hour or two by airboard. Perhaps, if he went there, he would find some indication of why he had not entered where he had expected to.

Remaining seated, he took the airboard out of hover mode, swung it to the right, and headed southeast. He cruised over the treetops, picking up speed as he went. He thought about standing. He wanted to stand. He wanted the familiar thrill of this test of balance. But when he was in a v-chamber, in god mode, there was no real danger. Now, the dangers might be grave.

He grabbed the sides of the board and lifted his knees up underneath him. It was a simple move, one he would normally execute without thinking. But now it made him feel a bit woozy, especially with the pain in his right wrist, and he instinctively pulled back, slowing the board.

"Oh please," he muttered, appalled at his trepidation.

Ignoring the pain in his wrist, he grabbed the board again and swung his feet beneath him, moving with the frustration-breaking resolve that blinds one to risk. Feeling steady, he released his grasp and started to stand. He caught sight of the foliage below, and the image of slipping off and smacking into a tree trunk demolished his confidence—he lurched left to catch his balance, then shifted right, stepping an inch wider with his right foot to improve his stability. He bent his knees to lower his body weight, but vertigo had already set in. He inadvertently tipped forward, looked straight down, then rocked up on his toes and threw his weight back. This quickly became a cycle of forward and backward adjustments, and he knew from experience that he had to get down fast. He turned to face forward and dropped down, his legs slipping over either side, and his sit-bones hit the board hard.

He let out a sigh of relief, then fell forward on the board, disgusted with himself.

"I should've just let myself fucking fall."

But even as these words came from his mouth, hope of figuring out what was going on flashed through his mind again. He owed himself at least the chance of figuring this place out.

"What if I actually did die, and this is some sort of punishment, but if I can figure it out I get to go free? Okay, that's ridiculous. But even I deserve some scrap of hope, right?"

Right?

His thoughts drifted over the truly bad things he had done in his life, and there were a few new items on the list. Spiking a man's arm to the ground, for example, and inflicting the trauma of his apparent death on Anya.

"Okay, maybe I don't *deserve* hope, but the fact is I have it. If there's something to be figured out here, I can do it."

Where he had failed at balance he made up with sheer speed. Transitions from jungle to swampland to cane fields flashed beneath him, his trajectory a roller coaster ride of downs and ups as he skimmed above the terrain at nearly a hundred miles per hour. The feel of the sun and the wind against his skin was enough to take his mind off everything else for an hour or so. He would open his eyes just the tiniest bit to check his position, make whatever small adjustment was necessary, then close his eyes again. He knew he had reached the Lomordian tributary when he saw the green stones that lined the stream's bottom, stones carried out of the Sai Ro foothills to the southwest. He dropped down and slowed to fifteen or twenty miles per hour, until he was so low he could drag his toes through the cool water. The stream twisted its way through the sub-tropical forest, and Raymond followed its path with zeal, shifting side-to-side through the turns.

The waterway grew wider and started to straighten; he was nearing the point at which it joined with the Soravia. That was where he had planned to enter Nurania from Home Base. He rose a few feet higher and sped up, anxious to reach his destination. He noticed giant boulders in the forest to either side and knew he was close. Soon he saw the familiar plateau of cobalt-blue rock ahead. The forest abruptly stopped where the blue cliff rose from the ground, and the stream disappeared into a tunnel in the rock face—a tunnel he knew, both by design and by experience, to be just tall enough to allow him to fly through it.

To prepare for his entrance into the tunnel, he lay down on his belly and shifted forward until his chin hung over the rounded edge of his board. He slowed to a near standstill, so slow that the stream was actually flowing past him, and stretched down to touch his forehead to the water—his way of measuring the perfect height. He then lifted his head, looked forward, and pushed the board faster, careful not to rise even an inch higher. The wall of rock loomed taller and taller above him as he approached. Without craning his neck, he could no longer see the sky. His heart started to race in anticipation of the thrill.

As he neared the mouth of the tunnel, he stretched his face forward to meet the cool air. He slipped into the darkness, and a smile broke across his face. Moist cave air swirled in eddies over his naked body. The air that filled his lungs carried smells of moss, wet stone, and floral sweetness. For years he had dreamt of this moment, experienced directly, without the inferior fidelity of a v-chamber, and it was everything he had hoped for—transcendently exhilarating. His eyes teared with pleasure, and he let out a wild howl.

By the glow of cave fish, he could just make out the tunnel's rock walls and ceiling. With his arms stretched along his sides and his fingertips extended, he arched upward in yoga's half-boat pose, lifting his head and hands and feet until the pads of his toes grazed the slick-smooth surface above him. He leaned gently to the right to follow the familiar curve of the tunnel, holding the pose until his limbs quivered from exhaustion and he could hold it no longer. He was impressed by how familiar his muscles felt—the physiological simulation seemed flawless.

As he came out of the curve, he saw light playing off the surface of the water ahead and knew he was close to the tunnel's end. He dropped the board to the water's surface and allowed it to simply float, then carefully flipped onto his back. Water lapped over the edges of the board against his shoulders, his flanks, his butt, his calves. At first it caused him to shiver a bit, but he soon grew accustomed to the temperature, and was able to close his eyes and focus on how it felt against his skin.

Through closed eyelids he detected the increasing light, but the moment he exited the tunnel was one of sharp transition, the bright sun causing him to close his eyes tighter and turn away. The warmth of the sun on his skin was delicious. As he drifted into the calm waters of the Soravia, the merging currents slowly spinning him, he felt drunk with pleasure. The heat of sunlight on his groin reminded him he was naked. He wanted to shamelessly enjoy his arousal, yet he couldn't help but open his eyes and look about him, instinctively fearing that someone might be watching. He decided this fear was sheer folly—he was more alone than ever. He reached down and adjusted himself, allowing his scrotum to hang more freely between his thighs. The luxuriously warm waters of the Soravia lapped against his skin. He decided to satisfy his longstanding curiosity about what a digital orgasm would feel like. He got up on his knees, spread his legs wide, and slowly dropped into a back-bend, his eyes closed, until the back of his head was against the board. The sun blazed, heating his skin—stretched taut across ribs and belly—and giving rise to erotic vitality. He imagined Anya, straddling him, her eyes closed and her head thrown back. He wanted to draw out the pleasure, as if trying to satisfy her first, but could restrain himself no longer.

He dropped to the board, exhausted, completely adrift with pleasure. Not a thought in his mind. Feeling, not thinking. With the smile of one who is at one with the present, he rolled off the board and into the water.

After a good swim, he pulled himself onto his airboard and flew back to where he had exited the water tunnel. Above the dark cave, carved out of the blue rock wall, was the alcove where he had planned to enter Nurania. It was mid-way up the wall, about twenty feet above the water, the perfect platform for a dive into the deep waters below. The arched entrance was closed off by gates carved out of the same vibrant blue rock, intricately detailed to allow fine rays of light to filter in. Another entrance was carved into the cliff just to the left of the Lomordia tunnel, where a steep rock staircase provided a means of climbing back up to the alcove after a dive.

Raymond chose to fly up to the higher entrance. He brought his airboard to a hover next to the gates, slid his fingers into carved slits, and pulled them open, backing out of their way. They swung smoothly open at the lightest touch, then slowly started to swing back closed, allowing him just enough time to slip through.

From the darkness emerged a young woman, as naked as Raymond—tanned and curvy, Polynesian in appearance. Raymond stopped short, shocked to see another person in Nurania. She stepped up to his board, smiling at him. A long braid of black hair curled around her neck and lay between her full breasts. She looked up at him on his airboard with pleading, playful eyes. Something about her seemed familiar, but he couldn't place it.

"How could you *tease* me like that?" she asked with girlish drama.

Raymond noticed a door at the back of the alcove, where there had never been one before. The alcove itself was strewn with flower petals, and there were cushions on the floor.

"Tease you?" he asked stupidly, taken aback by this scene.

"I was watching," she said in a pained voice. "And after you've been gone for so long! I wanted to come out and be with you, but you told me not to. Isn't this one of the airboards you didn't like?"

With this question, it clicked—she *was* familiar. She was a fantasy of his, made flesh. A gorgeous supplicant plaything. She stepped closer and ran a hand up his inner thigh. Much to his embarrassment, he was immediately aroused. He moved her hand away, toward his knee, and looked around for something with which to cover himself. She silently pet his leg.

"You're probably used to seeing me naked, aren't you," he said.

"Oh yes. Sometimes clothed, but mostly naked."

"Who do you think I am?" he asked. He was aware that this might ruin his opportunity to use her misunderstanding to his advantage, but the thought of having her as a plaything held little appeal now. And he had the uneasy sense that he knew what her answer would be.

"Why, Apollo, of course. Are you not Apollo?"

There was no fear or concern in her voice. She merely sought an answer.

"I look like Apollo, don't I," he said with an edge of despair. It was as he had feared—he had not even deemed his own fantasy woman worthy of knowing his real name. And he considered himself worthy of a god's name. This was a fantasy of his, brought to life. Seeing it from the outside, it seemed a little sick.

"Yes, very much. Except your face is marked again. Are you not Apollo?"

"For you, I am Apollo. But I'm confused. How long have you known me?"

"Since you created me."

He nodded. Possible explanations for his entire situation started to take shape in his mind, in quick succession, each one disintegrating under the scrutiny of reason. He got down off his airboard as if it were a horse and started toward the back of the alcove. The woman followed him.

"Is your name Venetia?" he asked.

"Of course," she responded.

Venetia was the name he most often attached to this fantasy woman of his. It had started as Venus, for the voluptuous body, but the name of a goddess seemed too noble for the baseness of his fantasy. By derivation, he had arrived at Venetia.

Raymond examined the new door at the back of the alcove. It was carved with patterns similar to the gates at the mouth of the alcove, but these carvings did not go all the way through.

"What's behind this door, Venetia?"

"Our palace, Apollo. You are confused, aren't you? Is there anything I can do that might help?" she asked suggestively.

He stopped and looked at her. He couldn't help but be tempted. What harm was there? She was a toy, and pleasing him was the game for which she had been built. But he knew she had somehow sprung from *his* fantasies with that game in mind, and he was ashamed of himself.

"How long ago did I create you?" he asked, pausing at the door.

"Eight months ago."

"Nuranian time, or real time?" he asked.

She looked at him quizzically.

Of course she would have no knowledge of her own virtual existence.

He cautiously pulled the door open. Sunlight flooded the alcove from the long, lush courtyard garden on the other side.

"By real time," asked Venetia, "do you mean time in your old world, where Anya is?"

Raymond spun around.

"You know about Anya?"

"Of course. She is the woman you loved in your previous life. You told me much about Anya."

"Like what?"

"You told me that sex with me was easy, but it was complicated with Anya—more exciting, but complicated. You told me that you felt like you could say anything to me but found it difficult to say things to Anya. You said it was partially because of the crime, and the secrets she couldn't know, but that she also made you feel judged and criticized. You said you felt like you had to hide from her, as much as you wanted not to, and you were glad that now you could have a new start in life."

Raymond was caught off guard. This woman was more than a plaything. She had clearly played the role of confidant, as well.

She knows me. She knows things I've never told anyone—things I've never even thought through.

He walked into the courtyard, intensely colorful with green foliage and huge white flowers against the polished blue walls. Venetia followed. He turned about slowly, gazing at the beauty of the place. He could feel that it was his own creation, yet he was impressed—it seemed more joyous than anything he had created before. He looked at Venetia, standing naked in broad daylight, relaxed, wanting nothing but to serve him.

"Did I ever tell you about uploading, or my life before uploading? You mentioned something about 'the crime'."

"You told me a little. I asked you once about the crime you committed in your previous life. 'Don't ask me about that,' you said. You told me you couldn't believe that uploading had really worked—you said that many times. You told me that you created this world, and now you got to live in it—but that you weren't done with it yet. You told me that Anya was still in the world of your previous life. You told me—"

"Okay," interrupted Raymond. "That's enough for now. How about a tour of the palace?"

"Certainly, Apollo, but you created the palace. Surely—"

"You know what? How about if you call me Raymond?"

"Okay, Raymond."

She led him through the halls and courtyards of the sprawling palace, all of it carved out of rock. It was an exercise in grace and peace, but there was an emptiness to it, a lack of life.

"Were there never more people here? Servants, or something?"

"You tried servants once, but you said you liked it better when it was just me."

"And how long ago did I leave?"

"Seven-and-a-half months ago."

"So I was here for two weeks. I see." His eyes fell again to Venetia's body. "What a curse to grow bored so easily."

"After the first week, when the palace was done, you came and went often."

"Did I ever leave Nurania?"

"Oh yes. You said there was another world that you went to when you were not here."

Someone was clearly here before me, and it seems like it was me, but I have no memory of being here. The last thing I remember was lying in the scanner, hoping the upload would work.

"I'm not the original Raymond," he muttered.

"What does that mean?" asked Venetia. Raymond had not intended for her to hear his comment, but neither had he thought of concealing it from her.

"You were designed to ask questions, weren't you, Venetia. To draw me out."

"I am always wanting to know you better."

"And how free I must have felt, speaking openly about myself. You probably learned more about me in two weeks than anyone else ever did."

His fantasies of life after upload had always revolved around enjoyment of the Nuranian wilderness and wildlife, free from people. But Venetia's presence in the world made perfect sense to him now.

It would be freeing, to speak openly to someone you know won't judge you—can't judge you.

"Venetia, I don't know if you will understand this, but I'm not the same Raymond who created you."

"You are not my Apollo?"

"Well, I am and I'm not. There seem to be two copies of me. And I'm the second one. The original one must have uploaded as planned, and entered Nurania here, with god powers. He must have saved the mental data from the scan and created another copy… but why?"

"Then you are not the one I am to please?"

"Well, I don't know about *that.*" He looked her over again. He was surprised he had given her big, full breasts. He preferred smaller breasts. Perhaps the first copy of him had wanted to save perfection for another woman. "If I told you that you should please yourself first, would that make sense to you?"

"Oh yes, you like to watch me please myself," she tittered, and she ran her hands up her belly and over her breasts, moaning pleasurably.

"No no, that's… that's not what I meant. Although I can see why I might like that." He watched her for a moment, marveling at how simple and predictable a creature he was. But he knew where it would lead if he continued to watch her, and he was enjoying his moral high ground too much to let this happen. "You should stop that, Venetia. That's really not what I meant by pleasing yourself first. I didn't think you would understand."

She immediately stopped and asked him if he would like to see more of the palace.

"Are there any clothes in this palace?"

"There are my clothes."

"Oh, so I let you have clothes?" he asked, snorting a laugh of self-disgust, embarrassed by the boyish crudeness of his own sexual fantasy. "Those should do. Show me the way."

He followed her back through the hall through which they had just been walking, through a maze of courtyards, a hookah room flooded with silk and cushions, a library of ancient texts, and various small rooms that seemed to serve no purpose beyond breaking things up and housing vases filled with flowers. As they walked, he kept watching Venetia, her long neck and tall torso, toned legs, the way she stepped lightly on the balls of her feet. He walked past a mirrored wall and saw his naked self, complete with erection, walking along behind her. "Do you have a bathrobe or something?"

"Oh yes, in the bathing room. I'll take you there."

They continued along through several rooms, eventually coming to a grand, splendid bedroom. Venetia passed through an archway to the left, into a small room, high-walled, with open sky above. He followed. Set into the floor was an elliptical pool of water. White towels and robes hung from pegs on the wall. Raymond grabbed one for himself and tossed another to Venetia, instructing her to put it on. Beside the entrance to this small room was a low stone bench, also carved out of the blue rock. He sat on it, crossed his arms, and stared absent-mindedly at the pool.

"Would you like for me to bathe you?" asked Venetia.

"No, Venetia. I don't want you to offer me anything anymore, okay? If I need something, I'll ask for it."

"Okay."

"So," he said, thinking aloud, "there's another copy of me. The first copy uploaded, had god powers… everything was fine. Then how on earth did *I* end up here? And where is he?"

Venetia sat down on the bench opposite and studied him curiously as he spoke.

"Maybe something went wrong," he said. "Or maybe this is me toying with me? Of course I would have kept a copy of my original mental data. In which case I could instantiate as many copies of myself as I had NBCs. Which would be two. Which means I must be running on Molly's NBC. But it would have to be serious for me to oust Molly. Unless… for all I know, many years could have passed by now, and the original Raymond scored another brainbox."

He looked up at the square of sky above, imagining the original copy of him looking down from on high.

"Are you up there, watching me?"

"Who are you talking to?" asked Venetia.

"I don't know. God. Myself, I guess. My other self."

"Are you not a god, like the Apollo who created me?"

He looked her in the eye. He was moved by how much and how little she seemed to understand.

"No, I'm not a god." An idea dawned on him—perhaps, as a character of this world, she would have administrative query permissions. "Do you know who is god right now?"

"Do you mean my Apollo?"

"I mean, can you ask who is god and find out? Do you have administrative query rights?"

"Administrative query rights?" She looked at him blankly.

"Never mind. It was a long shot. Do you have any maps of Nurania?"

"No."

"Have you ever left this palace?"

"No."

"I don't get it," said Raymond, leaning forward, his elbows on his knees and his hands clasped. "Why wouldn't I have instantiated my second self in a starter world? Why would I not have given myself god powers, unless it was some sort of game?" He looked up to the sky again and gave it the finger. "If this is a game, I don't like it."

He crossed his arms and sat back again, ignoring Venetia's puzzled gaze. He had long held the fear that he would upload into Nurania and grow bored with his powers, like a spoiled child. He wondered whether this was in fact what had happened. The image of the volcanic eruption in the Faralons sprang to mind. It was not difficult to picture it being the outcome of one of his destructive tantrums. Perhaps even Nurania could not escape his profound disregard for anything outside himself.

"So," he said, looking to the sky again. "Are you up there, wondering whether you can teach yourself a lesson? Is that what this is? Am I the second generation, burdened with the expectations of the first? Are you hoping I will succeed where you failed? That I'll find satisfaction where you could not?"

He looked at Venetia. He wanted to use her, demeaning himself to show his god copy that he was not to be used as a toy in some morality game. He wanted to anger and disappoint his god copy, perhaps even make him jealous. But the desire was fleeting. It seemed predictable and fruitless, damaging more to his self-image than to his god copy. If there even was a god copy.

Raymond's stomach growled, and he realized he was starting to feel hungry.

"Great, without god mode, how am I supposed to feed myself?"

Again he wondered whether he was subject to what would normally be fatal damage. Was it possible for him to starve to death? And if so, would he be able to come back to Nurania and start over, as if it were a game?

"Is there anything to eat in this palace?" he asked.

"There is fruit on the trees, in the courtyards. I used to feed my Apollo all sorts of fruits. He would create new ones and try them, and have me feed him the ones that he liked the best."

"Could you show me the ones he liked best?"

"Certainly."

Venetia led him back through several rooms and hallways, to one of the courtyards they had come through previously. It was dense with trees, short and small, from which hung all sorts of fruit. Some looked like fruits from the prime world—bananas, papayas, figs, limes, and oranges. Some were fruits that had long existed on Nurania. But he saw several that were unfamiliar—long plump violet fingers, small skinless green balls that glistened in the sun, and black-skinned things shaped like starfish.

"My Apollo likes these best," said Venetia, pulling down a bunch of the skinless green balls. "He named them yolo fruits." She turned the bunch upside down in her left hand and expertly pinched off one of the larger fruits, careful not to squish its fragile round body. She moved to feed Raymond; he pulled away slightly, but yielded and opened his mouth, accepting this as the best way to convey the fragile fruit.

The ball melted softly into a huge, sweet flavor, like honeyed skinless grape, but with a peach-like juicy richness.

"Mmm."

"My Apollo told me that Anya would be impressed, and this seemed to make him both happy and sad." She held out another yolo fruit, which he accepted without hesitation.

"Wow, that's delicious. Anya *would* be impressed."

"Does her name make you happy and sad, too?"

He paused. Again he was struck by how much Venetia seemed to comprehend. "Yes, I guess it does."

"You said you will let me know if you need anything."

"Right."

"I am just reminding you. My Apollo would sometimes forget things."

"You seem to have learned a great deal about your Apollo, for having only known him two weeks."

"Thank you, Raymond. My Apollo told me that it is one of my attributes."

"Wait a minute, if I'm in Molly's NBC, then her cage would be empty."

"I do not understand," said Venetia, with her now-familiar look of confusion and curiosity.

"That's okay. Do you want to leave the palace?"

"My Apollo told me that I am not to leave the palace."

"Did you hear that?" asked Raymond of the sky. "How about coming down here and telling her she can leave the bleeding palace?" He turned to Venetia. "If I took you away from the palace, would you fight me?"

"Of course not. I do not fight."

"Not even in bed?" asked Raymond suspiciously, knowing himself to like an occasional struggle in the sack.

"That is not fighting. That is playing."

"Oh, okay." He stood, and Venetia did so as well. "Well, tie your bathrobe around you good and tight, and lead me to the alcove, where I first met you. I'm going on a trip, and I need you to come with me."

"I cannot come with you. My creator told me that I cannot."

Raymond placed his hands on her shoulders and looked her in the eye.

"Venetia, I am your creator."

"But you said that you are a copy of my Apollo."

"Well, now I'm telling you that I am your Apollo. This has all been a test, to… to make sure that you really want to please me."

"Okay." She smiled brightly at him. "Did I pass the test?"

"You certainly did. You did a very, very good job. Now, do you understand that I need you to come with me on my trip? It would give me great pleasure." Saying those words, Raymond realized that it *would* give him great pleasure. He didn't recall ever having such an uncomplicated desire for someone's company.

The flight to Molly's cage took over an hour. The airboard that Raymond had found was not designed to hold more than one person. But it was still far faster than walking. Venetia rode behind him, her arms around his ribcage and her cheek leaned against his back. He couldn't help but feel that it was an expression of tenderness on her part, even knowing she was a simulated personality.

As he neared the spot where he remembered placing Molly's cage, his recollection was confirmed: he saw a perfectly square mesa poking out above the jungle canopy. He dropped down through the trees that surrounded it and brought the board in line with the bamboo fence. He started around the one acre square, looking for a spot where the fence had been opened.

Sure enough, a quarter of the way around, he came across a bamboo gate, wide open. He pulled to a stop near this gate and lowered the board to the ground.

"Am I to get off?" asked Venetia.

"Sure," said Raymond absent-mindedly. He slid forward off the board and walked through the gate.

"What is this place?" asked Venetia, trailing behind.

"This is the home I made for Molly, when I first uploaded her."

"You never mentioned Molly."

"No? I'm surprised." Raymond wandered about. There were signs that Molly had lived in the cage for a long time—piles of discarded palm nut shells, dried feces, and defoliated areas where she had probably sought food.

"Was Molly a woman?" asked Venetia.

"No." He chuckled at the prospect of keeping a woman in such a place, and was reminded of how much Venetia didn't know.

He called out for Hank the Handler, hoping he would have some answers, but there was no response. He finally came back to the airboard and directed Venetia to get on.

"Did you find what you were looking for?" she asked.

"No. This doesn't really help at all. If I had found Molly here, it would have told me that the first Raymond managed to get his hands on another NBC. Or that I'm in the original NBC, and the first Raymond is gone."

"What does that mean?"

"Um... you don't need to know." Raymond boarded the airboard, helped Venetia climb on behind him, and lifted off the ground. He was above the trees before he realized he had no idea where to go next. The sun was setting, and he was hungry again. He thought of simply returning to the palace, but he wanted to see more of Nurania, in hopes of finding some further clue as to its state, and his own. On a whim, he decided to ask Venetia if there were anywhere she would like to go.

"Over the mountains, to see your village," she responded excitedly. "You said that if you ever built the village, you would want me to see it someday. Or back to the palace, where I could please you."

"Village?" asked Raymond.

"The day that you left, you said that maybe you would build a village."

"Really," said Raymond significantly.

A village?

He had always conceived of Nurania as an escape from people. It made sense to him that he would create Venetia, to be his confidant and plaything. But a village?

"You said it was over the mountains," said Raymond. "Did I say which mountains?"

"No."

"Well, I suppose it wouldn't be too hard to guess." He envisioned lava flowing into the village, destroying it and all of its inhabitants.

The Faralons were far to the northwest of the palace, and they had flown more or less south to get here. They would have to cover a lot of the same ground again, and then continue on to the mountains. Raymond feared it would be dark before they could reach the village, if there was one. He would need daylight to find it, and to find his way back to the palace if he needed to. He didn't want to run the risk of sleeping in the wilds and being eaten by one of his own creations. He decided to return to the palace for the night and search for the village in the morning.

By the time they reached the palace, dusk was already turning to darkness. Raymond flew up over the vast blue rock wall and descended directly into one of the many courtyards.

He feasted on fruits, Venetia pointing out which ones he would like best—and she was right. He almost wanted her to be wrong, for the sake of his own individuality. She also mentioned that the black starfish fruits were designed to provide a balanced diet, and Raymond was pleased with his god copy for simplifying the often tedious task of nourishing oneself. He tried one. The skin was salty and fibrous, and the gooey inside tasted of lime-tinged black beans, with a fine vein of honey running through the center of each leg.

"How many of these do you have to eat per day?" he asked.

"Thirty, for your body weight."

"Oh god, I wish I'd spent more time on that." He tore off another mouthful and chewed away. "Do you eat, Venetia?"

"I can. Would you like for me to eat?"

"No, that's fine. Do you like eating?"

"I like learning the flavors that you enjoy."

"Naturally."

When he had eaten as much fruit as he could manage, Raymond asked Venetia to lead him back to the bathing room. He asked her to give him a bath. She told him that she would make it just the right temperature for him, then knelt at the water's edge and dipped her right index finger into the water.

"Okay," she said with a smile. "Your bath is ready."

Raymond smiled back at her. It was very nice to discover the features that his god copy had designed into her, rather than to expect them and seek areas for improvement. He took off his robe and stepped into the hot water, and enjoyed a combination bath-and-massage that left him relaxed and lightheaded. As she rubbed him all over with a towel, he announced that he felt ready to sleep. She finished drying him off, then went to the bed and turned down the covers for him. He slid his warm clean body between the delicious linens, and she tucked him in.

"Am I to sleep with you?" asked Venetia.

Raymond looked at her for a moment, realizing that sleeping with her felt like it would be cheating on Anya. His eyes fell to the floor—there was no more Anya. But there was the memory of her, which for him was still strong, regardless of the years that might have passed since his scan.

"It would please me to sleep alone," he said. "Is there somewhere nearby where you could sleep?"

"I could sleep on the floor."

"That's not what I had in mind. Do you have to sleep?"

"No."

"Do I?" asked Raymond.

"While you built the palace you did not sleep. When you were done, you said that you missed sleep."

Raymond felt sleepy now. His god copy must have experimented with the need for sleep, as he had planned to do.

"If you don't sleep," he asked, "what will you do?"

"I will wait for you to awaken."

He rolled onto his back. At first, this notion seemed silly, but an idea occurred to him. "Okay," he said. "I want you to stand guard outside the bedroom. If anyone comes into the palace, I want you to awaken me. Oh—and if he looks like me, ignore him and come straight here. Don't listen to a word he says." She nodded and left the room. It seemed unlikely that his god copy would choose to wander about, if his god copy were even alive anymore, but it was an easy precaution to take.

As he drifted off to sleep, he pictured the neuristors in his NBC sorting themselves out, as he roughly pictured the organic brain sorting itself out during sleep. He had never studied the topic, but he had overheard Anya and other scientists on the team postulating that this process would be necessary, to a lesser degree, in a computer brain. He wished he had at least enough access to his network to monitor the state of his NBC.

o-----------------------------o

Sleep, his first night in Nurania, was restless. He dreamt of himself as a puppet being operated by an evil version of himself. This dream transitioned abruptly into another, in which he was in the gallery of a courtroom, amid dozens of copies of himself. All of the copies were on trial for the negligent homicide of Mr. Tate, but only one was allowed to speak. Detective Brody was cross-examining that one copy, and he kept giving wrong answers. Raymond turned from side to side, looking to his comrades for the courage to speak out, but they looked at him with helpless eyes, their mouths sealed shut by an extra layer of skin. He tried to scream out that this was not fair, that someone must have brainwashed the copy that was representing them all, but he found that he couldn't open his mouth, either. He brought his hand up and ran it over the fresh new skin that stretched from his upper lip to his chin. He tore at the skin, trying at the same time to force his jaws open, but the skin was too tough. Then he saw that Anya was the judge. The copy of him that was allowed to speak was describing what it was like to drain the blood from the old man's body and cut it to pieces, feeding the meat and organs to caged rats and grinding the bone chunks into powder. Anya's face was white, distorted with sadness and disgust. She looked to the gallery, to him, shaking her head and mouthing the word "why". He bent forward, his head in his heads, and started to sob uncontrollably. And he awoke this way, lying on his side, curled tightly, shaking with heavy sobs.

"I didn't even kill him," he mumbled, slowly coming out of it. But he knew that what he had done was inhuman, and that he had never come to terms with it, never admitted to himself that it was wrong. "It was a symptom of some... deeper sickness." His concept of the sickness was vague, but he knew that it had to do with lies and concealment. "As if I could have concealed it from myself." At these words he started to cry again, tears of bitter self-awareness.

He lay awake for hours, uneasy with despair. He kept thinking of his relationship with Anya, and his failure to break through with her. He dwelled on his past until he could do so no more, and a desire to change arose within him. He threw the covers aside, got out of bed, and walked outside the bedroom. Venetia sat on a bench in the courtyard, doing nothing. At his approach, she stood up; he fell to his knees, embraced her hips, and leaned the right side of his face against her robed tummy.

"I am a worthless man," he said.

"No," protested Venetia.

"Yes. Please don't try to convince me otherwise, Venetia. I just want to tell you that I'm worthless. It feels good to say it out loud, to tell it to someone." He took deep breaths, enjoying how close he was to her reproductive organs. They were a symbol of strength for him, of humility and sacrifice. It occurred to him that they were probably non-existent in this particular woman, but he was willing to embrace this small delusion for the sake of his own peace of mind.

A heady floral aroma filled his nostrils. For a moment, he thought the scent to be coming from Venetia, but then he realized what it must be. He had always had a fascination with night-blooming flowers. He must have included some in this courtyard, just outside his bedroom, to be enjoyed on nights when he preferred not to sleep.

"You are worth something, Venetia, and I am worth nothing. You do only good. I've done so little good." She stood perfectly still, saying nothing, just as he had instructed. It made his speech seem to ring a bit empty, but it felt good to hear the words come from his mouth.

"I've done work," he continued, "but always with my own satisfaction in mind. You act to please others, and therein lies your pleasure. When have I ever done anything to please others? I have done work to please animals, I suppose. But that's different. When I work to please animals, I don't feel like I'm giving up anything of myself. Where people are concerned, it's like… my dignity is at stake. Why is that?"

"I don't know," answered Venetia.

Raymond loved that she wanted to answer his question. He opened her robe and sweetly kissed the skin that curved across her pelvis. "That's okay, Venetia. I don't expect you to know. I asked the question without expecting any answer."

Birds started to tweet in the trees around them. The first light of dawn had edged its way into the night. Raymond looked to the sky.

"You can already see fewer stars," he said. As these words came out of his mouth, a streaking ball of fire cut across the sky. It didn't fizzle out in the upper atmosphere—it kept going, clear across the sky, until it dropped out of view beyond the courtyard wall, followed a second or two later by an explosive impact that shook the ground.

"Oh no," said Raymond. He scanned the sky. About thirty seconds later, another meteorite tore across the night sky, this one closer. Its impact was closer, too, shaking the courtyard floor noticeably. "The beginning of the end. But… why would I have put a copy of myself into a world nearing its end?"

I'm not supposed to be here.

He looked to Venetia. "Stay here." He sprinted through the bedroom, grabbed his bathrobe, and returned. "Lead me back to the courtyard where we landed."

"Okay."

She started walking out of the courtyard. He commanded her to run, and he found that he could barely keep up with her. When they reached the courtyard, he laid eyes on the airboard and remembered how slow their last flight had been.

"I need a faster airboard," he said.

"I am unable to make one," responded Venetia.

A reddish golden light filled the sky. Light from a nearby forest fire, no doubt, started by the last meteorite.

"I wish you could. Venetia, this is the beginning of the end. Of Nurania. You're probably going to die."

"Okay."

"Oh Venetia. No, not okay. I want you to survive. It will give me pleasure if you survive. Do you understand that?"

"Yes, Raymond."

"Do you know how to get into the tunnel that runs beneath the palace? The tunnel with the stream that runs through it?"

"Yes. There is a passage into the start of the tunnel. You built it so that you could ride through the tunnel, and then climb back into the palace. The last time I saw you, before you came back, you went into the tunnel, and I waited for you to come in at the other end."

"For seven-and-a-half months," said Raymond, shaking his head. "You poor, non-autonomous program. Well, I want you to go into that tunnel and stay there. Do you know how to fly an airboard?"

"Yes."

"Good. If I get a chance, I'll send one to you, and I'll… I'll program it to come find me. Or something. Or I'll come back to get you. I don't know. But the most important thing is for you to be safe. That takes precedence over everything else, okay?"

"Okay."

"Oh, you beautiful thing. Why, why, why?"

Raymond rose up on the airboard a few feet. "It'll probably only be a few days before the comet hits. It's like the comet that hit Earth—the one that killed the dinosaurs. Only bigger. I remember once, a long time ago, I decided if I ever had to destroy Nurania, I'd do it with a comet. And this meteor shower is the lead-up."

He rose above the courtyard, watching Venetia as she ran from the courtyard, to what Raymond soon confirmed was the north. He pushed the airboard in the same direction, headed roughly toward Mount Lidral. To his left, he saw two great blazes, one closer than the other. These were the forest fires started by the first two meteorites. More meteorites would follow. Soon there would be dozens, eventually hundreds, raining fire out of the sky. He wasn't sure exactly what he hoped to accomplish now, but he figured he might find more clues in the village that Venetia had mentioned. It might have been destroyed by volcanoes, it might never have been built at all, but it was a lead.

CHAPTER 15

Using the rising sun as his guide, he cruised at the airboard's top speed, opening his eyes occasionally, making navigational corrections when he spotted familiar landmarks. Several more meteorites ripped across the sky. Taken out of context, they were quite beautiful. But for Raymond they meant the end of the only world available to him. Seeing them only made him wish he could fly faster.

After an hour or so, he spotted the Faralons in the distance. His trajectory was only slightly off—Mount Lidral lay a bit more to his left than he had anticipated. He swerved and headed for Mount Hawthorn, the volcano that lay beyond. It had died down somewhat. Lines of steam rose from several points on the mountain—what was left of it—but he saw no active eruptions. In the surrounding area, smoke rose from a sprawling network of smoldering fires.

Raymond slowed to a speed where he could comfortably keep his eyes open and leaned over to scan the landscape below. He was close enough to the mountains that this village could be anywhere. The Faralons were a vast range, extending roughly two hundred miles from Mount Lidral in the southwest to Mount Ionia in the northeast. It could take him days to cover the whole area. But it was unlikely that he would have created the village in a random location. It would be somewhere significant. Near his workspace on Mount Golgora, perhaps, or his favorite yoga spot at the bend of Orlea Brook. In the mountain meadows on the north face of Lidral, or near the milkleaf stands northwest of Hawthorn, where the friendly tigers lived. Or… near Anya's flower garden.

Of course—Anya's flower garden. At the very least, I would have visited there.

He had created the garden on the southern bank of the Ravello, the burgundy river that flowed through the valley between Lidral and Hawthorn. With this destination in mind, he tucked his bathrobe in beneath him and pushed his airboard to top speed again. Would the garden even be there anymore?

Far below, the trees were alive with morning birdsong, a painful reminder of all the death to come. Squawks and chirps and whistles of all manner faded behind him as he sped toward the ridgeline that ran eastward from Mount Lidral. Each time he opened his eyes to get his bearings, he was struck by the beauty of the tropical landscape in the golden morning light. To his left, the larger of the two Nuranian moons was setting as the sun ascended to his right. Sprawling orange and pink blooms in the treetops stood out against the greens of the foliage, brightening the scene all around. Ahead, the mountains loomed large.

When he cleared the ridgeline, Raymond slowed down to take in the view of the valley below, and was shocked by the sight of a bone-white tower, ornately carved, spiraling upward from an island in the middle of the Ravello. It was hundreds of feet tall. A cliff road wound up from the base, along the inner edge of which were white buildings, built into the tower wall, with tile roofs that jutted out like little red awnings.

"That's no village."

Raymond flew closer, taking it in. The river's course had been altered, and it had been widened to make room for the island. Raymond couldn't find Anya's flower garden. Perhaps the tower had been built atop the garden? This seemed an ominous turn. But, drawing closer, he spotted it, an orderly little burst of colors on the bank of the river. He flew down, intending to land next to the pond, at the spot he took Anya to, but he saw there was a small stone structure there now. He flew around it once, checking it out. It was a little building, with a stained-glass window on the pond side and a greenish bronze door on the side opposite.

"What is this, a mausoleum?"

He landed, left his board in the grass, and approached the door. Over the lintel, carved into the stone, was the word "Cordovil".

Oh my god, is Anya dead?

He stood gazing at the letters. Carved into stone, they had such a sense of permanence, of finality. He stepped away and looked around the garden. It was as he had left it. His willows still outlined the garden's edge. The peonies still bloomed where he had originally placed roses. The giant dahlia heads still wavered gently in the breeze. He ambled toward the pond and an amber frog leapt into the water.

How can anything go on as it was?

He felt himself tearing up. He felt like his core had been torn out and tossed aside. Standing seemed like too much effort; he plopped down in the grass, the presence of the building next to him an oppressive mass. He cast his gaze about as tears inched down his cheeks. Again he felt like a fool for throwing away his chance at a relationship with Anya, unwilling to accept that such a chance never existed.

"This is what I get instead—some bizarre exile, a surreal tour of psychological torture?" He picked at the grass, pulling up blades and throwing them away. "I don't know why it matters so much to know that Anya's dead. It's not like I was ever going to see her again."

He rolled onto his side and lay in the grass, sniffling. How had she died? He started imagining what might have happened, then told himself this was fruitless—the possibilities were endless, and he had no way of knowing. What did it matter, anyway? He imagined the original Raymond finding out, and constructing the mausoleum to symbolize the event for himself. To give himself a place to go to think about her, talk to her, and deal with the loss.

I must have still loved her.

He pictured himself going into the mausoleum to feel closer to her, and he wondered what he might have put inside. Back in the motor home, before he uploaded, there hadn't been enough time to scan any of his physical mementos of their time together. Would he have created replicas of them? Or maybe he had built new memories of her. He must have had Net access in order to find out she had died. Maybe he had watched her while she was alive, or even contacted her. Maybe she had even tried to upload, to be with him.

Yeah right. What are the chances of that?

He couldn't help but wonder what lay inside, but he feared he wouldn't like what he found. He would probably just discover that the original Raymond had been a Net stalker, recording footage of her private life, pretending she could love him again.

He lifted his gaze to the white tower city visible in the distance. It was hard to care about the greater mystery of his current situation.

"Come on, comet. Now would be good."

No wonder I programmed this world to destroy itself.

He stretched out on his back and just lay there. Eventually he gave himself over to despair and hopelessness and had a good cry, after which his mind seemed adrift in empty space. He lay there, and then lay there a while longer, and finally closed his eyes and just thought about his breathing.

When he awoke, the sun was high in the sky. He looked about him. Nothing had changed. The white tower-city still stood in the distance, hazier now in the mid-day humidity, and he found himself curious about it. He was relieved to find that his state of mind was a bit brighter, but he also felt as if this were a sort of betrayal—shouldn't he be burdened with interminable misery?

He looked to the mausoleum and thought of going in, but didn't think he could stand to. He arose slowly, sore from sleeping on the hard ground, brushed the grass from his bathrobe, and walked to his airboard.

"Onward," he said to himself half-heartedly, carried on by an ember of intrinsic motivation, the desire to master his situation.

He took off into the air and over the Ravello, toward the white tower.

Why would I have built a city? Was I lonely? Did I want to have someone to play god to? Is this my attempt at a utopia—was I trying to prove myself wrong about people? Or was I just tinkering, creating a complex system to entertain myself?

He slowed somewhat as he approached the city. In addition to the spiral road that ran around the outside of the tower, he saw tunnels that cut straight through it. The buildings reminded him of old coastal Mediterranean cities, built into rocky hillsides. They were narrow two- and three-story white houses and shops, the latter marked by signs. He saw cafes, a bakery, a grocer's, a delicatessen, a barber shop… but no people. He rose higher, circling once around the tower at its midpoint, and pulled the board to a hover. A breathtaking white city soared above him, apparently lifeless. He felt as though he had discovered a pristine ancient ruin.

Around the foot of the tower, colorful gondolas bobbed gently in the burgundy water, tied to the ends of long docks. Looking up, near the top, he spotted a pier jutting into the air from the side of the tower. At the base of the pier was a grand arched entrance. This, Raymond guessed, was his private landing strip. He decided to make his way for it, to check it out before continuing to the very top of the city.

Pennants fluttered on either side of the end of the pier. Raymond flew between them. Through the entrance he saw a long dark court, with a pool from one end to the other. Tall unlit golden torches leaned into the stately chamber from each side. They rested in carved white sconces built into the columns along either wall. He got off his board and turned to face the other direction. In the distance, straight off the end of the pier, was Mount Lidral. He wondered whether he had built some sort of private retreat there, so he could gaze upon his city from the mountaintop, altering it from afar to better please him, crossing the distance from there to here in a single godly step to admire his improvements.

A meteorite dropped from the sky to his right, headed beyond the western horizon. It reminded Raymond that the end couldn't be too far off. But he stood a moment longer, wondering again what he hoped to accomplish. He thought back to the bodiless existence he had experienced when he first gained consciousness, and the fact that he had entered Nurania directly, instead of the Home Base starter world.

This must have been a precaution of some sort. In Home Base, I would have access to the operating system. Someone doesn't want that. I'm on a ship in a bottle, and someone doesn't want me to get out.

He walked to the end of the pier and gazed down. It extended well-past the road below. Were he to jump, he would hit the rooftops of the next level down—a drop that would surely kill him. He turned away from temptation and walked along the pier, through the entrance and into the court. The air smelled oddly of lilacs, a smell his god copy must have applied artificially to the space.

"Light," commanded Raymond.

Flames sprang at once from every torch in the court. Between the columns on each side hung long silk curtains, concealing whatever lay behind them. At the far end, floating in the pool, Raymond saw a little island covered with cushions—a throne of sorts, he guessed, for his god copy.

He walked around the near-right corner of the pool to the closest of the curtains and drew it aside, revealing a spacious alcove, perhaps ten feet square, enclosed on all sides in red and orange silks. Above him, more silk hung from the ceiling, gathered up to a point in the center. The floor was piled high with pillows, and a hookah stood in the corner.

Raymond pulled the silk wall aside and found that it let into a similarly sized compartment, but this one had a dungeon theme, with manacles on the wall and a complicated bondage table suspended from the ceiling by ropes and pulleys. He walked through this space and into the next, finding himself in a spa shower. Metal hoses hung from the wall, with sprayer heads of different types, and there was a shiny metal column in the center, topped off by a bouquet of shower heads. This space seemed innocent enough, until he saw that there were ankle clamps at the base of the column, and wrist clamps hanging from the top.

He walked up and down the court—all twelve spaces were decorated and equipped differently, but all fit the theme of a sex den.

This must have been a harem, a hall of Venetias, each confined to her own cell. Did I create this entire city just to rationalize having a harem, so I could fulfill my sexual fantasies? And apparently one Venetia wasn't enough, I had to have a dozen more sexual playthings, to satisfy my desire for variation.

He pictured the women of his harem fawning over him and obligingly fulfilling his every desire, while others frolicked in the pool, and the people of the city went about their business.

Maybe it was the power trip?

He eyed the island of cushions, wondering whether there might be anything interesting on it. If his god copy spent much time there, perhaps he left a few useful items nearby. Raymond stepped to the edge of the pool and looked in, wondering if it was safe to swim to cushion island. There was something at the bottom of the pool—it looked like more cushions, but they appeared to be inside some sort of dome.

"Well what's that?"

He took his robe off and tossed it aside, then dipped a toe in the water. It was cool to the touch, but not too bad. And it didn't burn his toe off or anything. He sat down on the tile floor and dipped an entire leg in the water. It felt good. He dropped the other leg in, then pushed himself off the wall and fell all the way in, keeping a hand near the wall in case he had cause to get out quickly. But the water seemed fine, so decided to dive down and explore the bottom.

He opened his eyes underwater. It didn't sting at all, but it had the odd refractive qualities one would expect. There really did appear to be cushions on the bottom of the pool, and a fairly large blue-green ball. And light—a faint but pleasant light emanated from the space inside the dome. He swam closer, but his ears hurt, and he needed air, so he returned to the surface.

"Raymond?" called a young man's voice.

Raymond whirled around in the water, clearing his eyes as best he could with his wet hands, and saw the figure of a dark-haired, tan-skinned man in a swimsuit. He was carrying a bucket.

"Raymond, are you okay?" called the man.

"Yes, yes, I uh… I'm sorry, the weirdest things have been happening with my memory… I don't remember who you are."

"I am Tomás, your animal handler, remember?" He spoke with a clear, gentle voice. He looked and sounded young, maybe twenty.

"Okay. Hi Tomás." Raymond swam to the nearest edge of the pool so he wouldn't have to tread water. "Listen, this is really embarrassing, but uh… I'm not wearing any clothes."

"Oh, here's a bathrobe," replied Tomás. He picked Raymond's robe up from the floor. "Or I could get you something else."

"Could you? Wow, that would be great."

"Sure, no problem. Would you like me to let the otters in first?"

"The otters?" asked Raymond.

"The river otters. This is when I typically let them into the pool."

"Uh, how about you get me some clothes first. A swimsuit maybe, and something appropriate for the weather."

"Okay."

"Oh wait, before you go," started Raymond, but it was too late—Tomás vanished. And he took Raymond's bathrobe with him.

Raymond looked about for something else he could use to cover himself up. He could hold cushions in front and behind, but that would just be weird. He could tear down a silk curtain and wrap it around himself.

This is a harem. This guy's probably seen me naked plenty of times. And worse.

But it felt odd all the same. He decided he would duck into one of the alcoves and wait for Tomás to return. He looked around for a ladder out of the pool. Not seeing one, he lifted himself up onto the edge—it hurt to put that much weight on his right wrist, but it wasn't too bad.

"Here you go, Raymond," said Tomás.

The young man was already back, a pile of clothing tucked under his arm, holding a swimsuit out for Raymond to take.

Oh what the hell.

Raymond climbed awkwardly to his feet, dripping wet and stark naked, and took the swimsuit. He briefly looked Tomás in the eye, to see if he was checking Raymond out, and was relieved to see that he was not.

"I'll put the other things in a pile over here, okay?"

"Sure," called Raymond as he padded over to the nearest harem alcove. He pulled the curtain shut, stood amid an array of whips, crops, paddles, and instruments of sadomasochistic pleasure that he didn't even recognize, and tugged the swimsuit up over his wet legs. It fit well.

Raymond heard a splash and pulled the curtain aside. Tomás was not to be seen—he must have jumped in to let in the otters. Raymond walked to the edge of the pool and looked in. Tomás was halfway down, pulling open a sliding door. Before he was even finished, two dark forms came streaking through the opening. Raymond couldn't help but smile. The two otters chased each other in circles, then raced over to the corner of the pool where Tomás had left his bucket. Tomás popped up, not far behind them, and somehow pulled a shelf out of the wall of the pool, just beneath the surface. The otters were out of the water and on the surface in no time, turning in circles.

Raymond walked over to the bucket, and Tomás lifted himself out of the water right next to it.

"Fish?" asked Raymond.

"Crayfish," responded Tomás. He dumped the contents of the bucket onto the shelf, and the river otters proceeded to devour them, crunching happily on their afternoon snack.

"Tomás, I need your help. I need you to answer some questions for me. I, um… Something happened, and I have no knowledge of what has come before."

"You lost your memory?"

"Sort of. Tell me, when was the last time you saw me?" asked Raymond.

"Four months ago." Tomás answered directly, but he had a curious look about him that reminded Raymond of Venetia.

"What happened at that time?"

"That was the time of your anger," replied Tomás.

"The time of my anger—of course. I am a god after all. Do you know what I was angry about?"

"You said you were tired of the goodness of Faralonia and its people. You said that our selfless goodness bored you, that you were tired of being worshipped and you wanted a city of people who sought to serve themselves first. 'This contrived harmony is childish,' you said. 'It's pointless. And it's gotten so I feel pathetic and dirty every time I fuck one of you.'"

Raymond winced to hear such coarse language from this innocent-seeming young man. Tomás continued without the slightest sign of emotion.

"You were here, in your harem. 'It's like I'm screwing dolls,' you said. 'You're not real. You're too fucking compliant.' And then you left."

"Do you know where I went," asked Raymond, "or what I did?"

"No sir."

"Who was I talking to—was it one person, primarily, or several?"

"You said it to all who were present at the time, but perhaps you said it most of all to Salya."

"Salya?"

"She was your favorite."

"Was? What happened to her," asked Raymond.

"It is said that you took her away, after you left. It is said that you appeared once in the harem, late at night, and disappeared with her, without speaking."

"Really. And do you know where I took her?"

"No."

Raymond was surprised by how much Tomás knew—much as he had been surprised by how much Venetia knew.

"Do you understand my hand gestures?

Tomás looked at him questioningly. Raymond made his gesture for chimpanzee. "Like that? Do you know what that means?"

"No sir."

"Does anyone?" asked Raymond.

"Not that I know of. When you made the hand gestures, they were for yourself."

"Did I ever talk about another world? Reality prime?"

"Yes. Often."

"Did I mention a woman named Anya?" Tomás nodded. "Do you know if I ever looked into what she was doing? Was I ever in touch with her?"

"You said that you had to forget her, you could never go back."

Raymond thought of the mausoleum, and guessed at the deeper significance of this.

"Did I mention the bunker?"

"Yes. Early on, you would lie in your private space and you told us your mind would travel to the place you call the bunker. You would lie very still, sometimes for many hours. And you would make the hand gestures."

"My private space?" asked Raymond.

"The dome, at the bottom of the pool."

"And when I came back, would I talk about it?"

"No. But you would often want to be alone with Salya, or sometimes Scorpio. Perhaps you talked with them about the bunker."

"You know Scorpio?"

"He was your closest servant, the one of many forms."

Raymond started to pace.

"Tomás, is there a map of Nurania anywhere?"

"There is the globe, sir, in your private space."

"Really? Is it a dynamic globe?"

"I don't understand your question."

"Does it change? The globe. Does it change to reflect the current state of the world?"

"Yes, of course."

"Raymond?" asked Tomás. "What happened to the women? They do not sing or open their curtains to greet you."

Raymond stared at one of the curtains.

"The women weren't allowed to leave their… chambers, were they?" asked Raymond.

"Only when you requested them," said Tomás.

"I'm afraid I don't know what happened to them. I… don't remember."

And how is it that they're gone, but you're still here?

"So, this globe… how do I get into the private space?"

"You swim into it."

"I just swim into it? It's that easy?"

Tomás nodded.

"Okay," said Raymond. "Stay here."

Raymond dove into the water and swam straight to the dome at the bottom. He searched for a hatch or doorway, but saw nothing. He reached his hand out to touch the dome, but it slipped right through, into air. He felt like he would have to return to the surface for air soon, but decided to try what Tomás had said—swimming into the dome. He led with his hands, then his head, and soon found himself falling out of the water and onto the cushions.

He tentatively inhaled, then took a deep breath when he found that he could breathe without difficulty. Above him, the two otters were in the water again, playing. They must have finished their snack. Toward the end of the pool, he saw the turquoise underside of cushion island, drifting ever so slightly to one side.

Raymond liked this place immediately. He felt safe, and alone. He reached a hand out and touched the water. His finger came back wet. For the first time since entering Nurania, he wished he could just stay put awhile and enjoy the place.

He got up on all fours and crawled over to the globe, then knelt and looked at it. It was in a heavy stand, which looked to be made of bronze. The globe itself had an antique look to it, as if drawn by a Renaissance-era cartographer. It took Raymond a moment to make sense of the world, interpreting the skewed lines to match the world of his own creation. He found the Faralons, tiny drawings of mountains strewn along a southwest-to-northeast line. There was even a trail of smoke coming from Mount Hawthorn, to indicate volcanic activity. Between Lidral and Hawthorn was a dot labeled "Faralonia". He quickly surveyed the rest of the globe, looking for similar points of interest. He scanned the northern hemisphere and found nothing. He had always had less regard for the northern hemisphere, perhaps because it seemed familiar, having spent the whole of his life on Earth's northern hemisphere. He then went around the southern hemisphere more carefully. But he saw nothing until he had gotten all the way back to the Faralons. To the south of Mount Golgora was another dot, labeled "the Village". Then a third dot caught his eye, at the northeast end of the Faralons, with the name "Iniquita" written next to it.

"So, this isn't the village… And what the hell is Iniquita?"

Raymond examined the globe stand, looking for a way to remove the globe so he could bring it with him. He spotted a rod that ran through the center of the globe, from pole to pole. He unscrewed the bronze cap at the top and lifted out the rod, catching the globe in his left arm as it rolled out of the stand. He cast the rod aside, wrapped both arms around the globe, and launched upward, into the water. With the buoyant globe in his arms, he floated quickly to the top.

"Tomás," called out Raymond. "Catch."

He kicked with his feet to stay afloat and heaved the globe upward. Tomás deftly grabbed it out of the air. Raymond climbed out of the water.

"Tell me, Tomás, did I mention a place called 'the Village'?"

"Sure, lots of times. Hank was from the Village, and you put him back there once you were done creating me."

"Hank the Handler?" asked Raymond

"Yes."

"Did he take care of a chimpanzee named Molly?"

Tomás nodded.

"Do you know if he still does?"

"I don't know. I just work here in Faralonia."

"Hmm… do you know anyone else from the Village?"

"Salya and Bailey were from the Village."

"Who is Bailey?"

"She and Salya were friends. You put Bailey back in the Village, too."

"But you said I took Salya with me. There's another dot on the globe…" Raymond turned the globe in Tomás' hands. "Here. It's called Iniquita. Do you know what that is?"

Tomás shook his head.

"It's probably where I went when I left here. And from the way you described my departure from this place, I don't like the sound of it. If I know anything about my darker side, it will be a good deal more dangerous than Faralonia. I may need a companion. Would you be willing to accompany me there?"

"I cannot leave Faralonia, sir. No one can. It is forbidden."

Raymond noticed for the first time that there was a niche above the entrance to this hall, in which sat a blue bottle.

"Tomás, what's that bottle?"

"That is a bottle for putting messages into."

"I don't understand," said Raymond.

"You would create a message on a small piece of paper and place the paper inside a bottle. Then you would throw the bottle off the edge of the city, down into the river."

"You mean all the way down, to the water that surrounds the city?"

"Yes sir."

"And where would they go from there?" asked Raymond.

"I don't know."

"Hand me the globe for a second. There… okay, so the Ravello flows into the Moretti, which eventually flows into the Torian Ocean. They probably would have floated all the way to the ocean, and from there who knows where the currents would take them. Why would I throw messages in bottles out to sea?"

As he held the large sphere in his hands, he could tell that tiny changes were occurring. But they were hard to make out. He would notice some small transition, move to inspect it, and find that he didn't know what it had looked like before. He held the globe out at arm's length. Gradually, he gathered that areas of green were turning brown.

"Forest fires? The meteor showers must be moving westward across the planet as it turns." He pictured the intensity of the meteor showers increasing, a lead-up to the comet's impact. When the comet hit, all of Nurania would be destroyed. "As an animal handler… how many animals are there in Faralonia? Are they a-life?"

"There are twenty-seven thousand four hundred thirty-three animals, of which twenty-seven thousand three hundred fifty are a-life."

Raymond replayed the numbers in his head, wondering whether Tomás might have some sort of mental malfunction. Tomás must have seen the puzzled look on his face.

"That's including the ants."

"Ah…. Of course you would know how many ants there are. Excluding the ants, how many a-life animals are there?"

"Sixty."

"Sixty…" said Raymond, shaking his head. "All would be killed."

"Do you remember telling me that the animals would disappear?" asked Tomás, without indication of a sense of loss, or even any particular significance.

Raymond looked at him quizzically. "No… what was the context?"

"You told me, 'Tomás, one day the animals will disappear, and when they do it will be time for you to go.' I asked if you meant that I should terminate myself, and you said, 'yes'."

When I programmed the comet, I must have made a provision to save the a-life animals from experiencing the destruction. I let them live as long as possible and left them the Tomás persona as a keeper, perhaps with the hope that a new home could be found for them before the comet hit.

"Okay, that makes sense."

He imagined what would happen if the comet hit, with the a-life animals gone but the personas left behind. He had the sense that he actually wouldn't feel much at all—that it wouldn't matter. These were not real people, and they weren't a-life. They were logical processes in a computer, at risk of being terminated by another process which would simulate the impact of a really big, really fast rock.

He pondered what chain of events could have led the original Raymond to unleash total destruction on Nurania. He tried to imagine his god copy, alone in this world, seeking satisfaction in a society of personas, all of them motivated by artificial parameters that he could modify as he saw fit. His god copy had created the Village, and Faralonia, and apparently another place called Iniquita… why? All in the pursuit of finding a society that could satisfy a need to be around people?

Surrounded by people, yet entirely alone. Surrounded by pseudo-people, really. If you control everyone and everything around you, can you ever be satisfied? No wonder I was putting messages in bottles. But I couldn't risk throwing them out where any real person might find them—the FBI might get ahold of one and figure out I wasn't dead. So I sent virtual messages into a virtual ocean, on a computer nobody real could ever access?

He looked at the globe and found the mouth of the Moretti again, imagining hundreds of bottles afloat on the ocean's currents. He wondered what they might say. But did he really need to track them down? He felt like he knew what he would find.

"So, in Faralonia… there's this harem, and I saw lots of houses and businesses on the spiral road. I clearly spent a fair amount of time here in this hall. Is there anywhere else I spent a lot of time?"

"You spent a lot of time in your house, in the café, and in the upper garden."

"I have a house? Can you show me where that is? And the cafe, too? And what is the upper garden?"

"I'm already late to feed the leopards."

"Oh, I'm sorry—I didn't realize. Leopards? Cool. Will it take you long to feed them?"

"Two minutes," replied Tomás. "But I'm also late to feed the sea turtles."

"Great. How about if you bring me along."

Tomás picked up his bucket in his left hand and reached out to Raymond with his right. Raymond took it and was instantly transported to an outdoor space, under open sky. They were in an open garden space, surrounded by flowering trees of various types.

"The upper garden?" asked Raymond.

"Yes," said Tomás, and he walked toward the tree line.

"Are we on top of the city?"

"Yes."

Raymond watched Tomás walk up to a tree—a squat, sprawling tree that bore a star-shaped fruit similar to the one Venetia had introduced him to. Tomás looked up and made a kissy sound, and Raymond realized with a start that there was a leopard in the branches. It slowly stretched down and dropped to the ground. Tomás reached into his bucket, pulled out a hunk of red meat, and tossed it to the lanky cat. A larger leopard jumped down next to the first and started edging in on the meal. Tomás pulled another piece of meat from his magical bucket and fed it to the second cat, all the while cooing and softly speaking to them in Spanish.

"They're beautiful," said Raymond. "A-life?"

"Yes," replied Tomás. "Now for the sea turtles."

"Wait… are the leopards allowed to range? And isn't it odd for them to live as a pair?"

"You genetically altered their behavior to make them better pets."

Tomás took Raymond's hand, and Raymond found himself in a dimly lit, misty space filled with birdsong. His gasped and panicked for a split second when he looked down and saw that he wasn't standing on anything. He felt as though he should be falling. Then he saw Tomás kick away in a swimming motion and go drifting upward. Raymond reached out, and the motion pushed his body backward a bit, as if he were pushing against water. He tentatively breathed in, thinking the air might be too fluid to breathe, but it was actually quite nice—cool and moist against the roof of his mouth.

Tomás continued to swim away, and was disappearing from view. Raymond was still holding the globe under one arm, and found it awkward to swim, but he was able to kick hard and fast enough to get some speed up. He started catching up, and saw that Tomás was now just drifting. Beyond him, something large was slowly gliding toward them. Raymond kicked onward, and the thing started to take shape—it was a sea turtle. It gracefully moved its flippers up and down in a flying motion.

Something white whizzed past Raymond's head, flew alongside Tomás, and came to a slow-motion hover in the space between Tomás and the sea turtle. Raymond stared at it, disoriented by its presence.

"A seagull?"

It brought its wings in beside it and drifted, then flapped briefly to stabilize itself. Tomás pulled handfuls of glossy squid from the bucket and sent them flying toward the sea turtle. The gull spread its wings and launched forward, intercepted a squid, and disappeared from view.

When Raymond looked back to watch the turtle eat, it was gone. Tomás was alone, looking back at Raymond, and the squid were drifting from view.

"It's time for me to go," called Tomás.

"What? Wait." Raymond hurriedly kicked and paddled with his free arm to get closer to Tomás. "Wait, Tomás. That was just one turtle. What about the other animals?"

"They are gone, too."

"How do you know?"

"I just know. There are now zero animals in Faralonia."

"What about elsewhere on Nurania? This is too soon—the comet can't be coming already."

"I can't tell. But it's time for me to go," said Tomás.

"I created you. Don't go. I don't know where I am. I don't know how to get out of here. I need your help. I command you to stay."

"Use the globe. Goodbye Raymond," said Tomás politely. And he and his bucket vanished.

"Tomás!" yelled Raymond desperately. "Tomás, come back!"

He looked around. In every direction, nothing but mist. It was eerily quiet—the birdsong was gone.

"Oh my god. The animals disappeared. This place is about to be destroyed, and I'm floating in some weird-ass… aquarium thing. 'Use the globe.' Thanks a lot."

He thought about going up, thinking it would be good to get back to the upper garden and have a look around. Were the meteorites back? Was the comet about to hit?

"Wait, the globe!"

He held the globe out at arm's length, expecting to see some indication of what was going on. But it looked no different from before. He brought it closer and found the Faralonia dot. Immediately next to it, the ash cloud coming from Mount Hawthorn was bigger, and now there was one from Mount Lidral, too.

"They're gonna blow. Shit. If I don't get away from here… I have to get away from here!"

He started kicking upward. Then came the doubt—was up really up? He paused.

"I would have come in standing up, I should think. This has to be up, more or less."

He kept kicking and kicking. He considered ditching the globe to make better time, but it seemed too valuable to throw away.

Up, up.

A silvery shaft of light off to the left caught his eye. It appeared to be oriented in a more-or-less vertical line, so he corrected his direction to match it.

Curiosity got the better of him, and he altered course again to get closer to it. It was a column of glowing silver water, a foot or so across, falling… up?

"Shit. Am I going the wrong way after all? I'm dead—I'm never gonna make it out of here."

He reached out and touched the water, and it exerted just enough force to propel him into a slow spin. He paddled to right himself.

"Think. Think. Maybe I could use the force of the water to push me out of here. It has to go somewhere, right? Even if it's down, that would be better than being stuck in here."

He put his hand in again, and again he was launched into a spin. Again he made his way back to the column of water. But this time he sped up and he approached it, throwing himself into a sideways drift such that the water hit him in the belly. It pushed hard, causing him to double over as his torso was lifted upward. It felt funny and out of control, but it was working, and it didn't hurt. It pushed him along quite quickly, for quite some time, then tossed him a short ways into the air. It was as if he had been thrown into the air by a fountain. He briefly caught a glimpse of a vast white-walled interior space, then fell back into the obscuring mist. He kicked his way back to the surface, and his head and shoulders popped into clear air. The silvery water bubbled up several feet into the air next to him, and spread out in every direction, apparently turning into the mist. Overhead, a circle of daylight shown from the center of the far-away ceiling.

Raymond scanned the space around him, spotted something that looked like a deck overlooking the mist, and swam toward it. There was a closed door at the far side of the deck.

Thank god—a way out.

He clambered onto the deck, headed straight for the door, and pulled it open. It let into a long hall with a pool, and a floating island of cushions—the same court he had been in before. He saw his airboard, right where he had left it, and breathed a sigh of relief. But it felt odd to arrive here. He didn't remember there being any door out the back of the hall. He turned and saw that this side of the door he had just come through was flush with the wall.

Cool, a concealed door.

A massive rumbling from outside reminded Raymond of the urgency of his situation. He sprinted to where his airboard lay, scooped it up under his free arm, and headed for the entrance to the court. Just in time to witness an image of destruction he had never dreamt of seeing.

About two thirds of the way up Mount Lidral, a massive eruption blew out the side of mountain, and he saw the mountaintop slide down in an avalanche of inconceivable proportions. Mushrooming plumes of ash shot out, and the pyroclastic blast flattened the forest at the base of the mountain with stunning speed. It was headed his way, and the distance from the mountain to the spot where he stood suddenly seemed paltry.

"Shit."

He mounted his airboard, placed the globe in front of him, and flew out the entrance. The globe made it awkward to maneuver, but once he was aimed away from the mountain he was able to accelerate to a speed that felt manageable.

A shadow fell over him. He looked over his shoulder and saw a black cloud of ash now miles across. The mountain was completely blotted out, and the cloud was continuing to grow. At this rate, it would envelop the white city soon, and would overtake him seconds later. Even if he dropped the globe, he wouldn't be able to fly fast enough to outrun the pyroclastic cloud. His mind raced—what could he possibly do to take cover?

Use the globe!

It suddenly dawned on him that Tomás had given him the key. Raymond turned the globe in his hands until he found the Village. He put his finger on the dot and said, "I want to go there."

CHAPTER 16

Raymond looked up from the globe to find himself stopped dead, floating on his airboard above a placid old forest. He recognized Mount Golgora to his right, atop which he saw the speck of his workspace. Winding through the trees below was Orlea Brook, red as holly berries. Nearer the foot of the mountain, he saw the bend in the brook where his mossy yoga spot was. It felt good to be among so many recognizable places, away from the destruction—at least for now.

He looked straight down. Below was a roughly circular clearing, crisscrossed by foot trails, with a large thatched roof near the center. He descended in a sweeping corkscrew pattern to take a closer look.

"Raymond!" called out a boy's voice from somewhere in the trees, roughly level with Raymond.

Raymond pulled the board to a stop and looked for the source of the voice.

"Raymond, over here," called the boy again.

A bit of motion caught Raymond's eye, and he saw a tree house high among the branches. A smiling boy was hanging out of a window, one foot on the rough-hewn sill, the other dangling in mid-air. Raymond flew closer, cautiously surveying the area around him as he approached.

"Where have you *been*, Raymond?"

"Hello there," responded Raymond, uncertainly. "I'm sorry, something's wrong with my memory. Who are you?"

"Eddie! How can you not remember me? You got amnesia or something?"

Raymond drifted past several big leaf clusters, in among the branches, and stopped a safe distance from the boy.

"It's okay," said Eddie. "I'm your friend. Hey, what's that globe?"

I'm your friend?

Something about this phrase put Raymond on his guard. It triggered a memory. He associated it with a voice. A voice that wasn't to be trusted. But he couldn't put a face or a name to the voice. It was a man's voice, not a boy's.

"You alright?" asked Eddie. He had a disarming look about him. His thick eyebrows were bunched up with concerned inquisitiveness, while his wavy smile was at once goofy and skeptical.

"Sure. I'm fine," said Raymond.

"Come on, let's go to the clubhouse. I think I saw Diane headed in there. She'll be happy to see you."

Eddie withdrew through the window.

"Who's Diane?" called Raymond.

No response. From within the tree house, Raymond heard a sound of wood smacking against wood, as from a door closing. A moment later, Eddie dropped down from beneath the floor of the tree house, riding a wooden step suspended from a rope. The rope unreeled from within the tree house and the step descended with a smooth swinging motion, slowing to a stop at ground level, where Eddie stepped off.

"Come on!" he hollered from far below, and off he walked to the thatched-roofed building in the middle of the clearing.

Raymond was reluctant to follow, but his curiosity was piqued. He flew down, landed, and leaned his airboard next to the entrance of the building. It was a partially enclosed tropical pavilion with a relaxed, inviting feeling about it, like a summer-camp clubhouse. He pushed his way through the flimsy swinging door, globe tucked under one arm.

The interior was one big breezy room, with a bar at one end, a few tables and chairs in the middle, and a large holographic gaming table at the other end. Wicker-bladed ceiling fans slowly turned, out of sync with each other. Behind the bar, a middle-aged woman in a tank top was mixing drinks. She had graying brown hair, pulled back in a ponytail. The boy, Eddie, stood next to one of the tables, his arms crossed over his chest.

"I told you it was Raymond," said Eddie to the woman.

"Hello, Raymond," said the woman. "Can I make you a drink?"

"This is Diane," said Eddie to Raymond. "Raymond lost his memory," he said to Diane by way of explanation.

"I don't usually drink," said Raymond, "but I think I could use one now."

Eddie pulled out a chair, motioned for Raymond to take it, then plopped down in another. He slapped his hands down on the table. "I can't wait to hear your latest stories! How did you lose your memory?"

"I don't rightly know," said Raymond. He was too tense to sit, instead resting a hand on the back of the proffered chair while Diane made his drink. "In a sense, it wasn't mine to lose."

"What on earth does that mean?" asked Eddie, dramatically flabbergasted.

"I… wait, I'm the one who should be asking questions here. Do either of you have administrative access?"

"Administrative access," repeated Eddie. "What's that?"

"How about you, Diane?"

"Only you have administrative access," said Diane.

"Interesting," said Raymond. "So you actually know what I'm talking about. Do you have any access to external processes, or the operating system?"

"I'm afraid not, Raymond." She stopped stirring and looked at him. "You should know that."

"Is Hank the Handler around?"

"Nope," said Eddie. "He's out with the howler monkeys."

Diane joined them at the table, setting a tall glass in front of Raymond and another at her own spot. She sat down, and Raymond followed suit. He set his globe down on the floor and spun the glass in place on the table, enjoying the cool wetness of the condensation. It was a slightly cloudy drink, with gobs of bright green leaves in it.

"What, I don't get one?" complained Eddie.

Diane gave him a stern look. "You're thirteen years old."

Raymond took a good look at Diane. She seemed familiar. So did Eddie.

"Are you trying to remember who we are?" asked Diane.

There was a dry edge to her voice that clicked—he remembered who she reminded him of.

"Brody," said Raymond. "Of course. I must have wanted to feel like I was with people who meant something to me, so I added elements of real people. And Eddie is the Eddie from the Joliet Home, that kid I thought might be nice to get to know."

"You're doing that thing," said Eddie, "where you talk about us like we're not right here—like we can't hear you."

"Right, sorry. I guess I really tried to make you realistic." He took a sip of his drink. It was refreshing—carbonated, sweet, and minty, but with a bit of a kick to it.

"Mojito," said Diane. "You like it?"

"It's nice."

"I wonder if you can get drunk," said Diane.

"I wondered the same thing before I uploaded. Did I never get drunk while I was here at the Village?"

"No," responded Diane.

"How long did I spend here?"

Eddie looked to Diane to answer.

"Three months," said Diane. "This memory loss… have you noticed any other mental issues?"

"I wouldn't exactly call my situation a mental issue. I—"

Raymond stopped short when he heard the clubhouse door open. In walked an old southeast-Asian woman. On her back she carried a tall wicker basket full of vegetables. Her face lit up when she saw Raymond, and she nodded and smiled vigorously. Raymond raised his eyebrows and smiled tentatively in response. An old southeast-Asian man came in behind her, and he called over his shoulder in Vietnamese. Raymond guessed that they might be a family, as another old woman came in, followed by a couple in their late thirties or early forties and a couple of young girls. All smiled at Raymond, and some greeted him, but he had the sense they couldn't speak English. Those with baskets dumped their harvest on the bar and tables and set about cleaning and sorting everything.

"You don't remember them either?" asked Diane.

"Uh… no. Do you know if they speak English?"

Diane shook her head.

"Did you lose all your memories?" asked Eddie. "Do you remember who you are?"

"Sure, I just don't remember everything after I uploaded. Did I program you to ask me questions all the time or something?"

"Him, yes," said Diane. "You programmed him to be highly curious. You programmed me to scrutinize you and ask you the sorts of questions a psychologist might ask." She took a sip from her drink. "And questions of a more philosophical nature," she added. "For instance, do you regret uploading?"

Raymond absent-mindedly looked out the window, vaguely aware of the Vietnamese family laughing and sorting vegetables, and he let out a big sigh.

"Right now I do. I'm a stranger in my own world. Something is seriously screwed up, and I can't figure out what."

"Screwed up how?" pressed Diane. "And if things weren't so screwed up, do you think you would still have regrets?"

"I don't know. I'm so lost at this point, I don't know what to think. Anya's dead, apparently." He looked to them, wanting them to react to the significance of this, but their expressions indicated no sense of understanding or compassion. "I don't know how she died, and I don't know if I ever could have had a chance to set things right with her anyway. And Nurania certainly isn't what I expected."

"But you did it—you uploaded," said Diane. "That must make you proud."

"Proud? I don't know, should it?"

The door opened again, and a woman Raymond's age walked in. She looked as though she had just come in from a farm—overalls, long braided pigtails, tanned skin, and a broad floppy hat. She stopped short, a look of happy surprise at seeing Raymond.

"Hi, Raymond. What brings you back?" she asked in a friendly way.

She approached him with arms open. Raymond made a motion to stand, stopped, and asked who she was, explaining again that he had lost his memory. She put a hand on his shoulder.

"I'm Bailey. I can't believe you lost your memory—that's awful. It's so good to see you. Are you going to be here long? I'd love to have you over for dinner."

"Um, I don't really know. If I'm still around, where can I find you?"

"I'll be in the clinic, practicing my veterinary skills. I'm level 89 now."

"Level 89? There are levels?"

"Yeah, I'm 89 in veterinary skills, 56 in gardening, 40 in pottery, 40 in basket weaving, 35 in swimming… the list goes on. And, the Nguyen family here," she said, motioning toward the Vietnamese family, "they're like level one-hundred-something at gardening, and at cooking. You should try their mi quang! And I think Hank maxed out in animal handling and veterinary skills."

"Interesting that I introduced a skill system."

"Gives life a sense of structure," said Diane. "Having clear goals gives you a way to measure progress and compare yourself with others—a motivating spark."

"That makes sense," said Raymond. "Is there a robotics skill?"

"Sure," said Bailey. "You were almost level 27 the last time I saw you. You must be way up there by now."

"I have no idea. Hey, did I have a robotics lab?"

"Yeah, do you want me to show it to you?" asked Bailey.

"Yes!" Raymond grabbed the globe and stood up.

"Now, then?" asked Bailey.

"Yes—right away."

Raymond followed Bailey outside and across the clearing. Eddie came running out after them. Bailey gestured for Raymond to walk beside her.

"How's Salya?" she asked.

"Salya? I don't know."

"Oh, I'm sorry. I figured she would be with you." They walked a distance in silence. "You can see part of the lab there." She pointed up into the trees. Raymond spotted another tree house, and a rope bridge leading from it to yet another. "It's split up into five houses," she explained.

"Did I make anything cool?" asked Raymond.

"Well, I think so," replied Bailey. "You were never satisfied, but I think the robots you built were amazing."

They walked among the old trees. Above them was a vast network of platforms, ladders, and bridges. Raymond stopped a moment, to take it in. The more he looked, the more he discovered—ladders, slides, tubes, zip-lines, rope swings, pulley-contraptions.

"What's the bull's-eye for?" he asked, pointing to what looked like a red-and-white target suspended from a rope.

"Archery," replied Bailey, who had stopped a short distance ahead. "You want to try it?"

"No… sounds like fun, but I should check out the robotics lab."

Bailey walked a little farther, then looked straight up and called out, like someone calling for a far-off pet, "Ellie! Ellie!"

Raymond looked up. He saw something moving along the top of a branch—something small. It moved like a squirrel, but the light shown off it as if it were metallic. It ran to an open-air rope-and-pulley elevator and jumped onto the wooden platform, which rapidly descended and decelerated smoothly to stop a few feet from where Bailey stood. In the middle of the platform, perched on its haunches, sat a robotic squirrel, chattering away and twitching its spiky bottlebrush tail.

Eddie raced onto the elevator, and Bailey and Raymond followed. The squirrel plucked a metallic acorn from a slot in the floor of the platform—a slot clearly designed to hold the acorn—and the group rose into the air. The platform swung side-to-side, and Raymond and Eddie both grabbed hold of the ropes that connected the platform to the weathered wooden pulley above them.

"Been a while, Raymond?" teased Bailey, who stood completely unfazed by the motion.

"Yeah, I—hey he went for a rope, too!" said Raymond, pointing at Eddie.

"I think he was just being nice," said Bailey. "He rides this all the time."

Eddie grinned at Raymond. He swung one leg over the edge and put on an expression of mock panic.

"Yeah, yeah," said Raymond. "Whatever."

They reached the top, and Raymond saw a rope ladder leading up to the branch above. How the pulley system was powered was unclear, and Raymond guessed it was the magic of v-world mechanics at work. One by one, they climbed onto the broad flat-topped branch and walked single-file into the nearest lab building.

Raymond expected to find a cluttered workspace, components and half-built robots lying about on workbenches and in bins. Instead, he found a large open room, sparsely furnished—a few tables, a tall stool, and a cluster of chairs.

"Where's all the stuff?"

"It's all on-demand," said Bailey. She stepped up to one of the tables, and the tabletop rose to a comfortable working height. "Restore my 'whiskers' project," she instructed, and the work surface was instantly populated with dozens of small parts and tools, all neatly laid out. In the middle was a little white mouse-shaped robot with long metallic whiskers.

"Of course," said Raymond. "Not being in a v-chamber, I guess I kinda forget I'm in a virtual world. But I get so many of my ideas just sorting through junk."

"Oh, you do have a junk room," said Bailey.

She led the way outside and across a rope bridge, to another lab building, smaller than the first.

"This is more like it."

Strewn about the floor were wicker baskets of various sizes and shapes, brimming with arms, wheels, motors, gears, rods, pulleys, grippers, lights, cables, moldable plastic, snap-together components, clear boxes full of smaller components, and all manner of miscellany—some of which Raymond didn't even recognize. He squatted down next to one of the baskets and started going through it.

"What are you looking for?" asked Eddie.

"I don't know, exactly. Something useful. Some way to access the operating system on this machine. Or just something that might come in handy while I'm exploring. Like a weapon, maybe."

"Diane says you killed a man," Eddie blurted.

Raymond stopped what he was doing and looked at the boy.

"Is it true?" he persisted.

"No," said Raymond. Hearing the question from a child was off-putting. Raymond felt perceived as a murderer. "I did a very bad thing. If it weren't for me, an old man might have lived to be a little older. But I didn't kill anyone."

"Diane says you ground up the old man's bones and washed the powder down the sink."

"Wow kid—how about you shut the fuck up." Raymond went back to inspecting robots, trying to imagine how any of them might come in handy.

"Did you?" asked Eddie.

"Yes, as a matter of fact I did. To cover things up."

"And did you really feed the old man's flesh to rats, so they would digest it?"

"Yep. And I mixed their feces with fertilizer and had the lady bug robot push it down into the soil. What does your artificial intelligence make of that?"

"How old were you?"

"Seventeen, maybe?" replied Raymond.

"I can't believe a boy that age could do such a thing."

"I was scared," said Raymond. "The man was dead, and I was afraid I would get caught."

"Where did you even come up with such ideas?"

"Enough. Shut up, okay? I can see why I left this bleeding village."

"Sorry," said Eddie. "I wanted to hear it straight from you."

Raymond continued to look through the lab awhile longer, but came up empty-handed.

"Say, Bailey, where's the clinic you mentioned earlier? It seems like there's a good chance I'll be around for dinner."

Bailey led him back to ground level and showed him the clinic, a nondescript ground-level building that fit with the tropical village feel. Eddie continued to tag along, but was obligingly quiet.

"What are you up to next, Raymond?" asked Bailey.

"I'm gonna check out my workstation, up on the mountain. It's probably sealed up from the outside, the way it used to be, but it's worth checking."

"I could come along," offered Eddie a little sheepishly.

Raymond looked at him with one raised eyebrow. "I don't think so. Wait—are you allowed out of the Village?"

Eddie nodded eagerly.

"I'm not bringing you, but that's interesting. What about you?" he asked Bailey.

"Yes, to advance my skills," she replied.

Raymond nodded, considering this. "But you wouldn't be coming with me to advance your skills, Eddie. And you're still allowed out of the Village?"

"Well, it can't hurt to ask, right?" Eddie grinned at him.

"I see."

Raymond returned to the clubhouse, to fetch his airboard. Along the way, he glanced at the globe, looking for changes. Faralonia was gone. Mount Lidral and Mount Hawthorn both appeared as volcanoes now. The browning wave of meteorite fires continued spreading westward as the virtual planet turned. It appeared that the Village was directly in their path. Realizing he was now at roughly the same longitude as the coral-blue palace, he tried to guess when they would arrive.

They'll be here in the pre-dawn hours. If the comet doesn't hit first.

He straddled the airboard, set the globe in front of him, pointed at the area where his work cabin was located, and said, "I want to go there."

And nothing happened. He tried again. Apparently, he could only teleport to named places. He would have to fly. He secured the globe and circled upward, above the trees. A giant ash cloud could be seen drifting in from the west. The darkened landscape looked forlorn to Raymond's eyes, as if it knew the end was near.

CHAPTER 17

As Raymond flew away from the Village, the volcanic cloud crossed overhead, and a sparse gray snow of ash started to fall. Soon the air was thick with dust. He pushed his airboard faster, squinting and holding his right arm in front of his face to keep the gritty airborne ash out of his eyes. He held the Nuranian globe down with his left arm and gripped the board between his legs. All around, the valley and mountains that had once been so lush and beautiful were transformed into a sprawling realm of gloomy darkness. By morning, the meteor showers would have spread fiery destruction around the entire planet.

Everything I hoped for in uploading seems pointless. I'm a toy soldier in a toy tragedy. Why am I not just fooling around with Venetia and being fed yolo fruits till this whole thing ends?

He closed his eyes, seeking strength to continue. He thought of his old mantra, "self-control yields discipline, and the disciplined accumulation of power leads to freedom." How hollow it seemed now. He felt so powerless, and saw no means by which to improve his situation.

I must keep searching. Knowledge is the key. I just have to find it.

He opened his eyes and shook off his despair, determined to make the most of what might be his only opportunity to figure out what had happened, how he had landed in this paradise-turned-hell.

He passed over his yoga spot, then ascended steadily toward the peak of Mount Golgora. It took longer to cover the distance than he had expected, and the height made him nervous, but he eventually saw the familiar sight of his work cabin, surrounded by trees.

Raymond designed the cabin to be accessible only from the static gateway inside. At the time, it was the only building on the planet. It was meant to be a place of isolated viewing, pristinely apart from his garden paradise. Looking at it now, in the shadow of a cloud of smoke and ash, it seemed like a foreign object, a symbol of the universality of destruction.

With grit in his eyes and throat and a sense of despair flourishing within him, Raymond circled the cabin. He saw no indication of an entrance, and decided it was probably a dead end. But just as he started to turn the airboard away from it, breaking out of his circle of inspection, a spot of blue caught his eye. It was moving, fluttering just outside one of the windows.

Scorpio!

The name formed in Raymond's mind, in a flurry of exultation, and very nearly made it to his mouth. But he cut himself off, embarrassed by his emotions at seeing a digital persona.

It dawned on Raymond that he had never gone back and changed Scorpio's way of getting his attention when he was in the cabin. He sped straight at the cabin, and soon confirmed that there indeed was a blue jay pecking at the glass. Pecking, pecking, pecking. Raymond wondered how long the bird might have been there.

The bird did not stop its pecking. Raymond drew to within arm's reach of it, but it just kept hovering, a non-stop beating of wings, slamming its little beak into the glass in bursts of three or four hits. Raymond looked through the glass, to the dark room within, and could scarcely believe his eyes. Reclining in the chair, in the middle of the room, was a massively muscular naked man. He lay motionless, eyes closed. Looking past the man's bulging physique, Raymond turned his attention to the expressionless face. Initially in denial of its familiarity, he stared, fixated, and reluctantly acknowledged what he was seeing. Uneasy awareness stirred within him.

"That's me," he said. "That's my god copy."

He banged on the glass with both his fists and screamed, as if this might get the attention of the man inside where the blue jay's incessant hammering had failed. The man didn't move. Raymond banged with his knuckles. He rammed the front of his airboard into the glass, making as much noise as he could. No response.

"Can you hear me?" he asked of the bird. The bird continued to tap on the glass.

What, am I a ghost now? Or are these ghosts, empty animations put here to tease me?

Perhaps, thought Raymond, his god copy had jacked out and left this superhero avatar behind, an empty unresponsive husk. But why would Scorpio seek the attention of this non-Raymond? Scorpio always knew where to get in touch with Raymond. It was his privileged information, part of his programming as the head of HQ. Unless… if the Raymond that Scorpio knew were dead, what would Scorpio do?

"Something about this is weird," muttered Raymond.

He started to make the hand motion to summon Scorpio. In doing so, Raymond suddenly remembered that he had made this motion when he first awakened in the post-upload emptiness. At the time, it had seemed that nothing came of it. Now he wondered if it had in fact worked, but left Scorpio confused because he thought Raymond was dead. And now he was stuck in this endless pecking loop.

Raymond made the motion, this time completing the gesture. The bird stopped pecking and turned to face him, hovering on beating wings. In his right ear, he heard Scorpio's voice.

"He said there might be a copy."

"There is," said Raymond. "Damn am I glad to see you. Grant me god power."

"I don't take commands from you," said the voice. "If you are a genuine copy, you will have to prove it."

"Scorpio, it's me."

"Prove it."

Raymond used hand signals to spell out an elaborate password that he used to access HQ from remote servers, then instructed Scorpio to validate the password.

"Which elevator stops in the lower basement?" asked Scorpio. It was one of dozens of challenge questions that Raymond had established years ago, part of the authentication process.

By habit, Raymond spelled out the answer with hand signals: "service elevator three".

"Where is the chicken?" asked Scorpio.

Raymond spelled out the answer, "in the biscuit".

"Choose your weapon," instructed Scorpio.

Raymond tapped his index finger against his right temple, indicating that his mind was his chosen weapon.

Raymond sat on his airboard watching the bird, waiting for the next challenge question. A strong hand gripped his right hand in a handshake, but when he looked down he saw nothing but his own hand moving up and down. He recognized this as Scorpio's way of acknowledging Raymond as a true copy. The unseen hand released its grip, and—without thinking—Raymond grasped for it, as for an old friend, only to find it gone.

In a rush, Raymond suddenly realized all that Scorpio represented to him. Scorpio was a connection to his prior self, his physical self. He might also hold the secrets of the first digital Raymond, his god copy. He was the continuity starkly absent since uploading.

"We're not alone," said the voice in Raymond's ear.

"What do you mean?" asked Raymond.

"Don't speak. I detect unknown user accounts on this machine. And one of them is active."

Raymond instinctively looked around him, as if he might be able to spot the intruder. Then he looked up at the sky, wondering if he was being watched.

Raymond wanted to gush and ask all the questions that leapt to mind. He had to figure out a way to communicate with Scorpio without allowing anyone to eavesdrop. Scorpio's voice in his ear was typically something inaudible to others. But Raymond had no way of knowing the limits of the other users' listening power. He didn't know how much time had passed; it could be that his very thoughts were being tapped.

There's no way to know. The more secretive I am, the better. But I need to find out what Scorpio knows.

Raymond signaled to Scorpio, asking for the ID of the machine that was running this instance of the Nurania v-world. Scorpio responded by moving Raymond's hands to spell out the answer. It was the same machine that Raymond had planned to use after uploading.

Raymond's hand signals had been designed around giving instructions to his computers. They were not designed to serve as a general purpose language. He needed a way to have a serious conversation with Scorpio.

"Do you have access to a network?" signaled Raymond.

Scorpio shook Raymond's head from side to side in a "no", then spelled out "it might be possible" with Raymond's hands.

Raymond signaled for Scorpio to lead the way. The blue jay immediately took off flying. Raymond secured the globe and leaned forward, piloting the airboard in close pursuit. The bird flew faster and faster ahead of Raymond, continually accelerating until the airboard had reached its maximum speed. Raymond closed his eyes against the wind, opening them to a slit, just enough so he could track the bird.

"Too fast," signaled Raymond, and the bird slowed down. "Where are we going?"

His felt his hands spell out the response: "I-N-I-Q-U-I-T-A".

"Can you give me god mode?" signaled Raymond.

His head shook "no".

"Can you give me direct access to the operating system on this machine?"

His head nodded "yes".

Well, that may come in handy.

The other users on the machine might be able to detect his activity on the operating system, but there was always the chance they wouldn't—at least, not right away.

Raymond was reluctant to go to Iniquita. Knowing himself, it seemed like it might be a dangerous place. He wondered whether he might find the other users there, and it dawned on him for the first time that whoever was running this world might not know he had arrived in it.

"Can you give me a list of users on this machine?" asked Raymond. Scorpio's answer was "yes". Raymond instructed him to do so, and his hands formed the letters of usernames: "bquinn", "fgonsalez", "mbonner", "poverlord", "tranier". Raymond's horror grew with each new name—who were all these people?

"Which user is online now?" signaled Raymond.

"fgonsalez".

Raymond repeated the name over and over in his head, but it triggered nothing. None of the names meant anything to him.

"How many instances of me are you aware of?" he asked Scorpio.

Two fingers of his right hand extended forward.

"Including me?" asked Raymond.

His head nodded "yes".

"Are you in touch with the first one?"

His head shook "no".

"Did the first one die?" asked Raymond.

He felt his shoulders shrug and took this to mean that Scorpio didn't know.

"Did the first one communicate with Anya?" asked Raymond.

His head nodded "yes", and his right hand went on to make the gesture for "much", or "a lot". Forming the questions with his hand gestures and letters was a painstaking process, but the answers made it worth the effort.

Suddenly, it occurred to Raymond that it would be easy for someone to track him by his v-world entity ID. If he could switch IDs with another entity by inhabiting another body, it might throw off anyone watching him. It would allow Raymond to communicate freely with Scorpio, and to attempt network access.

"Is my old Raymond-mimic persona still on this machine?"

His head nodded "yes". With access to the operating system, he could use a v-world hack utility to take over another avatar and temporarily attach his Raymond-mimic persona to his own avatar. If someone really were tracking Raymond by his entity ID, that someone would be left watching the fake Raymond, instead of him, freeing him to explore and talk with Scorpio in relative secrecy.

"Stop," signaled Raymond. "I have a plan. Come with me back to the Village. Stay near, but don't act like you know me. We'll do an EID switch while it looks like I'm sleeping."

Raymond felt his head nod up and down—Scorpio's way of acknowledging the request.

"I'm so glad I found you, old friend," signaled Raymond.

Raymond flew toward the Village, the blue jay out of sight. Several times he signaled to confirm that Scorpio was nearby, and each time the answer was a nod of Raymond's head.

"Can you verify the EID switching utility is still available?" signaled Raymond.

Scorpio signaled that it was.

"Can you tell which avatar fgonsalez is using?"

Raymond's head shook "no".

Of course—Scorpio has operating system access, but he doesn't have administrative privileges in the v-world software. Which is why he can't give me god mode.

Raymond realized that if he switched EIDs and jumped to another avatar, there was some risk of accidentally bumping the fgonsalez user out of that avatar, at which point a savvy user would realize something is amiss and starting poking around to see who hijacked his avatar.

Who could this fgonsalez be? What if it's someone I've already met?

He ran through all the avatars he had come across. It could be anyone on Nurania, but it seemed pretty likely that the user would be someone interested in Raymond. It seemed like someone must have brought a new copy of Raymond's mental data to life, and they would have to have a reason to do so. Venetia was the first person he had come across, but she definitely seemed like an automated persona. Same with Tomás, although it was a little less cut-and-dried with him. With the Vietnamese family, he didn't have much to go on. It might make sense to occupy one of them, to make it easy to watch Raymond without having to interact with him. What about Eddie, Diane, and Bailey?

Eddie. "I can't believe a boy that age could do such a thing… Where did you even come up with such ideas?" I knew those seemed like weird questions for a persona to ask. It's got to be Eddie. Tricky, occupying a kid. Kids can get away with anything, right?

Who was this fgonsalez? Gonsalez was a Spanish last name, but that didn't really mean anything. And a first name starting with 'f'… Fernando? Federico? Or it could be a woman… Flora? Francisca?

"Scorpio, give me the full name for fgonsalez."

"fgonsalez," replied Scorpio.

That figures. Even the username could be an alias. Could be some FBI agent trying to get more information out of me. Could be… some Tate family member, taking revenge on me. That would explain Eddie's fixation on how I got rid of the body.

There was no way to know. He just had to figure out a safe avatar to occupy. Not Eddie, for sure. And probably not Diane or Bailey, since the whole point was to get away from the prying eyes of this fgonsalez user. Or any of the other accounts on the machine, for that matter. He needed to get away from the Village, into an avatar that nobody else was likely to occupy. Venetia seemed like the safest bet, but would Scorpio be able to get all the way to where she was?

"Scorpio, can you teleport?" signaled Raymond.

Raymond's head nodded "yes".

"Okay. When I give you the 'go' signal, move me to Venetia's avatar, move the Raymond mimic persona into my avatar, and then teleport Venetia's location."

"Do you want me to remain as a blue jay?" asked Scorpio.

"Yes, to be safe. I'll tell you when it's okay to switch."

Wait, if Scorpio can teleport, why am I wasting time flying around?

"Teleport to the Village," instructed Raymond. "I'll be right behind. Find me and stay close."

Raymond pulled his airboard to a stop and took a look at the globe. He found the dot labeled "the Village" and said, "I want to go there". It worked. He was immediately transported to a spot straight over the Village, as he had been before. Except this time he was higher up, at an elevation that matched how high he was when he told the globe to teleport him. He flew down and through the woods, and landed just outside the clinic.

"Bailey?" he called in through the open windows.

He opened the front door and stepped inside, into what appeared to be a cross between a lounge and an exam room. As he was setting down the globe and airboard, a swinging door at the opposite end of the room opened, and Bailey stepped through carrying a squirming animal in her arms. It was long and slender and furry and moved like a weasel or otter, its head popping out of every which way. Bailey couldn't help but laugh as she struggled to hang onto it.

"Do you remember Carly?" asked Bailey. She walked toward Raymond, and the animal's energy level surged even higher.

"No, is this Carly?" asked Raymond. He also couldn't help but smile, too. The animal had pale brownish fur over most of her body, with black mask-like markings around her eyes. She finally broke free of Bailey and leapt straight at Raymond, clearly expecting him to catch her, which he did.

"Well she clearly remembers *you*!" laughed Bailey. "Oh my god, she's so excited!"

Carly climbed onto Raymond's shoulder, circled around behind his head, put her front paws on his other shoulder, and sniffed his ear. He giggled and at the same time called out in a mildly scolding tone, "Carly! What are you doing!" She circled his neck again, then stood with her hind legs on his shoulder and her front paws on his head and paused, sniffing his hair.

"Is she a mongoose or something?" asked Raymond.

"Sort of. She's a modified meerkat, altered to be better suited as a domestic animal."

"A-life?" asked Raymond.

"Yes. I've been taking care of her while you were away, but she clearly prefers you. I made a point to feed her so she wouldn't be too much of a pest at dinner. I'm assuming you're here for dinner?"

"Yeah, I think dinner would be great. And then maybe I'll turn in early. Where did I sleep? Do I have a tree house?"

"You do. Actually, you slept in three different places. There's your main tree house, where I still find Carly sleeping sometimes. And there's the small one in the treetops, where you liked to watch the slammers. But you also slept at Salya's tree house pretty often. Let's eat and then I'll show you your options. I'll grab your stuff so you can give Carly the attention she's clearly dying for."

Carly wrapped herself around the back of Raymond's neck, her paws stretched along his right shoulder, and settled in. Her fur was kind of itchy on his skin, and he quickly discovered how hot it can be to wear a meerkat stole in the tropics. As he and Bailey walked together through the old forest to her place, Raymond scanned the area looking for Scorpio. He noticed a flash of blue and signaled with his hands, "I see you."

"That thing isn't going to eat me, is it?" came Scorpio's voice in his ear.

"Say, Bailey," said Raymond. "What does Carly eat?"

"Insects, mostly," said Bailey. "And sometimes lizards."

"She ever eat birds?"

"No. Insects are so plentiful, she usually doesn't need anything else. Meerkats do eat birds sometimes, but it's rare."

Raymond thought about boiling this down to a simple "no" for Scorpio, but decided to signal "I don't know" instead, to be safe.

Eddie came staggering out from behind a tree, tugging at a snake coiled around his neck and wailing dramatically, "Get it off me! Get it off me!"

Raymond stopped short, worried that Carly and the snake might be inclined to tangle.

"Ha ha," mocked Bailey. "That's Fiona, Eddie's pet snake."

Eddie immediately stopped his antics. The snake, remarkably unperturbed by the whole thing, flicked its tongue out in Raymond's general direction, giving him further concern about Carly's wellbeing. He tapped Bailey on the shoulder.

"You said I wasn't far off when I guessed that Carly was a mongoose. How do meerkats and snakes feel about each other?"

"These two know each other," said Bailey. "Normally, a meerkat would be terrified of a snake, and rightly so. I don't think meerkats attack snakes the way mongoose do. Fiona's well fed, and I've never seen her show any real interest in Carly. I wouldn't worry. Carly's smart enough to keep her distance."

"What you guys up to?" asked Eddie.

"We're headed to my place for dinner," replied Bailey.

"Can I come?"

Bailey looked to Raymond.

"Uh, sure…" said Raymond. "Why not?"

Maybe I'll learn something.

"Alright!" cried out Eddie, and he did a funny little dance, skipping in circles and flinging his arms this way and that.

o-----------------------------o

Bailey's tree house was spacious and closer to the ground than most, reached via a spiral staircase that wrapped around the trunk of the tree. It had the same rustic feel the other tree houses had—thatched roof, rough-hewn exterior, open windows, and the quirks and inconsistencies of a hand-built structure. Raymond found himself at ease in the space, despite its being unlike any place he had known before uploading. The furnishings were simple, made of branches lashed together with hundreds of little knots. Baskets and pots sat on shelves around the room.

"What's for dinner?" asked Eddie. "Can I have pizza?"

"Sure," said Bailey. "How about you, Raymond?"

"Oh, whatever."

"You always liked my acorn squash soup, with toasted mustard seeds and cumin. How about that, some chicken satay with peanut sauce, and a lemony white wine?"

"Wow. Okay—that sounds great."

Raymond found his mouth watering at this description of food, and realized he had hardly eaten anything.

"Are you hungry?" asked Eddie. "I am!"

"Yeah," replied Raymond. "Actually, I am hungry."

Bailey set a tray of drinks and hot appetizers on the bar that separated the kitchen from the living room.

"Eddie," said Bailey, "how about if you put Fiona out on the deck."

Eddie headed out through an open door.

"Here you go," said Bailey, handing Raymond a glass of white wine. She held her own glass out to toast. "It's great to see you again," she said, and they clinked glasses.

Raymond sipped the wine and was surprised to find that it really did taste lemony. He ate appetizers while Bailey set about cooking, magically producing all the ingredients she needed from the few cupboards she had in her small kitchen. Carly climbed onto the bar, stood on her hind legs and sniffed the air, then darted off to explore.

"So you and Salya spent time in Faralonia?" asked Raymond.

"Yes."

"What was that like?"

"Man!" interrupted Eddie. "That snake didn't want to get off me." He hopped into the seat next to Raymond, claimed his glass of bright pink juice from the tray, and started eating appetizers.

"Faralonia was beautiful," said Bailey. "And there were a lot more people there."

Eddie snatched the globe up and started looking at it. "Where's Faralonia?"

"You won't find it," said Raymond. "It's gone. It was destroyed by the eruption of Mount Lidral."

"Oh my god!" exclaimed Bailey. "Gone?"

"Did you destroy it?" asked Eddie, looking at Raymond curiously.

"I guess you could say that."

"Did the animals die?" asked Bailey.

"No," said Raymond. "They… got away. Before the volcano erupted. They knew it was going to erupt."

"What about the people?" asked Eddie. "Did you kill all the people?"

"No, the people were already gone. Except for Tomás, who was still there to take care of the animals, and he left when they left. But the others… I must have sent them away when I no longer felt they were… necessary."

"Where did the animals go?" asked Eddie.

"I actually don't know, Eddie. I don't have god power anymore."

"How do you know they didn't die then?"

"Because I think I programmed them to leave before they got hurt, and I wouldn't have done that just to kill them. Or maybe they did die, because there's no other computer for them to go to. Tell me, Bailey—is Eddie always like this?"

Bailey stirred the pot of soup. "He's always asking questions," she replied without looking up.

"Why did you destroy Faralonia?" asked Eddie.

"That's a good question. I don't know."

"Are you going to destroy the Village, too?"

"I think so. If you look at the globe, you'll see areas of brown spreading westward as the meteorites start fires. Eventually, I expect a comet will come and destroy everything." He took a sip of his wine.

"Will we all die?" asked Eddie, the tone of his voice still showing nothing more than curiosity.

"I expect so," said Raymond.

Bailey stopped what she was doing and looked up. "Why?" she asked. "Did we disappoint you?"

Raymond sipped his wine again, pondering this question as the others looked at him. He shrugged his shoulders. "I don't know. Since I created you, it's not really a question of whether you disappointed me." He looked closely at Eddie, watching for a reaction that would reveal deeper understanding than a persona could ever have. "It's more a question of whether I disappointed myself, isn't it."

"Disappointed yourself?" asked Eddie.

"Yeah, maybe I was disappointed because I couldn't create a world I was happy with. Or maybe I destroyed it because I didn't want someone else to get hold of it. You tell me, Eddie."

"Me?" said Eddie, his eyes opening wide. "I don't know!" He threw his arms up and cocked his head off to one side, cutely innocent in his ignorance.

"Should we be doing something different?" asked Bailey. "Maybe we could do something so you're not disappointed?"

"I don't know," said Raymond. "I would stop it if I could, but at this point there's nothing I can do."

"Do we need to help Carly and Fiona and all the other animals get away before the Village is destroyed?" asked Bailey.

"No, they'll just disappear, and go live somewhere else, I guess."

"And there's nothing we should do differently?" asked Bailey.

"Not that I can think of," said Raymond. "Enjoy yourselves, take care of the animals. Who knows, maybe I'm wrong and the comet won't come."

"Is there really nothing you can do?" asked Eddie.

"I don't think so." Raymond turned and looked Eddie straight in the eye. "Tell me something. If you could help me stop the comet, would you?"

"Of course."

Yeah, I bet you would.

Bailey served dinner on the deck. As Raymond wandered out that way, he saw Carly curled up in a chair in the living room. Outside, he looked for Fiona, and saw that she was wound around a tree limb, not far from the deck. He looked for Scorpio briefly, but didn't see him.

"What're you lookin' for?" asked Eddie.

"Just checking things out."

Raymond signaled to Scorpio, asking for confirmation that he was nearby, and felt his head nod.

Bailey topped off everyone's drinks, and they settled in to eat. The soup was fragrant and delicious, and went very well with the chicken and wine.

"Were you around," asked Raymond of Bailey, "when I came back to get Salya from Faralonia?"

"No, I was already back in the Village when that happened."

"But you know what I'm talking about?" asked Raymond.

"Yes. You told me about it once, when you visited the Village."

"Tell me what you know."

"I asked how she was doing, and you said, 'You don't want to know'. You said Anya was sleeping with another man, and it made you angry, so you took it out on Salya. You said, 'I took her to Iniquita and had her punished—had her treated like the whore she really is'. When I asked what you meant, and whether she was okay, you said she was 'okay enough', and that I shouldn't ask you any more questions about her. You said she was just a persona like me, so what did it fucking matter."

Raymond nodded. So Anya ended up with another man? Anger flared within him, and he could imagine how the original Raymond must have felt. He wanted to ask who it was, but thought better of it—he might not like the answer. It was probably someone she had been interested in even when they were together. And without her, what connection did he have to the real world? She was his sustaining force, and her betrayal would have felt like death.

Would have felt like death. Maybe that's what the mausoleum was about. Maybe she's not dead.

"Why did I visit the Village?" asked Raymond.

"You said you had to get away, that in creating Iniquita you realized how black your soul was, and that it was eating you from the inside out. But the next day you were gone, and I didn't see you again until today."

Raymond noticed that Eddie had stopped eating his pizza, and was staring at Raymond.

"What do you think of all this, Eddie?"

"Raymond," chided Bailey, "he's just a boy."

"Come on, Eddie," said Raymond, undeterred. "I want to know what you think of this?"

"It sounds like you're a bad man," said Eddie.

"It does, doesn't it. A lonely, angry killer."

Raymond wanted desperately to confront him, and ask whether he was fgonsalez. But he was afraid to. He was afraid they would give him even less freedom if he revealed that he knew he was being watched. They might even pull the plug on him. The boy went back to eating his pizza. Raymond looked at him, wondering whether there was a real person behind this avatar. There was no way to know for sure, without god power, but instinct told him 'yes'.

The rest of dinner was eaten in silence. Afterward, Eddie collected his snake and left, and Bailey took Raymond on the tour of his sleeping options, as promised. Carly came along, returning to her spot on Raymond's shoulders. They started with Salya's tree house, which was as it had been left when Raymond's god copy took Salya and Bailey to Faralonia. It was smaller than Bailey's and a bit higher up, accessed via any of three methods: a knotted rope, a hand-operated pulley-lift, or a zip-line from a distant tree house, which Bailey said was Raymond's. As with Bailey's tree house, the interior of this one was decorated with baskets and pottery, but Salya's were more colorful, with lots of reds, oranges, and yellows. Aside from these decorations, there were few personal items. Raymond went through cupboards and drawers looking for anything interesting, but came up with nothing. He rifled through the dresser, tossing all manner of women's clothing aside as he did so. He went through the closet, looked under the pillows, checked under the mattress. Nothing.

"Are you looking for anything in particular?" asked Bailey helpfully.

"No," said Raymond. "Anything interesting, I guess. But I won't know it until I see it."

A robotic monkey similar to Passe-Partout swung down from its perch near the ceiling and went about returning everything to its proper place.

"What's next?" asked Raymond.

Bailey took him to his own tree house. It was even smaller than Salya's, and more spare. There was a small sitting room with an adjoining deck on the bottom floor, and a ladder up to a sleeping loft, which Carly promptly claimed as her place to sleep for the night. From the deck there was a ladder up to the roof, where there was a yoga space and a hammock. Raymond thought back to the maze of palatial rooms Venetia had shown him, and he felt like this was his god copy's response to the self-indulgence of that first home.

And from here the self-indulgences increased—first Faralonia, then Iniquita.

He snooped around as he had at Salya's, but there was even less to explore here. Again he found nothing of interest.

"We'll need an airboard to get to the third one," said Bailey.

They returned through the darkness to the clinic, where Raymond had left his airboard, and both climbed on. Bailey held onto him from behind, and guided him up through the tree limbs, slowly, both of them ducking at times to avoid branches Raymond couldn't see until they were just a few feet away. Feeling her arm around him, Raymond noticed for the first time that she was a woman, and he a man, and felt some degree of attraction to her.

The treetop house turned out to be nothing more than a single glass-enclosed circular room with a surrounding deck. Inside were a couple of chairs, a mattress on a wooden platform, and another airboard, leaned up against the glass. The air at this height smelled of sulfur, and ash flakes floated down from the clouds above.

"I love it up here," said Bailey, as if unaware of the ash. "I came up here once with you and Salya, during slammer season, and we all watched the storms for hours, until we all fell asleep."

Raymond realized that if he asked her to, she would probably sleep with him now. Or would she? Her persona was complex enough that Raymond couldn't be sure. She would probably share a bed with him, to be close, but he wondered whether she would have sex with him. Not that he wanted her to—it was idle curiosity. She was clearly the parallel to Suma, as Salya was Anya's parallel, and he scolded himself for even thinking such a thing. But he couldn't help it.

"I think I like Carly's choice," said Raymond. "This is cool, but it feels disconnected. How about if I drop you off at your place, and then I'll sleep at my old place."

They returned to Bailey's. He wished her a good night, and was about to leave when she interrupted him.

"Don't you want your globe?"

"Right! Wow, I can't believe I almost forgot it."

She fetched it for him, and he flew to his god copy's tree house. He brought the globe and airboard inside, climbed up to the sleeping loft, and situated himself next to Carly.

"I can see why you like sleeping here," he said to the sleeping meerkat. "Cozy spot."

It was so cozy, he was tempted to let himself drift off to sleep. But this was his time to switch avatars. If he was right, whoever was watching him would continue to watch his avatar, allowing him to occupy Venetia and have a good talk with Scorpio.

CHAPTER 18

Raymond closed his eyes and signaled to Scorpio, to check in with him. Scorpio confirmed he was close.

"On my command," signaled Raymond, "move me into Venetia's avatar, connect the Raymond mimic to this avatar, and teleport to be near me."

Raymond felt his head nod—Scorpio's "affirmative".

Switching avatars is an old trick. They might be watching for it, whoever they are. They probably don't think I can, and it's the best hope I have.

He gave Scorpio the signal to switch—crossed fingers—realizing the double meaning only as he did so.

Raymond felt the change occur—he felt himself move into a woman's body. He stood in darkness, cool air swirling around his ankles. He patted his waist, felt terrycloth, and realized he was standing in the tunnel, where he had instructed Venetia to hide from the meteorites. Gradually, his eyes adjusted. He was standing on a rock ledge at the water's edge. In the water were the faint wavering lights of glowing cave fish. From the gentle shimmer he could tell the water was calm.

"Scorpio?" called out Raymond. "You can switch to human form. Scorpio?"

"I'm here."

Raymond was startled by how close the voice was. He reached out and felt Scorpio's leather jacket.

"Okay, tell me everything," said Raymond.

"What do you want to know?"

"First things first. Is Anya dead?"

"Not that I know of."

"Seriously?" asked Raymond.

"Seriously."

"Then what's the crypt all about?"

"You built it to convince yourself she was gone from your life forever."

"Then she might be alive!" exclaimed Raymond. "I mean, she's probably with this other guy, but she might at least be out there."

"I've watched your hopes rise and fall many times," said Scorpio. "Be careful. That said, you should probably know that things didn't work out with Tom."

"Tom?"

"That's the other guy, the one she dated briefly, and slept with."

"How do you know it didn't work out?"

"Because she told you."

"Okay, good. Right. Now, you said it might be possible to gain network access. What was that about?"

"When you knew the FBI agents were on their way to the bunker, you had a mote array sprayed onto the inside of this computer."

"Whoa—the FBI found the bunker?"

Scorpio nodded.

"Was I… arrested? What did they do with me?"

"I don't know," said Scorpio. "You said you were going to shut down your NBC."

"Shut down my NBC? You mean commit suicide?"

"No, you figured out a way to stop your brain activity and have it restored later."

"Did I tell anyone how to restore it?"

"You did," replied Scorpio. "You told Anya."

"Wow, I really broke the no-communication rule, didn't I? No wonder I was found out by the FBI. When did I start communicating with Anya?"

"You said you had to talk to her. You said Nurania could never work."

"I said that?"

"Yes. When you started speaking to me again, you—"

"I stopped speaking to you?"

"Yep. You told me you didn't want me to see what you had become, and that I should go away. But two weeks later you called me back, and you told me you needed to talk to someone who knew you when you felt real. You said that Faralonia felt fake, that Iniquita felt fake, that Nurania felt fake—that it would all feel fake, always, so long as you knew that the only society you really valued was one level down."

"One level down?" asked Raymond.

"Reality prime," said Scorpio. "You called it one level down. 'The foundation.'"

"So, I got bored and started talking to Anya?"

"First you started watching. Then you saw her with Tom. That's when you went back for Salya, and things started to get really bad."

Raymond leaned back and let his head rest against the rock wall. It felt as though he had just left the prime world a little over a day ago, but so much had happened.

"How long did it take before she started screwing this Tom?"

"About three months."

"About three months," repeated Raymond. He weighed in his mind whether this was a reasonable amount of time for her to have waited. "Okay. I mean, it's not like we were married."

"And she did think you were dead," pointed out Scorpio.

"Right. And things didn't work out with him, anyway. Okay. So, how did the FBI find the bunker? Did Anya squeal when I contacted her?"

"The FBI insider who erased your data from satellite surveillance history was found out, and your IID turned up in records of his computer activity. The link to Svensson was made. Agent Michaels was back on the case. You detected new FBI monitoring on Anya's network connection and figured out what had happened. Michaels uncovered Svensson's Minnesota property ownership and was then able to piece together enough intact surveillance data to obtain a warrant. That's when you actually contacted Anya, to tell her you were still alive, how Nurania was a failure, and how much you loved her."

"So, Michaels found the bunker on his own. How did I know to shut down? How did I know he was coming?"

"Bob contacted you. He told you he had been authorized by the FBI to take you into custody, and that if you cooperated he would see to it that you were taken care of."

"Bob? That doesn't seem very by-the-book."

"The day of the FBI raid," continued Scorpio, "you told Anya to restore you after shutdown, and you moved my process to the Nurania machine and shut it down. That was in May of 2070. The next time I was launched, it was February of 2071."

"And now?"

"June of 2071."

"Who turned me back on? Bob and Anya? No, that doesn't make sense. If someone simply restored my mental state, I would remember everything you're talking about. Whoever brought me to life this time clearly used the original copy of my mental data." Raymond mused on this for a moment. "The FBI would have seized every piece of hardware in the bunker. Maybe they turned it over to Bob, maybe they didn't. My guess is they would never actually do that. They might *promise* to give it to him, but they wouldn't actually do it—it would look bad. *Someone* has an instance of Nurania running on *my* hardware. And somewhere in the mix, there has to be an NBC, to be my brain. It's gotta be the FBI. But why would they bring me to life and then watch me? They wouldn't play around like this. They would be direct. I just don't get it."

Raymond chewed on the inside of his lip. He wanted to pace, but he couldn't—he was afraid he would fall in the water.

"So," said Raymond. "About this possible network connection. You said I had a mote array sprayed on the inside of this computer. If it's active, the FBI would have found it and wiped it."

"The array is set to wake on a signal, then go into listening mode without broadcasting anything that could be detected more than an inch or two away. There's some chance they never found it."

"Or they could have found it and ignored it, never suspecting that someone would bring me back to life. When I first asked about the possibility of a network connection, you started to lead me somewhere in Iniquita. Where were you taking me?"

"To the v-chamber in the Glory Hole. You can only access the network connection from a v-chamber."

"The Glory Hole?" asked Raymond.

"It's a sex club in Iniquita."

"Great. Is that the only v-chamber?"

"There was one in Faralonia, in the dome at the bottom of the pool, but it was destroyed along with the rest of Faralonia."

"No others?"

"There's also one in the work cabin, but there's no entrance."

"Is Iniquita as dangerous as it sounds?"

"It's dangerous," said Scorpio, "but I can get you where you need to go."

"Yeah, and rack up a body count on the way," said Raymond. "If there is someone watching us, they'll notice that for sure. And then they'll realize I switched EIDs. There has to be a way to get into the work cabin."

Raymond ran his hand through his hair, and was surprised to find Venetia's long silky hair.

"There's got to be a way. My god copy's superhero avatar was in there—how did he get in?"

"He had god power," replied Scorpio.

"Wait! His avatar is still in there! Can you move me into that avatar?"

"I expect so," said Scorpio.

"Boom! Done! Move me into that avatar, restore Venetia's persona into this one, and teleport to meet me at the work cabin."

"That should work."

"Wait—how much time do I have? You don't know when the comet's supposed to hit, do you?"

"You programmed it to impact in six days. You said God created the world in six days, so you would let the destruction last six days."

"And I've been here for about two, so with any luck I have four days left. And there's also the issue of my sleeping avatar, back in the Village. I need to reoccupy that avatar before Eddie or someone else comes visiting. And it would be nice if I could actually get some sleep. Wait, do I need sleep?"

"The original Raymond only needed a few hours each night. But you said it depends on the body simulation, and I don't know anything about your current body sim."

"Well I'm sure I can go one night without sleep. So here's the plan. Teleport back and forth between the work cabin and the Village. If you see someone approaching my tree house in the Village, or if it's time for me to wake up, come pull me out of the v-chamber in the work cabin and switch me back to my real avatar."

"Got it."

"Alright. Now let's see if you can switch me to my god copy's avatar."

Raymond found himself in a reclining position, in the chair of his work cabin. The muted moonlight coming in through the windows gave the room an unfamiliar eeriness. He looked down, his muscle-bound naked body barely visible, the moonlight being mostly obscured by the ash cloud. He flexed his pectorals and biceps, chuckling at the unfamiliar brawn. It felt downright ridiculous. Had his god copy just been screwing around, or did he really want to look like this?

"Computer," said Raymond. His voice came out extra husky. "Transition to v-chamber."

The scene around him transformed. His workstation appeared before him, and the computer instantly dressed him in exercise clothes. It felt backwards to enter his workstation from the mountaintop gateway; it had always been the other way around. He dropped his hands down and found his manuhaptic gloves, the familiarity an immense relief.

The computer asked him several challenge questions. Luckily, they were all old questions, and he was able to breeze through them. He then started poking around. Many of his workstation's features were missing, and he found it disorienting.

Of course. I'm not attached to my network. This is just a limited view, based on what's running on the Nurania machine.

Gradually adjusting to make the most of what was available, he searched for a way to signal the mote array, to awaken it so he could find out what kind of network traffic was out there. He eventually found what he was looking for, and issued the necessary commands. The workstation's networking view lit up, and Raymond smiled. His eyes moved rapidly from one display to the next, interpreting everything he saw. He discovered a great deal of activity, all encrypted. He chose to focus on a frequency typically used by the low-power transmissions of service equipment, and settled into the work of cracking the transmissions. Unfortunately, none of the tools he was used to were available. They had never been installed on this machine, and he had no connection by which to download new copies. His own development environment wasn't available either, so not even the tools he had written were at hand. He let out a big sigh.

"This is going to take awhile."

After several hours, using a combination of basic tools and some snippets of code he was able to reconstruct from memory, he finally got the break he needed: he identified the communications signature of Reikover cleaner bots.

"Well, there's a convenient oversight."

He had been hacking Reikover cleaner bots for years, and had discovered a backdoor documented nowhere on the Net, at least not that he could find. The bots had a service feedback mode that could be accessed via a skeleton-key password, a fairly standard practice among cleaning bot manufacturers. Naturally, Raymond knew this password. Being able to obtain service data was not much of a security hole, in and of itself. But the Reikover service mode had a bug where it gave the user the ability to delete the administrator password file. The next time the administrator logged in, the software would notice that there was no password file and reset itself to the default. Raymond also knew that password, which could be used to gain complete control over the bot.

Raymond executed the hack and gained access to one of the cleaner bots, a model with a full set of sensory input devices. He configured the bot's navigational system to give him direct control as soon as he said the word "override" and set the bot to transmit its optical data to him, giving him a view of its surroundings.

What he saw was a wall. A white wall. It filled his field of view, network monitoring data superimposed in low-contrast text off to his right. Pretty much what he would expect from a cleaner bot, except that the quality of light suggested it was an exterior wall. And as the bot moved down, Raymond saw areas where the paint was chipped away—definitely not what he would expect of an ultra-clean government facility.

He triggered an audio feed from the bot, and immediately heard voices. Two women were talking to each other, in a foreign language. They were speaking in short sentences, in relaxed tones, with frequent conversational spaces. There were birds singing, the tinking of a spoon in a teacup, a dog barking in the distance. He strained to recognize some informative snippet of what the women were saying, a name or place.

"No way," muttered Raymond. "They're speaking Portuguese."

Rage surged within him. Anya *was* involved in this somehow—she had to be. How could she watch him experience such pain, such hell, and not interfere?

This Tom guy was probably some corrupt FBI agent, and he seduced her and talked her into illegally continuing research. She told me things didn't work out with him, but that could have been a lie, to gain my trust.

He caught himself assuming the worst of her and tried to swallow his emotions. He had to gather information without jumping to conclusions.

He was quickly growing tired of watching the wall. As soon as the bot reached the end of its current run, he issued the override command. He smoothly spun the bot around, surveying the area. The bot was between two buildings, in a fairly narrow alley, two floors off the ground. Out the end of the alley he saw a cascade of red tiled roofs. Bougainvillea in full bloom climbed the wall of the neighboring building.

Raymond turned the bot toward the wall again and went into a straight vertical climb. He cleared the wall and found himself looking at a sun-drenched deck. Two olive-skinned, black-haired, middle-aged women sat on one side of a wrought iron table, drinking from white china teacups. They were looking off to Raymond's right, unaware of or unconcerned by the cleaner bot. They wore clean white blouses of identical cut, probably part of a uniform. French doors stood open behind them. Raymond spun the bot ninety degrees to the left and followed the edge of the wall, then turned again, headed for the open door. Before going through, he turned to the right, to get a look at the view these two women were enjoying.

In the distance, beyond a long expanse of tile roofs, lay the ocean. Raymond called up a screen of navigational information and saw that he was looking west. Additional evidence, he thought, that he was in Portugal.

He guided the bot through the French doors, across a handsomely furnished sitting room, and down a hall. There were closed doors to either side. He paused to listen at one after another. At the third one, he heard the tock-tock of high heels on tile. He listened a bit longer, then headed toward the staircase at the end of the hall.

"Coffee-banana shake," came a woman's voice from behind that door.

Raymond spun the bot around and returned to listen. Tock tock tock—the footsteps were coming toward him. The door, an old-fashioned hinged door, was pulled open from inside the room, and there stood Anya.

She stopped dead in her tracks, staring at him. She looked beautiful. Her hair was up in a bun, exposing her slender neck and pretty little ears. Her skin was tan. Raymond sighed. Seeing her, he couldn't believe she could have anything to do with his current situation. She had always been so good to him.

She raised her left wrist and spoke into her bracelet in Portuguese. Raymond caught something that sounded to him like "not functioning".

"Shit, shit. No!"

Anya ducked beneath the hovering bot and headed down the hall, toward the sitting room. Raymond suddenly remembered that this model of cleaner bot had text-to-speech capability, to ask people to move and such. He hurriedly hooked up a text input stream, half paying attention as he followed her down the hall. She was headed out toward the deck. He caught up with her just as she was about to go through the doors and got down close to her right ear, as if to whisper.

"Coffee banana," said the cleaner bot in a clear, polite male voice, not at all a whisper.

Raymond wasn't sure why these words had come to mind. Somehow, they seemed right, as if she would immediately understand the connection. Anya turned around and scowled at him—at the cleaner bot. The two women outside also turned around.

"Crap," said Raymond. He tried desperately to think of something that only Anya would associate with him, so as not to give himself away to the other women.

"Canal Street Home for Children of the State of Illinois," said the voice of the bot.

Anya's eyes opened wide, and she looked at the bot askance. One of the women outside asked a question, and Anya responded in Portuguese.

Raymond spelled out words with his manuhaptic gloves as quickly as he could.

"I am experiencing a malfunction. I need your help."

"Is that you?" asked Anya in a whisper.

Raymond moved the bot up and down like a nodding head. Anya said something to the women outside, then walked through the sitting room, back into the room where Raymond had first heard her. He raced after her, and she closed the door as soon as he was in the room, a small kitchen.

"Very cute, Raymond," said Anya. "How did you get network access this time?"

"This time," said the cleaner bot. Raymond had forgotten to add the question mark to the end of his sentence. He corrected it and tried again. "This time?"

"This isn't funny. If Henry finds out about this, he's going to kick me off the project, and his mad scientist friends will treat you like a lab rat."

"I don't know what you're talking about," announced the cleaner bot. "I don't know who Henry is. I think you must be talking about a different Raymond. I mean a different copy of me."

The spacious, polite voice of the bot couldn't keep up with Raymond's gestures. It was driving him mad. He sat waiting for the words to come out, dying to hear Anya's response.

She stared at him, clearly lost.

"Maybe I'm already a lab rat," said the cleaner bot.

Raymond heard a knock at the door. Anya's eyes opened wide, and Raymond saw her arms come up and wrap around the cleaner bot. The view went all streaky, as if from a dropped video camera, and then went black. A man spoke in Portuguese, and Anya replied. Raymond heard the door close.

Anya whispered from somewhere nearby. "Don't make a sound. Now… okay. Think. Okay, I'm going to ask you a question. If the answer is yes, spin clockwise. If the answer is no, spin counter-clockwise."

Raymond visualized these directions in his head, trying to figure out if it mattered whether the cleaner bot was right-side up or upside-down.

"Do you have access to the network?" she asked.

Raymond turned to the right.

"Right. Of course you do. Okay. Can you get onto my computer?"

Raymond turned to the left.

"Hmm. Damn it. How can this be? Henry said there was no way he could get a second NBC."

"How do I stop the comet?" asked the cleaner bot.

"Ssh!" hissed Anya. "If they hear you, they'll know you're in here."

Raymond knew that cleaner bots all broadcast location data. It ultimately wouldn't matter whether he made noise, now that they knew there was a malfunctioning cleaner bot.

"I need to stop the comet," repeated the bot, as pleasant as ever.

"I don't think you can," said Anya. "You told me you made it an immutable event, and you wiped out all your Nurania backups—you were so ashamed of—"

"Can you meet me on the deck in twenty hours?" asked the bot.

"Yes. No, no. In four hours. Or twenty-four. Both. Either."

"I'll try for four," said the bot. "Otherwise twenty-four. Leave the bot here. Say it looked lost. I love you."

"Oh, I hope you're okay."

Raymond saw light again—a sideways view across the floor—and heard Anya's heels tock-tock-tock out of the room and down the hall. He hurriedly wiped the bot's communication logs. He was just about to disable a key component of its navigational system when he realized he had made a mistake.

"Shit—I changed the password. Maintenance will see it was changed, and they'll know it was hacked. If they know anything about security… or maybe they'll just see that it was reset to the default and chalk it up to hardware failure. Oh, what do I do? I could make a run for it, and try to get the bot to a hiding place… no, then they might lock up all the bots until they figure out who stole this one. What do I do?"

He heard footsteps coming down the hall, getting closer.

"It's too late to run. It's back to the default password… I'll… that's it!"

He zipped through administrator screens. The footsteps stopped nearby, and he heard the door open.

"There it is." He issued the command to restore all factory defaults. "Bink—done!" His connection to the bot dropped, and he sat back and breathed a sigh of relief. They might take this particular bot out of service, making it impossible for him to hijack it again later, but at least this way they were unlikely to suspect hacking. He turned off the mote array, in case anyone decided to scan for unusual network traffic.

Raymond glanced at the clock. It would be at least a couple of hours before the meteorites reached the Village, at which point his real avatar would be expected to wake up.

"Time to think. But first I should switch avatars, in case someone comes to wake me up early. Computer, stop session."

He found himself in the recliner again, in the darkness of 3 AM. As his eyes adjusted, he realized he was looking at the silhouette of a man in a long coat, with arms crossed.

"I was just about to head back to the Village again," said Scorpio. "You done?"

"Yep. Go ahead and move me into my real avatar again, and switch back to the blue jay. And stay close enough to keep in touch."

"You got it."

Raymond was instantly transported to the sleeping loft. He lay on his side, curled up. He felt around him for Carly, but couldn't find her. He closed his eyes and listened to the sounds of the jungle's nocturnal life.

Henry. Who is Henry?

He signaled to Scorpio, asking to be awakened before the meteorites came, in case he fell asleep, and felt a nod in response.

So, the original me is still alive. And Anya didn't know I exist. She's working at a lab in Portugal, for someone named Henry. And his 'mad scientist friends'? Could those be the users on the Nurania box?

He signaled again to Scorpio, moving his hands beneath the covers, asking him to repeat the usernames of the other accounts on the Nurania server.

"bquinn, fgonsalez, mbonner, poverlord, tranier."

None of them start with an 'h'. But 'poverlord' stands out.

"Is poverlord online?" signaled Raymond.

Raymond's head shook side-to-side.

"Notify me when poverlord comes online," signaled Raymond. "Correction: notify me when any user comes online."

The other Raymond isn't allowed to have network access. And yet he's managed to get it. This lab doesn't seem to take security very seriously. They must not feel threatened. Maybe it's another academic project? Anya doesn't know I exist, but she does know about the other

Raymond. Maybe he's part of an above-board project, while there's a secret project underway at the same time—one that Anya doesn't know about.

Aware that he should try to sleep, Raymond closed his eyes. An abnormal chill was setting in, despite his having plenty of bedcovers. He knew he was tired, yet his mind raced. Anya's involvement gave the mysteries of his situation a greater sense of urgency. In only four hours, he would have another opportunity to contact her, assuming his network access wasn't discovered and shut down before then.

He felt like the name Henry should mean something to him. Had this name ever come up in connection with the FBI investigation? Did Bob have any colleagues named Henry? The name meant nothing to him.

CHAPTER 19

"Raymond," whispered Scorpio. "Wake up."

The sound of his name slowly worked its way into Raymond's consciousness, and he willed himself to stir. He wiggled a finger to let Scorpio know he was awake.

"fgonsalez has come online."

Raymond gave the "acknowledged" sign and let himself drift back to sleep.

"And the meteorites will be reaching the Village soon," said Scorpio.

With gargantuan effort, Raymond roused himself. He rolled onto his back and opened his eyes.

"How soon?" he signaled to Scorpio.

"Twenty minutes."

"Hey Raymond!" called a boy's voice from far away. It sounded like Eddie, calling up from the forest floor.

Okay, so Eddie must be fgonsalez.

"You up there?" hollered Eddie. "I'm comin' up."

Raymond threw the covers aside. The movement of air against his skin made him realize he was sweaty. He swung his legs over the edge of the bed, sat up, and ran his hands through his hair. Everything looked soft in the predawn light.

Twenty minutes until the meteorites reached the Village… it must be about 4:30.

He couldn't have slept more than an hour.

"Hi Raymond." Eddie poked his head up over the edge of the sleeping loft. "Looks like you're already awake?"

"Very astute of you," grumbled Raymond.

Eddie climbed up, knelt at the edge of the ladder, and pulled something out of his pocket.

"Here, catch."

He tossed a small object at Raymond, who instinctively went to catch it, but it seemed to disappear. No, it hadn't disappeared. Raymond squinted and leaned forward for a closer look—it hung motionless in mid-air.

"What the…"

"Stand up," said Eddie.

Raymond stood up, and noticed that the bed felt oddly solid as he pushed off of it. He turned around and saw a depression in the mattress, as if he were still sitting on it.

"What's going on?" asked Raymond. He looked at the object that hung in mid-air. It was a slender white flashlight, the kind Raymond used sometimes when working on robotics projects.

"Regional time freeze," said Eddie. "Listen, I got your message. How did you get network access?"

"Network access?" asked Raymond innocently.

Message?

Eddie looked at him with a distrustful scrutiny completely out of character. "Alright, I don't know if you're screwing with me. I don't see how it could have been from anyone else, unless… no, you it was clearly from you. Okay, listen. You turned out to be a lot different than I expected, and now that I've stopped recording, I might as well get this off my chest."

Recording—so they have been watching me.

Raymond quietly let Eddie proceed, pretending to understand what was going on.

"I'm so sorry," said Eddie. "I didn't think it was going to be like this. You're not the monster he made you out to be, as if that should matter—but it does, and I can't help it. And I've been having my suspicions about him, too—independent of what you said. I can't safely do much, but I can do this. I can only begin to imagine what you're going through. I don't know how much you know or don't know, but I'm starting to see your side of things."

"You don't know how much that means," said Raymond, trying to sound appreciative for something he barely understood. "You are Gonsalez, then, aren't you."

"Yeah. But don't let him know you know that. Don't let on to any of this, or any hope we have is lost."

"Henry doesn't need to know any of this," said Raymond, going out on a limb to test his understanding of what was going on.

"He's gonna be here in a minute."

So he must be talking about Henry, and there's dissent among the ranks.

"Sit down where you were," said Eddie, "and get ready to catch the flashlight. It's not really a flashlight. It controls the recording. You see, right now, with time frozen, the recording is stopped." Eddie leaned closer a bit, in a confiding way. "When you freeze time, the *recording* stops, too. That's why Henry wanted me to make him one of *these*."

Eddie held out his hand, showing Raymond a small disk, evidently the device Eddie had used to freeze the flashlight in mid-air.

"But when you click the switch on the flashlight, the recording will start again, even though time is stopped. And if we're lucky, he won't notice. Get it?"

"What exactly—"

"Ssh! Grab it!"

Raymond put his hand up, and the flashlight flew at him. He missed the catch, but was able to recover and grab it before it hit the floor.

"Flashlight—thanks, Eddie," said Raymond, trying to sound natural for the recording.

"So you can get around at night," said Eddie.

Scorpio's voice spoke in Raymond's ear: "poverlord is online".

Raymond stood up and pocketed the flashlight. From beneath the covers that hung off the end of the bed appeared Carly—she must have been nesting in the folds of a blanket. She stood on her haunches and sniffed.

"Well hello, Carly."

He bent down to pick her up, happy to see his new friend. She climbed eagerly up his arm, but suddenly faded from view and was gone.

"Does that mean we're gonna die?" asked Eddie.

"It means the meteorites are coming," said Raymond.

"And what of the Village?" called a woman's voice from the room below.

Raymond looked down and saw Diane looking up.

Well hello, Henry.

"If the animals are disappearing," asked Diane, "I'm guessing that means the Village is in trouble."

"I expect so," said Raymond.

Who are you, Henry?

"You'll be making your exit, then?" asked Diane.

"Yep." Raymond stepped over to where Eddie knelt. "Move aside, Eddie."

"What keeps you going?" asked Diane. "Your world is doomed, isn't it."

Raymond climbed down and walked right past Diane, ignoring her question. He grabbed his airboard and globe and headed outside.

"I actually want to know," said Diane, following him. "It's more interesting to me than you might imagine."

Raymond turned and looked at her. Had Henry reached the point where he was willing to break out of character, too?

"Why is that, Diane?"

"You're living out your worst nightmare. Instead of making the getaway you hoped to make, into a world of pristine isolation, you're living in a world controlled by someone else, and you never know who might be watching you. You lost your god power. Your world is about to be destroyed, and you can't do a damned thing about it. Someone has you by the balls, and you don't even know who. And yet you keep on going? In the midst of utter defeat, you seem to have boundless determination. Is it just in your blood to go down swinging? Or is there some kernel of faith that keeps you going?"

"You know an awful lot all of a sudden," said Raymond. "You aren't really Diane, are you?"

"Is it just blinding single-mindedness?" persisted Diane. "Do you lack the breadth of perspective that would lead most men to despair?"

A series of loud, sharp thunderclaps shook the tree house, as if an array of great cannons had been fired. A wicked hissing followed, and more thunderous rumbling. The meteorites were near.

"Let's cut the crap," said Raymond. "What do you want from me?" He mounted his airboard, ready to take flight.

"If you could point to one thing, Raymond, and say, 'that's what's keeping me going', what would it be?"

Raymond looked Diane in the eye.

"Keep watching, and you'll see."

"Still so naïve," Diane shot back at him.

"Still?" asked Raymond. "Do I know you?"

Diane's expression suddenly went placid. Scorpio's whisper informed him that poverlord had logged out.

"Fly away," urged Eddie, "before it's too late."

"Thanks," said Raymond.

He pushed his airboard forward, and sped up among the trees, through an opening in the foliage. He signaled to Scorpio to stay close. Something in the sky drew his attention upward. He glanced up and saw a black spot expanding in the cloudless blue sky. He pushed the airboard as fast as it would go and didn't look back. Seconds later, a horrific scorching sound, as if the sky had been torn asunder, sent him face-down on the board. The globe shot out from under him and was gone. A shock wave pushed him forward even faster, accompanied by a deafening explosion of earth as a meteorite penetrated the jungle's geologic underpinnings. Raymond gripped the board as hard as he could as he and the board cartwheeled through the air. A high-pitched whistling sizzle filled the air, seeping through eardrums that burned and felt like they might have burst. The pain brought tears to his eyes.

The airboard eventually righted itself, and Raymond clung to it, quivering, terrified, crying silently and expecting to be snuffed out of existence at any moment. Rock and mud dropped from the sky, but somehow none of it hit him. He flew on, consciously clearing his head and readying himself for death. But death did not come.

After some time, he slowed the board and dared a look back. Where the Village had been, quietly hidden away among the trees, he now saw utter devastation, a crater surrounded by a sunburst of blown-down trees and a multitude of fires. Two more dark spots appeared in the sky above him, and he sped onward, as far out of harm's way as he could get. These meteorites dropped further away. The oddly muffled sounds of impact made him realize he had indeed lost most of his hearing. One struck the mountain where his workstation cabin stood and decapitated it, the pinnacle sliding down the far side and out of view. Plumes of dust billowed into the air above. The other meteorite, much smaller, dropped into the jungle and sent up a spray of earth.

As Raymond flew away, it occurred to him that it was folly to think he could outpace the meteorites. The surface of the virtual planet turned at over 500 miles per hour. Without the globe, he would be caught among the falling rocks no matter what.

He pulled the board to a hover and turned to look back. From the lines of smoke rising from the landscape, he judged there to be hundreds of fires, perhaps thousands, burning in isolation. If conditions were right, they would spread and unite in conflagration. But, looking to the eastern horizon, he saw brown smoke clouds here and there—not the sky-blackening mass of smoke he would expect from widespread fire. If he flew straight east, in between the fires, he would actually shorten the amount of time he was in the meteorite shower.

Raymond signaled to Scorpio, confirming he was still in contact.

"Can you locate the meteorites?" signaled Raymond, spelling out "meteorites" because it was a word for which he had no gesture. "Can you warn me if there's danger?"

Raymond's head nodded in response, and he heard Scorpio's whisper, clear as ever—it wasn't affected by his hearing loss. "I'm already watching out for you," said Scorpio.

"I lost the globe," signaled Raymond.

"Yes," said Scorpio. "I tried to find it, but it was destroyed."

"Was the work cabin also destroyed?"

It took a while for Scorpio to respond.

"Totally destroyed," said the deep voice.

That leaves only one v-chamber. And I'm supposed to check in with Anya in less than two hours.

"How far to Iniquita?" signaled Raymond.

"Ninety-minutes."

"Lead me there. To the v-chamber."

An unrealistically fast-moving blue bird caught Raymond's eye, and he chased after it. Scorpio had resumed blue jay form. Together they flew, low to the ground, weaving left and right around forest fires. The air smelled of smoke, and grew smokier as they went, until Raymond felt his throat drying and his eyes starting to water. As best he could, he slowed his breathing and made his inhalations more shallow, to avoid coughing.

A meteor streaked down the sky and hit about a quarter mile in front of them. Debris rebounded up from the impact, a spray of soil and rocks shot high into the air. Raymond lowered his head to the board and shielded it with his right arm as bits of dirt and gravel rained down on him. After ten seconds or so, he emerged from the shower of debris and opened his eyes to find the blue jay streaking along undisturbed.

The sight of storm clouds on the horizon was a welcome one. It made the dryness in Raymond's throat and the burning in his eyes seem tolerable, an anguish to be endured for only a few minutes longer. A gray haze of rain spanned the distance from the expanse of clouds to the dark land beneath. Lightning flashed from within the stormy area, stirring concern in Raymond's gut. The blue jay held its implausible speed and continued in a straight line, headed right into the center of the darkness.

The rain started as a fine sprinkle, tiny pin pricks of water on Raymond's face. He looked down to see whether the forest fires persisted in the rain and was surprised to see that he was no longer over forested land. Beneath him was a vast swamp. He looked behind him and saw that the swamp extended quite a ways back. The smoke in the air was being carried from distant fires. He dropped closer to the ground, slowly, making sure the blue jay matched his descent. The air lower down was heavy and moist. Its taste of wet foliage and sulfur provided a surprising degree of relief.

The droplets that spattered Raymond's face and bare legs grew heavier and more frequent, until their painful sting was too great, and he had to slow down. The blue jay disappeared from view, lost in the thick precipitation.

"Don't slow down now," said Scorpio.

Raymond sped up, until he could see his guide again. A long bolt of lightning appeared far ahead of him, stretching from high above to a point near the ground about a mile away. Raymond was flying at an altitude of about three hundred feet, yet the bolt seemed to end at a point even higher. He wondered whether a mountain lay ahead.

Another bolt of lightning followed, coming from a different angle but striking what appeared to be the exact same spot. The tiny ever-flapping silhouette of the jay showed up in this new light, closer to him than he had expected. But the light revealed something else as well. Something that gave Raymond the sense that he would no longer need guidance to his destination.

In the blue-white glow of the lightning, Raymond saw a giant demon's head rising out of the swamp. A head the size of a mountain, with horns that protruded from either side and twisted upward in elaborate symmetrical curves, nearly meeting at the top. The eyes of the demon were slits, and its mouth curled ever so slightly at each end. The face had an air of lazy malevolence.

As the glow of lightning faded, the eyes of the demon flared with the same blue-white light. Raymond felt as though the eyes had seen him, seen through him. They reached an intensity so bright that he was forced to turn away, using his right arm as a shield. When he peered out again, the light was fading, with a flicker that gave the demon the shabby quality of a mechanical fairground attraction.

Lowering his arm, Raymond noticed that his heavy wet shirt, saturated by the downpour, was dragging his shoulders downward. He straightened up and drew in a breath, trying to focus on the invigoration of the rain. He looked at his right arm and saw that his skin was gray, nearly black. The smoke of forest fires had mingled with the rain, filled it with the soot of this doomed planet.

Raymond suddenly realized why his attention had been drawn to his arm. Light shone on his forearm from somewhere behind him.

"Go faster!" urged Scorpio.

Uneasy confusion caused Raymond to turn, just in time to witness the blazing streak of a meteorite. An ear-splitting screech brought his head down and his hands to his ears. An explosion of heat and light erupted beneath him, and an upheaval of swamp water launched him upward. He drifted up off his airboard, and his body was pummeled as he rose over a hundred feet on the mass of swamp-water displaced from the point of impact. He arced through the air in a prolonged somersaulting scream, and his body started to fall.

Raymond found himself roughly four hundred feet above the swamp, headed into freefall. Another bolt of lightning struck ahead of him, casting its eerie light over the dead trees that rose out of the swamp like spikes. In that moment before the crack of thunder arrived, Raymond lost all sensation. The world went silent, and his consciousness was occupied by a single thought: *I'm going to die.*

CHAPTER 20

"I assure you, he's not the same person. He's a copy."

"Such a perfect copy."

"I think he's coming to."

"I hope the drugs are working."

Voices. A man's voice… it was Scorpio. A woman's voice, another woman's voice. Raymond opened his eyes, then closed them against the red glare of light. He felt as though he were under a heat lamp. He struggled to sit up, but a hand on his chest pushed him back down. He tried to swallow, but his mouth was so dry he couldn't muster enough saliva, and he ended up with nothing but a miserable cough that tore his throat.

"Am I dead this time?" croaked Raymond, hoping for a merciful "yes".

A force shook his head from side to side, and one of the women said "no". He felt as though he might have shaken his own head, echoing her response, then realized it must have been Scorpio's response. He formed a question with his hands, asking for the time. His right finger extended and drew back, as if pawing at the cushioned surface beneath him—it was 1 AM.

"Raymond, do you remember me?" asked one of the women. Her voice was closer to him now, and the red glare that shown through his eyelids faded—she was blocking the light. Her voice was unfamiliar. He opened his eyes slightly, blinking. Compassionate eyes looked down at him, from a face crisscrossed with scars. The eyes were Anya's eyes, and the woman's dark hair reminded him of Anya's. But the voice was softer, more timid.

He closed his eyes and shook his head. He was exhausted.

I'm still in Nurania. Did I die and come back?

He posed the question to himself with a surprising degree of detachment. He was tired of the puzzle of his own mortality.

"Is he ready to move yet?" asked Scorpio.

"I don't think so," responded the other woman. Her voice was harder than that of the first woman, clinical, almost stern.

Raymond signaled to Scorpio for water.

"Could he have some water?" asked Scorpio.

"Sure."

Raymond opened his mouth when directed. He opened his eyes to see what was happening and found, a few inches from his face, a big pair of pinkish Caucasian breasts bulging out of tight white latex. A metal instrument was inserted into his mouth, and a fine mist was sprayed onto his tongue. It felt vaguely cool, then hot, giving him none of the expected relief. The instrument turned in his mouth, spraying the sides and roof. Raymond's tongue and throat contracted in a gag reflex, and the metal instrument was withdrawn. He closed his eyes again.

"Your mouth is a little burnt," said the woman. "Smoke inhalation. As the anesthetics wear off, it's going to feel like you gargled with boiling water."

Raymond tried to speak. He mouthed the words, "Where am I?" As his lips touched to form the 'W' in "Where", he sensed that they were stiff and cracked, and he generated nothing but a raspy whisper.

"Torture recovery ward C," answered the latex nurse.

"Iniquita," answered the other woman.

Raymond's hands started uncontrollably forming gestures, but in his numbed state he couldn't keep up with them. He noticed the words "thrown" and "carried", and guessed that Scorpio was explaining what had happened to him. Scorpio must have caught him when he was thrown by the meteorite's impact wave. And somehow he ended up here. But who was this other woman? He opened his eyes and lifted his head, looking for her. She was standing next to Scorpio, at the end of the bed. Raymond squinted against the red heat lamp.

He saw now that he was in a small room. An array of medical equipment hung from the ceiling on flexible arms. A grubby black mass of fabric lay wadded up in a chair by the closed door—his clothes, he guessed. He was covered by a translucent pink sheet that glistened in the light, like a pickled-ginger blanket. Scorpio was in human form, in the avatar he used in Seneca, wearing a heavily padded black protective suit and dark wrap-around eye gear. The woman next to him was wearing a torn ivory nightgown, streaked with blood stains. Her face and arms looked like they had been systematically mutilated with razors.

He sunk back. The signs of her suffering were repugnant. Whatever injuries she had received, she had received them here, in a world of his own creation.

"Anything broken?" he asked.

"Two ribs cracked," said the nurse. "Your right shoulder was dislocated when this guy caught your hand. Smoke inhalation. And first and second degree burns over much of your body, apparently from scalding. I repaired your ruptured eardrums."

Good pain killers. I wonder whether they were this good in reality prime.

"Sleep," said Raymond. He closed his eyes and turned his head to the right. But he slowly moved his hands, requesting that Scorpio locate another avatar for him to hijack. Forming the commands was slow and laborious, but Scorpio responded almost immediately with a "Done".

"Name of woman next to you?" gestured Raymond.

"S-A-L-Y-A," spelled out Raymond's hands.

The name seemed familiar. He had heard it in Faralonia. His memories gradually coalesced and resurfaced.

My favorite. The one my god copy took from Faralonia. And this is what happened to her.

He signaled to Scorpio to go to the avatar he had located.

"Salya, stay here with Raymond," instructed Scorpio. He then touched the door, and it slid open. From outside came regular drum thumps, at a high tempo, and faint droning music. The door slid closed behind Scorpio and the music was gone again.

Raymond felt fingers running through his hair. For a moment, he had the disturbing feeling it was a signal from Scorpio. He opened his eyes slightly and saw Salya's tattered nightgown. She had crossed to his side without his hearing her.

"He looks just like the original," said Salya.

"Does he?" asked the nurse.

"Oh yes. Did you never see the Creator?"

"The creator?" asked the latex nurse skeptically. "Did you have some god game going with this guy?"

There was a pause. Salya's fingers continued to run through his hair.

"I thought you might know," she said. "It seems like no one here knows." The nurse didn't respond. "The Creator created this entire world."

"Iniquita?" asked the nurse. Raymond heard footsteps, then running water. The nurse was going about her business.

"No, Nurania. He created the entire planet, when he was young. Before Iniquita, before Faralonia, before the Village. Before there were people. And then he came to it, to live in it, and left his own world behind."

Raymond felt his fingers move—Scorpio was in position. Raymond responded, telling him to wait a moment.

"So, you're saying there's a world outside Iniquita?" asked the nurse.

"Oh yes. A beautiful world. He would take me on his airboard and fly me to places that he wanted to show me. I was the Creator's favorite."

"I gather that didn't last?"

"Something went wrong. He started to call me by the name of his favorite from his old world. When I tried to please him, it made him angry. He would hurt me and tell me I was filthy, and then apologize and become depressed. It wasn't long after that that he went away to create Iniquita. He said he was tired of being god." There was a pause. Salya ran the palm of her hand over his hair, back from his temple. "Then one night he came and got me. He said it was time for me to be punished. He gave me to the men at Venom, and I never saw him again."

"Oh, you're the Venom torture-show girl?" asked the nurse light-heartedly.

Raymond had heard enough. He told Scorpio to prepare to carry out the entity ID switch, putting his old mimic persona in control of his real avatar, with instructions to sleep indefinitely.

He opened his eyes, and looked up at Salya.

"I'm sorry, Salya. For everything."

He closed his eyes, turned his head back to the side, and gestured to execute the switch.

Standing now, not lying down—on his toes, held up by something around his neck, like a thick rope. Total darkness, the feeling of his breath reflected back at him—his head was enclosed in something. His arms pulled behind his back, tied at the wrist. Uncomfortable tugging on the skin beneath his nipples. A vague sense of pain from his stomach, and from his groin, seeping through the pain-killers, making him nauseous. He could hear the droning music and thumping drum again, louder now, but muffled through the fabric over his head.

A thin asexual voice, like scissors cutting through cotton, whispered in both ears at once. "Take a deep breath. I'm going to drop you now."

"No you're not," said Scorpio.

Raymond heard a brief scuffle, which ended with the sound of a body hitting the floor. He felt strong arms lift him into the air. The pull of the rope at his neck was gone. His neck was still constricted, but he was able to draw in a short stuttering breath.

The rope fell away from his neck. He gasped in a lungful of air. The fabric over his head was pulled against his lips—he couldn't draw in a decent breath. He panted and coughed. Scorpio set him on his feet and released him. His knees buckled, but he leaned against Scorpio and was able to remain standing.

"Free my hands," he said between breaths. The words came out in a voice that was not his own. It was older, more gruff.

The binding at his wrists fell away. He brought his hands to his head and pulled desperately at the slick material that covered it, but his fingers were too numb to get a good grip. He expected Scorpio to help him, but there was no sign of help.

"Get this off my head."

The material was cut and fell away to either side. He hungrily inhaled, only to find that the air reeked of burning flesh. He saw a figure in the pulsing red light, arms bound above him, head hanging limp. There was a flash of fire from behind the man, then something between a moan and a scream, and Raymond felt a wave of heat.

"Free me," mumbled the man.

Raymond turned to Scorpio.

"Free him," he instructed miserably. "I can stand on my own."

Scorpio crossed to the whimpering burn victim. A long blue lightblade appeared in Scorpio's right hand, and he used it to cut the chains that suspended the man, catching the man in his left arm as he slumped.

"Can you have someone sent down to look after him?" asked Raymond in his new voice. "We need to get out of here."

He followed up with a hand signal: "To the v-chamber."

Scorpio nodded. He spoke into his lapel, calling someone down from torture recovery, then quickly led the way out.

Raymond allowed himself to be led through a maze of dark corridors until they reached what appeared to be a dead end. Scorpio stooped to the ground, picked up a bit of metal, and tossed it at the stone wall. When it hit, it made a ringing sound of metal on metal, and a small round bronze hatch appeared. Scorpio turned the wheel of the hatch and pulled it open. Inside was a small ornately decorated room, like an old-fashioned train compartment. There were bench seats on either side, and a red velvet curtain across the far wall. A long, angular bronze lamp hung in the center.

Raymond stepped through the hatch and dropped onto the cushioned bench on the left. Scorpio followed, pulling the thick metal door closed behind him. Raymond let out a long, groaning sigh. The pain killers were starting to wear off.

"Any surveillance?" signaled Raymond.

"No," said Scorpio. "Not here."

"If I kept the pain killers when I switched entity IDs with this avatar," said Raymond, "does that mean that my mimic ended up with all the pain of cracked ribs, a dislocated shoulder, and a body covered with burns?"

"It has shown no sign of pain," responded Scorpio.

"Well that's a convenient bug. Good. Okay. I need to bounce some things off you."

"Shoot," said Scorpio.

"First, nice job picking an avatar for me to occupy. What the hell was that?"

"Breath torture," responded Scorpio. "Your first copy got a big thrill out of it."

Scorpio pulled a brass mouthpiece out of the wall and spoke into it. "Glory Hole," he said. The room lurched slightly, and Raymond realized they were in fact in some sort of vehicle.

"Did I really create this fucked up place?"

"Iniquita, sir?"

Raymond nodded.

"You created Iniquita."

"Good lord. Was there something wrong with my NBC?"

"Not that I know of. You created Iniquita as an antidote to the boredom you felt at Faralonia. You gave the people here darker desires and made them want to serve themselves first, not others. You started to experiment with control, to see if losing control would make life here more fulfilling. You would deny yourself god mode for a while and put yourself on the same level as the people of this city. At first, it was just for a few minutes at a time, then hours, and eventually days."

"Did it work?"

"For a while," said Scorpio. "But you started to struggle with shame. You would revel in the sex and—"

"Wait," interrupted Raymond. He put his feet up and sat sideways on the bench, rubbing his head. "First things first. Do you know who this Henry is?"

"Naturally, I am aware of thousands of people named Henry, but I see no clear link from you to someone named Henry."

The vehicle they were in lurched to a stop. Raymond looked to Scorpio expecting him to make a move, but he sat still, as before, watching Raymond.

"This is… what did you call it? The Glory Hole?"

Scorpio nodded. "It's a sex club, and you put one special v-chamber in it." He pulled the red curtain to the side, revealing a window.

Raymond gazed out on a vast dark space filled with transparent bubbles, floating lazily about, each one filled with light. Lights of different colors and intensity. Human figures moved within the bubbles, too far away to be seen in detail, but Raymond could guess what they were doing. He looked down, he looked up—the space appeared to be endless in both directions.

From beyond the bubbles came a sudden flash of bluish light, by which Raymond saw a distant landscape, a flat swampland, far below.

"Close your eyes!" shouted Scorpio.

Before he could do so, Raymond witnessed a blindingly bright flash of the bluish light. It filled the space outside the window, overwhelming his vision. He reflexively turned aside and closed his eyes, but the light seemed to burn.

"Holy shit that's bright!" he exclaimed. He opened his eyes after a moment, facing away from the window. Black spots floated in both eyes, leaving him nearly blind.

"So," he said, "we're in one of the demon's eyes, and that was a lightning strike?"

"Yes. The right eye of Iniquita."

Raymond rubbed his eyes. Slowly, he regained the ability to make out shapes. A bubble drifted past. In the center of the bubble, awash in orange light, a man and woman dressed in powdered wigs and frilly eighteenth century outfits were going at it. The man had the woman against a wall, the poofy skirts of her dress hiked up around her waist. They spun slowly as the bubble turned through space. From behind the woman, it looked as though her dress was pressed against a plate of glass.

"Okay, so where's this v-chamber?"

"It's one of the bubbles."

"One of the bubbles is a v-chamber?" asked Raymond.

"They are all v-chambers, but only one permits external access. The exterior of each v-chamber is a display of the people inside, including their virtual costumes and any items they're holding."

"Of course. For my voyeuristic pleasure."

"If a bubble is empty, its exterior plays a randomly selected recording of some previous session."

"Never a dull moment in Iniquita."

Scorpio arose from his seat and opened the brass hatch. He gestured Raymond through the opening. As Raymond stood, he felt a sharp pain in his right shoulder.

"Shit. The pain killers must be wearing off."

"The v-chambers are all capable of dispensing drugs. You should be able to request anything you want."

Raymond shook his head. "So, my god copy turned into a druggie?"

"An occasional user," replied Scorpio.

"How do I find the right bubble?"

"I'll take care of that."

Raymond stepped through the opening onto a black marble floor. To either side of him, a brass railing ran around the perimeter of what appeared to be a massive floating platform. Bubbles docked at breaks in the railing, a constant motion of arrivals and departures. The entire seemingly-endless space was filled with throbbing ethereal music. Across from Raymond, in the center of the platform, was a curved bank of mahogany lockers. Men in various states of undress were milling about, laughing and talking, boasting of the sexual conquests they had just made or were about to make.

Raymond watched a naked man step through the entrance into one of the bubbles. The door slid closed, restoring the bubble's seamless exterior, and Raymond could see the man alone inside it, doing squats, as he drifted off in the direction of another platform.

"Take your clothes off," said Scorpio, "and I'll call your v-chamber."

"Take off my clothes?"

"The ride ends with a shower. Plus, it's club rules. No clothes, no weapons, no solo flights, and the first one in the bubble gets to pick the theme."

Raymond raised an eyebrow, but it was lost on Scorpio, who turned, placed a hand on the brass railing, and spoke a command to call the special bubble. Raymond walked to the lockers. A couple of the men smiled at him congenially, most paid no attention to him. He chose an open locker and started to undress.

"Hi," said a man next to him. Raymond turned to see that the man, a sinewy naked white man with bleached hair, was extending his hand to Raymond. Not wanting to stand out any more than he could help, Raymond shook it. "Flip Johnson. Care to go in on a three-way?"

Raymond smiled wanly at the man. "Uh..." He swallowed. "Not today. I'm, uh, here for a little one-on-one, if you know what I mean."

"Sure, no problem."

Raymond proceeded to take his clothes off. He looked down at the body of his avatar. His torso was covered in an abundance of dark hair. Looking further, he saw scars across the tops of his legs and across the shaft of his penis. He winced at the thought of what must have been done to him. He remembered Salya's face and arms and realized the damage probably didn't end there.

"This place is fucking sick," he muttered.

He closed the locker. There appeared to be no lock on the door.

"Oh well."

He walked back to Scorpio. Still nobody paid particular attention to him. Apparently, his scars were wholly unremarkable.

"Here it comes," said Scorpio, looking down over the railing. "Oh look, it's Catherine."

Raymond looked down and saw a bright blue bubble headed toward him. Inside was a woman in a shiny blue dress, seated with her legs crossed. Her jet black hair rose up from her head, a towering coiffeur.

"Catherine?" asked Raymond.

"She was your first dominatrix."

"How do I get rid of her so I can... do what I need to do?"

"She likes tying people up. Just tell her to take her time and leave your hands free."

"What?" exclaimed Raymond. "Can't I just pause her persona or something?"

"Maybe. Try it. She's also good at deep-tissue massage."

"Right. By the way, is everything okay back in... the room?"

"Yes."

Raymond watched with trepidation as the bubble drifted up to the edge of the platform. "Why the hell did I put the v-chamber here?"

The bubble docked, and the door slid open. Catherine sat inside, in her blue dress, giving him a devilish look.

"Woof," said a man just to his left. A hand cupped his right butt-cheek and gave it a squeeze. Raymond jumped. He turned and saw that it was Flip Johnson.

"You sure you don't want to go in on that three-way?" asked Flip.

Raymond wanted to deck the guy, but he was afraid it might be against club rules. He glared Flip's cheesy smile off his face, entered the bubble, then had a thought. He turned to Flip.

"Sure, get in."

Flip and Catherine kept each other occupied while Raymond took pain killers and then went into workstation mode again. He issued the command to awaken the mote array, and was relieved to find the network displays light up with activity. He was even more relieved to find that there were still several Reikover cleaner bots in service.

Raymond checked the time and date, wondering how long he had been unconscious. He must have been out all day and into the night. Already, nearly twenty-four hours had passed since he had last seen Anya. He had missed his first rendez-vous with her, of course, and his second window of opportunity was fast approaching.

He chose one of the cleaner bots at random, and used the same hack to take control of it. This one turned out to be sitting idle at a charging station, at the end of a long windowless room cluttered with boxes. The feel of the space was nothing like what Raymond had seen last time. It was bright, spacious, and messy. It looked like a low-rent laboratory space in the midst of being packed up.

From somewhere to his right, he heard two men talking.

"Anything interesting today, Fidel?" asked one.

Raymond was surprised to hear English.

"The end is near for this one," replied the other, with a hint of a Spanish accent.

The two men walked into view. Both were older, in their fifties or sixties, dressed in slacks and short-sleeved shirts.

"You almost sound sad," said the first, the older and lighter-skinned of the two.

"Not sad," said Fidel. "A little sentimental, I suppose—he's the first one I've really had a chance to spend time with."

"Will he be done by the time we move? Not that it matters, I guess."

"Yes, with time to spare. The comet hits in just a few hours."

A few hours?

"What's Henry's take? Is he satisfied with R2? Do you think there will be many more?"

"You know," said Fidel, "it's hard to say. I'm sure Henry will want us to instantiate another Raymond when we get to the new lab, just to make sure the hardware is all still good. But I'm not sure what he gets out of all the time watching and interacting."

"It'll be nice to have him out of our hair awhile, so we can conduct the experiments in a more rigorous fashion. He'll be in London, what was it, three weeks?"

As much as Raymond wanted to keep listening, he had to try another cleaner bot—this one didn't seem to be in a good place to reach Anya. He decided to keep his connection with this one open, in case he had to come back to it. Leaving it sitting in the charging station would draw no attention. He checked the signals of the others, scanned them looking for information that might help him choose one, and ultimately concluded that picking one at random was really the best he could do.

The next one he chose turned out to be right next to the first one, also on the charging station. He left his connection open to this one, too. A glance at the clock showed that he was now running a couple of minutes late—he needed to hurry up and find a way to meet Anya.

"Third time's a charm."

He chose another, and was immediately pleased with his choice. His view was filled with a white sunlit wall—he was clearly outside. Within a few seconds, he had his bearings. He guided the bot to the patio where he had first heard the tink of spoons in teacups, just in time to see Anya headed in through the same door he had entered last time. He flew the bot across the deserted patio, through the door and down the hall after her. She must have heard the whirr of the bot approaching—with her hand on the knob of a door, she turned and paused, looking straight at Raymond. She then opened the door and stepped through, leaving the door open long enough for him to get through. Raymond scanned the small room briefly, checking for other people. It was a small wood-paneled office, with a tall open window and a closed door in the corner. Anya crossed to the window and closed it.

"Tell me it's you," said Anya.

"It's me," said the bot in its cheery voice.

"Oh thank god. Every time I see a cleaner bot, I keep looking at it, hoping for some signal that it's you. It's driving me out of my mind. And you won't believe everything that's happened. Where have you been?"

"I was nearly killed by a meteorite," announced the bot pleasantly. "In a few hours, the comet will hit, and I'll be dead."

"A few hours!" exclaimed Anya. "Oh no. There might not be enough time."

"For what?"

"Wait. First, R1 set things up so you should be able to contact my v-chamber directly. I think he was kind of jealous, but—"

"R1?" interrupted Raymond.

"R1 is the other copy of you, the one I'm working with. I can explain all that later. Check for a direct v-chamber connection. He said you would recognize the signal."

Raymond looked to the network traffic display. Sure enough, there was a direct session invite.

"Got it," said Raymond. "See you there."

He guided the cleaner bot underneath the desk and put it into local cleaning mode, so it would be inconspicuous, and left this bot connection open along with the others. He then initiated a session connection with Anya's v-chamber. His workstation environment was replaced with a sun-filled living room, brightly decorated, with windows on three sides. All three windows looked onto a lake. He appeared to be in some sort of floating home. Flip and Catherine, thankfully, were gone.

Anya appeared out of nowhere, seated on the long orange sofa in front of one of the windows. She was wearing a broomstick skirt and a long sweater. She jumped up and gave him a hug. Raymond held her tighter than ever before.

"Okay, we don't have much time" said Anya, gently backing away. "Brody thought you might be able to—"

"Brody?" asked Raymond. "She's involved?"

"Yes! Isn't that great? R1 managed to get external access and contact her. She thought you might be able to catch Henry with his guard down. Did Fidel give you the recording switch?"

Fidel... of course—fgonsalez!

"I have the switch," responded Raymond. "Not on me... crap, it must be in my pants."

"You're... not wearing pants?"

"No no, I am. This avatar is. But my real pants... oh, never mind. How does Brody fit in?"

"Right, okay—I'm sorry, so much has happened, I forgot how much you don't know. R1 managed to hack Fidel's account—"

"Who is Fidel?"

"Fidel... Fidel used to work on my team, then left, supposedly to take some time off to be with his father, but it turns out he really went to work on the secret project where they restored you from the original mental backup. Son-of-a-bitch had another NBC after all—Henry, I mean, not Fidel. Anyway, R1 hacked Fidel's account, and it turns out Fidel has been doing some of his own research on Henry, and Henry apparently has a lot more going on than anyone knows. We think he's involved in some sort of underground political stuff in London, some kind of subterfuge to stir up civil war in South Africa. Maybe more. I can't believe I've been working with this monster."

"And Brody?" persisted Raymond.

"So R1 found evidence that Henry was up to something big, and he was worried about me, so he captured what he could and contacted Brody to ask for help. And she got in touch with me, and she's been great! It turns out she's been part of a related investigation for months. They've been trying to put together various pieces, and it seems like Henry might be the key to it all. Apparently, he was high up at the FBI, with unlimited surveillance access, and there are signs that he tampered with a lot of surveillance records—satellite surveillance and stuff. And if you put it all together, there's a pattern. It all seems to relate to underground political activity. Terrorist plots, coups, training of insurgents. There's a pattern of concealment, like he's been covering the tracks of people stirring unrest throughout the world. For years. Maybe decades."

Oh my god—this must be Manolo's contact on the inside.

"Does R1 know about all this?" asked Raymond.

"Not yet—not all of it."

"Tell Brody there could be a connection with Manolo."

"Manolo?" asked Anya.

"Underworld guy. He said he had FBI connections, and he could clean up the surveillance records that linked me to the Svensson property. And now Henry has hardware that would have been seized by the FBI as part of the investigation."

"Ohhh… it sounds like you might be onto something. But Jacob Falls was the one who did the satellite surveillance cleanup for you. He was found—"

"Anya," interrupted Raymond, "you have to get out of here. You're in way over your head."

"No—I mean, I will, but not yet. Brody thinks you might have a chance to catch Henry with his guard down. To record him saying things he wouldn't say to anyone else, because he thinks he has you completely under his control. And Fidel's helping us. He's closely monitoring the recordings, and he's going to grab anything incriminating and get it to Brody right away."

Wow—I didn't know Eddie had it in him.

"This all happened in the past twenty-four hours?" asked Raymond.

"No, apparently it's been going on some time. R1 was just trying to protect me. He's been gathering information for over a week, but when he realized what he had on his hands, he knew he couldn't deal with it all himself. But listen, if you get a chance to get information out of Henry, give it your best shot—if we can nail him, we might be able to stop his plans to foment civil war in South Africa. Raymond, you could stop a war before it starts."

"What makes you think Henry's not listening to this conversation?"

"Fidel says he's paranoid about internal surveillance. He doesn't want any record of his own actions. But he overlooked the Nurania recordings."

"Did Fidel tell you what they're trying to accomplish with whatever experiment they're doing on me?"

"I think Henry plans to upload. He talked to me early on about replicating the scanner we had at the old lab, and then never mentioned it to me again. He probably plans to upload into the NBC you're in right now, and he wants to make sure it's safe to reuse it. Which it isn't, in my opinion. I don't think the neural flush—"

"Anya," interrupted Raymond. "I love you."

"I know. R1 keeps telling me that. He built a model of me in his new v-world, which frankly gives me the creeps."

"No, you don't understand. I'm not talking about infatuation. You are life to me. Nothing else means anything. My love for you is the greatest emotion I've ever felt. If I knew you loved me as much as I love you, I could die happy."

Long pause.

"And why do you keep calling the original Raymond R1?"

"Oh, R1 isn't the original Raymond. R1 is the copy of you I'm working with."

"The one you thought was controlling the cleaner bot at first?"

"Yes. There's R, which was you before you scanned yourself—your original organic self. Then there's R-sub-0, the first upload copy, and R-sub-1, which is the copy here at the lab. And now I guess you're R-sub-2. Or R2, for short."

"There are two other copies of me?"

"Yes, apparently. Well—"

"And you created a nomenclature to keep them all straight?" asked Raymond.

"Yes. For the legal papers, originally, but I've found it useful for my notes as well."

"Legal papers?"

"Yes. Oh, you don't know any of it, do you. Okay. How to make this story quick… Well, R scanned himself, was of course destroyed in the process, and everybody thought that was it. But R0 uploaded into a computer at the Svensson property, and lived in Nurania for a while with no Net access."

"Right," said Raymond. "Lying low, as planned. It's so nice to have a conversation with you in person."

"I'm just glad it's working. Well, then Jacob Falls was discovered—your satellite clean-up friend at the FBI."

"Jacob Falls? You said that earlier, didn't you. Okay—I never knew his name."

Anya cocked her head off to one side, puzzled. "R1 said the same thing. I wonder if it's some kind of localized amnesia, something that was lost during the scan."

"I don't think so. I mean, I don't feel like I've forgotten anything."

"You could easily not know that you ever knew. Besides, he had your IID, and there are records of your written communication with him."

"Well then they were faked. I communicated with Manolo, not the cleanup guy. Unless… maybe Manolo and Jacob Falls are the same person."

"Were," corrected Anya. "Jacob Falls turned up dead in an FBI bathroom the day he was found out. Suicide."

"That doesn't sound like Manolo. Wait, how do you know all this?"

"From working with your attorneys. I managed most of your court case. I mean, R-sub-0's court case."

"You did? You did that for me?" Raymond experienced a rare and precious moment of humble, joyous gratitude.

"Well, Bob's credibility was compromised, and he had his own trial to worry about."

"What!"

"Turned out, when the Jacob Falls thing was blown open and they figured out where you were, he and Agent Michaels worked out a deal to seize all the hardware from the Svensson property and cover the whole thing up. And turn you into a government proof-of-concept project for big-wigs in the intelligence community who want to upload."

"Like Henry?" asked Raymond.

"I guess. But then Brody had a feeling Michaels was up to something when he came around asking for police reports, months after you had apparently died. She had her own connection in the FBI, and she contacted him to blow the whistle. Michaels was already under observation, so they put an internal watchdog team on him and caught him red-handed, right at the Svensson property."

"Wow. I'm guessing Bob got off pretty easy, given all he's done for the feds?"

"Easier than R-sub-0 did, that's for sure. Bob was fined, the university fired him, and he fell off the map. But I've since heard he's heading up some Army project now."

"And R-sub-0?" asked Raymond.

"Over a hundred years in prison, for negligent homicide, two counts of identity theft—"

"Only two?"

"I don't want to hear it," responded Anya. "Seven or eight counts of theft, and more counts of fraud than I can remember. And this is going to sound bizarre, but I count that court case a real victory."

"I thought you said you were on my side of the case!"

"I was. Getting your case into court at all was huge. It set the precedent for the rights of an uploaded human. It was a landmark case, really."

"This Jacob Falls guy… was there any connection between him and Henry?"

"Possibly," said Anya. "I'll mention it to Brody. I should actually get in touch with her right away."

"Wait," interrupted Raymond. "Is Molly okay?"

"She is. She was held for a month while they sorted through all the hardware at the Svensson property, but she was eventually returned to the university. She's with Bento now."

"And Suma?"

"Actually, she and Alfonso are on the team looking after Molly and Bento."

Raymond found that this gave him considerable peace-of-mind.

"And how did you end up working with Henry?" asked Raymond.

"Oh, right. Part way through the legal case, he contacted me with an offer. He said that with my help he could give you the chance for a new life."

"Who is he? Aside from the FBI connection, what do you know about him?"

"I had no idea about the FBI connection at the time. All I knew was that he's a wealthy American ex-patriot. Majorly connected. So, he sent me this confidential offer to be the head scientist on a continuation of the upload project. I told him I was interested, and it turned out he had managed to buy a bunch of our old hardware from the government, once the case was over, with the stipulation that the continued research be pursued quietly, in another country—with no further scans of humans."

"What aren't you telling me, Anya?"

"What do you mean?" she asked somewhat sheepishly.

"You don't buy hardware seized by the FBI and used in a landmark case. And you haven't told me how you were able to get a copy of my mental data."

"Oh, it was still on one of your backup storage devices."

"Again. What aren't you telling me?"

There was a long pause.

"It does seem kinda… too good to be true, doesn't it?" She winced, embarrassed by her own naïveté.

"The original backup of my mental data was heavily encrypted," said Raymond. "There's no way the FBI would have sold that hardware, there's no way they would have left data on it if they did sell it, and it wouldn't be easy to crack that data without my giving you access."

"I guess I've been trying to ignore the shady side of all this," admitted Anya. "But you did give me access. 'There are men too gentle to live among wolves', with eights between the words, then the same thing backwards with the first eight abbreviations from the periodic table between the words. Sound familiar?"

The sound of someone saying these words sent a shock of vulnerability through him. That was the keyphrase that unlocked the store of his most private data encryption keys. It was a very personal and very sacred symbol of his secrecy.

"I told you that?"

"R0 told me that. When... well, I'm not sure how much I should tell you."

"The scientists who brought me to life here don't exactly know what they're doing, do they?" asked Raymond.

"Yes and no. They—"

"Anya," interrupted Raymond, "I could die anytime. I'm guessing that the mad scientists club got as far as they did by trial and error. By your nomenclature, I might be R-sub-20. I don't think there's any point in hiding anything from me."

"Okay. R-sub-0 wasn't exactly sent to prison. It was more like solitary confinement. He sat in a white room, by himself."

"*Was*? Wait—the original me is dead?"

"He... he was only allowed personal visits, and—aside from Brody—I'm the only one who ever visited him. When I visited him to tell him we'd found a copy of his mental data, he told me he'd written me a letter, in his head. He'd been in his cell for two months. Alone." Anya's voice caught. "He proceeded to recite the letter to me, word for word, looking me straight in the eye with this... spooky, hollow determination." She paused, crying. Raymond reached out and held her hand. "It was an apology letter, but it was so... bleak, so hopeless. And how could it not be?" She paused, collecting herself. "When he was done, he asked me if there was any way he could kill himself. I told him there was. He told me that if I could bring him a letter from R1, saying how happy he was to be in the lab, under my care, he would want to die, knowing that R1 had a better life. And then he told me that passphrase."

"Anya, you've done so much for me."

She looked at him through tear-filled eyes, then looked down and gripped his hands.

"A month ago, I visited R0 again. I memorized the response letter from R1, because I wasn't allowed to bring anything with me, and I recited it for him. He smiled and nodded the whole way through the letter. When I was done, he told me I was the most beautiful person in the world. And he told me I should never come back. I got word the next day."

Anya broke down, weeping uncontrollably. Raymond held her, and she talked into his chest, between sobs.

"When I first realized," she continued, "that the cleaner bot wasn't R-sub-1, I thought it might be him. I thought somehow he had figured out how to make another copy of himself and get out of prison, and just make it look like he died. God, this is getting to be too much."

"Wait a minute," said Raymond. "How could you not know about Manolo? Are you sure R0 never mentioned him?"

"Yes."

"The hacker's mutual protection code is pretty sacred, but it seems a little weird that he wouldn't have mentioned Manolo at all. Manolo is a high-stakes hacker with a reputation for befriending anyone who's against the FBI."

"He used inside connections to interfere with investigations?"

"Yep. And he must have had deep connections. He might even be an ex-agent. Or a current agent, for that matter. What was Henry's official motive for funding your project?"

"Pursuit of politically disfavored science, for the advancement of mankind. He rattled off a long list of projects where he's an anonymous donor."

"Gotta love anonymity. He probably just wants to upload himself, and his cronies. He's just one of those government big-wigs you mentioned, who just want to upload themselves. How old is he?"

"I don't know. Late sixties, maybe early seventies."

"You've met in person?"

"Sure. He likes to visit the lab."

"Mosby," whispered Scorpio, "poverlord just logged in."

"Shit, I have to go!" said Raymond to Anya.

"Okay, I'll let Brody know how little time you have left. She's trying to get Interpol into the lab, to seize hardware before Henry knows he's been fingered."

Raymond jacked out and signaled to Scorpio to get him back into his real avatar, fast. The transition was instantaneous; he lay on his side, his eyes closed. The only sound was the soft hum of medical equipment.

CHAPTER 21

Raymond heard the soft shoosh of a door opening, the tok-tok of high heels on tile, the quiet fff-thunk of the door sliding back into place.

"Hello, Raymond," came a woman's voice, abrupt—not at all quiet or gentle.

Raymond opened his eyes. Salya looked down at him from beside the table.

"I'm surprised to find you sleeping."

The hum of the machines stopped. Raymond glanced at the clock on the wall. It was 8:53:49… and it wasn't changing.

"Sleeping away your final hours before the comet hits? Did it break your spirit to see what you did to me?"

This is it—he's stopped time.

"To see the scars?" she continued.

Raymond moved to grab the flashlight, reaching by force of habit to where he expected a pocket to be—and remembered he was naked under the moist translucent blanket. His clothes were bunched up in the chair.

"You created me as a proxy for the woman you loved, didn't you?" asked Salya.

"Yes," said Raymond, feeling like his lack of interaction might be suspicious.

"And yet you had this done to me. Curious to see how far it goes?"

Salya reached her fingers into one of the rips in her nightgown and tore it further, revealing a gruesome hatchwork or scars over her pelvis and down her thigh. Fresh scabs stood atop the scars, red parallel lines as from razor-sharp claws. Raymond reflexively turned away, sickened by the sight.

"I'm sorry, Salya," he said.

He gestured to Scorpio under the covers, instructing him to teleport in, grab the flashlight, and teleport out as fast as possible.

"I see your hands moving under the blanket, Raymond. Who do you think you're talking to? There's nobody here but me."

"Just a habit," said Raymond. "It's how I talk to myself."

"Mosby," whispered Scorpio. "I can't get in. Time freeze. Only real logins can move within your region."

"I could give you what you wanted," said Salya. "I could give you back your life, with all its isolation. The freedom to create your own perfect world and live in it with your made-up friends."

Maybe Fidel sees what's happening, and he's turned the recording back on without me. But he's not logged in. And without the recording, he probably can't monitor what's going on—that's why he gave me the flashlight.

"The chance to make everything just the way you want it," continued Salya. "But you had that, didn't you? You've seen it—you've seen what you created. And it doesn't look so good, does it?"

Salya turned in place, modeling her wreckage for him.

"No, it doesn't." He swung his legs over the side of the table opposite Salya and sat up, pulling the blanket along with him. "Something must have been wrong."

"I don't think so," said Salya. "That's what everyone said—'something must have gone wrong with his NBC.' But I've spent a lot of money to satisfy myself on that point, and I find no support for that argument."

Raymond scooted forward and extended his feet to the ground. He tested putting his weight on his legs and had the sense it would be very painful if it weren't for the medication. He wrapped the blanket around his waist and crossed to the chair. He saw the end of the flashlight, protruding from the pants pocket atop the heap of clothes.

"Where are you going? You can't put your clothing on—I've stopped time, and you can't interact with the objects in this region. Except for the burn blanket, apparently."

And the flashlight, apparently, since I just flipped its switch.

Raymond turned around. Salya was staring at the blanket wrapped around him. "It must get special treatment, as clothing worn on your person."

"Stopped time?" asked Raymond. He staggered back to the table and leaned against it.

"Yes, I'm putting things on pause. It has the side effect of shutting down surveillance temporarily, and I'd like to have an off-the-record conversation."

"Why do you want to talk to a loony like me?"

"They say something went wrong with your NBC, but that really doesn't seem to be the case. Everything tests out okay. R1 has been running for months now, on hardware that's essentially identical, and he seems to be doing fine. Considering what he had to start with, of course."

"R1?" asked Raymond, pretending ignorance.

"He—he's your other self, shall we way. Another test instance. Some people say that it wasn't the hardware, it was *you*—that you're a special case. Unloved child. You were nuts from the get-go, and it's only natural that a madman would create a mad world. Granted, you did have… difficult circumstances, but all things considered, I'd say you came through okay. You're smart, you're tough, you're self-critical, you've got determination—hell, you've got more spirit than just about anyone I know. And you've got one hell of a woman who loves you. You know that? Anya would do just about anything for you."

"Anya?" asked Raymond. "What do you know about Anya?"

"Oh, everybody knows about Anya. She's the brilliant scientist who threw all rational consideration aside to fight for the rights of her digital man. Blinded by love, she couldn't see that you were nothing but a simulation. A crazy one, at that—a machine gone wrong. You're the subject of much confusion."

"So you've turned me into an experiment, to get to the bottom of it? You treat me like I'm disposable."

"Just this copy of you. And so far, I'm not buying that shit about you being a loony. The more I get to know you, the more I think—"

"This is your idea of getting to know me?"

"The way I see it, you just went into the whole upload thing all wrong, with the wrong ideals. You set out to create your own isolated utopia, but that's just not something that can be done. We're social animals, Raymond. We define ourselves in relation to others. We get our footing by leaning on some people and pushing away from others, and eventually we find people to *hold onto.* Without that, we flail, we lose ourselves completely."

"But I *did* have others," said Raymond. "Eddie and Diane, Bailey—"

"Not others that mattered," interrupted Salya. "There was nobody you were afraid to let down. No one you really wanted to impress. Even in the real world, we don't really care about most people. To some extent we do—I mean, you don't want to make an ass of yourself. But it's when you have someone you really care about that life takes on meaning, becomes electric. It's hard for you to form that kind of bond, isn't it?"

"Yeah," said Raymond. He couldn't help but find himself a little touched. "Yeah, it is."

"Someone who needs you and whom you need. Someone you want to impress. And you found that in Anya, didn't you?"

"Yeah, sure. Okay. What about you?"

"You see, that's where I'm better off," said Salya. She had started to pace, and was gesturing with her arms. "You were trying to hide from people, but I'm good with people. You were on the run from the law, from society. Whereas me, I'm just trying to escape my body."

"You want to upload, don't you? But you want to make sure it works first."

"I'm an old man, Raymond. An old man with a diseased body, and the doctors all tell me I've got very little time left. You know where I am now? Headed to London, to see another doctor. I've gone to the best—the very best—and all they can do is apologize. If I upload, I can give this lemon of a body the slip. And I'm not going into hiding. Quite the opposite. I'll be more connected than ever. *If* I upload. I didn't foresee not being able to get hold of the scanner, and I never thought it would take this long to make a new one. They say I could die any day. I could last a year, I could core-dump right now. All that stands between me and uploading is some nanoware. And while I'm waiting, I might as well have you do me the favor of participating in a few experiments, to make sure the kinks are all worked out. It's the least you could do for me, really. If it weren't for me, you'd be nothing but data, a brain on ice in some FBI archive. When I made time to see you in Delta Nuevo, didn't you think it was odd?"

"No way. You aren't just… associated with Manolo. You are Manolo."

"Yes, and so much more. You have no idea. And who the hell were you to warrant an audience with a man like me? Of course, you had no idea who you were dealing with, but still… Didn't it seem odd? But I'm smart." Salya slammed her fist down on the table. "I learned a long time ago not to underestimate people. I said, 'who is this kid to think he deserves my time?' So I did a little research. And it turned out you were on this upload project I'd never heard of, and I thought, 'I wonder how far off they are from uploading?' When I saw how close you were, and I figured out what you were up to, I thought you were nuts. But I figured, if this shit works, I can flip the Grim Reaper the bird. And you know, if I live long enough to pull this thing off, I'm not going to upload to some godforsaken v-space fantasy land. I know how to make people do things. I know how to make myself important, how to be that person others want to impress—how to wield power. You were running from the law. I toy with the law!"

Salya nearly shouted this, and the transformation shocked Raymond into action. He had to get Henry, or Manolo, or whoever this person was, to spill concrete details that could lead to his conviction.

"So what," he started, "Michaels was a pawn? A pawn in a game you set up so you could upload?"

"Michaels was a self-important, overly ambitious rookie. It was a matter of time before *someone* sacrificed that piece. Might as well be me."

"And Brody? What ever happened to her?"

"The last thing I needed was a real detective on the case."

"You can pull strings like that?"

"That's child's play."

"And Bob?"

"It's amazing what an inventor will do when you take his brainchild away." Salya smiled, basking in Raymond's amazement.

Brody was right—I really am in a special position to get this villain to open up.

"Seriously," said Raymond, "I know Bob wasn't entirely on the up-and-up, but how did you coax him into collusion with the FBI?"

"Oh, that was all Michaels. All I did was plant the seed in his greedy little mind: think of the glory if you could deliver this technology into the hands of the Old Men, and keep the Bureau's best investigative minds alive? Not to mention the monetary potential as they all paid him off."

"Old Men?"

"Heathcliff, Sneider, Mankewiecz—all the Old Men's Club. Semi-retired agents who still consult with the Bureau, and still have a good deal of clout. And money, from the deals they cut through the years. They've all got one foot in the grave, and not one of them would be above bending the rules for digital immortality."

"And you're not one of the Old Men?"

"No, I'm not FBI. Are you kidding? I get all the benefits of an insider without the sticky difficulties."

"I don't follow," said Raymond, hoping for something more material. "How exactly did you pull that off?"

"I sold them their surveillance systems, and I ran the team that built them. Ever heard of a company called GSI?"

"No shit."

"Funny the jobs they'll give a hacker, no? And when it came time for a security audit, who do you think they hired?"

"Didn't they do it themselves?"

"Hell no. They don't trust their own talent to do it right, dumb sons of bitches."

"Surely they didn't hire the same company that built the systems."

"No, but they might as well have. They hired Femus, a little auditing firm I did the hiring for. Half the Femus auditors were on my payroll at GSI. I set Femus up with clean samples, Femus conveniently neglected to look any further, and they greenlighted the whole thing."

"And now you use your backdoors to manipulate surveillance data?"

"That's just the tip of the iceberg."

"That's a nice racket you've set up for yourself. You've probably got some pretty big-name clients."

"Everyone from Ernesto Claudio to the CIA to… Saudi princes."

"You say you're not on the run like I was, but with clients like Ernesto Claudio, it seems like you'd be quite a target yourself ."

"I've got blackmail on every major terrorist group in the world. Another good reason to upload."

"But then… you are on the run."

"There's a difference between a smart defense and being on the run. You ever dreamt of putting your NBC up in space?"

"Sure."

"Well I could actually do it. If I wanted to. And without giving up a damned thing. I'd still be in touch. I'd still be connected with my people."

"Your people?" scoffed Raymond. "You have people?"

"You'd be surprised."

"Name one."

"I'm not about to defend my self-worth to you."

"I'm not challenging your self-worth. I'm challenging your worth to others, and whether anyone's really worth anything to you? Who would you give your life for? Who loves you? Who's your Anya?"

Pride welled within Raymond: Anya really did love him, and he would give anything for her. He suddenly glimpsed himself as part of something bigger, and it was a joyous revelation despite knowing it would quite probably cost him his life.

"Mere rhetoric," said Salya dismissively.

"You don't have anyone, do you?" challenged Raymond, trying hard to corner his captor. "You're as adrift as I was, aren't you? Only I was relatively harmless."

"Harmless?" cried our Salya. "Look at me!" She tore her gown even further, revealing most of her torso. "Look at what you did to this woman!"

"And I see that now, and I'm sick with guilt," said Raymond straight-on. "Even though she's not real. While you—you're fucking with real people, and you don't seem to care."

"I just wipe out data."

"Bullshit. You can't deny the results of your actions. You conceal assassinations, you hide the deeds of low men—for money. You're as bad as they are."

"Enough!" shouted Salya. She stepped swiftly around the table and lunged at Raymond, placing a strong hand on his throat and driving him backwards against the wall. He fell backwards over the chair and landed hard on the floor.

He scrambled to his feet, and she allowed him to put some distance between them. He looked around for something with which to defend himself, but knew it was futile.

"I could kill you right now, you know that?" asked Salya, as if reading his mind.

"You could, couldn't you?" asked Raymond pointedly. "You've done it before. And not just me. You killed Jacob Falls, didn't you?"

"Jacob Falls knew too much. He turned on me, and he thought… Wait a minute." Salya looked at him with narrowed eyes. "Your mental data predated your upload. You shouldn't know who Jacob Falls is."

Raymond realized his misstep. "You thought you could reuse my NBC?" he asked, and was mortified as his voice cracked. "You thought none of my memories would endure, but I do remember things." His lies were utterly see-through, and he knew it.

"I didn't reuse your NBC," said Salya slowly. "Not the original one. It's Fidel, isn't it. I was a fool to trust him. I shouldn't have brought anyone over from Anya's team. He and Anya are tight, aren't they. And he's my surveillance man—he's in the perfect position to talk to you and hide it from me. You know too much."

Salya produced a disruptor from nowhere and pointed it at Raymond's head.

"Time to die."

Raymond signaled to Scorpio for emergency assistance, but it was too late. The last thing Raymond saw was a burst of blue light—at point blank.

CHAPTER 22

Nothing. No Salya, no medical equipment, no feeling. No eyes with which to see the nothingness.

The void. I've been returned to the void.

He tried to exhale and panicked. No lungs to push out air, no air to be pushed out. Gradually, panic gave way to a sense of relief.

The disruptor blast didn't kill me. It must have just kicked me out of Nurania.

His visceral fear had faded, but a deeper anxiety started setting in. A moment before, he had expected his life to be snuffed out, but he was still alive—and vulnerable to a far worse fate at Henry's hands.

Manolo turned out to be much bigger than Raymond had ever suspected—a giant in the world of shady hackers. Had any of their final conversation made it to Brody? Even if it did, had he given her enough to go on? And was there anything she could do against a man with such powerful connections? Alone in the void, Raymond had no way of knowing.

Did I just sacrifice myself for nothing?

His mind turned to his own situation.

How was that even a sacrifice? I was going to be killed by the comet anyway. To imagine myself a hero is sheer vanity.

It was fitting to be killed by Salya, after everything he had done to her. Seeing what had come of himself and his world after uploading, he was disappointed. Yet it was disappointment at a distance.

It was my god copy—it wasn't really me.

He wondered again whether his god copy's NBC had malfunctioned, driving his psychology into the twisted darkness necessary to create Iniquita. It was hard to accept that this was what his own self could become, that this was merely the darkness of a man utterly alone. His god copy had voluntarily subjected himself to Iniquita. In fact, it seemed as though he had embraced it, craving the suffering as an antidote to the shallowness and inherent insignificance of Nurania's simulated populace. As if brutality and darkness could fill in where meaning was absent.

Time ran on. Raymond's thoughts turned to the brief time he had had with Anya. Seeing her, he knew now that she still cared for him. She was protective of him, willing to take a risk to talk to him. Thinking of her, he wanted to smile.

Having no face to show expression, no lips to turn up in a smile, his happiness felt muted. He pictured her face, smiling on his behalf. Unable to smile himself, her imagined smile felt empty, left him feeling even flatter. But he persevered in thinking positive thoughts about her. Her life seemed balanced and productive. Her thoughts were outward, his were inward. She gave of herself, and she expected him to give of himself in return, but he had always been secretive and selfish.

He wondered again whether he was about to die. Would it be bad if he did? What loss would there be, other than to himself? There was another copy of him, in Anya's care. What right did any man have to live more than one life?

Especially me. I can die. There can be zero copies of me, and the world will go on, no worse off than before.

He thought back to his childhood. He was jealous of children who had had more than he, children who had grown up taken care of. The State of Illinois had given him food, shelter, occasional supervision, and sufficient computing resources to provide himself with an education. When he got to the university, everyone seemed so confident, outgoing, energetic. Positive. Loving, and loved.

He wanted to release himself into Anya's care, this time with nothing to hide. He wanted to lay his head in her lap and close his eyes, and have her pet his head and say pleasant things, about her day, or her plans for the summer, or fond memories of her father. He wanted to throw himself into the arms of a woman who could rebuild him as an innocent.

At least once, I came through. I went out on a limb to get Henry. Success or failure, I did it. I got a glimpse, at least, of myself as part of something bigger. If I do somehow come out of this alive, I'll always have that.

The void persisted for what seemed like forever. He started to engage in mental exercises, attempting to recall details of people, places, music, events—anything he could conjure from memory and attempt to reconstruct in his mind's eye. Perhaps the void, this world of nothing but his thoughts and words, was to be his place of immortality. He tried to imagine specific sensations. Cold vs. hot, lying down vs. standing up, air moving over skin, taking a deep breath. The smell of coffee. The feeling of swallowing hot liquid. Tightening groin muscles to hold in pee.

He started to worry that this state really would never end. What if his message hadn't gotten out, and Henry had chosen to leave him running in isolation indefinitely—at least until managing to upload into the NBC himself.

He imagined knife-fighting with Hammers in Delta Nuevo, single-handedly defeating groups of three and four attackers. He tried to remember the rules of card games he had played as a child, in the Joliet Home. He imagined he was with his karate instructor again, showing her all the moves he knew. He made up elaborate series of moves. He imagined rain. Gentle rain, on water, on leaves, on pavement.

o------------------------------o

"Raymond?"

Raymond came to at the sound of Anya's voice. He realized he must have lost consciousness at some point. Perhaps he had fallen asleep?

"Raymond?" gasped Anya, desperate, nearly panicked. "Can you hear me?"

He tried to open his eyes. He had no eyes. He was still in the void. He wondered whether he had imagined hearing her voice. It would be impossible to hear anything without being connected to a body. He could have been dreaming.

"I'm seeing aural and linguistic activity," she said. "You should be able to hear me. It looks like you just woke up? Oh Raymond, if you can hear me, please talk to me. Imagine you're talking to me. I should be able to transmit the neuristor activity through a speech converter."

"Anya?" asked Raymond. "Is that really you?"

"Raymond! Oh thank god. I did it."

"Are you hooked up directly to my NBC?" asked Raymond.

"Yes. I've made some advances since you uploaded. Listen, we may not have much time. Your NBC was badly damaged in the explosion. Something caustic got into the case—some kind of acid or something."

"Explosion?"

"Henry must have had more security measures in place than anyone realized. Fidel tried to let me in, but his code access had been revoked. We went back to get what we could from the main lab, and then we heard an explosion. Fidel thinks it was Henry's attempt to cover his tracks. But we found your NBC in the rubble. The bands that lock it to the ground must have protected it from the blast. But it's still locked down, and I can't get it out to clean out the acid. I need to—"

"Did Fidel get any of what Henry said?" interrupted Raymond.

"Yes, all of it. He got it straight to Brody, which is how Interpol got involved. They're on their way. You did it, Raymond. We've got Henry on the run."

"Are you sure you're safe?" asked Raymond. "And your father? Henry won't go down easily. He could have men on the way, to finish the cleanup. And he probably has inside connections with Interpol."

"We'll be fine. My father's already under protection."

"Did my other copy survive—R1?"

"Yes. Nothing in the original lab was destroyed."

"You said my NBC was damaged? I can't feel it."

"I don't have the tools I need to run diagnostics, but there's clearly damage. The case of your NBC was smashed in at one corner, where it's not protected by the banding. Listen, I'm worried the acid could seep in further."

"Well, as long as you're okay, I don't care."

Silence.

"Did you really just say that?" Raymond heard Anya draw a breath. "You *do* love me, don't you?"

"You're so much more than I am, Anya. I would suffer a thousand deaths for you. And… actually, I may be the first person for whom that's not an empty assertion."

Raymond heard Anya's laugh. Just one laugh squeaked out before she stifled it, but she had laughed. Again he wanted a face with which to smile.

"I'm sorry," she said. "I shouldn't laugh."

"No, you should. It makes me happy. I wish I could see you laughing."

"But then you'd see that I'm crying at the same time." He heard her exhale heavily.

"So," said Raymond. "Are you and Fidel gonna blow this thing open? Maybe the ESW will see that they can't stop upload research. They've just driven it underground. It's going to be done, and it should be done in legitimate labs, under the scrutiny of society at large."

"Maybe. I mean, we'll try, but the media has portrayed you as a criminal, a crazed hacker—a peripheral member of society. I'm not sure even my father could get your story into any of the respected journals. Not the ethical story."

"Well, if you can get your hands on the Nurania recordings, maybe you can share them and they'll see that there's more to me. Like Fidel did."

"Maybe… It looks like a lot of hardware was destroyed. We'll see what Interpol can turn up when they get here."

"Anya, do you love me?" asked Raymond.

"I… I do. I love you, R-sub-2."

Silence.

"I'm sorry," said Raymond. "I shouldn't have asked."

"No, really—I do, I do. And I'm so proud of you. You've shown such courage."

Raymond felt a bizarre sense of cold come over him.

"Are you still there?" asked Anya.

"Yes. I'm scared."

"Oh god, Raymond, I'm scared, too. I wish I could get your NBC out! I wish I could hold you. Are you okay? I'm seeing some activity that concerns me."

"Anya, you've got to get out of here. What if Henry has men on their way? Or bots?"

"I can't just leave you here."

Raymond thought about asking her to simply destroy his NBC.

"Wait a minute," said Raymond. "You said my NBC is locked to the floor? *How* is it locked to the floor?"

"There are four metal rods sunk into the floor, and metal banding around the sides and over the top. You'd have to have a heavy cutter to get through it, and you'd probably destroy the NBC in the process."

"No way! Oh, that's so classic. They didn't lock down the NBC. They locked down the case!"

"What do you mean?"

"Break the case! It's made of the same composite material IBM uses for all their academic research cases. Most of their cases, actually. It's designed to splinter on sharp impact, rather than denting inward and damaging the important bits inside. That's why the one corner broke. Crack it open more, and you should be able to get the core out."

"There's got to be a safer way."

"I don't think there's time. Smash the case. Give it a good whack, with a hammer or something. Expand the hole."

"I don't see anything like a hammer."

"Is there a table with removable metal legs? Lab tables are usually assembled onsite."

"Um, no. It doesn't look like it. There's so much rubble in here. Wait! What about a fire extinguisher? I brought one in with me."

"That sounds like it might be too big."

"No, it's a little one. I think it will work. But—what if it doesn't? I could kill you."

"Well, the alternative seems to be death by acid. Or major brain damage."

"Wait, does the NBC core have its own power source?"

"Yes," answered Raymond. "I should be good for at least a couple weeks."

"Okay, I guess," said Anya hesitantly.

"Wait," said Raymond. "Is R1 happy?"

"Sure, he's happy."

"That doesn't sound very convincing."

"No, he is. It's just… it's hard. He dreamt of flying solo, free from everything, and now he's, well, he says he feels like my mental patient. Which he is, I guess. And, you know, things between us… I mean, under the circumstances, I've kept things kind of… clinical. To protect myself, and him."

"That's cuz I'm the real Raymond, right?" joked Raymond.

"Right," chuckled Anya. "Of course you are."

"Do you think a person could ever be happy uploaded?"

He heard Anya let out a long sigh.

"I do," she said at last. "Absolutely. But not alone. And you just… you went into it with a lot of growing up to do, Raymond—and no one to help you. If you'd had a chance to work things out yourself, who knows."

"I'm ready," said Raymond. "Give it a try."

"Okay," said Anya.

Waiting, Raymond felt oddly serene.

"Are you still there?" asked Anya.

"I am. Did it work?"

"No. I hit it pretty hard, but the core's so close to the surface—I'm afraid to damage it."

"Anya, I'm getting these weird cold feelings. I think the acid is seeping in. You're gonna have to hit it harder."

"Okay, here goes nothing."

Raymond felt a ghostly cold sensation and his thoughts turned hazy. He felt as though he were falling, falling, falling; he braced for his existence of thoughts and words to suddenly stop, and the thought made him wish he could cry.

He struggled to form a single word, pretending to move a mouth he didn't have.

"Anya?"

CPSIA information can be obtained at www.ICGtesting.com
Printed in the USA
BVOW08s1734170716

455873BV00001B/34/P